PROLOGUE

The sign scabbed to the dog-yellow wall read:

FOR SALE—VIABLE HUMAN EMBRYO
GENUINE TERRESTRIAL STRAIN

"This is the place, Bella," Raff Cornay said. "By God, we're a long way from home."

Bella smiled up at him and bit at her dyed lips. Having them dyed hadn't really made her look twenty years younger—or even a year younger. She moved closer to his side, put lean, grayish fingers on his thick, brown arm, looking up the dark ravine of the stairway.

"Raff, it's so . . ." she started, and then left it, because when you've been married twenty years all those words aren't necessary.

Raff hitched at the harness that crossed his heavy, rounded shoulders, brushed with a finger the comforting bulge of the short-barreled power pistol.

"We'll be all right, Bella." He patted her thin hand, moved ahead of her to the high, narrow steps, worn into hollows pocketing oily puddles. The heat and sounds of the plaza faded as they climbed through layered odors of decay and alien cookery, passed a landing railed with twisted iron, reached a towering, narrow doorway hung with a dirt-glazed beaded arras that clashed softly as Raff held it aside.

There was a leathery rustle, a heavy thump, the clack of clawed feet. An enormously tall, stooped figure in ornately decorated straps and bangles minced forward from yellowish gloom, ruffling molting plumage. It settled itself on a tall stool, clattering stiff, flightless feathers, blinking translucent eyelids from Raff to Bella.

"What do you want?" the Rheops chirped. "There is no charity here."

"There's a lady here'd like to sit down too, maybe," Raff said sharply.

"Then sit."

Raff looked around. There was no other chair. He looked at the proprietor, eyeing the red, leathery neck, the tarnished beak.

"I never knew one like you before," he said. "What are you, you don't know how to treat a human lady?"

"Human?" The alien clacked its beak contemptuously, staring at Bella's gray Yill skin.

"Don't, Raff." Bella put her hand on his arm. "We don't care nothing about him. All we want's the baby." Through the ill-fitting youth suit he had bought for the trip, she could feel him forcing himself not to care. Maybe he was too old for the legal adoption agency, but he was as good as any man a hundred years younger.

"We've got money," Raff said tightly. "We're here on business."

The big eyes blinked at him. "How much money?"

"Well—almost five hundred credits."

The tall creature on the stool closed its eyes, opened them again. "I can offer you something in a sturdy mute, guaranteed I.Q. of 40 . . ."

"No," Raff and Bella said together. "No defective stock," Raff went on. "Your sign down on the square said Genuine Terry Strain."

"Too much intellect in a slave is undesirable. Now, this line of stock . . ."

"You think we'd make a slave of a human child?" Raff

Henry gripped Roan's shoulder with a hard hand. "Listen, boy: a Man's got to live. I started off in the Terry ghetto on Borglu, kicked around, spit on, worked like a tun-lizard in the wood mines. There wasn't a day they let me forget I was a Man—and that all I'd ever get was a Man's share—the scraps, and the kicks, and the curses. They used to call me in and laugh at me; they'd tell me how once the Terry Empire had stretched across half a Galaxy, and how Terries had been the cock of the walk in every town on ten million worlds, master of everything. And how I was a slave now, and just about good enough, maybe, to wash their dirty clothes and run their errands, and maybe some day, if I was a good worker, they'd get me a half-breed wench and let me father a litter of mules to slave for them after I was gone.

"Well, I listened—and I got the message—but not the one they had in mind. They didn't know Terries, boy. Every time they'd show me a book with a picture of a Terran battle officer in full dress, and tell me how the Niss had wiped out the fleet—or hand me an old Terran pistol and tell me how their great grandpap had taken it off a starving Man—it didn't make me feel like a slave. It made me feel like a conqueror. One day one of them made a mistake. He let me handle a Mark XXX hand blaster. . . .

KEITH LAUMER AND ROSEL GEORGE BROWN

EARTHBLOOD

BAEN BOOKS

EARTHBLOOD

This is a work of fiction. All the characters and events portrayed in this book are fictional, and any resemblance to real people or incidents is purely coincidental.

A Baen Book

Baen Publishing Enterprises
260 Fifth Avenue
New York, N.Y. 10001

First Baen printing, August 1987

ISBN: 0-671-65348-2

Cover art by Alan Gutierrez

Printed in the United States of America

Distributed by
SIMON & SCHUSTER
1230 Avenue of the Americas
New York, N.Y. 10020

snapped. "Can't you see we're Terries—Terry stock, anyway," he added, as the round eyes flicked over him, then Bella. She stirred and wrapped her cloak closer.

The dealer clacked its beak contemptuously. "Five hundred credits—and for this, I should produce perhaps a conquistador, complete with Sc.D. certificate?"

"Just an ordinary boy," Raff said. "Just so he's normal. Earth normal. We don't mind if he's maybe color blind—"

The dealer cocked its head, eyed Raff. "What kind of citizenship do you have?"

"What? Why, we're Freeholders, from Granfont."

"You have papers?"

"Sure. Otherwise we'd never . . ."

The dealer half turned, raised its voice in a sharp cry. A small slave in trailing rags came in from a side room.

"Bring benches for my valued customers—and brandy. The Fleon, '49." It turned back to Raff, its hooded eyes sharp and interested now. "A happy blending of rain, sun, sulphur, and fungi . . ."

"We don't need the buildup," Raff said. "We didn't come here to socialize . . ." He stopped. It wasn't a thing you could put words to. *We came to buy a human child . . . to buy a son . . .*

"Ah, but I like people with resources. I confide in them." The dealer was beaming owlishly now. "You wish an heir. I understand. You have come at a fortunate time. I can offer a most exceptional embryo—a son fit for an emperor."

"We're not emperors," Raff said. "Just plain folks. We want a plain Terry boy . . ."

"So." The dealer ruffled limp shoulder plumes indifferently, its expression abruptly cold again. "If you want to rear inferior stock, I can sell you something cheap—"

"Good. How much?" Raff rose, resting his hand on his credit coder.

"Wait!" Bella cried. "I want to know what he means. What's the . . . the other kind you was talking about?" She pulled Raff into his chair as the slave returned with a tray bearing a clay pot and bell-shaped glasses.

The dealer placed spidery, plucked-chicken fingers together, waiting while the slave poured and withdrew. It cocked an eye at Bella.

"As it happens, I am in a position to offer top price for freehold citizenships—"

"Are you crazy?" Raff started. "How'd we ever get back—"

Bella picked up a glass and said, "Wait, Raff." She made a great thing of sipping the brandy, making it a compliment.

"Sell our citizenships!" Raff snorted. "It takes us for ignorant rubes, Bella."

The Rheops hunched on its stool, fragile feathers raised in a halo around its head, eyes on Bella now.

"I happen, at this moment, to have in my tanks," it said with impressive gravity, "a prime-quality fetus intended for the personal service of—a most high official. A magnificent blastosphere, large, vigorous, and of a superior intellectual potentiality."

"What's wrong with it, this high official didn't take delivery?" Raff asked bluntly.

The round eyes blinked. "Alas, the Shah is . . . er . . . dead—together with his heirs and assigns. One of these annoying uprisings of the rabble. By great good luck, an agent of mine— But no matter. I lost two valuable servants in the acquisition of this prize, which now, frankly, must be transferred soon to a suitable artificial placenta, or be lost. I confide this in you, you see."

"This is just sales talk, Bella," Raff said. "To build up the price."

"A rustic's shrewdness is the merchant's joy," the dealer quoted sharply. It raised its head and shrilled for the slave again, chirped instructions. Raff and Bella waited. The slave returned, toiling under a small, glittering, stone-encrusted box. At a sign from the dealer, it handed the casket to Raff. He took it; his hands sagged under the unexpected weight.

"This golden incubator, set with diamonds, awaited the favored tot," the dealer said. "Now heavy-footed bucolics haggle for his destiny. The price is two thousand credits—or two freehold citizenships."

"That's twice the going black-market price," Raff said weakly, overwhelmed by the box and what was in it.

"You're not bargaining for black-market goods now," the Rheops screeched. "I'm a legitimate trader, licensed by the Sodomate!"

"I'll give you one citizenship," Raff said. "Mine. I can earn another with a few years' work."

The dealer snapped horny lips together. "I'd decant this jewel among lads into the hive sewers before I'd cut my price a demi-chit! The descendant of kings deserves no less."

"Raff . . ." Bella said, appeal in her voice.

"How do we know he's telling the truth, Bella?"

"I have a license to protect, outlander," the tall creature said. "You think I'd risk my reputation for your paltry custom? The Shah paid fifty thousand Galactic credits—in rhodium ingots—"

"But if you don't sell it quick—"

"I've told you my price. Take it or leave it—and then get out!"

"Well . . ." Raff hesitated.

"We'll take it," Bella said.

They moved through the noise of the plaza, Raff leading the way among hawkers' stalls, Bella clutching a two-inch glass cylinder to her lean chest. Yellow dust swirled, stirred by a fitful desert wind. The second sun was low in a bronze-black sky.

"We shouldn't have spent all that credit," Raff said. "How're we going to get back, Bella?"

"We'll find a way," Bella said. "But first, we got to find a Man doctor."

Raff halted. "Bella—you ain't coming down sick?"

"We got to have the baby implanted—right away, Raff."

"Bella, you know we can't afford that now. We'll wait till we're on Granfort, like we planned—"

"We thought we'd have time, Raff—but we don't. He'd never have sold so cheap if time hadn't been short—awful short."

"But we were going to use Len's stock brooder. Where'd we ever find a mammal brooder here? And we'd have to stay nine months—"

"We won't have to stay, Raff. I'll have the baby implanted—in me."

Raff stared at her. "Bella—you sure? I mean, could you . . . could it . . . ?"

She nodded. "I asked Doctor about it once—a long time ago. He said—first he took a lot of tests—and then he said I could."

"But, Bella, you're . . . you're not . . ."

"He said I could—even if I'm not human." Her vertical-slitted eyes were bright in her still piquant face. "I'll be the mother of our son, Raff. He'll be our human boy, born to me . . ."

Beside Bella, Raff raised his head suddenly. He moved closer to Bella, put a protective arm around her.

"What is it, Raff?"

"Bella—somebody's following us."

"Following . . . why?"

"I don't know. Give me the boy. And stay close."

They turned into a canyon hung with harsh lights, pushing through the jostling crowd. Alien hands plucked at their sleeves, alien eyes stared, alien voices implored, cursed, begged, threatened. The dust rose, hot and corrosive.

"Down here," Raff gasped. In the shelter of a narrow way they clung together, coughing.

"We shouldn't have left the main plaza," Bella said. "Tourists don't come here . . ."

"Come on." Raff led the way, thirty feet back, where the twisted path ended between high walls in a cul-de-sac. They turned—

Two figures, one squat, one tall, both wrapped in heavy, dun-colored togas, waited at the alley mouth.

"Stay behind me." Raff tucked the cylinder in a harness pouch, put his hand inside his tunic to rest on the pistol butt, started forward; the short creature came to meet him, waddling on thick, bowed legs. Ten feet apart, they halted. Raff looked down into dead eyes like black opals in a face of bleached and pocked wood.

"We are stronger than you," the alien grated. "Give us the royal slave and go in peace."

Raff brought the gun into view. There was blue stain across his throat where the cheap dye of the youth suit had dissolved in sweat.

"Get out of our way." His dry mouth made his voice rasp.

There was a moment of silence. Then:

"We will pay," the alien said. "How much?"

"I'll sell you nothing. Just clear out of my way." Raff licked sweat from his upper lip.

The tall alien had moved up behind his dwarf companion. Beyond, a heavy, lizard-bodied cuspoid with a scaled hide painted in garish colors moved into view, and behind him were others.

Raff took a step forward. The gun was almost touching the dusty folds of the other's toga. "Out of my way or I'll shoot sure as hell—"

A stumpy arm whipped out; Raff fired—a momentary flare of blue; then the gun was flying as the weight of the alien slammed against him, and he reeled back, grappling for a hold on horny hide. He caught a sinewy arm, twisted with all his strength, heard gristle creak, snap. He hurled the alien from him, leaped past him, swung at the tall one, missed as he leaned aside. The gun lay two yards away; he dived for it—and a vast weight slammed against him, driving out his breath in an explosive grunt. He was aware of the roughness of the cobbles against his face, a fiery pain that rolled in waves from his shoulder. Far away, Bella's voice wailed.

Raff rolled over, came to his knees; a wide foot in a ragged sandal smashed at his face. He caught at it, held on, dragged a kicking, fighting body down, hearing himself cry out at the agony in his shoulder; and then he found a grip on yielding flesh and clung, crushing, feeling cartilage crackle under his thumbs. He grunted, hunching his shoulders as talons raked his face once, twice, then scrabbled and fell away. Hard hands hauled at him, threw him on his back. He struck out blindly, rolling over to protect the cylinder with his body. A red-hot vise closed on his leg. He tried to crawl toward the gun, but a boulder, falling from an immense height, had crushed his body and his lungs were charred pits in his chest. His arms and legs moved, though he had forgotten now why he must crawl . . .

At last, brilliant light flared and died into bottomless darkness, and Raff felt himself fading, fading, winking out . . .

He lay on his back, hearing their voices.

"This one fought like a scalded dire-beast!"

". . . cartilage like rods of granite!"

"Break them . . ."

The blows were remote, like distant thunder. The beating went on for a long time. Raff didn't notice when it stopped; he floated in a silence like a sea of molten lead. But voices penetrated the silence. There was the deep rumble of one who demanded, and a thin cry . . .

Bella.

Raff moved an arm, groped over his face, wiped blood from his eyes, feeling broken flesh under his fingers. He blinked, and through a red blur saw Bella, held pinned against a wall by a cloaked figure. Its arms rose and fell, rose and fell again . . .

Raff reached, groping. His hand fell on the power pistol. He tried to sit up, coiled away from agony like a worm on a hook. He dragged the gun around, leveled it on the yellow cloak, and fired. The cloak crumpled. Another caught at Bella, whirled her around as a shield.

"You will kill your woman," a thin voice said flatly. "Give us what we seek and go your way. We are stronger than you."

Raff was watching Bella. She hung in the grip of the alien, small, limp. He saw her hand move—

"Why do you struggle so, foolish one?" the alien grated.

Bella's hand was at her girdle. Light glinted on steel. Raff saw the thin arm grope, finding the vulnerable spot between plates of scale-armor . . . and then the sudden movement—

There was a grunt from the creature who held Bella. He leaned, fell stiffly, the handle of Bella's rattail poniard against his side. Behind her, a dark shape moved. Raff fired, a near miss. But the alien halted, called out in a strange tongue. Raff blinked gummed eyes, aiming . . .

"Wait, Raff," Bella called. She spoke rapidly, incomprehensibly. The alien answered. Raff held the gun aimed at the voice.

Bella was beside him. "Raff, this one's a Yill—like me. He gave me his parole."

"Parole, hell!" Raff croaked.

"Raff, if we spare his life, he'll be our slave. It's true, Raff. It's the Yill law. And we need him . . ."

The gun fell from Raff's hand. He tried to reach for it, to curse the weakness, but only a thin moan came.

There was a babble of alien talk, Bella's voice a thin thread against the rumble of the other. Raff tried again.

". . . Bella . . ."

"Yes, Raff. It'll be all right now. T'hoy hoy will take us to a place . . ."

"Use the gun," Raff gasped out. "Make sure of the rest of 'em—all of 'em."

"Raff—if we just go now—"

"No good, Bella. No law in this place. Taking no chances. There'll be no wounded devils tracking us . . ."

Afterward, there was a confused memory of strong arms that carried him, and pain like a blanket of fire, and the bite of the night wind, suddenly cold; and later, voices, the clink of keys, and at last a nest of moldering furs, and Bella's hands, and her warm breath against his face.

"Raff . . . poor Raff . . ."

He tried to speak, gasped, tried again. "Our boy," he said. It was important to explain it to Bella, so she'd see how it was. "Our boy: bought with money and bought with blood. He's our boy now, Bella . . ."

Leaning heavily on his cane, Raff looked down at his wife and his newborn son while the slave T'hoy hoy washed out rags in the tin tub by the door.

"This ain't the way I meant it to be," Raff said. "Here in this fallen-down shack in the ghetto. Gee, Bella . . ."

"When you get more able you can paint it. Pretty and white. And it's on the other side of Tambool from the bazaar. They won't look for him here. Roan."

"My son," Raff said, touching one tiny, curled fist. "In fifty years, maybe, he'll be a full-grown human Man."

1

Roan was bored watching his mother wash dishes.

"No," she said. "I can't take you outside now. After I do the dishes I got to grind the grits and then shell some snails and clean your daddy's brushes so's he can do some spring painting when he gets back from that job in town. And then . . . stop that!" Bella cried.

Roan tried to stick the paper back on the wall but it wouldn't stay.

"Daddy fix," he said. His nose was running and he wiped it on the end of the curtain.

"*Not* on the curtain," Bella said. "I just washed them and I didn't make no more soap yet."

Roan reached for the salt cup. Salt was a nice thing to taste, a little at a time. Only it all came over on him.

"The *salt*!" Bella screeched. "Now that's the end! Raff worked all day one day just to get that salt for you and there it's all over the floor and how'm I going to wash salt?"

Roan began to wail again. Everything he did was bad.

"All right," Bella said. "All right. I guess maybe you could go out in the back. You stay right near the house.

11

And don't get into no trouble, and leave them chunck flowers alone. That juice don't wash out."

Roan ran out into the sunshine with a whoop of joy. He could taste the sun all over him except where his clothes were.

Oh, what lovely chunck flowers! Purpler than purple-fruit, redder than blood, greener than grass.

Mustn't pick the chunck flowers.

He wandered to the other side of the yard where it trailed off into a dusty lot beyond the careful picket fence that Daddy was going to paint again soon. Roan liked to pick the flakes of old paint off it, but today something more interesting was there.

On the other side of the fence were a bunch of wiry, leathery little gracyl children, and oh, what fun they were having!

"Hello!" Roan called. "Hey! Hi! Come play!"

Some of them looked up.

"You're not a gracyl three," one of them said.

"*Here* is where the three year gracyls dig, not *there*."

"I can help," Roan said. "Help dig."

He began to clamber over the fence. It was hard work and he tore a long strip off his shirt on the top of a picket.

Then, once over, he was suddenly shy and stood and watched the gracyl threes burrowing into the ground, their sharp claws working quickly.

"Me, too!" he cried then, and started in on a gracyl's burrow. The gracyl kicked him disinterestedly and kept on burrowing, and Roan burst into tears and went to help another, and got kicked again.

"Dig your own burrow," one of them finally said, not unkindly. Roan could see he was a little different from the others. One embryonic wing had failed to develop.

"You don't got a wing bone," Roan said. "Where's your wing bone?"

The gracyl stretched out his one good wing into an infant fan. "They grow later," he said. "You don't have *any* wings."

Roan tried to feel beneath his arms but he couldn't find anything.

"I'm going to grow my wings later," he said excitedly. "Then I'll fly. I'm Roan."

"I'm Clanth," his new friend said, and then noticed the others had already burrowed ahead of him. "Shut up and dig."

Roan began to dig and found out almost immediately it wasn't as easy as it looked. The dirt at the top was loose, and came right out, but underneath the ground got damp and harder.

"Mama cutted my fingernails," Roan said bitterly. He *knew* she shouldn't have cut his fingernails and now look—he couldn't dig like everybody else.

Roan went and found a sharp stick and began to do a little better. He hit hard with it and suddenly a hole opened up all by itself. A nice, big hole and Roan crawled into it and a gracyl came up and punched him and said, "Dig your own burrow, you freak."

Roan took his stick and began digging down some more.

"You're doing it wrong," the gracyl said, and went on lengthening his burrow.

But as Roan gouged at the earth, it fell in again, and he was in another burrow and it was quite dark and a little cold, but Roan crawled further along into the burrow and then he ran into something furry that he couldn't see in the dark.

"That's funny," Roan said aloud and laughed, because something was tickling the inside of his mind.

"Here it is lovely and cool and dark and no winds blow. Here live we Seez and who are you?"

"I'm Roan," Roan said aloud.

The See put out a soft claw and felt Roan. *"You do not feel like you look in your mind,"* it said. *"There are no wings and no digging claws. Tell me again what you are."*

"I'm Roan," Roan said, and laughed again. And then there was a silence in Roan's mind while the creature felt around in it, and he waited, feeling the strange sensation.

"There's something amiss with you," the See said. Roan felt him backing off. *"You can't tell me who*

*you are. And some terrible power lurks there in your
mind. And such enormous puzzles, and things that are
strange . . ."*

Roan could feel a shudder from the creature's mind
and then it was gone and he was alone. Alone in the
dark cold, with all those strange things the See said
were in his mind. And the ground smelled dead and
damp and wormy and there might be Charons crawling
through the burrows to eat dead things and suppose
they thought he was dead?

Roan started to back out and found he was scared and
all he wanted was Daddy or Mama and his own bed.
He sat down and opened his mouth and howled.

The tears poured out of his eyes and he felt dirt in his
mouth and he screamed with all of his body and he was
wet, now, too, and that made everything worse.

Then he felt Raff's strong hands on him and even
though he knew it was Raff he had to go on screaming
to show how scared he had been.

"Boy," Raff said when he got him out and the screams
quieted to sobs. "Boy, I been looking all over for you."
Daddy sounded funny. Daddy was scared, too.

"And I'm going to do something I never done before.
I'm going to give you a good lickin'."

And he turned Roan over his knee, but Roan didn't
mind the licking. By the time it was over he'd stopped
crying altogether and he got up and looked solemnly at
his father and Bella, who was hysterical and hollering
for Raff to bring Roan in for a bath.

Roan wiped his nose on the back of his hand and
said, "What am I?"

"You," Raff said, "are a human boy. And some day
you'll be a human Man. Pure Terran you are, boy."

"But I got funny ears," Roan said, feeling one ear,
because suddenly it seemed as though it was mostly his
ears, his funny, rounded ears on the side of his head,
that might be causing all the trouble.

"What's Terran?" Roan asked T'hoy hoy, as the Yill
slave carefully washed him in a big wooden tub of hot
water, while Bella hovered, checking.

"Terran?" T'hoy hoy echoed. "Well, a Terran is from Terra."

"Unca T'hoy hoy know a song about Terra?" Roan asked hopefully. Roan knew from his voice that he did. T'hoy hoy had a special way of pronouncing things he knew stories about. Sort of singsong, like he said the stories, speaking the ancient, melodic language of the Yill.

"Yes. And if you stand still while I wash you and then eat all your dinner and go right to bed, I'll be telling you the story."

"Oh yes!" Roan said. "Yes and yes and yes and yes!" And he made a big splash in the water, but then he really was still and T'hoy hoy began his story.

"Once upon a time, longer ago than the oldest creature in the oldest world can remember now, there was a world called Terra."

"Is it still there?"

"We'll get to that later. A long time ago, and so far away you can't even see its sun in the sky from Tambool, there lived people on the world named Terra, and these people all looked just like you."

"Like me!" Roan's eyes grew wide, and he stood even stiller than he needed to. "With funny ears?"

"Your ears aren't funny," T'hoy hoy said. "Not to a Terry. Now, one day these Terrans built the first spaceships that ever were. A whole new kind of thing that had never been built before. Only Terrans could do that. Then the Terrans went to other worlds in their spaceships and after thousands of years, creatures all over the universe learned that those twinkles in the sky were stars with worlds around them. Because previously each world had thought it was the only one. And each thought it had the only God, whereas there are actually nine Gods.

"And Terrans learned to live on those many worlds, but some of them changed, and on many worlds they met other beings, not human, but not too different, so that they could think some of the things Terrans think, but not all of the things."

Roan sat down in the warm bath water because he was getting goose bumps standing in the cold air. "You not a Terran," he said, touching T'hoy hoy's Yill ear.

"No, I'm all Yill, as far as I know. But these people began to build things of their own and do many Terran things. And since these worlds sold things to one another, and visited each other, pretty soon they also began to have wars, because each wanted to be the strongest. So the men of Terra decided to rule the universe and keep the peace."

"I got soap in my mouth, Roan said. "Tastes terrible."

T'hoy hoy carefully wiped the inside of Roan's mouth with a damp cloth.

"Then something very unhappy happened. Strange people came, from far away—on the other side of the Galaxy—or maybe even from another Galaxy—and their weapons were strange but powerful and they challenged Terra for the overlordship of the universe. And they fought a great war that lasted for a thousand years."

"Naughty," Roan said. He could tell from the tone of Uncle T'hoy hoy's voice. "*Very* naughty."

"Yes, indeed," T'hoy hoy said. "These bad people were called the Niss, and such was their power that even great Terra couldn't defeat them."

"Did they kill the Terrans dead?"

"No. They put a circle of armed Niss spaceships around the planet Terra. And after that no one could get to Terra and the Terrans couldn't go anywhere. So nobody has been to Terra in five thousand years."

"What's five thousand years?" Roan asked, jumping from the tub into the drying cloth T'hoy hoy held for him. Roan loved to be dried off in the lovely, warm cloth and he liked to wear it wrapped around him while T'hoy hoy got his clothes together.

"A long, long time. I'm not even sure how long. But the story says five thousand years, so that's what I say."

At dinner Roan crammed food into his mouth with both hands and Raff and Bella were too exhausted to make him try to use his spoon.

"This how *Terrans* eat," Roan said, to excuse himself.

"Terrans do this." And he filled his mouth so full his cheeks bulged out.

"Terrans do *not* do that," Raff said. "And beginning tomorrow night you'll always eat like a Terran."

And T'hoy hoy began to tell Roan how Terrans eat and what Terrans eat, but Roan was asleep before T'hoy hoy could get past the hors d'oeuvres.

2

Roan's turn came.

The others were already across. Except the gracyl who'd fallen, and was probably dead by now.

Everybody's wings had worked, the young, pink membranes fanning out along their torsos, along under their arms—all but Clanth's. He hadn't even tried. He had looked down into the ravine and then gone home alone.

They were all laughing, on the other side of the ravine. First at themselves, because it was so much fun, and then at Roan, because he was hesitating.

It had been easy. They were proud of their wings, amused because that one gracyl had managed his wings badly and fallen. *He* hadn't been clever. Now they watched Roan, the only one not over.

"Roan is the dumbbell of the sevens," they began to chant, flapping their wings at him. "Roan is stoo-oo-pid."

"I'm going to do it," he called. "Just watch me."

But still he hesitated. He didn't *have* any wings.

The idea was to take the rope vine, which was just long enough to swing three-fourths of the way across Endless Ravine, and swing out into the dizzy air, and then sail the rest of the way across on your own power.

Roan tested the rope vine, swinging softly on it, looking up to where it hung from high, high in the

18

purplefruit tree, and then looking across Endless Ravine, across the impossible distance to where the other seven yearers stood.

Roan's pink face was drenched with perspiration, his tunic pasted to his childish body, his whole being drenched with fear.

He clung to the swaying rope and thought of how it would be if he just let go and ran home. Ma would say, "What did you do today?" and he'd say, "Nothing," and the day would end, just like any other day.

"Stoopid!" they called. "Roan is a dumbbell."

They'd said that before, that way, about other things, and Roan had decided it wasn't going to happen again. No—he'd show them, show them, show them—and some day there'd be something *he* could do that they couldn't do.

Roan made himself relax, muscle by muscle, as Ma had taught him to do when he was angry and couldn't go to sleep. All I think about is getting to the other side, he said to himself, and didn't mention the ravine. He measured the distance with his eyes and gauged the swing of the rope vine with his whole body.

With luck, he'd make it.

Roan ran back with the rope vine, as far as it would go. Then he clung, feeling himself part of the arc of the swinging, willing the swing to be far enough, forcing himself to know when the top of the arc came, to let go at just the right moment.

The air was in his ears and the mouth of the ravine opened to swallow him, but his eye was on the soft pasture grass of the other side, and he let go at the apogee of the swing. Then, not knowing whether he would land or not, he relaxed himself for the landing, feeling the whistle of the air . . .

He struck, rolled freely to lessen the impact of the earth on his soft human body, hardly feeling as his foot caught briefly, then rolled free with him.

He laughed up at the group of empty faces. Somewhere inside of him something was pumping him in and out, as if he were a pair of bellows.

"Yah, I did it better than any of you," he said, and

jumped up to walk off and show it hadn't been anything, to jump over a ditch.

"Yah," he said.

And fell down and went black.

He awakened slowly, into red and green flashes of pain, and he couldn't see anything but glaring sunlight. The other children had gone. They'd figured he was just dead.

If this was what death was, somebody ought to care.

Ma and Dad would care.

Roan started pulling himself along by his hands and his right knee. His left foot pulsed with pain that flared up his leg and into his groin. He had to peer through the brilliant sunshine as though it were a fog, to see which way home was. He would have to crawl to the swinging bridge over Endless Ravine, and across it, and then across more countryside to home.

Up the hillock and down, his dead, screaming foot dragging uselessly behind him. Roan wanted to die at home. Or not die, if Dad could fix him. But he wasn't going to lie and die where he was, as the gracyls did.

His foot bumped over a sharp stone, caught in a prickle bush. The prickle bush uprooted and clung to the dragging foot like a great insect. Like the Charons that cleaned the flesh off gracyl bodies.

That gracyl at the bottom of Endless Ravine. He'd be thick with them.

Roan stopped to retch, and he thought of removing the prickle bush from his foot but it was too much to do anything else except crawl toward home.

He came to the swinging bridge and here the crawling was worse, infinitely worse, because his hands slipped on the smooth, worn boards and it was possible that he'd slip off, between the ropes along the sides, and always the bridge swayed nauseously.

The wood smelled dry and hot and burned his arms and hands and the prickle bush made an arid, insistent rustle, scraping along with the dead foot.

He crawled forever through the hot, bright fog, his whole leg burning like a torch. He reached home and crawled up on the stoop and called, "Ma! Dad!" and went black again, still calling through the infinite dark corridors of his unconsciousness.

Ma was saying, "Drink this," and he drank it.

"Raff!" she called. "He's awake."

Dad was there, his big, broken body looming in the doorway. You knew he was big, but he stood shorter than Ma.

"Stop that sniffling, Bella," he said. "I'll do it good."

Roan was gladder of Dad. Ma was so old. Like curled leaves. Like things the winds toss up.

Raff sat down heavily, arranged himself on the chair, his bent legs awkwardly set back and his twisted torso facing to one side so that his face was over Roan's, his good eye bright and concerned.

"Don't worry, boy," he said. "It's all right."

"I'm broken, Dad," Roan said, and realized something suddenly. "Like you." And began to cry.

"Oooh!" Ma said, almost whistling it. "Oooh."

"Get out of the room, woman," Dad said, looming over to pat Roan's shoulder. "I'll fix you, boy. Shut up, Bella. My hands are good. I don't have anything else left, but I've got that."

Raff felt softly of Roan's foot. Roan screamed.

"The drink'll help some, boy," Dad said. "But this is going to hurt. There's no help for it. Let it hurt."

Roan was shaking all over and Ma was sobbing and saying, "Stop, Raff, stop, I can't stand it." And Dad was doing something to his foot and Roan shuddered and shuddered and finally thought, I'm going to die, Dad is killing me. Dad is killing me because I'm broken.

The first day that Roan was outside exercising his foot the gracyl sevens came by. Roan was carefully limping. Putting even a little weight on the foot hurt.

"He's *alive!*" one of them said, and they all stood still and gaped at him, and came close and then edged back a little.

"Go ahead, *walk*," Dad said to Roan.

Roan limped painfully.

"Put your weight on it. It doesn't matter how much it hurts. *Use* it. Show 'em."

"He ain't natural," a gracyl child said.

"He was dead," another added.

"His father ain't natural, either. Look at 'em. They're both dead people walking around alive, that's what they are."

The children edged back some more, flapping their skinny arms excitedly, showing the pink membranes of their developing wings.

One of them picked a bright orange chunck-flower pod from the front garden. It missed Roan and made a garish stain on the little house Raff so carefully whitened every spring.

Another child threw a brown one and Roan ducked and a green one hit him over his right eyebrow and hurt and the acrid juice dripped into his eye and stung.

Dad started after the gracyl and the child laughed and spread its wings and flew off in little jumps. Raff swore at his twisted bones and useless muscles and tried to catch the children, and, forgetting himself, fell and lay there futilely trying to twist himself over like a turtle.

"Roan's old man is broken," they chanted. "Roan's a freak, and he's broken, too . . . ." They howled with glee and tossed the chunck-flower pods as fast as they could pick them, and when the pods began to run out they used gobs of mud.

Bella came to the front door and screamed.

Roan forgot his foot. He didn't even know it hurt. He ran to the nearest gracyl and wrested the pod from his hand and smeared the juice in his eyes. Then he grabbed the next one and did the same thing.

They were all upon him, but they didn't fight together. They didn't have one hold him while another hit; Roan fought them one at a time. He kicked one gracyl and caught another around the neck with his hands, and bit a third that fell against him.

Finally those who hadn't gotten hurt bounded off, in their half-flights, and the rest lay there to see whether they were going to die or not.

That evening before dinner Roan took off his tunic and looked at himself in the mirror, examining himself carefully all over. He felt of his hair and poked at his teeth. He twisted around and examined his back minutely and then moved his arms and poked his wing bones in and out, seeing the sharp edges move beneath the thin skin.

He went down to dinner, but he didn't look at the food on the table; he looked at Ma and Dad. And he asked, "What am I?" He always asked, but he never understood.

"You," said Dad, "are a human being. And don't you forget it." That's what he always said.

Roan looked at the steaming plate Ma put before him and didn't want it. "Then that's why I'm so stoopid. Why I can't do anything the gracyls can do."

Raff and Bella exchanged glances.

"That's why you can do everything the gracyls can't do," Raff said. "Or that anybody can't do."

"You cost two thousand Galactic credits," Bella said proudly.

"I cost that much!"

"You were special," Bella said. "Very special."

Roan thought of the insignificant white body he'd just examined, and how it got so easily hurt and broken and how he didn't have any wings and how he'd had to learn how to burrow and swim instead of just knowing as the gracyls did, and how he couldn't just let himself die when he was broken but had to cause everybody a lot of trouble . . .

"You got gypped, didn't you?" Roan said, and ran to his room to cry alone.

But when he'd finished crying he was hungry and he went down and ate and Raff talked to him about what a great thing it was to be a human—and of the original Terry strain. Roan kept trying to believe all the things Raff told him.

Raff was enjoying this talk with his son, and thinking how more and more his son would be a companion to him, and how it had been worth the trouble and the expense of adopting Roan and seeing him through the difficult years of babyhood—and hadn't the boy grown fast!

"You weren't born to be a slave. The Shah could have those a dime a dozen. Or for a common soldier because they were easy come by, too. You were something special . . ."

"But when will my wings grow?" Roan asked, watching Raff's wide, brown face.

Raff shook his heavy head. "You don't need wings, boy. You've got something better: you've got your humanness—"

"Oh, don't try to explain him all that, him only seven years old, even if he is big for his age," Bella said, coming in with another hot dish.

"He's old enough to understand he's a Terry—a real Terry, genuine Terrestrial strain," Raff said. "Not mutated, like me . . ." He nodded proudly at the boy. "And not just humanoid, like your ma." He leaned toward Roan. "Some day you'll know what that means. Real Terry—the breed that settled the whole universe—that built the empire, long ago."

"I thought they were all stuck on Terra," Roan said. "That's what T'hoy hoy says."

Raff looked confused. "Yes, but . . . you were a special case."

"And if I'm a real Terry, why do we have to live in the ghetto with a bunch of old gracyls, and—"

"Here, don't go worrying your mind about all that," Raff cut in. "You're genuine, all right. I can tell. I've seen pictures. Look at you: pale skin, like skim-ice, and hair the color of wineberries, and—"

"But how did I get here, and where are the other real Terries, and—"

"Raff, I told you it wasn't good for the boy to get talking about all those things."

"Some day when you're older," Raff said. "Now just eat your dinner, and take my word for it: you can hold your head up anyplace in the Galaxy and be proud. You're a Terry. Nobody can take that away from you."

T'hoy hoy had come in to put Roan to bed. "I didn't

mean to upset the boy," he told Raff, "telling him about the Terran blockade and all the old Terran legends."

"Tell him the legends," Raff said. "I want him to know. Tell him your stories, T'hoy hoy."

"Then, Roan, tonight I tell you the song of Silver Shane the warrior, who defeated a Niss dreadnought single-handed by crawling up through the waste ejector and holding a fusion bomb while it exploded."

It was winter and the incontinent rains of Tambool swept across the hills and found out a hole in the ceiling of the Cornays' house and Roan heard it drip, drip and it was the last straw, to try to read with that drip, drip happening and the frowsy house smelling of age and poverty, the house they could have because nobody else wanted it.

"It's nasty outside," Bella said.

"It's nastier inside," Roan said, and flung his book across the room. "I'm through."

"You haven't even started," Raff said. "Sit back down."

Roan stood at bay before his parents. Bella set her bone-white lips and began picking irritably at the shedding skin on her thin arm, and Raff tried to work up a temper over the boy, but he couldn't. He's beautiful, Raff thought. No other word for it. Beautiful. Standing there tall for his ten years and glowing in his anger and with the dark red curls tumbling over his forehead.

"Everything," Roan shouted. "I have to do everything the hard way. I'm tired of it. *They* don't study, study, study. They know how to read just looking at the graffiti."

"They're only gracyls," Raff said. "Charons know how to build mud houses without learning. It's the same thing."

"I want to do whatever it is humans know how to do without learning. A two-thousand-credit Man ought to be able to do *something*."

Raff pounded his right fist into his left hand and wished he could flex words the way he could flex his hands. "I've tried to make you understand. I don't know how to say it so's you'll see. Humans are superior, but that doesn't mean everything's easy for you. But you can do things no gracyl can do—"

"One thing humans don't do is read," Roan interrupted. "I hate reading."

"But you can read *good*," Bella said. "You read better than me. Better than Raff. And you can read Gracyl and Universal and those Terran books we kept for you."

"I know he can read good," Raff cut in. "I want him to read better. Good isn't enough."

"Humans *aren't* superior," Roan said. "They're—"

"That's enough, boy," Raff said sharply. He rocked in his chair, watching Roan sliding his foot in a puddle of rainwater on the floor. Bella went to the crockery shelf and took down a bowl to put under the leak in the roof. "Suppose you can't read for Studies? You'll get sent away from home with the Junior Apprentices."

Raff frowned, watching her mop up the floor with the dish towel. "Of course he can read good enough for Studies. If only he don't trip up on a word we haven't come across in the gracyl graffiti yet. Even so, a gracyl that develops seventy per cent literacy goes for Studies. Roan's reached that by now."

Bella straightened painfully from the floor and rubbed at her shedding skin with the dish towel. She looked at Roan and bit at her lip, an old gesture that had once even been cute.

"He's been working so hard, Raff. Maybe we ought to let up on him some."

Roan went to the door.

"Here! Where are you going, Son?"

Roan looked defiantly at Raff. "I'm going to do what humans can do and gracyls can't. And it isn't reading and it's not flying." And he was out of the door into the rain.

"Raff, stop him!"

"Don't worry. He's human. He knows what to do even if he doesn't know he knows."

They both sat by the strip of cloudy plastiflex window and watched the rain on the garbage dump, waiting. They didn't reach for each other any more. Only for the boy.

* * *

The ten yearers were hilarious with the game of swoop ball in the rain when Roan came over the hill in sight of them. It was a simple game. The idea was to keep hold of the ball. They played in a grove of scattered trees, and whoever decided to take the ball would swoop down on whoever had it and take it away and then another would swoop down and take it from the second one, if possible in mid-air. And when you took the ball, you also knocked the gracyl out of the air, which was easy, and if possible into the yard-deep ditch of muddy water that ran along the edge of the little grove.

Roan leaped lightly across the muddy ditch.

The gracyls were delighted to see him. The gracyl with the ball tossed it to him and then four of them swooped straight at him and their momentum shoved him back, straight down into the mud of the ditch.

"OK," Roan said, climbing out of the oozy mud. "OK. I just wanted to be sure I was in the game."

One of the trees was a young purplefruit tree, and Roan found a straight rope vine and cut off a good length from it, several times longer than he was tall. He tied a slip knot in one end and then coiled the rope and slung it in his belt. At the edge of the grove by the ditch, he picked a quarter-grown sapling and climbed up its straight trunk, hanging by his hands when it began to bend, and edging along the length of the young, springy tree until the top of it bent down to the ground. Then carefully, using his full strength, he bent the tree all the way back on itself and used a length of rope to tie the top to the lower part of the thin trunk. He still had plenty of rope left.

The gracyls gathered around and jeered. "That's a silly game," they said. "Who ever played that?"

"It's part of swoop ball," Roan said. "You just watch."

"Yah, yah," said the gracyl who had the ball at the moment. He was up in a nearby tree and he swooped to a lower branch. Then another gracyl swooped the ball away from him and Roan was twirling his rope as the last gracyl was flying across the grove with the ball.

He caught the gracyl around the leg in a beautiful loop and drew him in squawking.

Roan calmly took the ball away and threw it to another gracyl to start the game again, and trussed the lassoed gracyl to the sapling and slipped the rope, so the gracyl went sailing away over the ditch.

Roan climbed up the sapling and bent it again. It no longer stood straight but there was plenty of spring left in it. He looped his lasso again and caught the next gracyl that came sailing by.

"I seem to keep winning," Roan said, trussing the next gracyl to the tree and slipping the rope again. This one landed right in the ditch and scrambled out and made for home.

The gracyls could have played swoop ball higher up in the trees, where Roan's lasso couldn't reach them. Or they could have moved the game. But they didn't; *this* was where gracyls played swoop ball.

Roan took care of two more gracyls. "Give up?" he asked the rest.

"Yah, you can't even fly," they said, and kept on playing exactly the same way. No one tried to take his rope away. No one tried to keep him from bending the sapling.

Pretty soon there were no more gracyls. The last one went sailing over the ditch and hopped off home, whining.

All except Clanth, of course, with his one undeveloped wing. He'd learned to sit and watch games.

"That was fun," Clanth said.

Roan tossed his rope into the muddy ditch and leaped across it and turned back to watch the deserted spot where the swoop ball game had been. He rubbed the mud off his hands down the sides of his trousers.

"I won," he said, and grinned, and went home to practice his reading.

3

Roan sat on the stoop of his house with a large book spread in his lap. It was entitled *Heroes of Old Terra*, and it was packed with shiny tri-D pictures of men and ships and great towering cities. It was a very old book, and some of the pages were missing, but the pictures were still bright.

"Hey, c'mon," someone said. Roan's mind swam out from the book. Clanth, who was the nearest thing Roan had to a friend, stood waiting.

"Where?" Roan asked.

"Where!" Clanth flapped his one, useless wing. His black, leathery gracyl face was alight with excitement, the round amber eyes asparkle. "It's the spring pre-mating. Out in the grove."

Roan's fair cheeks flushed, back to the roots of his deep red hair. "Don't be ridiculous," he said. "But . . . good flying," he added, so as not to offend his friend. It might have been an offensive phrase to Clanth, because of his disability, but Roan had found that Clanth preferred for him not to be sensitive about it.

"I . . . Oh, I'm not like the others, either." But Clanth was handsome, gracyl handsome, and well developed for fourteen, and you noticed that before you noticed about his wing. And since he was in Studies, not Labor, it didn't make so much difference about the wing. "C'mon, Roan . . ."

"What would I do there?" Roan asked. "Provided I could get a female up a tree to begin with?"

"Well . . . wings aren't really necessary. At least I hope not. Look at me." And he raised his wingless right arm.

"I'd rather not try." Roan pictured the black, screeching little gracyl females. He was glad he didn't want one, because she'd laugh at him if he did. Sneer at him. Flap her wings at him.

"But gee, here you are fourteen years old," Clanth persisted. "What are you going to *do?*"

"I'll wait," said Roan.

"For what?" Clanth asked, and didn't wait for the answer, for a gaggle of fourteens went by and Clanth ran off to join them.

Roan watched them go, then sat with the book in his lap, gazing at the clouds and trying to picture a human female. The portraits in his books, the descriptions he'd read; he tried to put all his knowledge together, but it wouldn't add up to a definite picture. Every time he thought he had it, it slipped away from him.

Day wore into evening and still Roan sat, and he thought about human women and then about human men, and the old heroes of his book, who left human women to go out and find new worlds, and died showing there were places besides earth where human men could bring human women.

Human women were not like Ma. They were . . . Roan couldn't find the thought. He didn't know.

The gracyls had finished going by. The crowds of young males had gone out, and the crowds of ripening females. The first moon was still white in the sky, but it was brightening and soon the sickle anti-moon would come up and the ceremonies would begin and Roan wished Clanth well and hoped his female would not laugh too much at his poor wingless arm.

Another group of youths was coming along; there was

a low mutter of talk and laughter among them—and they were not gracyls.

"Supper!" Ma called. And came to the door. "What are you doing reading in that light?"

Roan peered through the gloom to see who was coming. The Veed. What were they doing out of their ornately decorated quarters in the heart of the town?

"Has there been a Veed murder or something?" Roan asked, because Ma always managed to know, without talking to anybody, what was going on in the adult world.

"If there has I don't want to know about it and neither do you," said Ma, retreating further behind the front door. "You come on in. You don't want to tempt that trash to stop here."

But Roan waited to watch them go by, the young Veed, their scalesuits glittering faintly even in the tarnished twilight. They walked upright, looking almost human, talking their Veed talk.

"They're children," Roan said, and went in finally. "About my age."

"About fifty years old," Ma said, spooning stewed limpid seeds onto the grits on his plate. "That would be about half mature, for them."

"One of them was an aristocrat. I saw the iridion quadrant on his cheek." What magic lives they must lead, Roan thought, those Veed, with their painted porches and their gardens and their endless games of slots and colored beads, and their lives that stretched on forever.

"When will I die?" Roan asked, and Dad dropped his knife with a helping of purplefruit balanced on it.

"What made you ask that?"

"Nothing. I just wondered. I mean the Veed take forever to grow up and gracyls die if they get broken badly, but what about me?"

"You," Dad said. "Well, I've always answered you straight. You'll live a long time yet. Take me. I'm a hundred and eighty, and still got lots of years ahead. You'll live longer yet. You're prime Terry stock, boy."

"Even if I don't get broken or something? That's all I'll live? I'll just die?"

"There's a story," Raff said, picking up his knife and scraping the dirtied fruit off on the side of his wooden plate, "an old, old story that at the beginning of time the nine Gods called all the species of intelligent beings together and asked them which they preferred, a long life or a glorious one. Only Man chose the glorious life. And he's always been proud of it."

There was another sibilance of Veed going by outside and Roan scurried to the dark front window and saw a second group, headed the same way, toward the gracyl mating grove, the grove of trees by the ditch, where long ago Roan had used his lasso to win a game of swoop ball. The sapling was a tree with spread limbs now, and maybe Clanth would be waiting in it to drop down and catch his female.

The moonlight showed yellowish pink now, and the garbage dump outside the window was jeweled with it. It was Veed garbage, Roan thought, and for some reason this made him love the gracyls and hate the Veed.

"There's going to be trouble tonight," Roan said, and finished his dinner thoughtfully.

Raff silently got down his big hammer and nailed a panel and a bar of wood across each plastiflex window.

"No," said Roan, when Raff started to nail the door bolt from the inside. He wiped the last of the grits off his knife and stuck it through his rope vine belt. He pulled his tunic up short, so that it draped over his belt and left his legs free for running. Raff looked at him.

"Clanth's out there," Roan said. "I'll be back after a while."

"Now, boy," Raff started. But Roan was already gone, out into the moonlight and the warm spring night.

"Why did you tell him that silly story?" Bella asked, sitting in the darkened house and miserable at the thought of the long, dark hours before Roan might come home.

"Because," Raff said, "I think it's true."

*   *   *

Roan knew something the Veed didn't know. He knew every shack and rock and ditch and garbage pile in the slum. As he came out of the house he sensed another group approaching, and he ducked into a tunnel through the heaped garbage.

They were speaking Veed, their hushed, hissed tongue, so Roan could not tell all of what they were saying, though they passed so close he could have spit on them. But he did catch "gracyl" and "moon," which were the same in all their languages.

If it were only the children out, that meant it was a lark, not a hunt in retribution for some crime or suspected crime. "Ten half-breeds for one Veed," was their rule. Half-breeds included anybody that wasn't Veed.

But this. This was children playing. Or practicing.

Roan gave the Veed a good head start.

He went through the backyard of the funny old voiceless couple that kept mud-swine, and around another garbage heap, and through a series of gullies, and then crept up the knoll that overlooked the ditch and the grove of trees where the gracyls were sporting.

In the grove, where the moonlight could pick them out through the trees, Roan could see the running gracyls, and hear their high, shrill calls. They had no thought for anything but each other. He even thought he could make out Clanth, flapping grotesquely in the tree that Roan had known as a sapling. And he thought he saw something else, very strange. It looked like a white figure, high in one of the trees, looking on very still.

Around the grove, in the ditch, the Veed boys were gathered in full force, a ditch full of glittering Veed, swaying silently in unison. They must be almost ready for the attack.

Roan leaped to the top of the knoll and filled his lungs. "Danger!" he screamed, and the gracyl began running about in the grove in confusion and making for the treetops.

The Veed attacked immediately and furiously. No

one seemed to have noticed that the scream had not come from within the grove. Roan was through the ditch and at the grove in seconds.

The Veed filled the grove now, furious, slashing about with their razor-sharp wrist talons. They had planned to catch the gracyls on the ground. With the gracyls in the branches of the dark trees it was going to be harder, and less fun.

Roan crept forward and into and up the side of the dry ditch.

And got caught by a Veed as he started up the purplefruit tree on the edge of the grove. He'd thought it was a tree that brought him luck.

The Veed's raking hands curled around his thigh and he felt the blood spring out into a thin line of pain and he jerked the knife free of his belt and slashed the coarse Veed flesh and felt the hands recoil instantly.

In the brief moment this gave him, Roan was scrambling up, swinging on a rope vine to the next tree. Around him gracyls fluttered and squawked. The cry of the wounded Veed had brought his fellows to his side; and there were indignant conferences and hisses of outrage. No gracyl had ever dared to use a weapon against a Veed.

Roan listened, catching a word here and there. They were out without permission, because young Veed were always carefully protected. So they couldn't complain to their elders about the wounded Veed. This meant they had to take their vengeance on the spot.

But they couldn't get up into the trees because their bodies were too awkward for climbing and they couldn't throw things up into the trees without hitting each other.

Several of the Veed went over to one of the slenderest of the trees, where three gracyls hung in the branches like clumps of moss, and began pushing the trunk back and forth. The gracyls screeched, clinging tighter in their panic, and as the tree gained momentum, one of them fell to the ground, too panicked to try to fly.

The Veed were gleeful. It was like shaking the purplefruit off a tree.

Several Veed grabbed the gracyl and Roan carefully didn't watch what they did with him.

"Fly to the next tree," Roan called to the other two gracyls. "All you have to do is stay calm."

But they couldn't. They could only cling and screech, the way gracyls always did when they were frightened. They couldn't change, even to save their lives.

Another gracyl fell.

Other Veed were starting on other trees.

"Make for the thickest trees," Roan called. "They can't shake the thickest ones."

But no gracyl moved. Roan burned with the frustration of it all, the helplessness of the gracyls and the blunt cruelty of the Veed. Where was Clanth? Perhaps he was already safe in a broad-trunked tree.

"Clanth!" he called, but there was no answer. Perhaps Clanth couldn't hear him, or perhaps he was clinging to a tree, squawking with terror, like the other gracyls. But he had always been a little different; surely he would save himself. Then Roan remembered. Clanth couldn't fly.

Roan's tree began to sway.

He looked around for a rope vine, to make it to the broader trees toward the center of the grove, but there was no rope vine. He cursed himself for not having cut one and looped it through his belt when he was in the first tree. But it was too late.

Well, it would be easy enough for him to hang on. He stood on one branch and held on to the next, watching the gleeful Veed below, their teeth gleaming as they smiled their crocodile smiles, their crests swaying contentedly.

Something dropped past Roan and fell into the waiting arms of a Veed. They gasped to see it and so did Roan. It was all white and for a moment Roan thought it must be a human child.

That was the moment he leaped.

He leaped for the back of the Veed holding the screaming white creature and he drove his knife deep into the Veed's right eye, through to the brain, and the Veed died beneath him.

Roan pulled the knife out and stood on the dead Veed, the white creature clinging to his neck, and stood to meet the slashing blows of the other Veed.

But they backed away from him.

They were in awe and fear of him, that he had wounded one Veed and killed another. They had seen many a gracyl die, and that was funny. But they had never seen a Veed die before; they hadn't thought anybody could kill a Veed.

They fled to take revenge on more gracyls. It was safer.

Roan pulled the white creature from his neck and looked at it.

She was a white gracyl.

"I'm not dead," she said wonderingly. Gracyl fear didn't last long when the danger was over. "I knew I was going to be broken and I prepared to die and . . . now I feel as though I must have died and here I am still alive."

"You're a half-breed?" he asked. "Or a mutation?"

"I'm an albino," she said. "You saved my life, didn't you? You did that on purpose."

Then they were silent a moment, looking at each other in the little moonlight. Caught in the brief bond of savior and saved, they tried to meet minds across the deeps and dimensions that separated their aliennesses.

"I belong to you now," she said, and clung to him, and he held her close and felt her whiteness and kissed her strange, cold mouth and it was all a part of the swaying darkness and the hissing Veed and the dying gracyl and the death that Roan had made. The dead Veed and the victory.

Roan had lost the threads that bound him to himself and all that was left was the white gracyl woman under his hands in the sickle moonlight.

Across the grove, the gracyls were screaming as they fell but Roan was not thinking of them dying, only of the distant music of their voices.

"That one was Clanth," she said dreamily. "I was going to be his female and now . . ."

"Clanth!" Roan cried, and came to himself.

"Yes. Only Clanth. After all, I just took him because nobody else wanted me and now it doesn't matter."

"Doesn't matter!" He yanked her savagely to her feet. "Show me which way the scream came from! Show me where Clanth is!" He had not been listening. He had not been caring. He had been as bad as a gracyl. Worse, because they couldn't help it and he could.

He saw the Veed beginning to leave the grove as they made their way through the trees. Either they had had all their fun or it was time for them to get back before their parents discovered they were gone.

"There he is," said the white gracyl female. "What do you want with him?"

One last Veed, seeing Roan, gave Clanth a parting slash and moved sinuously off. Roan knelt by the dying gracyl. "Clanth, I couldn't find you. I couldn't help." But he hadn't looked.

"I'm broken," Clanth said. "But, Roan, I had a female."

"I brought her to you," Roan said. He stood and put his knife at the white female's back until she came over to Clanth. "You can die in her arms."

"That was silly," she said when Clanth had died.

The gracyls, those that were left, were coming down from the trees now and incredibly starting their mating ceremonies again.

Roan walked away through the grove, and out into the white moonlight. He climbed to the top of the tallest garbage heap and sat, looking down on the ghetto, not listening to the happy gracyl sounds, thinking about what a human woman might be like.

4

Here on the high ledge, the wind was sharp with sand particles, buffeting angrily like a gracyl when you held him upside down to show him that even if you didn't have wings, you weren't something to throw chunck flowers at. Roan got to his feet, holding on tightly to the tiny fingerholds of the wind-worn carving, feeling with his toes for a firm grip. He was high enough now: over the tops of the purplefruit trees, he could see the glare panels strung out across the arena gate, spelling out:

GRAND VORPLISCH EXTRAVAGANZOO!!!
Renowned Throughout the Eastern Arm!!
Entrepreneur Gom Bulj Presents:
Fabulous Feathered Flyers!
Superb Scaled Swimmers!
Horrific Hairy Hurlers!
A Stupefying Spectacle of Leaping Life-forms,
Battling Boneless Beasts, Wingless Wizards of Wit,
Frightful Fanged Fighters!
See Iron Robert, Strongest Living Creature—
Stellaraire, the Galaxy's loveliest creation!
Snarleron, Ugliest in the Universe!
ADMISSION, G. CR. .10 plus tax.

Roan's hand twitched, wanting to go to his credit coder to check once more; but he restrained it. He knew what it would show. The balance gauge would barely glow. Even the five demi-chits he'd earned stacking bread-logs for the Store was gone, spent for dye-wood billets for carving. He'd have to be satisfied with what he could see from here—not that that would be much. He could hear the noisemakers faintly, but the dusty grounds of the arena were mostly obscured by the trees and the high wall, crumbling along its top like all the Old Things, but still high enough to shield the marvels from his view.

But on the other side, there, where the great white-boled Never-never tree grew . . .

It was beyond the Soetti Quarter, where Dad had told him never to put a foot—but it spread wide, almost to the rubble-littered top of the wall, where it dipped down in a sort of notch.

He wouldn't really be going into the Soetti Quarter—just passing through . . .

Ten minutes later, Roan perched in an arched opening, just above the lower gates, breathing a little fast from the quick climb down. He checked to be sure no heavy old gracyl mares were stretching their atrophied wings on nearby balconies; then he jumped, caught at ancient green-scaled tiles, scrambled up to a position astride the steep gable of the first house. From the balconies below, he heard a clatter of food troughs, a few shouts, a lazy pad of feet, the slam of a door; the oldsters' early-evening siesta was under way and everyone else was at the Extravaganzoo. Roan rose, ran lightly along the ridge tiles, jumped the gap to the next house. There were carved devils at ten-foot intervals here; he had to drop flat at each one, work his way under, then up again. At the end, he swung down under the eave, dropped to a shed below, then swarmed up the carved gable end of the next house; but then it was easy; a series of wind-god altars, like stepping-stones, led to the end of the last house before the high, black-glazed Barrier. He jumped for a drain ledge, worked his way along to a down gutter, held on with his fingers, and slid quickly to the yellow dust of the path. Roan grinned to himself. All those years of playing with gracyls had almost taught him how to fly.

The burrow under the Barrier was almost choked with rubble and blown prickle bushes; it had been a long time since he and Yopp, a Fustian eggling, had last explored it. Maybe he was too big now; he grew so fast—like a Soetti, Raff had said once, grumbling at having to cobble new shoes so soon after the last ones . . .

But it was all right; once the last prickle bush was dragged clear, Roan went in head first, pulling himself along with his hands until he came to the straight-up part; then he stood, put his back against one wall and his feet against the other, and walked up.

The iodine smell of the Soetti was strong, even before he reached the top and pulled himself out into the hazy, late orange sunlight, filtered dark by the great, sagging, patched nets the Soetti used to hold in their kind of air. Roan lay flat, breathing close to the ground; when he had his lungs full—even though they burned a little, from the bad Soetti air—he jumped up, ran for the high fences barely visible in the gloom at the far side of the quarter.

He was halfway there when a big Soetti—almost five feet high—in greaves, a flared helmet with black eye shields, and a heavy cloak, popped out of a hut in his path, blocking his way, heavy pincers ready. Roan slid to a stop, watching the violet-freckled claws. They looked too massive for the short, spindly Soetti arms, but Roan knew they could cut through quarter-inch chromalloy plate.

From burrows all around, bright Soetti eyes winked, ducking back as he looked their way. The warrior advanced a step, snapping his claws like pistol shots, *pow! pow!* Roan stooped, picked up a four-foot stick of springy boolon wood. He waved it at the Soetti; it hissed, its arms twitching in instinctive response to the movement. It saw what Roan was trying to do, and backed quickly; but Roan moved in, flicked the stick almost under the Soetti's faceted eyes; the pincers flashed, locked on the wand, as involuntarily as a wink; and Roan jerked the stick, hard, throwing the warrior off balance. He dropped the stick and sprang past the creature, sprinting for the board wall, laughing as he ran.

The Never-never tree was three yards thick at the base, rising like a column of buttressed white stone set with daggers of crystalline lime. It wasn't hard to climb, as long as he just held on with his knees and elbows and didn't touch the spines; and the branch, the one that reached out to the wall—it wasn't very big, but it would probably hold all right—even with the weight of a sixteen-year-old Man on it.

Roan started up; the first fifty feet was simple enough, the spines were as big as Roan's wrist, set well apart; he could even use them as footholds.

He reached for a higher grip—and a spine broke under his foot. His hand snapped out to seize a razor-edged spine while his knees gripped the narrowing buttress between them. Pain tore through his hand and snaked down his arm, red pain and blood. Roan hated the dumb way his hand had grabbed, like the Soetti's claws, at whatever came near. The Soetti's claws couldn't learn but maybe Roan's hand could, if it hurt enough. And it did hurt enough and now it was slippery as well.

Pain was a taste of death in Roan's mouth, like the time he'd broken his foot. But something else Roan could do was force himself to forget things. He ignored the hand and went on.

The branch that stretched over the wall had patches of peeling bark adhering to it. Roan brushed them away before stepping out on it; he couldn't take a chance on losing his footing; with his slippery hand, he might not be able to hold on if he fell. He wiped his hand again on his tunic, then clenched it to hold in the pain and the blood. The branch moved gently underfoot as he walked out on it, swaying to the gusty wind, and dipping now under his weight. Raff was right; he did grow too fast. He was heavier than an old gracyl brood master. The tip of the branch was level with the top of the wall now; and now it dipped lower, the shiny blue leaves at its tip clattering softly against the weathered masonry. But he was close now; the whine and thump of the noisemakers were loud above the chirp and bellow of the crowd beyond the walls, and he could see the blue-white disks of the polyarcs glaring on the dusty midway.

The last few yards were hard going. The tiny spines were close together here—and sharp enough to stab through his bos-hide shoes. If the slender bough sank much lower under his weight, he wouldn't be able to reach the wall. But he knew. He knew from the gracyl games how much weight a tree limb could hold.

Balancing carefully, Roan started the branch swaying, down, up, in a slow sweep, down, heavily, then shuddering up . . .

On the third upward swing, Roan jumped, caught the edge of the wall, raked at loose rubble, then pulled himself up and lay flat on the dust-powdered surface, still hot from the day's sun. He opened his hand and looked at it. The blood had formed a blackish cake with the dust. That was good; now maybe it would stop running all over things and spoiling his fun. He patted it in the dust some more, then crawled to the edge of the wall and looked over into the glare of the grounds—

Sound struck him in the face like a thrown chunck-flower: the massed roar of voices, the shrill clangor of the noisemakers, the rustle of scaled and leathered bodies, the grating of feet—shod, horned, clawed, hooved. The cries of shills and hucksters . . .

It was dark now. Twenty feet below Roan, the heads of the crowd stretched in a heaving sea of motion, surging around the pooled light of the midways, alive with color and movement. There, a jeweled harness sparkled on tandem hitched bull-devils; there a great horned body, chained by one leg, pranced in an intricate dance; and beyond, caged dire-beasts paced, double jaws gaping.

Roan forgot to breathe, watching as a procession of scarlet-robed creatures with golden hides strode into view from a spotlighted arch, fanned out to form a circle, dropped the red cloaks, and rushed together,

cresting up into a living pyramid, then dropping back to
split and come together like a wave breaking against a
wall, and then . . .

He had to get closer. He raised his head and looked
along the broken wall, following its great arc to the far
side where it loomed black against the luminous amber
twilight. He could jump down easily enough, but not
without landing on a bad-tempered gracyl or a wide-
jawed Yill.

He rose and moved off, stepping carefully among the
rubble. It was almost full dark now. Ahead, he made
out the heavy sagging line of an anchor cable, its end
secured to a massive iron capstan set in the stone
coping. He clambered up, followed the cable with his
eye as it dipped, then rose up to meet a slender tower.
This was almost too easy: the base of the tower was
hidden in shadow behind a cluster of polyarcs. No one
would notice if he walked across and slipped down
there . . .

He stepped out on the taut cable; it was much easier
than the branch had been; it was only as big as his
finger, but it was steady. No one looked up from below;
he was above the polyarcs, invisible against their glare.

He walked out across the crowd, reached the tower,
swung quickly down—

A hand like an iron clamp locked on his ankle. He
looked down. A face like a worn-out shoe blinked up at
him. Gill flaps at either side of the wide head quivered.

"Come down, come down," a curious double voice
said. "Caught you—ought—you good—ood."

Roan held on and pulled; it was like trying to uproot
an anvil tree.

"Let go," he said, trying to make his voice sound as
though it were used to being obeyed by beings with
old-shoe faces and hands like ship grapples.

"You're—re—going to see—ee the boss—oss." The
iron hand—which was bright green, Roan noticed, and
had three fingers—tugged, just gently, and Roan felt
his joints creak. He held on.

"Want me—ant me to pull—ull your leg—eg off—
off?" the hollow voice echoed.

"All right," Roan said. He lowered himself carefully until his other foot was on a level with his captor's hand. Then he swung his free leg back and kicked the creature in the eye.

The grip was gone from his ankle, and he leaped clear, landed in dust, turned to duck away—

And slammed against a wide, armored body that gathered him in with arms like the roots of the grizzly-wood tree.

It was dark inside the big tent, and hot, and there were odors of seaweed and smoke. Roan stood straight, trying not to think about the way his hands were numb from the grip on his wrists. Beside him, the shoe-faced creature flapped its gills, blinking its swollen eye. "Ow-ow," it said, over and over. "Ow-ow."

The being behind the big, scarred, black-brown desk blinked large brown eyes at him from points eight inches apart in a head the size of a washtub mounted on a body like a hundred gallon bag of water. Immense hands with too many fingers reached for a box, extracted a thick brown cigar, peeled it carefully, thrust it into a gaping mouth that opened unexpectedly just above the brown eyes.

"Some kind of Terry, aren't you?" a bass voice said from somewhere near the floor.

Roan swallowed. "Terry stock," he said, trying to sound as though he were proud of it. "Genuine Terrestrial strain," he added.

The big head waggled. "I saw you on the wire. Never saw a Terry walk a wire like that before." The voice seemed to come from under the desk. Roan peered, caught a glimpse of coiled purplish tentacles. He looked up to catch a brown eye upon him; the other was rolled toward the gilled creature.

"You shouldn't have hurt Ithc," the deep voice rumbled. "Be quiet, Ithc." The wandering eye turned back to Roan. "Take off your tunic."

"Why?"

"I want to see what kind of wings you've got."

"I don't have any wings," Roan said, sounding as

though he didn't care. "Terries don't have wings; not real original Terrestrial stock, anyway."

"Let's see your hands."

"He's holding them."

"Let him go, Ithc." The brown eyes looked at Roan's hands as he opened and closed them to get the blood going again.

"The feet," the basso voice said. Roan kicked off a shoe and put his foot up on the desk. He wriggled his toes, then put his foot back on the floor.

"You walked the wire with *those* feet?"

Roan didn't answer.

"What were you doing up there?"

"I was getting in without a ticket," Roan said. "I almost made it, too."

"You like my little show, hey?"

"I haven't seen it—yet."

"You know who I am, young Terry?"

Roan shook his head.

"I'm Gom Bulj, Entrepreneur Second Class." One of the broad hands waved the cigar. "I'm owner of the Extravaganzoo. Now—" The heavy body hitched forward in the wide chair. "I'll tell you something, young Terry. I haven't seen a lot of Terries before, but I've always been a sort of admirer of theirs. Like back in ancient times, the wars and all that. Real spectacles." Gom Bulj thumped his desk. "This desk—it's made of Terry wood—*woolnoot*, I think they call it. Over six thousand years old; came out of an old Terry liner, a derelict on—" He cut off.

"Never mind that. Another story. What I'm getting at is—how would you like to join my group, young Terry? Become a part of the Grand Vorplisch Extravaganzoo! Travel, see the worlds, exhibit your unusual skills to appreciative audiences of discerning beings all over the Western Arm?"

Roan couldn't help it: he gasped.

"Not much pay at first," Gom Bulj said quickly. He paused, one eye on Roan. "In fact, no pay—until you learn the business."

Roan took a deep breath. Then he shook his head. Gom Bulj was still looking at him expectantly.

"No," he said. "Not until I ask Dad . . ." Suddenly Roan was remembering Ma, waiting, with his dinner ready now, and Raff . . . Raff would be worried, wondering where he was . . .

"I've got to go now," he said, and wondered why he had such a strange, sinking feeling.

Gom Bulj drummed his tentacles under the desk. He sucked on a stony-looking tooth, eyeing Roan thoughtfully.

"No need to trouble old Dad, young Terry. You're big enough to leave the burrow, no doubt. Probably he'll never miss you, new litters coming along—"

"Terries don't have litters; only one. And Ma only had me."

"You'll write," Gom Bulj said. "First planetfall, you'll write, tell them what a mark you're making. A featured sideshow attraction in the finest 'zoo in this part of the Galaxy—"

"I'll have to ask Dad's permission first," Roan said firmly.

Gom Bulj signaled with a finger. "You'll surprise him; come back some day, dressed in spangles and glare-jewels—"

Ithc's reaching hand grazed Roan's arm as he ducked, whirled, darted for the tent flap. Something small, with bright red eyes, sprang in front of him; he bowled it over, ran for the tower, darting between the customers milling in the way between the bright colored tents under the polyarcs. He veered around a cage inside which a long-legged creature moaned, jumped stretched tent ropes, sprinted the last few yards—

A hulking, gilled figure—a twin to Ithc—bounded into his path; he spun aside, plunged under an open tent flap, plowed through massed gracyls who hissed and struck out with knobbed wing bones. A vast gray creature with long white horns growing from its mouth teetered on a tiny stand; it trumpeted nervously and swung a blow with a heavy gray head-tentacle as Roan darted past; then Roan was under the edge of the tent, up and running for the wall. Behind him, an electric voice crackled, deep tones that rattled in a strange tongue.

He saw the gate rising up, light festooned, above the surging pack. To one side, another of the gilled creatures worked its way toward him, knocking the crowd aside with sweeps of its three-pronged hands. Roan threw himself at the mass before him, forcing passage. Another few yards—

"Roan!" an agonized voice roared. By the gate, Raff's massive white-maned head loomed over the crowd. "This way, boy . . . !"

"Dad!" Roan lowered his head, threw himself against the slow-moving bodies in his way. The gill thing was close now—and there was another—

And then he was at the gate, and Raff's hand was stretched out to him above the crutch—

The gilled creature thrust itself before Roan, arms spread wide. Roan whirled—and saw the other—and beyond, a third, coming up fast. He feinted, dived between the two nearest—

The steel grip caught his arm; he looked up into the old-shoe face, swung his doubled fist—

Both hands were caught now. He kicked, but only bruised his toes against the horny shins.

And then Raff was there, his brown face twisted, his mouth open. Over the mob roar, Roan couldn't hear what he was shouting. He saw Raff's thick arms swing up, and the crutch came down in a crashing arc on the gilled head, and for an instant the grip loosened and Roan pulled a hand free—

And then a gray-green figure loomed behind Raff, and a three-fingered hand struck, and now Raff's face was twisted in a different way, and he was falling, going down, and the white head was flushed suddenly crimson, and he lay in the yellow dust on his face, and Roan felt his throat screaming—

His hand was free, and he struck, felt something yield, and he ripped at it, feeling his jaws open, teeth hungry for the enemy, and then both hands were free, and he smashed at the old-leather face, seeing it reel back, and then the other was at him with three-taloned hands clutching, and Roan seized two long fingers in his two hands and tore at them and felt them break and rip—

And then he was falling, falling, and somewhere voices called, but they were far away, too far, and they faded, and were gone . . .

And he was alone and very small in the dark.

5

Gom Bulj's diamond stickpin glittered like his eyes, and he smoked his cigar as though he had tasted and wearied of all other cigars in the universe.

"You're a wild one, Terry," he said, both eyes staring at Roan. "What was the idea of crippling up Ithc? You should see his hand. Terrible!"

"I hope he's ruined," Roan said, not crying, not thinking about the ache that made the side of his head feel as big as Gom Bulj's. "I wish I'd been able to kill him. I *will* kill him the first chance I get . . ." He had to stop talking then, remembering Dad, trying to help, then falling . . . and the dust on his face . . .

"There was no need for the dramatics; no need at all. If you'd come along quietly, you'd have found life in the Extravaganzoo most rewarding—and I'd still have the use of Ithc. Did you know you nearly tore his finger off?"

"He killed Dad," Roan said, and now there were tears; his face tried to twist and he felt dried blood crack on his skin; but he stood as straight as the Ythcan's grip on his arms would let him and looked Gom Bulj in one eye, the other being busy now with some papers spread on the desk.

"I know everything you're going to say," the entrepreneur said, "so don't bother to say it. Just let me indicate to you that you are a very lucky Terry, Terry. If you weren't a valuable Freak, I'd put you out the nearest lock for the trouble you've caused me. But I'm a businessman. You'll start in as a scraper-punk and double in greenface." He jerked his huge head at the three-fingered guard. "Take him along to a cubicle on number two menagerie deck with the other Freaks— and see there's a stout lock on the door."

Green arms like cargo cranes turned Roan and propelled him into the corridor. The vibration of the engines and the stink of ozone were more noticeable here than in the deep-carpeted office of the 'zoo owner. For a moment Roan felt a surge of excitement, remembering that he was aboard a ship, in deep space. He wanted to ask where they were bound, how long the voyage would last, but he wouldn't ask the Ythcan. He might be one of the ones who'd helped to kill Raff. Roan couldn't tell them apart. But there was one he would recognize . . .

Roan sat in the limp hay that was his bed. The metal-walled cell smelled of animals and old air. He was sore all over but his mind was clear, and he listened to the sound that had awakened him with a feeling of suspense that was almost pleasurable. Something was working at the latch to his door, and he looked about for a weapon, but there was nothing. Nothing but four stark walls and the used hay. Not even clothes: they had taken his tunic away; and he thought, I'll have to fight with my hands and teeth, and he crouched, ready.

But the door didn't open; instead, a metal panel swung back and suddenly Roan was looking through bars into ocher eyes in an oval face with skin as pale and smooth as a tay-tay leaf, and a cloud of soft hair the color of early sunshine.

She laughed, a sound like soft night rain, and Roan stared at the tender red mouth, the white teeth, the tip of a pink tongue.

"You're . . ." Roan said, "you're a human woman . . ."

She laughed again, and he saw a delicate purple vein that throbbed faintly in her white throat. "No," she said in a voice that seemed to Roan like the murmur of evening wind in the crystalline leaves of the Never-never tree. "I'm a mule."

Roan came close to the barred window. He looked at her: the slender neck, the shapes of yielding roundness under the silver clothes, the tiny waist, the long, slim lines of her thighs.

"I've seen pictures," Roan said. His voice seemed to catch in his throat. "But I never, ever saw . . ."

"You still haven't. But Pa said I could pass for Pure Strain in a bad light." She put her hands on the bars, and they were small and smooth, and Roan put out a hand and touched her.

"A mule's a cross between two human strains that never should have got mixed up together in the first place," she said carelessly. "Mules are sterile." She looked at him.

"You've cut your head. And you've been crying."

"Will you—" Roan started, and swallowed "—will you take your tunic off?"

The girl looked at him, still smiling, and then the pale cheeks quite suddenly were pink. She laughed, but it was a different laugh.

"What did you say?"

"Please—take off your tunic."

For a long moment the ocher eyes looked into Roan's blue ones. Then she stepped back from the door, her soft hand slipping from under Roan's for a moment. She did things to the silver garment and it fell away, and she stood for a moment poised and straight, and then she turned slowly, all the way around.

Roan's breath came hard through the turmoil in his chest.

"I never dreamed anything could be so beautiful," he said.

The girl drew a quick breath, then bent, snatched up her garment, and was gone. Roan pressed his face to the bars, caught a glimpse of her as she darted past a lumbering, bald humanoid who turned and stared after her, then came clumping up to the cell door. He looked angrily at Roan.

"What the hell's wrong with Stel?" he barked. He looked down, clattering keys. "All right, Terry, the vacation's over. I'm Nugg. You work for me. I can use some help, the devil knows . . ."

The door clanked open. Roan stepped out, measured the alien's seven foot height. The creature raised a fist like a stone club.

"Don't get ideas, runt. Just do your work and you'll get along. You'll need some shoes, I suppose. And a tunic. Around this place clothes are the only way to tell the Freaks from the animals."

"Who was she?" Roan said. "Where did she go?"

Nugg glared at him. "Keep your mind off Stel; Stellaraire, to you. She dances. She's got no time for Freaks and scrapers. I know about you; you're a mean one. You watch your step, Terry, and tend to your scraping—and your greenface. Now come on."

Roan followed the hulking humanoid along the echoing corridor, noisy with the rumble of ventilators, the clamor of voices, the thump of feet, to a dingy room of shelves heaped with equipment. Nugg hauled a large duffel bag of used clothing from a locker, dumped it out onto the floor.

Roan discarded a bra affair that might have fitted a midget Stellaraire, a zippered tube that seemed to be made of human skin, a hexagonal wired corset, and a gauze veil before he came up with a simple buttoned tunic only a few sizes too large. But he found a marvelous belt made of flexible metal links that fitted itself perfectly to his slim waist. He also found a pair of heavy hide sandals.

Nugg grunted. "Get down to C deck. One of the boys will tell you what to do." He gave Roan directions. "And stay out of trouble!" he added.

Roan rode down the lift, stepped out into a sour reek of stables, a vast, steel room echoing with grunts, squeals, and the shuffle and clatter of hooves and the pad of horny feet. Through bars he saw shaggy pelts of black and pink and tan, glistening hides, scaled, knobbed, smooth, the flash of light on horns, tusks, fangs, the curl of sinuous tails, the reach of taloned limbs, and tentacles that groped restlessly.

"You—oo son of a bitch—itch," an echoing voice said. Roan turned. On the other side of a massive grill a seven-foot Ythcan glowered, one three-fingered green hand thrust through the bars, the thick fingers closing futilely an inch from Roan's tunic. The other hand was a round knob of dirty bandages.

Roan stepped back and looked around for a weapon. Ithc raised his maimed hand and shook it. "It wa—as my skilled—illed hand—and. You—oo've ruined it for life—ife."

"Good," Roan said. "I'm going to ruin the other one too."

"You—oo wait there—ere," Ithc said, moving along the grill. "I'm—mm coming to kill—ill you—oo."

There was a long-handled pitchfork against the bulkhead with straw and dung matted in the tines. Roan clanged it against the steel wall and ran to meet Ithc. A wide gate at the end of the grilled wall stood open. The Ythcan halted just beyond it and Roan stepped through, the pitchfork raised.

Ithc made a sudden motion and the heavy, motor-driven grill slammed against Roan, knocked him off his feet, pinning him in the opening. The Ythcan planted a horny, three-toed foot against Roan's chest and with his good hand drew a knife from behind him. He clicked a catch and the blade guard dropped off the knife and what was left was a glistening razor that made Roan bite his teeth to look at.

"I'll—ll cut your wrist tendons first—irst," Ithc said. He leaned close, just out of reach of Roan's hands. His gill flaps rippled, flushed pink. "Then—en I'll do—oo your eyes—ss . . ." He held his bandaged hand before him for balance, weaving the blade to and fro.

Roan was watching the dagger. Every time it moved, he had his hands ready to grab. With a sudden, unexpected motion the Ythcan jabbed for his shoulder; Roan struck out—and the Ythcan jumped back, holding his bandaged hand. A red stain grew on it. Roan's hand tingled from the blow he had struck.

"Ow—ow," Ithc keened. "Ow—ow." He stepped back, holding the dagger by the point now and lining it up with Roan's left eye. Roan got ready to dodge, then realized that was what he was supposed to do. The Ythcan would throw for some other spot.

There was the clank of a door, then the sound of running feet along the corridor.

Stellaraire's woman-voice rang. "Ithc, you smelly animal! Get away from that gate. Let him up!" She was standing over Roan, long, slim legs planted astride him, fists on rounded hips. Ithc held up his bloodstained bandage.

"Because of him—im I lost—ost my job—ob. Now I'm just a dirty scraper—rr."

"You'll be worse than that if I tell Gom Bulj about this!" She pushed at the heavy gate.

"He hurt me—ee," Ithc said. "Ow—ow." But he let the gate come open. Roan rolled over and sat up. He looked at the pitchfork, and the girl followed his look.

"Terry, you've got to promise me you won't start it again . . ."

"I'm going to kill him . . ." It was hard for Roan to breathe. His ribs hurt.

"He would have killed you if I hadn't made him let you up. Now call it square!"

Roan looked at her. "Maybe he would and maybe he wouldn't. He doesn't move very fast."

"Look, you've got to forget what happened. He's too dumb to hate."

"Hey—ey," Ithc started.

"You shut up," Stellaraire snapped. "Now go on, get out!"

Roan watched Ithc move off, holding his bad hand in his good one. "All right," he said. "I'll leave him alone—until the first time he bothers me." He lay back against the cold metal floor, wanting to moan, but not wanting the girl to see how much pain hurt him.

Stellaraire's hand was cool on his forehead. "You take it easy a minute, honey . . ."

"I have to get to work."

"You're a *real* sucker for punishment! You stay where you are, till you get your breath."

"He's still walking. So can I."

"You don't have to tell me, sugar. You're a tough one. I saw the fight when they caught you. The Ythcans don't have much brains, but they're awfully strong. I saw Ithc's hand before they bandaged it. It's ruined for life. I've never seen anybody fight like that before, and believe me, I've seen a lot of fights in my carny days. What made you so mad?"

Roan sat up, remembering, feeling the hot tears ready behind his eyes. "My father," he said. "They killed my old man."

"Ah, sweetie, that was a lousy thing to do . . ." She was kneeling, cradling his head in her arms. "Go ahead; it feels better if you cry. But you fixed that Ithc good. He can't be on Security any more; not with that hand. Gom Bulj has already sent him down here as a scraper."

"He didn't have to kill Dad," Roan said. "My father was a cripple. He was crippled defending me before I was born."

"How much real Terry strain do you have?" Stellaraire asked. "Your mother?"

"I'm all Terry," Roan said. "Raff was only my foster father. Ma wasn't really human. They lived all their lives in a garbage dump on account of me and Dad got killed on account of me. And Ithc walks around with nothing but a bad hand."

"My folks were a funny pair," Stellaraire said. "Pa was a water miner on Archo Four. He came of one of the Ganny crosses; real short-like, and he could go fifteen minutes without taking a breath—and o'course real coarse skin. Mother came from Tyree's World; she was dark, with light hair, and real slender. I've got her eyes, but outside of that, I'm kind of a throwback, I guess."

"You're beautiful," Roan said. "I love your eyes. If . . . if it wasn't for Dad, I'd be glad they kidnapped me."

"That's right." Stellaraire smiled. "Just think about the good part."

"I've never had a friend before," Roan said. "A real friend."

"Gee," said the girl, and her eyes grew round like a child's. "Gee, I could make you a list ten miles long of all the things men have called me since I've been with the 'zoo, but this is the first time it was 'friend.' " Her hands moved gently over his chest and arms. "There are the oddest things about you. This fuzz; what's it for?" She touched his cheek. "And your face is prickly."

"That's my beard. I have to shave nearly every day."

"I like it. It gives me nice shivers to get scraped with it. But I wonder what kind of adaptation it was supposed to be for. Open your mouth." The girl looked at Roan's teeth.

"You have such nice, white teeth—but so many of them . . ." She counted. "Gosh, thirty-two." She looked thoughtful, moving her tongue around inside her mouth. "I only have twenty-six."

"The better to eat you with, my dear—"

The grilled door slammed open. A thick, boneless gray arm with a mouth at the end of it reached in, groped over Stellaraire, then curled around her and pulled her to the door.

"Stellaraire!" Roan gasped, and jumped to his feet, grappling the arm.

But Stellaraire was laughing, perched in the curve of the massive tentacle. Beyond the doorway, Roan saw a vast creature like a mountain of gray rock. The girl put a foot on a great curving tusk, stepped up to the enormous head.

"It's just Jumbo. He knows how to work the lift and sometimes he gets loose." Jumbo reached his mouthed arm into a bin and came out with a wad of hay, which he stuffed into the other mouth, under his single tentacle.

"Stel!" a rasping voice called. "Get that damned bull back down where he belongs." The bald humanoid Nugg came stamping up. He looked angrily at Roan.

"Stel, this Terry's dangerous. You stay away from him—"

"You're not talking to your scraping crew now, Nugg," Stellaraire said sharply. "Don't go giving me orders. And you'd better keep an eye on Ithc. He started trouble with the kid here."

Nugg looked angrily at Roan. "All right, you. Get to work. I told you—"

"He's not working today. He might have busted ribs; that damned Ythcan goon slammed the door on him. I'm taking him to the vet."

"Look here, Stel—"

"Tell it to Gom Bulj. Come on, Terry."

Roan looked at the elephant, then up at Stellaraire. He put out a hand and touched the gray hide, then stepped into the curve of the trunk and was lifted up beside the girl.

"This is the strangest-looking creature I ever saw," he said, trying to sound casual. "And you don't have to call me Terry. My name's Roan."

He held on as the bull turned ponderously, swayed off along the corridor.

"And I don't need to go to any vet," he added. "I'm all right."

"Suits me. I'll take you to my room and clean you up. You smell like a scraper already. And I want to see to that cut on your face."

Roan's eyes opened wide when he saw Stellaraire's quarters. The single room, three yards by four, had a low ceiling which shed a soft light on three walls decorated with patterns of flowers and a fourth which was a panel of greenish glass behind which small vivid fish waved feathery fronds, moving with dream-like slowness through an eerie miniature landscape. There was a low couch by one wall, a table of polished black wood, a carpet of soft gray into which Roan's feet seemed to sink ankle-deep.

He drew a breath, wrinkling his nose. "It smells— pretty," he said. "I never smelled a pretty smell before."

"It's just perfume, silly. Sit down—over there on the bed. I'll get some medicine."

Roan waited quietly while the girl cleaned the deep

scratch on his cheek, painted it with a purple fluid that burned like cold fire, and sprayed a bandage in place.

"There. I'm as good a vet as Grall any day. I ought to be—I've done enough of it. Now go in there"—she pointed—"and take a bath."

Roan went to the door and looked in. There was a large basin in the floor, with glittering knobs and spouts around it.

"I don't see any water . . ."

Stellaraire laughed. "You're such a baby—except when you're mad. Here, just turn this . . ." Water churned into the tub.

"Now take off your tunic and get in. You *do* know how to rub yourself, I hope."

Roan stepped into the warm water. "This is strange," he said. "Taking a bath—inside a room. I always used to go to the river."

"You mean right outside—with fish and things bumping into you? And mud? How could you ever do it?"

"It was nice. And fish don't bump into you. I could swim right out across the water to the other side, and lie on the bank, and look up at the sky. But this is nice, too," he added.

"Here, I'll do your back. That Nugg, putting you in that dirty pen where they used to keep the mud-pig until he died! I'm going to tell Gom Bulj a thing or two. You'll have a room right by mine. You're a valuable Freak, Roan. What's your act?"

"Walking a wire. Gom Bulj said Terries aren't supposed to be able to, but I don't have any trouble."

Stellaraire shuddered. "I'm afraid of heights. But you said you grew up among those flying things—grapples or whatever they are—I guess that makes a difference. What's he paying you?"

"I don't know. Nothing, I guess, until I learn the business."

"Ha! We'll see about that. Why, you're the only real Terry in the show. Don't say anything to Gom Bulj about the extra teeth and he'll never know the difference."

"I don't want anything from him. I'm going to get away as soon as I can, and go . . . go . . ."

"Yeah, sweetie, go where? You'd have to earn passage money back to Tambool—and believe me, it costs plenty. You'd better stick with the show at least until you've saved some money—and I'll see that you're paid what you're worth."

"I don't want you to get in trouble."

"Don't worry about Gom Bulj. He's really a kind of a nice old cuss, after you get used to that tough talk. He's so used to these tough Geeks he thinks he has to talk that way to everybody—but he doesn't try it with me."

Roan dried on a huge soft towel that smelled as sweet as the room and dressed in a clean tunic that Stellaraire took from a locker filled with bright clothes.

"Come on," she said. "I'll show you around the ship. It's over five thousand years old . . ."

For an hour Roan followed the girl along endless corridors filled with hurrying creatures, sounds, colors, odors, through vast, echoing halls which Stellaraire said had once been ballrooms and dining areas, up wide staircases and down narrow companionways, to a broad, curved room with a wall of ink-black glass set close with brilliant points of colored light.

"You mean . . . that's the sky?" Roan said, and watched the fantastic array of slowly proceeding lights, realizing for the first time what it meant, to be in space. So much nothingness there. He looked around the rest of the room—a vast array of instruments and dials and a door with a red glare that said BATTLE CONTROL—AUTHORIZED PERSONNEL ONLY.

"What's all that?" he asked. "And who does the controlling in that room?"

"All that's not anybody's business. Nobody goes in that room and nobody knows what all that's for. It's separate from the guidance system. This was originally a Terran warship and all that's for fighting. Gom Bulj says it works automatically if we run into another warship. But that isn't likely. The thing to remember is not to touch any buttons or switches and not to go into that little room."

Roan went over to look at the instrumentation closely. *His* people had built this ship and old heroes had flown them, fought in them.

"I've got something a lot more interesting than that to show you," Stellaraire said. "Come on. I want to show you Iron Robert."

"Who's Iron Robert?"

Stellaraire laughed and shuddered at the same time. "Wait and see."

They rode a lift, passed along a hall which vibrated with the thunder of the idling main drive, went through a high-domed room where several dozen ill-assorted beings sat in a group, puffing and thumping strange implements. Roan winced at the din of squealing flutes, blatting horns, clacking tambourines, whining strings.

"What's all this noise for?" he called over the cacophony.

"Oh, a band is traditional with a 'zoo. It goes back to Empire days. The Old Terrans always used to have noisemakers with social events. Some of our instruments even date from then."

"It's terrible!" Roan watched a short, many-armed being in yellow silks puffing away at a great brass horn. "It's like some kind of battle."

"Gom Bulj says the Terry noisemakers used some kind of charts, so they all made the same noises together, but our fellows don't know how to read the charts. They just make any old noise."

"Let's get out of here!"

Nine decks below, in an armor-plated hold where heavy cargo had once been stored, Stellaraire took Roan's arm, nodded toward a wide aisle which led back into gloom.

"It's along here," she said. "He has the whole last bay."

"Why are you whispering?" Roan was looking around at the battered bulkheads. "I didn't know anything could make dents in Terry metal. What happened?"

"This is where Iron Robert exercises for his fights; and who's whispering? Come on . . ." She led the way along the unlit passage, stopped before an open bay which was a cave of deeper gloom.

"He's in here," she whispered. She was still holding Roan's arm, tighter than before. He went closer, wrinkling his nose at a faint odor of sulphur, peering into the darkness. He could see dim walls, an object like an oversized anvil in the center of the floor, and near one wall an immense lumpy shape that loomed up like an incomplete statue in gray stone.

"He's not here," Roan said. "There's nothing here but an old boulder."

"Shhh—" Stellaraire started.

The boulder moved in the shadows. It leaned forward, and Roan saw two bright-faceted jewels near the top, which caught the light and threw back a green glint. There was a low rumble that seemed to come from the bottom of a volcano.

"Why you wake Iron Robert up?"

"Hello, Iron Robert," Stellaraire said in a squeaky voice. "I . . . I wanted our new Freak to . . . to meet you . . . He's a Terry, sort of, and he's going to do a wire-walking act and double in greenface . . ." Her voice trailed off. Her fingers were digging into Roan's arm now. He wanted to take a step back, but she was half behind him, and he would have to push her out of the way, so he stood his ground and looked into the green eyes like chips of jade in an ancient idol hewn from lava.

"You mean new Freak want to look at old Freak. Go 'head, Terry, take good look. Iron Robert strongest living creature. Fight any being, anytime, anyplace." The giant's voice was a roll of chained thunder.

Stellaraire tugged at Roan's arm.

"We . . . uh . . . didn't mean to bother you, Iron Robert," she said breathlessly. She tugged again, harder. But Roan didn't move.

"Don't you have any lights in this place?"

The dark shape stirred, rose up in the shadows, nine feet tall, massive as a mountain.

"Iron Robert like dark. Sit in dark and think of old battles, old days." He took a step and the deck boomed and trembled under Roan's feet. "You come meet Iron Robert? OK, you shake hand that can tear leg off bull-devil!" He thrust out a vast, blunt-fingered, grayish-brown paw. Roan looked at it.

"What's matter, Terry, you 'fraid Iron Robert tear arm off you?"

Roan reached up, put his hand in the stone one before him. It was rough and hard and warm, like rock in the sun, and it made him feel as soft and weak as a jelly-toad. Iron Robert flexed his fingers, and Roan felt the grating slide of the interlocking crystals of the incredible hide.

"You small, pale being," Iron Robert rumbled. "You really Terran?"

Roan tried to stand up straighter, remembering that once Terrans had ruled the Galaxy.

"That's right," he said. He looked up at the rough-hewn face above him and swallowed. "Why do they call you Iron Robert instead of Rock Robert?" He hoped his voice sounded bold.

Iron Robert laughed, a deep, gutsy laugh. "I come of royal ferrous stock, Terry. See oxidation?" He turned his arm so that Roan could see the flakes of rusted iron in the silicon of his skin.

"You look as though you'd last forever," Roan said. He was thinking suddenly of mountains and how they weathered and endured, and of his own soft, inadequate flesh and the maybe two hundred years he had left.

"Why not?" the giant said, and he took his hand away and turned and went back to the cast-iron slab that was his bed. Roan's eyes were accommodating to the dim light now, and he saw a wall plaque over the bunk, a carved design of growing flowers. One of the blossoms, half-blown, leaned, dropped a petal that fell with a gritty crunch, crumbling into dust.

"Petals all gone soon," Iron Robert said. "Then last remembrance of home gone. Flower getting old, Iron Robert old, too, Terry. Last long time, maybe, but not forever."

"Well, 'bye, Iron Robert," Stellaraire said, and this time when she tugged at Roan's arm, he went with her.

That night Stellaraire made Roan a pallet in a small room near her own. She dressed the scratch on his face again, and the other, deeper one on his thigh, adjusted the blanket under his chin, did something nice to his mouth with hers, then went away and left him alone in the silence and the dark. For a while he thought of the strangeness of it, and suddenly the loneliness was almost choking him, like the bad air in the Soetti Quarter. Then he thought of Stellaraire, and of suddenly having a friend, something he had almost forgotten since Clanth had died so long ago.

Then he slept, and his sleep was tortured with vivid, dying images of Dad . . . of Dad's sad corpse, crying for blood.

6

Roan awoke with a foot digging into his side.

"So here you are," Nugg growled down at him. "Let me tell you I got better things to do than look all over the ship for you, Terry! Here!" He dropped a box on the floor by Roan.

"Chow's been over for an hour. What do you think this is, a vacation cruise?"

Roan sat up, rubbed his eyes, feeling the cold, early-morning feeling, even here in a ship in space, far from any sun, with a temperature controlled by machines so that it never varied, year in and year out . . .

He picked up the box Nugg had tossed to him, got the lid off. Inside were two lumpy-shelled eggs, a slab of coarse, gray bread, a fruit that looked like a small purplefruit; there was also a lump of raw, greenish meat and a red, coagulated pudding that almost turned his stomach in spite of the sudden hollow hunger feeling.

"Thanks, Nugg—" Roan started. But Nugg cut him off with a snort.

"If you don't eat you'll be too weak to work. Hurry it up." While Roan ate, Nugg went on grumbling about dangerous Freaks, malingerers, and interference with discipline by privileged characters. Roan finished, then

pulled on his tunic, feeling the pain as he stretched his
wounded flank. It hurt more than a deeper wound
might have, and it reminded him of Ithc. The feeling
of hatred warmed him. It made his heart thump and
his body ache. He hated Ithc worse than he loved
Stellaraire—

Love, he thought loudly. That's what love is.

He stood, doing up buttons and thinking of the slender mule, and how it felt to love a girl who was human,
or almost human—

"I'm taking you off scraping. You'll work in Stores.
It's only a short hop to Chlora, and there's inventory to
take."

Roan buckled on his belt. It made him feel strong,
the hard embrace of the belt, and he wondered if this
were why there were so many stories of magic belts,
like the ones Uncle T'hoy hoy used to tell him.

"If I have to work all the time," he asked as he
followed Nugg out into the corridor, "when do I practice my wire-walking act?"

"Practice? What's that?"

"I need to get ready for the show. Gom Bulj said—"

"You're supposed to be a Terry who can walk a wire
like a vine-rat; that's why Gom Bulj took you on. You
either can or you can't. Practice! Hah!"

Roan followed Nugg through the din of the Freak
Quarter, past the bumps, hisses, shouts, the dragging
of boxes, and the commotion of people doing things in a
hurry. He stared at furred and scaled and feathered
faces, massive bodies that clumped on short legs, and
lean ones that jittered on limbs with too many joints,
tiny things that scuttled, and here and there the bald,
clumsy-looking shape of a Minid or a Chronid, or some
other creature with some faint claim to a trace of natural Terran or humanoid blood.

He looked around for Stellaraire but there were only
strangers everywhere, all hurrying and shouting to each
other, their faces hot and busy-looking. He passed Gom
Bulj at the center of a crowd, snapping out orders and
smoking two cigars at once. The entrepreneur saw him,

waved a nine-fingered hand, and called out something
Roan couldn't hear.

They went down, down, into smellier and less crowded
levels. In a vast, noisy storeroom, Nugg pointed out a
skinny, scruffy being like an oversized and wingless
gracyl.

"He's foreman of the shift. Do what he tells you. And
stay out of trouble." He walked off and left Roan standing alone.

The foreman had been watching from the corner of a
moist eye. He stalked over to Roan, looked at him,
then gave a shrill cry. The workers who had been
crawling over the heaped goods stopped what they
were doing and gathered around. Others appeared from
aisles. Altogether there were fifteen or twenty of them,
no two alike. They all stared at Roan.

"What are you?" the foreman whistled. "Never saw
one like you before."

"I'm a Terran," Roan said.

Somebody hissed.

The foreman clacked his shoulder blades together
and ruffled out a fringe along the sides of his neck. "I'm
Rik-rik and I'm the boss here," he whistled. "Now,
you're new. Your job will be to carry out the slop jars.
And some of the boys don't have sphincters; you'll take
care of the diapers. And o' course, some of the gang are
messy eaters, regurgers, you know. *That* has to be
cleaned up. And—"

"No," Roan said.

The circle around him moved in closer. Something
plucked at Roan's tunic from behind.

"I'm boss here, Terry," Rik-rik shrilled. "You'll do
what I tell you, right, fellas?"

The tug came again, and Roan whirled, grabbed at a
snaky tentacle that was wiping something slimy on him.
The being who owned the member yanked angrily, but
Roan hauled it close, then suddenly shoved it back. It
fell. The others made excited noises. Roan faced Rik-rik.

"I didn't ask to be here," he said, "but I'm here
anyway. I'll work, but I won't carry slop. Your men can
clean up their own messes."

"You're the newest one," Rik-rik squeaked. "You're supposed to carry the slop. The newest one always does . . ."

"Not me," Roan said. "Leave me alone and I'll work as hard as anybody. But don't think you can pick on me." He looked at the being who was shifting from one of its eight or nine feet to another and snorting softly through its trunklike tentacles. "And if *you* ever touch me again, I'll tie a knot in that arm of yours."

"Spoilsport," someone grumbled.

Rik-rik stared at Roan angrily. "You're a trouble-maker, I can see that. Probably you'll want off three or four hours in a cycle to hibernate; most of you would-be Terries do."

"I sleep eight hours a day," Roan said, "in a bed."

"And you'll want food every day, too—"

"Three times a day."

"Maybe it'd like to join our sex circle," a bulbous being suggested. "We have a vacancy in—"

"No, thanks," Roan said. "We Terries prefer our own kind for that."

"Chauvinist," a gluey voice said.

"Hah," someone else commented. "Thinks he's something special, I guess."

"All right," Rik-rik said sharply, taking charge again. "Back to work all of you. And as for you . . ." He gave Roan a threatening look. "I'll have my eye on you."

"That's all right," Roan said. "As long as you keep your hands off."

For the next eight days Roan worked sixteen hours at a stretch among the stacks of supplies, lifting heavier weights than he had ever lifted before, climbing long, wobbly ladders, counting, tallying, arranging boxes and cans and jars in even rows which the issue clerks promptly disarranged. When he left the storeroom to go to the mess hall or to his room, he looked for Stellaraire along the corridors and in the rooms he passed, but he never saw her. She's forgotten all about me, he thought miserably. She fixed up my cuts like you'd try to help a scratched gracyl who was lying on the ground expecting to die. Now she was busy with other things—and other people.

On the ninth day Nugg came to the warehouse, signaled to Roan.

"We're coming into Chlora; planetfall in a few minutes. Plenty to do: tents to set up, midway to lay out, rigging to stretch . . ." Roan followed while Nugg talked in his usual grumbling way.

"I need to know more about what I'm supposed to do, if I'm going to put on a wire-walking act tomorrow," Roan interrupted.

"Tonight," Nugg corrected. "What do you need to know? Does a Flather need someone to tell it how to fly? You're a Terry wire-walker; so walk the wire . . ."

There was a sharp change in the ship's gravitation, and Roan caught at a handrail to keep from falling. His feet were like lead, suddenly, and his breakfast was heavy in his stomach.

"What's the matter?" Nugg called. "Never felt high-G before?"

"N-no," Roan said. He swallowed hard, twice.

"You'll get used to it," Nugg said carelessly.

The gravity pulled and the deck trembled and vibrated. There were noises and sudden tiltings underfoot. A roaring whistle started up, went on and on. There was a final, violent shudder, and the ship was abruptly still. The gravity was worse now, if anything.

"We're down," Nugg said. He stopped at a door, unlocked it with a big electrokey, motioned Roan into a dingy storeroom. He hauled a heavy wooden mallet and a vast bundle of plastic stakes from a shelf, shoved them at Roan.

"Go ashore and help stake-out. There'll be Mag to show you what to do. You do your job and stay out of Ithc's way, see? When you finish, go to tent three, cell 103, and get ready for your stunt." He walked off, and Roan shouldered his load and went looking for the debarkation deck.

A stream of circus creatures were pushing into an elevator, each carrying a box or piece of equipment, and Roan, caught in the press, went into the elevator with them, and along the long central corridor of the ship and down the ramp, out into the strange smell of another world.

He started sweating almost immediately. The heaviness felt worse outside, in the heat, and Roan didn't like not knowing where he was supposed to go and having only a vague idea what he was supposed to do.

He was walking across a landing field. Not an official, well-groomed one, but more like an abandoned launching pad; just a flat, cracked concrete ramp. Beyond, a garbage dump of a neighborhood crawled up a hillside. It reminded Roan depressingly of home.

Beyond the garbage dump neighborhood reared a blue metal city, flashing harshly in the merciless sunshine. A flat, shining sky loomed overhead.

The crowd from the circus ship thinned out, everyone hurrying to an appointed task.

Miraculously, the incredible, monstrous tents began to go up. Roan walked toward them. A diminutive red-eyed creature scurried up to him, pulling a heavy cart that bumped over the cracks in the concrete. It stopped in front of Roan and jumped up and down, chattering, waving a stick overhead. "Mag! Mag!" Its voice was like fingernails on dry wood.

"I guess you're Mag," Roan said. "Where do I go?"

Mag started off with the cart again and Roan followed him across the field where the garbage was being cleared off as the tents went up.

Mag pointed with his stick to a spot marked with powdered chalk and Roan pounded the first stake in. The hammer felt like a tree trunk and he brought his whole body down with it when he struck.

After the first stake, he wanted to throw the mallet down and sit on the ground and catch his breath, but Mag chattered and waved his stick and danced toward the next chalk mark, and Roan followed. There were other stake drivers at work, big, thick-armed humanoids mostly. They swung their mallets with effortless ease, knocking a stake into the hard soil with two or three easy-looking blows and moving on to the next.

Roan struggled with the heavy mallet, raising it and letting it fall. Sometimes he missed the stake completely. After each stake, he promised himself he would rest—but the others never paused, and somehow, he didn't want to be the first to stop work. His aim got worse and worse. He broke one stake with a glancing blow, and Mag jumped up and down and his screeching went up into the supersonic. Roan leaned on his mallet and breathed dust, then started in again.

For hours in the blinding sun, Roan drove stakes. All around, the magic tents rose, cables arcing to their high peaks, pennants breaking out to flutter against the steely sky. Zoo people came and went carrying props, equipment, tools. Processions of ambling animals with caked dung on their flanks went by, driven by cursing menagerie keepers; a few curious locals wandered along the now dusty paths between the canvas tops, ogling the show people. Once Roan looked up to see Ithc standing twenty yards away, eyeing him, fingering the butt of a nerve gun strapped to his birdlike hip. His injured hand behind him, the tall alien came closer, his gill flaps working nervously.

"I'll—ll be watching—ing tonight when you walk the high wire—ire," he said. "Maybe—aybe you'll fall—all . . ."

Roan made his face smile. "Some day I'll catch you alone, without a weapon, Ithc," he said, trying not to breathe hard from the stake-pounding. "Then I'll kill you."

Ithc showed a gristly ridge where teeth should have been and walked away with his queer, gliding walk that reminded Roan of the Veed and the smell of alien hate and cruelty. Ithc wants revenge, Roan thought, watching him go. But he doesn't really know what wanting means.

The stakes were all driven at last, and Mag squeaked and took his cart away, without even looking back.

Roan found tent three, and in room 103 he found two Freaks. Two other Freaks, he thought wryly. One was a transparent post, and it wasn't until it moved that Roan saw it was a creature at all. The other was a thing with a hide like a skinned tree, covered with orange polka dots, and with a double-faced head set on one shoulder. Its modesty section was apparently approximately at the left knee, for it was carefully covering it with a little patch of black plastiflex. As far as Roan could tell, all it was covering was an orange polka dot exactly like all the others.

Roan settled for arranging his tunic into a skirt, pulling it around his belt.

A bell rang—they seemed to ring every few minutes—and he followed the first creature out into the dust and heat of the midway. The creature ambled stiffly over to a row of cages, got in one, and reached a flipper around to close the big, fake lock, which was supposed to indicate that the Freaks were dangerous. It motioned Roan to the next cage.

Roan looked curiously at the sign on the bars. PRIM-ITIVE MAN, it said in Panterran, the fifth legend in a long row, all in different scripts. He climbed in and clanged the door shut and sat on a wooden bench. This part of the job was easy enough. It felt good just to sit and rest.

Roan sat in his cage for two hours. The ponderous creatures of Chlora crowded past, pointing and making noises. One Chloran stood in front of Roan's cage for a long time, making sketches and taking notes in a curious script. Once a child prodded him with a long stick. But they didn't seem to find Roan very spectacular. Most of the Freaks were much larger and more colorful.

Roan hardly noticed the Chlorans filing past because he had fallen to musing about himself again. Some day I'll find out, he thought. I have to know who I really am, who my parents were, where my people are—my home.

Home. Somewhere was home for him, and it wasn't Tambool.

I'll take Stellaraire with me and there's where we'll live. Among our own kind. Surely Stellaraire was near enough human so it wouldn't matter.

Another bell rang. Dusk had fallen, Roan noticed.

The days were short here on Chlora. The Freak exhibit was now empty of spectators, a garish and lonely place under the polyarcs glaring far above.

Roan got stiffly out of his cage. He'd sat too long and his thigh had stiffened a bit again.

Mag was there waiting for him, the little red eyes catching a glitter from the arc lights; he chattered and hopped on his spidery legs, clutching his stick, and Roan followed him through the huge, billowing tents. It was much cooler now that evening had come. Almost cold when the wind blew, ballooning out the tents and flapping against the poles.

Roan walked through the dizzying flickers of colored lights and blasts of noise from the noisemakers and the twirling of weird creatures.

At the base of a vast mast as big around as Roan, Gom Bulj appeared from the crowd, his walking tentacles rippling as he hurried over.

"Ah, there you are, young Terry! You're on! Now, I'm expecting great things of you! See that you perform in a style worthy of the Extravaganzoo!"

"What am I supposed to do?" Roan asked. "I don't know anything about being in a 'zoo. Don't I wear a costume?"

"Do? Costume?" Gom Bulj popped his huge eyes at Roan and drummed on his wide torso with his thick fingers. "You're the first Freak I've had who wanted freaking lessons. You have expensive ideas, young Terry!" He plucked a cigar from the flowered weskit that stretched across his chest, stuck it in his mouth.

"Later on, we'll see; for the present, you're on probation. Oh, it's a gamble, taking on new talent! Never know how the public will receive 'em." He drew a tremendous breath that made the cigar burn bright yellow, letting the ash fall with the insouciance of those who never have to clean up after themselves.

"It wasn't my idea for you to kidnap me," Roan said.

"Tush, tush! I'm going to forget you said that, young Terry." Gom Bulj flung his red-lined cloak about him and rippled his legs. "Good luck—and if you *should* fall, do it nicely, as though it were part of the act." He loosed a vast cloud of smoke from his air-discharge orifice and hurried off.

Mag pointed with his stick to the rungs set in the pole. Roan looked up. He couldn't see it, but somewhere up there, in the backwash of the cacophony of circus sounds and colored lights, there was a tightrope . . .

Ithc strolled up, tall and alien, his gills moving in and out, his greenish face shadowed sharply black in the harsh light. He was still wearing the nerve gun.

"Go—oh up—up," he said. "All—ll the way—ay up—up."

"I'll go up," Roan said. "You couldn't do it, but *I* can. I'm a Terran." A short life and a glorious one, he thought, looking up the swaying pole. Stellaraire would be here somewhere; maybe she'd be watching him. He'd have to throw off the tiredness now, and forget the stiffness in his leg. He wanted to do his act smoothly, just as though he'd been with a 'zoo all his life. He wanted her to be proud of him.

He stopped to rest halfway up. He didn't want to be tired or breathless. It was going to be hard, walking the rope with that gravity pulling at him. And he already felt hot and dizzy and his leg ached.

Roan looked down. Ithc was still there at the bottom of the ladder, a toy Ithc, far off, looking up. If he shot Roan with the nerve gun, everyone would assume Roan had merely fallen.

Roan climbed slowly now. He was safer on the high wire. Ithc's gun couldn't reach him that high up. But he felt eyes on him and looked back again. A bright spotlight was on him and so were a million eyes. A voice was booming over the loudspeaker, in Chloran, and Roan knew it was announcing him. He heard the word "Terran."

There was noise for him, loud and insistent.

He forgot the eyes and the noise and kept climbing. The metal of the ladder was cold, from the wind blowing on it, and slippery in his sweaty hands.

He reached the platform at the top. A few feet above

him the top of the tent billowed and flapped. The noise
of drums rose to him, commanding him on, and the
spotlight felt like a ray of heat. Everything seemed to
spin slowly, and he held onto the flimsy rail for support.

There was nothing to catch him if he fell.

Roan put a foot on the wire and inadvertently looked
down. The world fell away endlessly at his feet. He
pulled his foot back and felt his stomach sweating coldly
inside, and the fear reaching to hold his body rigid.

He held on to the bars around the edge of the platform and shook. He was afraid even to stand there on
the little platform. I'm a coward, he thought with horror. But he couldn't do anything about it. All he could
do was hold on for dear life and wonder how he was
going to get down—and knew that Ithc was waiting
below with the nerve gun in case he tried to back
down, hoping he'd fall . . .

Roan wanted to die—but not by falling. Just to die
now, without effort.

"Roan!" a voice called, faint and clear from the middle of the air. Roan looked. Stellaraire was on the
platform at the distant, other end of the tightrope. She
was dressed in gold skintights now, from head to toe,
and she called, "If you don't come here, Terry, I'm
going to come there."

Roan held on and looked at her. He remembered
how she had shuddered when he told her what his
specialty was. But she had climbed up here to the
crow's nest to watch him. She had known he might
need her.

He let go of the rail. Falling wasn't anything. He
would just die—like Dad. But to fail, and have to go on
being alive . . .

He went to the taut, black cable, stepped out on it,
stood balanced on the wire that swooped down and up
again to the blob of light and the golden figure. Then
he was laughing aloud, with relief that he wasn't a
coward, and with love for his woman, with the deep joy
of life.

He walked right across the tightrope, stopping in the
middle to wave to the invisible faces below; he was

master of the crowd now, tuned to the strong noise of the drums.

Then he was at the other end and Stellaraire caught his hand and pulled him close, looking up at him, and there were tiny flecks of gold dust in her hair.

"Would you have done it?" he asked her afterward, when they were back on the sawdusted ground among the black shadows from the high, hazy polyarcs.

"I would have tried," she said. "Now it's time for my dances." She squeezed his hand and slipped away in the crowd. As Roan turned to follow, he saw Ithc's yellow eyes watching from the shadow of a ticket booth.

Stellaraire's act was terrific. It was an erotic dance in five cultures, and the Chloran part must have been crude enough for the crowd to understand, because they roared with enjoyment.

But part of the dance was for Roan alone, out of the thousands. He liked it; he liked her being his woman, when everybody else wanted her.

"Even I," said a bald, purplish Gloon standing by, "even I can find her attractive. She can dance in such a way as to seem a regal bitch of Gloon. She can be anything you want her to be. Anything you pay her to be. A tramp of rare talent."

Roan whirled with his fists clenched, but the Gloon was already moving off, not even noticing Roan.

He watched the dance to the end, not enjoying it now. There had been other men for Stellaraire, he knew that—even creatures not men. But one other thing he knew: she wasn't any tramp. And there weren't going to be any more men except Roan.

After the dances he watched to see which way she went, but she disappeared through the crowd along one of the aisles.

Half an hour later he was still looking for her, along corridors of smelly canvas and rope, among sagging, faded banners and garish lights and the shouting of hucksters and the blare of noisemakers and the clamor of the crowd that seemed to be everywhere now, flowing among the tents and stalls and poles like a rising flood of dirty water. A grossly fat being in a curly silver wig directed him to Stellaraire's dressing room, after he had asked and been ignored or insulted a dozen times.

But Stellaraire wasn't in her pink, tawdry tent room. Roan stood there undecided, feeling an uneasy sensation washing up inside of him. He wanted her—the reassurance of her. He recalled that she smelled of young trees.

"Where did she go?" he asked Chela, one of the girls who shared the dressing room. "Did you see her?"

Chela was a tiny, graceful saurian, faintly humanoid, with long, heavily made-up eyes. She flapped her artificial lashes at Roan and showed her little teeth.

"Ithc came and got her. He wanted her for something." She looked demurely at the floor and by some trick of musculature curled her eyelashes back.

"There's always me," she added.

"Wanted her for what?"

"Really!"

"Where did they go? Did you see?"

"No. But Ithc lodges in Quadrant C." She was putting purple paint on her lip scales now, bored with Roan's questions.

He made his way through the rings where shows were going on, pushed through the crowds on the other side. Once, he saw Nugg's heavy, ugly face, and heard him call, "Here, where you think you're going . . . ?" but he ignored him, pushed on through the crowd.

There was a taste in his mouth that was part fear and part something else, he didn't know what. The uneasy feeling was like a sick weight inside him.

A clown was shot from a cannon and the smell of gunpowder spread through the tent. Lights went off and on, and colored spots were a kaleidoscope of dancing patterns. Roan went through a slit in the back of the huge tent into cold night air, crossed a path, and went into a smaller one where most of the roustabouts quartered.

"Where's Stellaraire?" he asked of a wrinkled olive-colored being who was sitting on an upturned keg, nursing a vast clay mug with both hands.

The oldster let out a long breath. "Working," he said, and winked.

"Where?"

"In private."

There was a sound—a kind of animal moan—from the adjoining room. Roan flapped through two stiff partitions, came into a dim, cluttered room with a mud-colored rug, beaded hangings on the walls, the reek of a strange incense. Ithc stood across the room, the nerve gun gripped awkwardly in his good hand, his gills working convulsively. Stellaraire stood before him, her golden costume torn off one shoulder. One arm seemed to hang limp.

"Dance—ance," Ithc commanded, and aimed the gun at her as though he would shoot. The double voice issuing from his gills seemed to send a shudder through the girl. There were several circus people ranged along the far wall: an underdirector whom Roan recognized, a pair of Ythcan laborers, some minor creatures in second-string clown costume. One with a dope stick blew a cloud of smoke at Stellaraire.

"Come on, dance," he urged carelessly.

Stellaraire took a step back.

"Come—umm here—ere," Ithc said.

She turned to run, and Ithc's finger tightened on the firing stud of the nerve gun, and as Stellaraire fell Roan heard the animal noises again.

Roan's body hurt with hers, but he held himself rigid, hidden in shadows. This wasn't a time for gestures. Whatever he did now had to count. He stepped softly back, whirled, ran across the tent where the old being hiccuped into his beer, out into the dark. There were tent stakes stacked there, somewhere. They were pointed at one end and knobbed at the other, and heavy. He groped, stumbling among tent ropes, feeling over damp ground, lumpy refuse, hitting things in the dark. His hands fell on a bundle, and he ripped the twine away, caught up a yard-long, wrist-thick bar of dense plastic.

He ran around the tent to the side that opened on the alley, lifted the heavy flap, stepped into the smell of snakes and Ythcan dope smoke. A small clown in colored rags was just in front of him; beyond, Ithc stood, tall, lean, slope-shouldered, long-necked. He was holding his bandaged hand close to his side, and the other with the nerve gun was held awkwardly out. That was the first danger. Against the gun Roan would have no chance at all. There was no question of fair play; it was simply necessary to save Stellaraire from what was happening to her, in any way possible. And he would have to do everything right, because he wouldn't have another chance.

He gripped the club carefully, stepped quickly past the ragged clown, set himself, and brought the club down on Ithc's gun hand. He had decided on the hand instead of the obvious target, the head, because he wasn't sure where Ithc's brains were; hitting him on the head might not bother him much.

It was surprising how slowly the gun fell. Ithc was still standing, holding his hand out—but now the hand was oozing fluid, and the gun was bouncing off the dusty rug and falling into a pile of dirty clothing, and Ithc was bringing his hand in and starting to turn. Roan brought the club up again—how heavy it seemed—and aimed a second blow at the back of Ithc's neck; but Ithc was turning and ducking aside, and the blow struck him on the shoulder and the club glanced off and jarred from Roan's hands, and then he was facing the tall, pale-green, mad-eyed Ythcan, seeing the dirty yellow of the gill fringes as they flapped, smelling the penetrating chemical odor of Ithc's blood.

"Owww—owww," Ithc moaned, and brought a foot up in a vicious kick, but Roan leaned aside, caught the long-toed member, and threw all his strength into twisting it back and around, driving with his feet to topple Ithc. They fell together, Roan on top, Ithc's sinewy body buckled under him, and his knobbed knees battered against Roan's chest. But he held on, twisting the foot, feeling the cartilage crackle and break, remembering Dad, and the sounds Stellaraire had made, and he twisted harder, harder . . .

Ithc roared a vibrating double roar, fighting now to escape, but Roan reached after him, caught the other foot, tore at it, twisting, tearing, while the now helpless creature fought to crawl away. Then Roan was on Ithc's back, his arm locked around the other's throat, crushing until Ithc collapsed, fell on his face, his legs twitching.

Roan got to his feet. He was only dimly aware of the faces watching, of Stellaraire still moving on the floor beyond her fallen tormentor, of the stink of alien blood and burning dope. He looked around for the club, saw it tangled among unwashed garments on an unkempt heap of bedding by the sagging canvas wall. He caught it up, turned back to Ithc. The alien lay half on his side, his broken feet grotesquely twisted, his gills gaping convulsively. A deep, reedy vibration of agony came from him. Roan brought the club up, and paused, not hesitating, but picking the best spot—the spot most likely to kill.

The yellow eyes opened. "Hurry—urry," Ithc said.

Roan brought the club down with all his strength, noting with satisfaction that the Ythcan's limbs all jumped at once. He hit him twice more, just to be sure Ithc would never bother him again. The last blow was like pounding a side of meat hanging in a kitchen. He tossed the club aside, picked up a dirty blanket and wiped the spattered yellowish blood from his face and hands. He looked around at the circus people who watched. Two of the small clowns were edging forward, looking Ithc over, a little saliva visible at the corners of their beaklike mouths.

"Nobody helped Stellaraire," he said. "Nobody helped me. Anybody on Ithc's side can fight me, if they want to." He glanced toward the club, flexing his hands. He was breathing hard, but he felt good, very good, and he was almost hoping the other Ythcan would step forward, because it had been a wonderful feeling, killing Ithc, and he felt as though he could beat anybody, or all of them together.

But no one moved toward him. The one with the

dope stick ground the smoke out on a horny palm, tucked it in a pocket of its black polyon blouse.

"It's your fight. Gom Bulj won't like it; Ithc was a valuable piece of livestock. But who'll tell him? He may not even notice. Who cares?"

"We'll take care of the remains," the small clowns said, clustering around the body.

The others were leaving, wandering off now because the fun was over. Roan went to Stellaraire and lifted her in his arms. He was surprised at how light she was, how fragile for all her sumptuous curving flesh; and how sharp was his need to take care of her.

She smiled up at him. "He . . . must have gone . . . crazy."

"He won't bother you any more, Stellaraire."

Out in the cold night, the blaze of stars, the rise and fall of the mob noise, Stellaraire's arm went around his neck. Her face was against his, and her mouth opened hungrily against his.

"Take me . . . to my tent . . ." she breathed against his throat, and he turned and walked along the shadowy way, aware only of the perfume and the poetry and the wonder of the girl.

7

In the gray light of Chlora's dawn, Roan worked with the others, dismantling the tents, folding the vast canvases, coiling the miles of rope, stacking and bundling stakes, striking sets, and packing props and costumes. The wagons puffed and smoked, and hauled everything back up the ramps into the ship, and then they lowered their scraping blades and pushed all the garbage back into the circus grounds where it belonged, with the stripped yellow bones of Ithc at the bottom.

Later, in Stellaraire's room, she poured Roan a glass of wine and sat on his lap.

"I never knew how much I loved you, until you fought Ithc for me," she said.

"Nobody's said anything about him," Roan said. "Aren't they going to investigate his death?"

"Why should anyone bother? He wasn't much use with a ruined hand, anyway."

"But what about his friends . . ."

"You're talking like a Terry," Stellaraire said, and sipped her wine appreciatively. Roan tasted it, too. It was a blossom-pink Dorée from Aphela and it tasted like laughter.

*   *   *

Algol II was a wonderful pale green gold-edged mountain that filled half the immense view screen in the dusty old room that had once been the grand observation salon.

"I've got an idea," Roan said, standing with his arm around Stellaraire's slim waist. "I've been thinking about what you said, about there being a lot of mutant Terrans here, and about the climate being like Terra. Why don't we stay here? When the show pulls up, we'll disappear. Gom Bulj wouldn't go to the expense of coming back after us—"

"Why?" the girl asked, raising her violet-penciled eyebrows. "What would we do on Algol II?"

"We wouldn't stay—just until we made enough credit to leave. I have to get back ho—back to Tambool. Ma's still back there, all alone now."

"But the 'zoo is my home! I've never been any other place, since I was ten years old. It's safe here; and we can be together."

"And besides," Roan went on, "Ma will know all about where I came from; maybe who my blood father and mother are. I have to find out. Then I'm going to Terra—"

"Roan—Terra's just a mythical place! You can't—"

"Yes, I can," he said. "Terra's a real place. I know it is. I can feel inside that it's real. And it's not like other worlds. On Terra everything is the way things should be. Not all this hate, and not caring, and dirt, and dying for nothing. I've never been there, but I know it as though I'd spent all my life there. It's where I belong."

Stellaraire took his hand, leaned against him. "Ah, sweetie, for your sake I hope it's really there—somewhere. And if it is," she added, "I know someday you'll find it."

The 'zoo went well on Algol II. Roan was sure-footed and nimble on the high wire in the light gravity, only three-fourths ship-normal, and Stellaraire's dance was an immense success with the mutant Terrans, who were odd-looking dwarfs with bushy muttonchop whiskers and bowed legs and immense bellies and no visible difference between the sexes; but they appreciated the erotic qualities of her performance so well that a number of the locals occupying ringside boxes began solemnly coupling with their mates before she had even finished.

Afterward, Roan found Stellaraire by the arena barrier, watching Iron Robert in his preliminary warm-up bout.

"I've planned a route for us," he said softly. "As soon as—"

"Shhh . . ." she said, and put a hand on his arm, her eyes on the spotlit ring, where the stone giant was strangling a great armored creature with insane, bulging eyes. It was already quite dead, and he was mauling it for the amusement of the crowd, which had no way of knowing the beast had died minutes before.

"Listen," Roan insisted. "I have clothes and food in a bundle; are you ready to go?"

She turned to look up at him. "You really mean it? Now? Just like that, just walk off and . . ."

"What other way is there? This is as good a time as any."

"Roan, it's crazy! But if you're going, I'm going with you. But listen. Wait until after Iron Robert's act. We can slip away while the tops are going down. Somebody might notice if we tried it now—and whatever we do, we don't want to get caught. Gom Bulj has some pretty drastic ideas about what to do with deserters."

"All right. As soon as the fight's over and the noisemakers come on, we'll mingle with the marks and go out gate nineteen. There's a patch of big plants growing over on that side, and we can duck in there and work our way to the town."

There was scattered applause as Iron Robert tossed his victim aside and raised his huge, square hands in his victory sign. He came over to where Roan and Stellaraire stood, accepted a towel tossed to him by Mag or his twin brother. He wiped pale pink blood from his face and hands, then took a scraper from his belt pouch and began to clean himself, frowning as he worked. He was very neat and meticulous and it made a tooth-cracking noise.

"How you like fight, Terry?" he asked suddenly, scraping his arm with long strokes.

"I didn't really see it," Roan answered. "When I got here it was already over."

Iron Robert chuckled, a sound like a boulder rolling downhill. "Fans like see plenty action," he said. "Iron Robert kill too quick, have to ham up act little, give everybody money's worth." He finished his toilet and put the scraper away.

"Next fight different maybe," he said. "Parlagon easy. Tear up whole parlagon with bare hands. Chinazell next. Never see chinazell before. Chinazell pretty tough, some say. What is chinazell? Who care? Tear him up, too."

"I guess you can beat just about anything they put in against you," Roan commented, looking around to see if Gom Bulj was in sight. It wouldn't do to have him watching when they made their try.

"So far, Terry," the giant said. He looked at Roan with an unreadable expression in his green-glass eyes. "Iron Robert meet all comers. Some day meet being too tough to kill." He waved a hand at the stands. "That what all come, hope for. Some day they see. Maybe today. Maybe next year. Maybe hundred years. Meantime, fight to win. Iron Robert born to fight. Fight until die."

A horn blew long, nerve-shredding blasts. Crews were hauling sections of heavy fencing into the cleared arena. The PA system boomed out a description of the coming battle. Iron Robert took a gallon-sized swig from a bottle, tossed it aside, stalked out into the center of the ring under the glare of the lights. Jumbo appeared, hauling a vast, iron-barred cage. Its sides trembled as something inside slammed against the bars. The crowd fell suddenly silent. An immensely tall, thin being dressed in green silks that flapped about its long shins pulled a rope and the end of the cage fell aside.

A triangular, scaled head poked out, swaying inquiringly on its serpentine neck. The chinazell bounded from the cage and shook the ground when it landed. It was an incredibly monstrous creature, a primitive world dinosaur type with bony plates along its high-arched spine. But the fearsome thing about it was the gleam of intelligence in the small, glittering eyes. It paused a moment, surveying the sea of faces behind the barriers, and gauging Iron Robert, half its size, who stood watching it and gauging it back.

Roan heard Stellaraire's quick intake of breath. "No wonder the betting was so high," she said. "Gom Bulj said a syndicate was importing something special from Algol III, just for the fight. It's a high-G planet, and that monster's used to weighing twice as much as he does now. Look at him! I don't think I want to watch this . . ."

"You're not really worried, are you?" Roan asked. "I mean, it's fixed, isn't it?"

Stellaraire whirled on Roan. "I've known Iron Robert ever since I was a little girl," she said. "I've seen him go up against the awfullest fighters and the cruellest killers on a hundred worlds, and he's always won. He wins with his strength and his courage. Nothing else. Nobody helps him—any more than they helped me—or you!" She looked back toward the arena, where the chinazell watched Iron Robert now. It gathered its legs under it, watching him standing with his back to his opponent, his arms raised to the crowd in the ancient salute of the gladiator.

"I'm afraid, Roan," Stellaraire said. "He's never fought anything like this before!"

The chinazell moved suddenly; it rose up on its hind legs and charged like a huge, ungainly bird straight toward Iron Robert's exposed back. Stellaraire's fingers dug deep into Roan's arm.

"Why doesn't he turn . . . !"

At the last possible moment, Iron Robert pivoted with a speed that seemed unbelievable in anything so massive, leaned aside from the chinazell's charge, and struck out with a clublike arm. The blow resounded against the beast's armored hide like a cannonball striking masonry; it staggered, broke stride, sent up a spray of dust as it caught itself, wheeled and pounced. The vicious triangular head whipped down with open jaws that clashed against Iron Robert's stony hide, dragged him from his feet—

His arms encircled the scaled neck, hugging the monster close. In sudden alarm, it braced its feet and backed, and Iron Robert held on, twisting the broad head sideways, his fingers locked in the corners of the clamped mouth. The heavy reptilian tail slammed the ground in a roil of dust; sparks flew where the bright talons of the creature's short arms raked Iron Robert's invulnerable chest and shoulders. Then it opened its jaws, whipped its neck, flung Iron Robert aside. He rolled in the dust, and before he could come to his feet, the chinazell sprang to him, brought an immense hind foot down in an earthshaking kick.

Roan coughed as dust floated across from the scene of the battle.

"I can't see . . ." Stellaraire wailed. "What's happening?"

Iron Robert was on his feet again, grappling a hind leg nearly as big as himself. The chinazell, its weight down on its stunted forelimbs, sidled awkwardly, trying to shake its attacker loose. Its head came around and down, striking at Iron Robert. He hunched his head closer to his shoulders and reached up for a higher grip.

"The thing's too big for him," Stellaraire gasped. "He can't reach a vulnerable spot . . ."

With a surge, the chinazell raised the trapped leg clear of the ground and dashed it down. Iron Robert slammed against the concrete-hard clay—but he kept his grip.

"He's hurt!" Stellaraire choked. "It's all he can do to hold on—and that isn't doing him any good. But if he lets go, it will kick him again—"

"At least its teeth aren't hurting him," Roan said. "He's all right. He'll hold on until he tires it, and then—"

"It won't tire—not in this light gravity . . ."

The chinazell stood, its ribby sides heaving, its head on its long neck twisted to look at Iron Robert, who shifted his grip suddenly, leaped, caught a bony boss that adorned the dino's withers, and hauled himself across the creature's back, his weight bearing it down. Its legs sprawled out, and it plunged violently, striking with its yard-wide jaws as dust rose up in a dense cloud . . .

The chinazell came out of the dust cloud, wheeled, and charged down on Iron Robert as he came to his feet. It bounded past him and struck him with its immense tail, a blow like a falling tree. Iron Robert went down, and the dino galloped away, circled, and Roan saw that its tail was broken, the hide torn, blood washing down across the scales, caking the dust. The head writhed on the long neck as the voiceless creature shuddered its pain. It came to a halt, the broken tail dragging now. Its head whipped from side to side as though seeking some escape from its torment. Fifty yards away, Iron Robert came slowly to his hands and knees.

"He's hurt!" Stellaraire cried. "Oh, please, Iron Robert! Get up!"

The chinazell moved heavily, painfully. It walked to Iron Robert, stood over him. It maneuvered into position, raised a leg like an ironwood log set with spikes, brought it down square on Iron Robert in a blow that shook the ground.

"Gom Bulj has got to stop it!" Stellaraire screamed. "It will kill him . . ."

"Wait!" Roan caught her arm. "He's not finished yet! Look!"

The chinazell was moving awkwardly sideways, its head held low. Iron Robert's mighty arms circled the lean neck. As it dragged him, he freed one arm, raised it, drove his stony fist into one small, lizard eye. The chinazell bucked, tried to shake free, but Iron Robert held on, twisted, struck at the other eye. The dino reared and plunged desperately, and Iron Robert dropped away, lay on his back. He raised his bloody fists, let them fall back.

The blinded chinazell stopped, squatted; thick blood ran down the triangular face; the primitive mouth opened in voiceless agony. It rose, ran a few yards, dragging its dead tail, then squatted again, its small cunning gone with its eyes. A murmuring ran through the silent crowd, and someone started a hissing, and at the sound the chinazell leaped up, crashed aimlessly against the thick fence. People scrambled back in fright, screaming, and the panicked beast lunged, brought down a section of the barrier, then turned and blundered back, struck the fence again. There was a blare of noise from the PA system, and Gom Bulj appeared, a vivid, bloated figure in scarlet capes, carrying a heavy power gun. He took aim, blew the head off the maimed beast. It fell over sideways like a mountain, kicked out once, twice, then lay still. The headless neck twitched as blood pumped out to puddle in the dust like black oil.

Gom Bulj walked over to Iron Robert, stood looking at him, still holding the gun in his hand; he raised it . . .

"No!" Stellaraire was around the barrier, running toward the entrepreneur.

"You can't!" Roan heard her voice, almost drowned in the angry shouting of the crowd that had seen the two most deadly fighters in the Galaxy maim each other, and still felt cheated because there hadn't been more blood and agony.

As Roan came up, Gom Bulj was holding up a wide, many-fingered hand.

"As you wish, my dear," he was rumbling. "I merely thought—"

"Iron Robert's not just another wounded animal," Stellaraire flared.

"But of course he is," Gom Bulj boomed, lighting up a foot-long cigar. "What else would you call him? But no matter, say your farewells or whatever, and then back to work, eh?" He turned away.

"We'll have to get a crew over here," Roan said. "He's too heavy to lift—"

"Leave him where he is," Gom Bulj said. "Disposal is the locals' problem. And now I really must—"

"Aren't you even going to try to help?" Roan demanded, standing in front of the bulky businessman.

Gom Bulj waved his cigar, blinking at Roan. "Ah, you Terries," he chuckled. "So impractical . . ." He rippled quickly to one side and past Roan and the crowd of hurrying circus hands swallowed him up. The audience was melting away and almost before they were clear the seats were going down, and the crews had started on striking the top. Stellaraire was bending over Iron Robert.

"Good-by," she said sadly. "You fought awfully well, Iron Robert; he was just too big for you."

The stone giant opened his eyes. "Chinazell . . . tough fighter," he said in a gritty, labored voice. "Dirty . . . trick . . . gouge . . . eyes." His craggy face was contorted and his huge chest labored with the effort of his breathing.

"Do you think you could stand?" Roan asked. He gripped a massive arm and pulled, but it was like pulling on the trunk of a fallen tree. "We've got to get help," he said, looking over toward the ship that was visible now where the tent had been peeled back. A crew was folding up the arena partitions, and a group of busy locals were setting to work to skin out the chinazell. There was no one else near.

"No one will help," Stellaraire said. "They just . . . don't help. And anyway . . ." She paused, looking at Iron Robert as he lay sprawled out on his back.

"Anyway . . . no use," the giant growled. "Iron Robert bad hurt. Bone in back broken. Legs . . . not move. You go now, Gom Bulj not like you be late."

A bald, thick-necked humanoid came up, cradling Gom Bulj's power gun in his arm.

"Get moving, you two," he ordered. "There's work to be done. Gom Bulj said—"

"Don't you give me orders, Bulugg," Stellaraire snapped at him. "Anyway, we were just going—"

"I'm not leaving him here like this," Roan said. He looked helplessly around. The skinners were lifting a sail-like flap of horny skin from the chinazell, exposing the bone-white flesh of the dino's flank. No one was paying any attention to Iron Robert's plight, Roan saw. No one cared. Beyond the busy throng folding canvas, the animals were moving up the aft gangplank into the ship. There was a holdup as a humped animal decided to sit crossways and someone yelled for the electric goad. Then Roan saw Jumbo heaving over the 'zoo grounds like a ship in a slow sea.

"Get Jumbo," he said to Stellaraire. "I'll find some rope . . . !"

"But, Roan—"

"Do as I tell you!" he snapped. He started away and the guard said, "Hey!" and brought the gun around.

"Shut up, Bulugg!" Stellaraire said. "And don't get any ideas with that gun. You're just supposed to hold it and scare people."

Roan looped the thick, oily plastic cable under Iron Robert's arm, tied it in a vast knot. Stellaraire was perched on Jumbo's head with her legs hanging down over his gray, furrowed forehead. The pachyderm moved his trunk restlessly as Roan tied the cable to his leather-and-chain harness. Looking toward the ship, Roan saw that the animals were almost all aboard now; the last of the yard wagons were puffing away toward the greenish blaze of the setting sun with their loads. A shrill whistle sounded from the ship.

"Hey, shake it up!" Bulugg called. "That's minus a quarter. Whatta, ya wanna get left?"

"Pull, Jumbo!" Stellaraire cried. "Hurry! Pull!"

The elephant took a step and jolted to a stop. He looked back over his shoulder, puzzled, and flapped his ears.

"Pull, Jumbo," Stellaraire called; and Jumbo leaned into his harness and pulled, sensing the necessity of something more than ordinary effort. Iron Robert budged, dragging a furrow in the ground, and Jumbo strained, putting his back into it, placing his great feet and thrusting, hauling the dead weight of many tons across the dusty clay of the empty arena.

At the gangplank, Bulugg jumped at the sound of the shrill last-warning whistle. He waved the gun nervously.

There were faces at the port above, looking down curiously.

"Five minutes to the Seal Ship bell," he blustered. "You can leave that hunk of rock right here and get aboard . . . !"

Jumbo put a foot on the wide gangway, started up. A loudspeaker was chanting checklist orders. Gom Bulj appeared above, looking out from the cavernous hold.

"Here, here, what's this?" he bellowed. He waved his arms, staring around as if outraged. Iron Robert's vast inert weight dragged in the dust like a broken monument, reached the end of the gangplank—and jammed. Jumbo heaved, the harness taut across his chest. A rivet popped from it and clattered against the hull. Roan ran to the fallen giant, caught up a long pole, levered at the stony shoulder. Jumbo rocked twice, then heaved again—and Iron Robert bumped up on the gangway, grinding along the incline with a noise like a wrecked ship being hauled off a launch pad.

Then they were in the hold and Gom Bulj was rippling his walking tentacles, muttering loudly, and the others were staring and then walking away, bored quickly with Terry foolishness. Stellaraire's lavender powder was caked with sweat and two of her gold-painted, so-carefully tended fingernails were broken off, but Roan looked at her and found her beautiful, with dust in her ocher eyes and streaks down her face, and her gold tights plastered against her body. The port clanged shut, and the ship's lights came on, and they stood and looked down at the great body they had salvaged.

"Well, there went your chance to run away from the 'zoo," Stellaraire sighed. "What are you going to do now? Just leave him here?"

"We'll get the vet to look at him; he'll know how to fix him. You and I will bring him food and scrape him. After a while he'll be all right again."

The girl looked into Roan's face curiously. "Why?" she asked. "He was nothing special to you—you hardly knew him . . ."

"Nobody should be left alone to die just because he's hurt," Roan said shortly.

"You crazy, funny, Terry," Stellaraire said, and then she was crying, and he held her, wondering if it was because she was a mule and not a real Terran that she was so hard to understand at times.

For two months Iron Robert lay in the canvas-hung compartment Roan and Stellaraire had arranged for him in the cargo hold, with his lower body encased in massive concrete casts to remind him not to try to move. Every day Roan or the girl went over him with a scraper, and assured him he was as handsome as ever. Now and then Gom Bulj came down to stare at the huge invalid, rap his nine knuckles against the casts, and mutter about expense.

When the day came that the vet said the casts could come off, Nugg came down and helped Roan work carefully with a jack hammer, freeing him. When they finished, Iron Robert sat up, then got to his feet and stood, whole again.

"Terry customs strange," he rumbled, looking down at Roan. "Not call you Terry now. Call you Roan. Iron Robert your friend, Roan. Not understand Terry ways, but maybe good ways. Maybe better ways than Iron Robert ever know before."

Gom Bulj appeared, puffing two cigars. He looked Iron Robert over, shaking his head.

"A remarkable thing, young Terry. It appears you were right. A valuable property, and good as new—I hope. I'm a fair being, young Terry, and I have decided to reward you. Henceforth, you may consider the mule, Stellaraire, as your personal concubine, for your exclusive use—except when I have important Terry-type guests, of course—"

"She's not yours to give away," Roan said sharply.

"Eh? What's that, not mine?" Gom Bulj blinked at Roan. "Why, I paid—"

"No one owns Stellaraire."

"See here, my lad, you'd best remember who it is you're addressing! Are you forgetting I could have you trussed up in leathers and flogged for a week?"

"No," Iron Robert rumbled. "No one lay hand on

Roan, Gom Bulj. Iron Robert kill any being that try—
even you."

"Here . . . !" Gom Bulj backpedaled, staring around
wildly. "What's the cosmos coming to? Am I to be
threatened by my own property?"

"Iron Robert not property," the giant rumbled. "Iron
Robert of royal ferrous strain, and belong to no being.
And Roan my friend. Tell all crew, Roan friend to Iron
Robert."

"And since you can't give me away," Stellaraire put
in, "Roan still has a reward coming. I think it's time you
gave him full Freak status and started paying him. And
he should be freed from all duties except his high-wire
act. And he should eat in the Owner's Mess, with the
other stars."

"Why, why . . ." Gom Bulj stuttered. But in the end
he agreed and hurried away, still muttering to himself.

8

There had been a party celebrating Iron Robert's successful defense of his title against a Fire-saber from Deeb, and Roan had drunk too much and not left Stellaraire until almost ship-dawn, and now he struggled out of a dream in which he fought against iron arms that closed on him, hearing the beloved voice that called by the arena gate. His eyes were open now, and he could hear his own breath rasping in his throat, and the voice was the wailing of a siren, but the crushing weight still held him, flat on his back with the edge of the bunk cutting into his arm, and a wrinkle in the blanket under him like a sword on edge. Far away, bells clanged, and a tiny glow grew behind the black glass disk above the cabin door, swelling into a baleful red that flashed on, off, on . . .

Roan moved, dragged an arm like an ironwood log across his body, turned under the massive pressure and fell with stunning violence to the floor from the bunk.

Lying on his face, he felt the deep vibration through the deck plates. The engines were running—here in deep space, four parsecs from the nearest system! He rose to his feet, his bones creaking under the massive acceleration—three gravities at least. Far away, over the bellow of the engines, the clang of bells, the whine of the siren, he thought he heard the sound of Jumbo's trumpeting . . .

He made his way across the room, into the corridor, dragging feet like anchors, while the noise swelled, crimson lights screamed red alarm, faraway voices called. At the end of the corridor the lift door waited, open. Inside, he reached to the control panel, pressed the button for the menagerie deck. For a moment, magically, the weight went away and he drew a breath—then massive blackness clamped down while tiny red lights whirled . . .

He was lying on the floor of the car, smelling the salty sea smell of blood. Through the open door under the blue-white glare of the ceiling, he saw the long white corridor, the barred doors. Crawling again, he made his way along the passage, feeling the slickness underfoot, seeing how the pattern spread from under the doors, blackish red and harsh green mingling in a glistening film that trembled in a geometric resonance pattern.

All around him, over the mind-filling Niagara of the engines, there were bellows, groans, grunts of final agony. Roan went on, not looking into the cages as he passed them one by one, seeing the film of blood-dance spreading.

The high, barred door of Jumbo's stall was bulged outward, the two-inch steel rod sprung from its socket. Behind it, the elephant lay, blinded, ribs broken, one tusk snapped off short. Blood flowed from the open mouth, from under the closed eyelids. Roan could see the animal's massive side rise in a tortured heave as it struggled to breathe.

"Jumbo!" he choked.

The heavy trunk groped toward him. The great legs stirred; a moan rumbled from the crushed chest.

Roan looked at the power rifle clamped in a bracket beside the stall door. He pulled it free, checked the charge, raised it against the relentless pull, aimed between the closed and bloody eyes and pressed the firing stud . . .

*   *   *

Alarms jangled monotonously in the carpeted corridor outside the quarters of Gom Bulj. Roan dragged leaden feet past the fallen body of an Ythcan, lying with one three-fingered hand outstretched toward the door of the patron's apartment.

Inside, Gom Bulj lay sprawled, his body crushed against the floor, his eyes bulging from the pressure. He moved feebly as Roan came to him and went heavily down to hands and knees.

"Why are you . . . killing us all . . . Gom Bulj?" Roan asked, then stopped to breathe.

"No . . ." The entrepreneur's voice was a breathless wheeze. "Not me . . . at . . . all . . . young Terry." He drew a hoarse breath. "Old battle . . . reflex . . . circuits . . . triggered . . . somehow. Maximum acceleration . . . three . . . standard . . . G . . ."

"Why . . . ?"

"Ah, why indeed . . . young Terry . . ."

"What . . . can we do?"

"It's . . . too bad . . . too bad, young Terry. No help for us. The time has come . . . to terminate . . . the biological process . . ."

"You mean . . . die . . . ?"

"When the . . . environment becomes . . . hostile . . . a quick demise . . . is greatly . . . to be desired . . ."

"I want to live. Tell . . . me what to do . . ."

Gom Bulj's massive head seemed to sink even deeper into the compressed bulk of his body. "Self-preservation . . . an interesting . . . concept. A pity . . . we won't have . . . the opportunity . . . to discuss . . . it . . ."

"What can I do, Gom Bulj?" Roan reached to the bulbous body, gripped a thick arm. "I have . . . to try . . ."

"I suggest . . . you suspend . . . respiration. Five minutes . . . should do the trick . . . As for me . . . I may thrash a bit . . . but pay . . . no attention . . ."

"I'll turn off the engines," Roan choked. "How . . . ?"

"No use . . . young Terry. Too far . . . Even now . . . blood runs . . . from your nostrils . . ."

"Tell me what to do . . ."

"On the war deck . . ." Gom Bulj gasped. "Command . . . control panel. A lever—painted white . . . But . . . you can't . . ."

"I'll try," Roan said.

It was an interminable time later, and Roan's hands and knees left red marks against the gray decking as he pulled himself across the raised threshold of the door above which the red glare panel warned: BATTLE CONTROL—AUTHORIZED PERSONNEL ONLY.

Across the dusty room, the dead gray of the great screens had changed to vivid green-white on panels alive now with dancing jewel lights. A dark shape moved on the master screen; below, mass and proximity gauges trembled; numbers appeared and faded on the ground-glass dials. Roan pulled himself to the padded Fire Controller's seat, spelled out the symbols flashing in blue: IFF NEGATIVE.

A yellow light blinked suddenly in the center of the panel. Red letters appeared on the screen, spelling out words in archaic Universal:

MAIN BATTERIES ARMED

The words faded, changed:

MAIN BATTERIES FIRE, TEN SECONDS
ALERT . . .

The auxiliary panels blinked from yellow to red to white.

FIRE ALL, the panel spelled out. Through the seat, Roan felt a tremor run through the ship, briefly rattling a loose bolt in the panel. Before him, the banked controls sparkled row on row, telltale lights blinking insistently, gauges producing readings, relays closing, clicking, as the robot panel monitored the action. Roan's eyes blinked back haze, searching for the white-painted switch . . .

It was there, just to the right of the baleful crimson dial lettered MAIN RADAR—TRACKING. He reached out, forcing his heavy hand up, grasped the smooth lever, threw it from AUTO to MANUAL.

The war lights blinked off. He searched the instruments before him, found a notched handle lettered EMERGENCY ACCELERATION, threw it to ZERO.

A thousand noises growled down to silence. Roan seemed to float upward from the chair as the pressure dropped to the ship-normal half-G. In the stillness, metal popped and groaned, readjusting to the reduced stresses. Distantly, someone screamed, again and again.

Roan thought suddenly of Stellaraire, alone in her cabin . . .

He ran, leaping down the companionways, along to her door. It stood ajar. He pushed it wide—

With a sound like the clap of gigantic hands, the room exploded in his face.

He was a dust mote, floating in a brassy sky. Somewhere thunder rolled, remote and ominous. Somewhere, a voice called to him, and he would have answered, but his lungs were choked with smoke as thick as syrup. He fought to clear them, and then his eyes were open and he saw broken metal, the fragments of a flower dish and of a yellow blossom, and a white hand, limp, the fingers curled.

He was on his feet, choking in an acrid reek of burned metal, throwing aside a shattered chair, heaving at a fallen fragment of paneling, coughing as dust boiled up from the rubble of insulation, charred cloth, smashed glass and wood and plastic.

She lay on her back, her eyes closed, her face unmarked, her platinum hair swirled across her forehead. "Stellaraire . . . !" He knelt, feeling scorching heat against his face, brushing away dust, splinters, paper—

The duralloy beam lay across her pelvis, pinning her tight. Roan felt his throat close as he gripped the cold metal, strained at it, felt its massive inertia. On his knees, he wrapped his arms around the metal section, heaved back until the room swam red. The odor of smoke was stronger now. Roan stood, hearing the ringing in his head, seeing the pale yellow flames that

licked at scattered paper and torn cloth. Twisted wires
and broken conduits sagged from the broken wall. Water trickled from a ruptured pipe, and beside it a stream
of sharp-odored liquid poured down.

The little colored fish from the tank lay stiff on the
floor.

Too late, Roan whirled, threw a quilt over the burning paper. With a whoosh! the coolant fluid ignited, and
now red fire boiled black smoke, and a wave of heat
struck Roan's face like a whip. He seized a blanket,
thrust it against the broken waterline, then threw the
wet cloth over Stellaraire's body. It hissed when it
touched the floor beside her. He threw himself down,
not noticing the searing pain against his back, braced
his feet, set his shoulders against the beam, and pushed.
It was like pushing at a granite cliff. The air he breathed
burned in his throat.

There was fallen length of a duralloy channel under
his hand. He thrust it under the beam, levering until
the shirt split across his back. The channel buckled.
When he tossed it aside, there were yellowish-white
burns on his palms.

Stellaraire's hair was burning, the platinum-gold strands
blackening and curling. Roan stumbled to the door, out
into a smoke-blinded corridor. He would find Iron Robert, and together they would free Stellaraire . . .

In the thick-rugged chamber of Gom Bulj, the entrepreneur lay where Roan had left him, in a puddle of
blood, heavy lids half closed over dull eyes.

"You succeeded, young Terry," he said, his voice
a thin echo of its old rumble. "Too late for me, I
fear . . ."

Roan swayed on his feet. "Where is Iron Robert,
Gom Bulj . . . ?"

"Alas, I don't know." The dull eyes turned to Roan's
hands, his blackened clothing.

"You are burned, poor lad. Now you will die, there's
a clever boy. Too bad. I had great ambition for you,
young Terry. One day . . . I would have billed you . . .
as the Galaxy's greatest Freak . . ."

"It's Stellaraire," Roan said, talking now through a black mist that closed ever tighter, ever tighter. "I need Iron Robert . . ."

A wall annunciator crackled and a strange voice spoke: "Attention all hands! Assemble in the main dining hall at once! Bring no weapons! Disobedience is death!"

"What voice is that?" Gom Bulj said faintly. "Are we boarded then?"

Roan made his mind work. "I saw a ship," he said, "on the screens. We fired—and they fired back. I think they won."

"Yes," Gom Bulj blinked heavy lids. "I knew it. I felt the shocks. Alas, in her day *Belshazzar* was a mighty dreadnought of the Empire—but now she has fought her last action . . ." His voice faded to a whisper.

"What should I do, Gom Bulj?" Roan cried.

The heavy body stirred; a last hoarse breath sighed out.

Roan looked down at the still body.

"Gom Bulj is dead," he said aloud. "Jumbo is dead . . . and . . . and . . ." He whirled, ran into the corridor and toward the dining hall.

All around, sounds of destruction echoed along metal halls. A muffled blast shook the deck plates underfoot. Harsh odors of hot metal and things that burned caught at Roan's throat. He came to the arched entry over the two wide steps leading down to the broad dining room with its threadbare eternon carpets and blackened gilt fixtures, and stopped, seeing overturned tables, huddled bodies, and standing among them, legs braced wide, cradling weapons, five creatures in coats covered with tight-curled hair.

"Help me!" Roan called.

The nearest creature whirled, swung his weapon around in an easy gesture. There were horns on his head, and his eyes were black stones.

A big creature in a radiation mask stepped to the horned creature's side, knocked the weapon aside, then turned the power pistols gripped in his big fists on Roan, looked him over through the slits in the mask.

"Don't burn this one, Czack. Can't you see he's a Terry?"

"To the pit with Terries," the other snarled—but he lowered his gun.

"It's Stellaraire!" Roan said. "Help me!"

The tall creature holstered one pistol and took off the mask. Roan looked into wide gray eyes, saw the thin nose, the edge of white teeth between the thin lips . . .

Roan stared.

"You look like pretty pure stock, kid," the tall Man said. "Where you from?"

"You're a Terran," Roan said. "Help me. The fire—"

The horned creature stepped close, swung a wide hand against Roan's head. He staggered; the room rang . . .

"—hands off the kid," the Man said. Roan shook his head, blinking back a blurring film.

"But I asked you a question, kid. Henry Dread doesn't ask twice." The pistol was still centered on Roan's chest.

Roan turned, started back up the steps. A horned humanoid blocked his way, swinging a slow blow that Roan leaned aside from.

"Get out of my way," Roan said. "I have to find Iron Robert . . ."

"Hold it." Henry Dread had both guns in his hands now, and he turned to the arched doorway. A tall, green-skinned Ythcan stood at the top of the two steps. Beside Roan, Czack brought his power rifle up. There was a deafening *ba-wam!* and a flicker of blue light— and the Ythcan spun back, fell, kicked, and lay still.

"See if there's any more," Henry Dread snapped. A hair-coated creature with hunched shoulders and a bald skull moved past Roan, sprang up the steps. Beyond him, Roan saw a wide silhouette looming against the corridor's glare.

"Iron Robert!" Roan shouted. "Run!"

Facing Iron Robert, the bald creature fired at point-blank range. Roan saw the flicker of blue light that played for an instant against Iron Robert's broad chest, heard a deep grunt; then Iron Robert took two steps, plucked the bald one from the floor, whirled him high, and threw him against the wall. He rebounded, lay utterly still, his face oddly flattened, blood dribbling from his ear.

"Stand clear," Henry Dread barked. "My blasters will take him."

Roan struck with the edge of his hand at the horned one's arm, caught the power rifle as it fell, swiveled on Henry Dread.

"Don't shoot him!" Roan said.

Iron Robert stood, his eyes moving from one to another of the six weapons aimed at him. Beside Roan, the horned creature snarled.

"What are you waiting for? Kill him!"

Henry Dread looked at Roan. He turned slowly, bringing his guns around to aim at Roan's chest.

"Drop it, kid."

"No," Roan said.

The Man's mouth twitched. There was sweat on his forehead. "Don't try me, kid. I'm supposed to be fast—and you're covered. Now let the gun down nice."

"Roan," Iron Robert's deep voice rumbled. "I kill this one?" He took a step toward Henry Dread. Six guns tracked him.

"No, Iron Robert. Go to Stellaraire—quickly!"

"I kill him easy," Iron Robert said. "Have only two small guns."

"Help Stellaraire, Iron Robert!" Roan shouted. "Do as I tell you!"

Standing straight, Roan forced himself not to think about Stellaraire or about the burns on his hands and body, or about the smell of charred flesh, but only about holding the gun aimed at the pirate's chest. And Iron Robert understood and he turned and went.

"Be smart, kid," Henry Dread said between gritted teeth. "Drop it, before I have to burn you . . ." He was tall and solid, with a scarred face and thick fingers. He stood, two guns aimed at Roan, tense and ready, and the sweat trickled down his face.

"Try it," Roan said.

Henry Dread's mouth twisted in a sort of smile. "Yeah, you're fast, kid. Nobody ever took a gun away from Czack like that before. I don't think he likes you for it—"

"Why don't you kill the muck-grub . . . ?" The horned one stood in a half crouch, eyes on Roan.

"Go ahead, jump him, Czack. Even if I put two through the head, I'll bet you a keg he'd nail you on the way down. Want to risk it?"

The other answered in an incomprehensible language. Henry Dread barked an order. His creatures stirred; two of them filed carefully past Roan and out into the corridor.

"Don't let them try to hurt Iron Robert," Roan said. "If he doesn't come back, I'll shoot you."

The pirate licked his lips, his eyes on Roan's. "What's that walking Bolo to you, kid? You're human—"

"He's my friend."

"Friends with a Geek?" Henry Dread sneered.

"Why are you killing everyone?"

"This tub fired on me first—not that my screens can't handle museum pieces like you tossed at us." The Man's eyes narrowed. "Nobody lobs one into Henry Dread and gets away with it."

"You killed Jumbo—and Gom Bulj—and maybe . . ." His voice broke.

"Don't take it so hard, kid. With me it's business. I needed fuel and ammo . . ." The voice seemed to fade and swell. Roan held his eyes open, leaning against the wall just slightly, holding the gun steady.

". . . this tub happened along. That's life."

There was a movement in the corridor behind Henry Dread. Iron Robert stepped into view. Behind him, a hair-coated creature stepped from a door, brought up a gun—

Roan swiveled and fired, and was back covering Henry Dread's belt buckle in a movement quicker than the eye could follow. The gunner fell and lay still.

"Wait there, Iron Robert," Roan called.

The big Man lowered his pistols, tossed them aside. He looked shaken. "Holding these things is likely to be dangerous," he said. "Kid, you move like a fire lizard on Sunside. But you're burned pretty bad. You need to have my medic take a look at you. Now, just aim that blaster off side, so no accidents happen, and we'll talk this thing over."

Roan held the rifle steady, listening to the surging in his head. In the doorway, Iron Robert waited.

"Look, kid, you put the gun down, and I'll guarantee you safe conduct. You and the one-man task force, too. You can't hold the iron on me forever."

Roan looked at the Man's eyes. They were steady on his.

"Will you give me your word as a Man?" Roan asked.

The Man stared at him. "Sure, kid." He glanced at Czack and the others.

"You heard that," he said flatly.

Roan lowered the rifle. Czack moved in, snatched it away, brought it up and around—

Henry Dread took a step, slammed a gnarled fist against the horned head. Czack dropped the rifle and spun against the wall. Henry Dread massaged his fist. "This slob didn't think I meant it." He looked at Roan. "I guess us Men got to stick together, eh, kid?" He bent and scooped up a gun. Iron Robert came toward him, a blackish stain on his shoulder.

"Shall I kill this one now?" he rumbled.

"No . . . Iron Robert . . . Stellaraire . . ." Roan leaned against the wall, feeling the dizziness rising. Iron Robert caught him.

"No, Roan." The great ugly head shook slowly. "The Fair One is gone away now. Now she dances for the Gods in their high place, above all sorrow . . ." The deep voice seemed to come from far away.

"Take Roan to your doctors, Man."

"Yeah—the kid's in bad shape. You better come too, big boy. You're a tough one. You took a blaster on half-charge at five paces, and you're still walking and ready to eat 'em alive. Maybe I can use a Geek like you at that . . ."

9

They were alien hands, gentle but impersonally insistent, and they poked and prodded with a feel of slick, scaly hide, and hard, too-thin fingers. There was no comfort in alien hands; they weren't like Stellaraire's hands, warm and soft and—human. Roan moved to thrust the hands away, and searing pain flashed through his body and he gasped, not at the bodily agony but at the sudden vivid remembrance of hands that would not touch him again, and white-gold hair, and smiling ocher eyes . . .

"He wakes," a reedy voice said. "A tenacious organism. Not like some of these beings, who seem almost eager to flee to the long darkness. I feel their souls tremble and shrink under my hands, and they are gone like a snuffed candle. But not this one . . ."

"Make Roan live, Man doctor," Iron Robert's basso rumbled. "Make Roan live strong."

"Yes, yes. Stay back, you great ugly lout. Now, the wounds are clean. And I have here . . ." There was a sound of rummaging . . . "Aha! Now, we'll see—"

Roan stiffened as a sensation like molten lead poured across his chest. He was aware of white lights glaring through his eyelids. He moaned.

"Eh, he feels it now: Lie easily, Terran. It is only pain . . ."

"You make pain go away, Man doctor!"

"I've yearned for a proper patient for these medicines, ugly giant! A fabulous pharmacopeia, all made for Terrans ages dead; long have I saved them. Henry Dread likes to fancy his rogues have human blood, but my knives know all their secrets. Half-castes, mutants, humanoid trash! Now, this lad's different. He's almost a textbook example of your pure Terry stock. A rare creature . . ."

The thin voice rambled on, and the hands probed and the fire touched, flamed, and faded into a dull numbness. Roan let out a long breath and felt drugged drowsiness creeping over him like warm water rising in a tub.

"This skin," the voice went on, far away now. "The texture! How nicely the blade slides through it! And the color. See, look at this illustration in my book . . ."

"Does he sleep, Man doctor? Or . . . ?"

"He only sleeps, monster. Faugh, I'm pleased I have no need to take a scalpel to that horny hide of yours . . . Now, get back. I've two hours of close work ahead, and no need of your rusty bulk to hinder me."

It was many hours later; Roan opened his eyes and by a faint light filtering through a barred transom saw the massive silhouette beside him.

"Iron Robert . . ." Roan's voice was a weak croak.

"You wake now, Roan. You sleep, good. Man doctor small foolish creature, but he fix you good, Roan."

"I should have shot him, Iron Robert . . ."

"No, Roan. He fix you."

"I mean the Man. He killed Stellaraire. I should have killed him. You should have smashed them, smashed their ship—"

"Then Roan and Iron Robert die, too, Roan. Too soon to die for you. Too many strange things to see yet, too many places still to go. Long life ahead for you still, Roan—"

"Not for me. I'm only a Terry Freak, and I'm almost dead already. Dad told me. Humans only have time to start living and they die. And living's no fun—not any more . . ."

"Sure, lots of fun still to come, Roan. Many great jugs to drink, and far suns to see; many females to take, and enemies to kill, and whole universes to see and smell and taste. Plenty time to be dead after."

"All my friends are dead. And Stellaraire . . ."

"I still alive, Roan." Iron Robert moved and Roan heard a soft metallic clash. "Iron Robert your friend, sure."

Roan raised up on one elbow, ignoring a tearing sensation in his bandaged arm, peering in the dim light. Massive chains lay across Iron Robert's knees, and his wrists were circled by shackles of finger-thick metal.

"Iron Robert—you're chained to the wall . . . !"

"Sure—Henry Dread scared of me, you bet. I let him put chains on me if he send Man doctor to you."

Roan pushed himself upright, ignoring the pulse that started up, drumming in his temples. He swung his feet heavily to the floor. A blackness filled with whirling lights swelled to fill the room and he gripped the edge of the bunk, waiting for it to go away.

"I'll make him take them off," he heard himself saying. "I'll make him. . . . It was a Man to Man agreement . . ."

"No, Roan, you lie down! Bad for you to move now . . ."

"I don't want to lie down. Call him. Call Henry Dread . . ."

"Roan! You got to do like Man doctor say, otherwise you get bad sick . . ."

Roan was on his feet, feeling the floor sway and tilt under him.

"Henry Dread," he called, hearing the words emerge as a croak.

"Wait, Roan. Somebody come . . ."

There were metallic sounds in the corridor; a splash of light glared suddenly; long shadows crouched away from the door that swung wide, and a tall, broad figure stood squinting into the room.

"You yelling for me, were you, boy? Hey—on your feet already—?"

"You chained Iron Robert. You didn't keep your word."

"Henry Dread always keeps his word, you . . . !"
The Man's wide shape seemed to blur; Roan blinked
hard, wavered, caught himself.

"Unchain him. He's my friend . . . !"

"You better crawl back in that bunk, boy; you're
raving! I'm captain aboard this vessel; you're a slave of
war. I let the sawbones patch you up, but don't let it go
to your head . . ."

Roan advanced toward Henry Dread on uncertain feet.

"Unchain him, liar! Keep your word, murderer!"

Henry Dread's eyes narrowed. "Why, you lousy
little—"

Roan lunged, and Henry Dread leaped back, jerked
his pistol from his hip holster and aimed it. Iron Robert
came to his feet in a clash of chain.

"I'm aiming this right between your eyes, Terry boy,"
Henry said between his teeth. "One more step, and so
help me I burn you down."

"I don't care about that," Roan said, taking a step.
"That isn't anything."

"No, Roan!" Iron Robert boomed. "You do like Henry
Dread say now, Roan!"

Roan tried to take another step, but the floor tilted
and he gritted his teeth, and willed himself not to fall,
willed the blackness to retreat . . .

"I wear chains for you, Roan. You do this for me."

"Kid, you're crazy . . . !" Henry Dread's voice barked.
"You'll kill yourself!"

"You wait, Roan," Iron Robert said. "Later, when
you get well, then you have chance to kill this one."

Henry Dread laughed, a harsh snarl. "Yeah, listen to
your sidekick, kid. You kill me when you feel better."

Then the shadows moved and the light narrowed
down and was gone in a clang of metal, and Roan sank
down, groped, found the bed, fell across it.

"He's a Man, Iron Robert. A Terry—almost like me.
But he's not like Dad said the Terries were."

"Henry Dread mighty scared Man, Roan," Iron Robert rumbled softly. "And maybe he not such mean Man
like he make out. He come plenty quick, first time you
call. Maybe Henry Dread wait outside, hope you call

his name. Maybe Henry Dread plenty lonely Man, Roan . . ."

The bars welded across the doorframe of the warhead storage room were as thick as Roan's wrist and close together. He leaned on the mop and looked through the bars at Iron Robert, who sat on a duralloy slab that sagged under his weight, almost invisible in the shadows of the lightless cell.

"The Minid they call Snaggle-head is the worst," Roan said. "He's about seven feet tall and he smells like a Charon's mud-hive. Yesterday he tripped me and I almost fell down the aft companionway."

Iron Robert's chains clanked. Roan could see his small eyes gleam. "You be careful, Roan. You don't let riffraff get you mad. You do like I say; wait."

"I don't want to wait. Why should I wait? I—"

"You wait cause you got plenty bad burns, not healed up yet. You want to get crippled for life? You wait, don't pay mind to anybody teases you."

"I don't mind, though. I know which ones I'm going to kill first, just as soon as—"

"Roan, you stop that fool talk, you remember how you promise to do like I say."

"I'll keep my promise. Just because Henry Dread's word is no good doesn't mean I'm a promise-breaker, too."

"You wait a minute, Roan, you too much angry against Henry Dread. He keep promise, all right. He say you and me, he won't kill us. Well—both of us alive, all right."

"I'm going to tell him if he doesn't free you, I'll steal a gun the first chance I get and kill him."

"You do that, you big fool, Roan. I don't mind sit here in dark, rest. Not much rest for me, long time. I sit and think about old days, back home, time Iron Robert young being, have plenty fun. I got pretty good eidetic recall, remember all smells, tastes, sounds, faces. Sure, I got plenty good memories, Roan. First time I got time really look at them good."

"You're stronger than any of them—" Roan took a

breath and made his voice angry to cover up the break. "You let them chain you, you big dumb hunk of scrap iron—"

Iron Robert rumbled a laugh. "Plenty easy sit here with chains on. Tough for you, Roan, have to stay outside and let Snaggle-head push you round. But you show you got brains, Roan. You stay quiet, you wait. One day you heal up good, then maybe we see."

Roan looked along the corridor. A hatch clanged as three Minid crewmen emerged from a cargo hold.

"Well, you'll get a chance to see how they operate now, Iron Robert." Roan felt his throat turn dry. "You'll see how much good ignoring them does."

"OK, Roan, you go now, quick, don't have to wait for herd of mud-pigs—"

"I'll take it without hitting back," Roan said between his teeth. "But I won't run from them, I don't care what you say." He began working the mop, eyes on the floor.

The leading crewman hooked his thumbs in his sagging pistol belt and started toward Roan, laying a trail of oily sandal prints across the shiny expanse of freshly scrubbed floor. He had thick bowed legs and a hairless skull and there were wide gaps in the row of spade-shaped bluish teeth he was showing in what might have been a grin. Three loops of rough-cut yellow jewels hung against a grimy gold-braided tunic. He stopped two yards from Roan, plucked a dope stick from a breast pocket, bit off the cap and spat it on the floor, sniffed it appreciatively with wide nostrils, and said:

"Hey, boys, looky what's here . . ." He pointed with the dope stick, his wide mouth forming a loose-lipped O of mock amazement. "What is it, a itty bitty baby boy playin' like a growed-up Geek?"

"Naw, it's a cute little pansy-pants, talking to its sweety through the bars," a second crewman offered. "It thinks that rusted-out Freak is mighty sexy—"

"Hey, don't talk dirty in front of it," another said. "It might learn a dirty word and use it in front of its mama and get 'panked."

"Always thought old Henry wasn't as tough as some thought," Snaggle-head stated. "Now he's got hisself a play-dolly." He chuckled, a sound like gas escaping from a sewer. "Next thing, Old Cap'n'll get hisself a little Terry bitch and start in breedin' 'em." He haw-hawed, hawked, spat on the floor at Roan's feet. Roan stopped mopping, stood looking at the wide mural on the lounge wall, with its audiovision of a rolling sea-scape. In the silence the crash and hiss of breakers was loud. Snaggle-head chuckled again, took a final puff, and dropped the dope stick on the floor.

". . . but I notice he still don't trust him far; not since he held that gun on his belt buckle. I think his little pet plumb scared him that time—"

Casually, Roan slapped the wet mop across Snaggle-head's sandal; the big crewman jumped back with a yell, stamping his wet foot against the deck. The grin had vanished from the loose mouth; the other crewmen watched with bright, interested eyes. Snaggle-head drew his massive head down close to his burly shoulders. His mouth was open, his brow creased in a black frown.

Ignoring him, Roan thrust the wet end of the mop into the filter unit, watched the rollers close and open, went on with his mopping.

Snaggle-head stepped in front of him; his grimy fin-ger prodded Roan's chest. Roan looked into the over-sized face, spotted here and there with coarse hairs sprouting from inflamed warty blemishes.

"What you think you're lookin' at, punk?"

"It looks like the hind end of a crundle-beast," Roan said clearly, "only hairier."

The coarse face tightened; the finger jabbed again, hard. "You take a lot of chances, softie—"

"Whatever it is, I'll remember it," Roan continued. "Some day I'll put my foot in it."

Snaggle-head's eyes narrowed. "It's a mean-talking one," he said softly. "Too bad it ain't got the guts to back up the talk." The heavy hand swung in a short arc, slammed Roan's head against the metal bulkhead. He staggered, caught himself with the unbandaged arm, shook his head to clear it.

"Is that . . . the best you can do?" he asked blurrily.

"I guess you're scared to get too rough; there's only three of you . . ."

The crewman shook clawed hands, palms up, under Roan's nose.

"One of these days, pansy, I'll put the thumbs in, where it counts. I'll put 'em in till the blood squirts—"

Roan looked into the pale eyes. "You will, eh? You think Henry Dread will let you?"

The wide mouth dropped open. The pasty face turned a dull pink. "Whatta I care about Henry Dread? As soon as I get ready to croak you, rube, you'll know it—and to the Nine Hells with Henry Dread."

"Careful," Roan said, nodding toward the others, "they're listening."

"Huh?" The heavy head swiveled quickly to look at the two crewmen. They looked at the ceiling.

"All right, you slobs. Let's get moving. We ain't got all day to gab with sissy-britches here." The two filed past in silence.

"I'll get to you later, cull," the lead crewman grated.

"Roan," Iron Robert's voice rumbled from the cell. "You got to learn keep mouth shut sometimes. That space rat hurt you much?"

"He didn't hurt me." Roan's face was white in the gloom.

"You not be so dumb, you not talk back, you don't get hit."

"It's worth it."

"Maybe some day he get really mad, hit too hard."

"He hasn't got much of a punch."

"Maybe he got better punch than you think. Maybe what you said not so far off true."

"What do you mean?"

"Maybe Henry Dread better friend than you think, Roan. I think he tell all Gooks and Geeks, hands off human boy. I think he have plans in mind for you, Roan."

10

The surgeon clicked his lipless mandibles, peeling off the protective film under which the burns on Roan's shoulder and arm had been healing for many weeks.

"Eh, pretty, very pretty! Pink and new as a fresh-hatched suckling! There'll be no scars to mar that smooth hide!"

"Ouch!" Roan said. "That hurts."

"Ignore it, youngling," the surgeon said absently, working Roan's elbow joint. He nodded to himself, tried the wrist, then the fingers.

"All limber enough; now raise your limb here." He indicated shoulder level. Roan lifted his arm, wincing. The surgeon's horny fingers went to the shoulder joint, prodding and kneading.

"No loss of tone there," the surgeon muttered. "Bend over, stretch your back . . ."

Roan bent, twisted, working the shoulder, stretching the newly healed burns. Sweat popped out on his forehead.

"At first it may feel as though the skin is tearing open," the surgeon said. "But it's nothing."

Roan straightened. "I'll try to remember that."

The surgeon was nodding, closing his instrument case.

"You'll soon regain full use of the limb. Meanwhile, the hide is tender, and there'll be a certain stiffness in the joints—"

"Can I—ah—do heavy work now?"

"In moderation. But take care: I've no wish to see my prize exhibit damaged." The surgeon rubbed his hard hands together with a chirruping sound. "Wait until Henry Dread sees this," he cackled. "Calls me a Geek, does he? Threatens to put me out the air lock, eh? But where would he ever find another surgeon of my skill?" He darted a final, sharp glance of approval at Roan and was gone. Roan pulled his tunic over his head, buckled his belt in place, and stretched his arms gingerly. There was a wide header over the doorway. He went to it, grasped it, and pulled himself up carefully. The sensation reminded him of a Charon he had seen stripping hide from a dead gracyl . . . but the injured arm held his weight.

He dropped back and went out into the corridor. There was a broken packing case in a reclamation bin in the corner. Roan wrenched a three-foot length of tough, blackish inch-thick wood from it. He looked toward the bright-lit intersection of the main concourse. A steward in soiled whites waddled past on bowed legs, holding a tray up on a stumpy arm. Henry Dread and his officers would be drinking in the wardroom now. It was as good a time as any . . .

Roan turned and followed the dull red indicator lights toward the lower decks.

He was in a narrow corridor ill lit by grimed-over glare panels. Voices yammered nearby: shouts, snarls, a drunken song, a bellow of anger; the third watch break hour was underway in the crew quarters. Roan hefted the skrilwood club. It was satisfactorily heavy.

Feet clumped in the cross-corridor ten feet away. Roan ducked into a side passage, flattened himself, watched two round-backed barrel-chested humanoids high-step past on unshod three-toed feet, bells tied to their leg lacings jingling at each step. When they had passed, he emerged, following the tiny green numbers that glowed over doors, found one larger than the others. Roan listened at the door; there was a dull mumble of voices. He slid the panel aside, stepped in; it was a barracks, and he wrinkled his nose at the thick fudgy odor of unwashed bedding, alien bodies, spilled wine, decay. A narrow, littered passage led between high bunks. A dull-eyed Chronid looked up at him from an unkempt bed. Roan went past, stepped over scattered boots, empty bottles, a pair of six-toed feet in tattered socks sprawling from a rump-sprung canvas chair. Halfway along the room, four large Minids crouched on facing benches, bald heads together. They looked up. One of them was Snaggle-head.

He gaped; then his wide lips stretched in a cold grin. He thrust aside a leather wine mug, wiped his mouth with the back of a thick, square hand, got to his feet. He reached behind his back, brought out a knife with an eighteen-inch blade, whetted it across his bare forearm.

"Well, looky what's got loose from its string—" he started.

"Don't talk," Roan said. "Fight." He stepped in and feinted with the club and Snaggle-head stepped heavily back, snorting laughter.

"Hey, looks like baby face got hold of some strong sugar-mush." He looked around at the watchers. "What'll we do with him, fellers—"

But Roan's club was whistling and Snaggle-head jerked back with a yell as the wood smacked solidly against his ribs. He brandished the knife, leaped across a fallen bench; Roan whirled aside, slammed the club hard against the Minid's head. The crewman stumbled, roaring, rounded on Roan, a line of thick blackish blood inching down his leathery neck. He lunged again and Roan stepped back and brought the club down square across the top of the bald skull. Snaggle-head wheeled, kicked the bench aside, took up a stance with his feet wide, back bent, arms spread, the blade held across his body. He dashed blood away from his eyes.

"Poundin' my head with that macaroni stick won't

buy you nothin', Terry," he grated. His mouth was set in a blue-toothed grin. "I'm comin' to get you now . . ."

He charged, and Roan watched the blade swing toward him in a sweeping slash and at the last moment he leaned aside, pivoted, and struck down at the Minid's collarbone; the skrilwood club hit with a sound like an oak branch breaking. Snaggle-head yowled and grabbed for his shoulder, spinning away from Roan; his face twisted as he brought the knife up, transferred it with a toss to his left hand.

"Now I kill you, Terry!"

"You'd better," Roan said, breathing hard. "Because if you don't, I'm going to kill you." Roan moved in, aware of a layer of blue smoke in the muggy air, wide eyes in big Minid faces, the flat shine of Chronid features, the distant putter of a ventilator fan, a puddle of spilled beer under the fallen bench, a smear of dark blood across Snaggle-head's cheek. The Minid stood his ground, the knife held before him, its point toward Roan. Roan circled, struck with the club at the knife. The Minid was slow: the blade clattered from the skinned hand, and Roan brought the heavy bludgeon up—

His foot skidded in spilled beer, and he was down, and Snaggle-head was over him, his wide face twisting in a grimace of triumph; the big hands seemed to descend almost casually and Roan threw himself aside, but there were feet and a fallen bench, and the hands clamped on him, biting like grapple hooks, gathering him into a strangling embrace.

He kicked, futile blows against a leg like a tree trunk, hearing the Minid's breath rasp, smelling the chemical reek of Minid blood and Minid hide, and then the arms, thick as Roan's thigh, tightened, and Roan's breath went out in a gasp and the smoke and the faces blurred . . .

". . . let him breathe a little," Snaggle-head was saying. "Then we'll see how good his eyeballs is hooked on. Then maybe we'll do a little knife work—"

Roan twisted, and the arms constricted.

"Ha, still alive and kicking." Roan felt a big hand grope, find a purchase on his shoulder. He was being held clear of the floor, clamped against the Minid's chest. The Minid's free hand rammed under Roan's chin, forced his face back. A blunt finger bruised his eye.

"Let's start with this one—"

Roan wrenched his head aside, groped with open jaws, found the edge of a hand like a hog-hide glove between his teeth, and bit down with all the force of his jaws. The Minid roared, and Roan braced his neck and clung, tasting acrid blood, feeling a bone snap before the hand was torn violently from his grip—

And he struck again, buried his teeth in Snaggle-head's shoulder, grinding a mass of leather-tough muscle, feeling the skin tear as the Minid fell backward.

They were on the floor, Snaggle-head bellowing and striking ineffectually at Roan's back, throwing himself against the scrambling legs of spectators, kicking wildly at nothing. Roan rolled free, came to his knees spitting Minid blood.

"What in the name of the Nine Devils is going on here?" a voice bellowed. Henry Dread pushed his way through the crewmen, stood glaring down at Roan. His eyes went to the groveling crewman.

"What happened to him?" he demanded.

Roan drew breath into his tortured chest. "I'm killing him," he said.

"Killing him, eh?" Henry Dread stared at Roan's white face, the damp red-black hair, the bloody mouth. He nodded, then smiled broadly.

"I guess maybe you're real Terry stock at that, boy. You've got the instinct, all right." He stopped, picked up Snaggle-head's knife, offered it to Roan. "Here. Finish him off."

Roan looked at the Minid. The cuts on the bald scalp had bled freely, and more blood from the torn shoulder had spread across the chest. Snaggle-head sat, legs drawn up, cradling his bitten hand, moaning. Tears cut pale paths through the blood on his coarse face.

"No," Roan said.

"What do you mean, no?"

"I don't want to kill him now. I'm finished with him."

Henry Dread held the knife toward Roan. "I said kill him," he grated.

"Get the vet," Roan said. "Sew him up."

Henry stared at Roan. Then he laughed. "No guts to finish what you started, hey?" He tossed the knife to a hulking Chronid, nodded toward Snaggle-head.

"Get the vet!" Roan looked at the Chronid. "Touch him and I'll kill you," he said, trying not to show how much it hurt to breathe.

In the profound silence, Snaggle-head sobbed.

"Maybe you're right," Henry Dread said. "Alive, he'll be a walking reminder to the rest of the boys. OK, Hulan, get the doc down here." He looked around at the other crewmen.

"I'm promoting the kid to full crew status. Any objections?"

Roan listened, swallowing against a sickness rising up inside him. He walked past Henry Dread, went along the dim way between the high bunks, pushed out into the corridor.

"Hey, kid," Henry Dread said behind him. "You're shaking like a Groaci in molting time. Where the hell are your bandages?"

"I've got to get back to my mop," Roan said. He drew a painful breath.

"To hell with the mop. Listen, kid—"

"That's how I earn my food, isn't it? I don't want any charity from you."

"You'd better come along with me, kid," Henry Dread said. "It's time you and me had a little talk."

In his paneled, book-lined cabin, Henry Dread motioned Roan to a deep chair, poured out two glasses of red-brown liquid.

"I wondered how long you'd take the pushing around before you showed you were a Man. But you'll still have to watch yourself. Some of the boys might take it into their heads to gang up on you when they think I'm not looking."

"*I'll* be looking," Roan said. "Why do they want to kill me?"

"You've got a lot to learn, lad. Most of the boys are humanoids; I've even got a couple that call themselves Terries; I guess they've got some Terry blood, but it's pretty badly mutated stock. They don't like having us damn near pure breds around. It makes 'em look like what they are: Gooks." He took a swallow from his glass, blew air over his teeth.

"I don't like to work around Gooks, but what the hell; it's better'n living with Geeks."

"What's the difference between a Gook and a Geek?"

"I stretch a point: if a being's humanoid, like a Minid or a Chronid, OK, give them the benefit of the doubt. Maybe he's descended from mutated human stock. You got to make allowances for Gooks. But a life-form that's strictly non-human—that's a Geek."

"Why do you hate Geeks?"

"I don't really hate 'em—but it's them or us."

Roan tried his drink, coughed, put the glass down. "What's that? It tastes terrible."

"Whiskey; you'll learn to like it, boy. It helps you forget what you want to forget."

Roan took another swallow of the whiskey, made a face.

"It doesn't work," he said. "I still remember."

"Give it time," Henry Dread growled. He stood and paced the room.

"How much do you know about Terry history, boy?"

"Not much, I guess. Dad used to tell me that once Terries ruled the whole Galaxy, but then something happened, and now they're scattered, what there is left of them—"

"Not 'them,' boy. 'Us.' I'm a Terry. You're a Terry. And there are lots more of us. Sure, we're scattered, and in lots of places the stock has mutated—or been bred out of the true line—but we're still Terries; still human. And it's still our Galaxy. The Gooks and Geeks have had a long holiday, but Man's on the comeback trail now—and every Man has to play his part."

"You mean murdering people like—Stellaraire and Gom Bulj—"

"Look, that's over and done. To me a Geek's a Geek.

I'm sorry about the girl, but what the hell: you said she was only a mule—"

Roan got to his feet; Henry Dread held up a hand. "OK. No offense. I thought we had a deal? Let's lay off this squabbling. We're Terries: that's what counts."

"Why should I hate Geeks?" Roan finished his drink, shuddered, put the glass on the table. "I've got reason to hate you, but I was raised with Geeks. They weren't any worse than your Gooks. Some of them were my friends. The only human I ever knew was my father— and I guess maybe he wasn't all human. He was shorter than you, and wide through the shoulders, and his arms were almost as thick as a Minid's. And he had dark brown skin. I guess that couldn't be real Terry human stock."

"Hard to say. Seems like I read somewhere that back in prehistoric times, Men came in all kinds of colors: black, red, yellow, purple—maybe green, I don't know. But later on they interbred and the pure color strains disappeared. But maybe your old man was a throwback —or even descended from real old stock."

"Does anybody know what a real Terry looks like?" Roan took a lock of his thick dark red hair between his fingers, rolling his eyes up to look at it. "Did you ever see hair that color before?"

"Nope; but don't let it worry you. Everybody's got a few little flaws; hell, Men have been wandering around the Galaxy for over thirty thousand years now; they've had to adapt to conditions on all kinds of worlds; they've picked up everything from mutagenic viruses to cosmic radiation to uranium burns; no wonder we've varied a lot from the pure strain. But pure or not, us humans have got to stick together."

Roan was looking at the empty glass. Henry filled it and Roan took another drink.

"He wasn't really my father," he said. "He and Ma bought me in the Thieves' Market on Tambool. Paid two thousand credits for me, too."

"Tambool; hmmm; hell of a place for a Terry lad to wind up. That where you were raised?"

Roan nodded.

"Who were your real parents? Why did they sell you?"

"I don't know. I was only a fertilized ovum at the time."

"Where'd those Geeks get hold of Terry stock?"

"I don't know. Dad and Ma would never talk much about it. And Uncle T'hoy hoy either. I think Ma told him not to."

"Well, it doesn't matter. You're the closest thing to pure Old Terry stock I've seen. I've made you a member of my crew—"

"I don't want to be a member of your crew. I want to go back home. I don't know if Ma's still alive, even, with Dad not there to look after her. I miss Dad. I miss Stellaraire, too. I even miss Gom Bulj—"

"Don't cry into your beer, kid. What the hell, I've taken a liking to you. You play your cards right and you'll do OK. You'll live well, eat well, see the Galaxy, get your share of loot, and some day—when I'm ready—you may be in on the first step toward something big—bigger than you ever dreamed of."

"I don't want loot. I just want my own people. I don't want to destroy. I want to build something."

"Sure, you've got a dream, kid. Every Man has. But if you don't fight for that dream, somebody else's dream will win."

"It's a big Galaxy. Why isn't there room for everybody's dream?"

"Boy, you've got a lot to learn about your own kind. We've got the drive to rule—to conquer or die. Some day we'll make this Galaxy into our own image of Paradise—nobody else's. That's the way Men are."

"There's billions of Geeks," Roan said. "But you're the only Man I've ever seen."

"There are Terries all over the Galaxy—wherever the Empire had an outpost. I mean to find them—one at a time, if I have to. You think I'm just in this for the swag? Not on your life, boy. I could have settled down in luxury twenty years ago—but I've got a job to do."

"Why do you want me? I'm not going to kill Geeks for you."

"Listen, kid, goon squads are cheap; I can hire all I want for the price of a good dinner at Marparli's on Buna II. But you're human—and I need every Man I can get."

"I still haven't forgotten," Roan said. "That whiskey's a fake. So are you. You killed my friends and now you think I'm going to help you kill some more."

Henry gripped Roan's shoulder with a hard hand. "Listen, boy: a Man's got to live. I started off in the Terry ghetto on Borglu, kicked around, spit on, worked like a tun-lizard in the wood mines. There wasn't a day they let me forget I was a Man—and that all I'd ever get was a Man's share—the scraps, and the kicks, and the curses. I hung around back doors and ate garbage, sure. A Man's got a drive to live—no matter how. And I listened and learned a few things. They used to call me in and laugh at me; they'd tell me how once the Terry Empire had stretched across half a Galaxy, and how Terries had been the cock of the walk in every town on ten million worlds, master of everything. And how I was a slave now, and just about good enough, maybe, to wash their dirty clothes and run their errands, and maybe some day, if I was a good worker, they'd get me a half-breed wench and let me father a litter of mules to slave for them after I was gone.

"Well, I listened—and I got the message—but not the one they had in mind. They didn't know Terries, boy. Every time they'd show me a book with a picture of a Terran battle officer in full dress, and tell me how the Niss had wiped out the fleet—or hand me an old Terran pistol and tell me how their great grandpap had taken it off a starving Man—it didn't make me feel like a slave. It made me feel like a conqueror. One day one of them made a mistake. He let me handle a Mark XXX hand blaster. I'd read a book or two by then. I'd studied up on Terran weapons. I knew something about a Mark XXX. I got the safety off and burned old Croog and two bystanders down and then melted off the leg band . . ." Henry Dread stooped, pulled his boot off, peeled back his sock. Roan stared at the deep, livid scar that ringed the ankle.

"I made it to the port; there was a Terry scout boat there, dozed offside, buried in the weeds. I'd played around it as a kid. I had a hunch maybe I could open it. There was a system of safety locks—

"To make it short, I got clear. I've stayed free ever since. I've had to use whatever gutter scrapings I could find to build my crew, but I've managed. I've got a base now—never mind where—and there's more battlewagons ready for commissioning—as soon as I get reliable captains. After that— Well, I've got plans, boy. Big plans. And they don't include Geeks running the Galaxy."

"Iron Robert's a Geek—and he's my friend. He's a better friend than any of those Gooks of yours—"

"That's right, boy. Stick up for your friends. But when the chips are down—will he stick by you?"

"He already has."

Henry Dread nodded. "I have to give him credit. I admire loyalty in a being—even a Geek. Maybe old iron pants is OK. But don't confuse the issue. A good, solid hate is a powerful weapon. Don't go putting any chinks in it."

"Iron Robert is a good being," Roan said. "He's better than me—and better than you, too . . ." Roan stopped talking and swallowed. "I feel kind of sick," he said.

Henry laughed. "Go sleep it off, kid. You'll be OK. Take the stateroom down the hall from mine here. A Terry crew member doesn't have to sleep with Gooks anymore."

"I've got some rags in the corridor outside Iron Robert's cell. I'll sleep there."

"No, you won't, kid. I can't have a Terry losing face with Gooks—for the sake of a Geek."

Roan went to the door, walking unsteadily. "You've got a gun," he said. "You can kill me if you want to. But I'm going to stay with Iron Robert—until you let him out."

"That animated iron mine stays where he is!"

"Then I sleep in the corridor."

"Make your choice, boy." Henry Dread's voice was

hard. "Learn to take orders, and you live a soft life. Act stubborn, and it'll be rags and scraps for you . . ."

"I don't mind the rags. Iron Robert and I talk."

"I'm *asking* you, kid. Move in next door. Forget the Geek."

"Your whiskey's no good. I haven't forgotten anything."

"What's the matter with you, you young squirt? Haven't I tried to treat you right? I could send you below decks in lead underwear right now to swab out a hot chamber!"

"Why don't you?"

"Get out!" Henry Dread grated. "You had a big credit with me, kid—because you looked like a Man. Until you learn to act like one, keep out of my way!"

Outside in the corridor, Roan leaned against the wall, waiting for the dizziness to go away. Once he thought he heard a sound—as though someone had started to turn the door latch—but the door stayed shut.

After a while he made his way down to Iron Robert's cell and went to sleep.

11

Iron Robert shook the bars. "You big fool, Roan, go on raid with riffraff, maybe get killed. What for? You stay safe on ship—"

"I'm tired of being aboard ship, Iron Robert. This is the first time Henry Dread has said I could go along. I'll be all right—"

"What kind gun Henry Dread give you, Roan?"

"I won't need a gun. I won't be in the fighting."

"Henry Dread still 'fraid give you gun, eh? He big fool, too, let you go in combat with no gun. You small, weak being, Roan—not like Iron Robert. You stay on ship like always!"

"There's a city on this world—Aldo Cerise—that was built by Terrans, over ten thousand years ago. Nobody lives there now but savages, so there won't be much of a fight—and I want to see the city—"

"Extravaganzoo play on Aldo Cerise, once, long time 'go. Plenty natives, plenty tough. Have spears, bows, few guns too. And not fools."

Roan leaned against the bars. "I can't just stay on the ship. I have to get out and see things, and listen and learn, and maybe some day—"

"Maybe some day you learn stay out of trouble—"

A wall annunciator hummed and spoke: "Attention all hands. This is Captain Dread. All right, you swabs, now's your chance to earn some prize money! We're entering our parking orbit in five minutes. Crews stand by to load assault craft in nine minutes from now. Blast off in forty-two minutes . . ." Roan and Iron Robert listened as Henry Dread read the order of battle, feeling the deck move underfoot as the vessel adjusted its velocity to take up its orbit four hundred miles above the planet.

"I've got to go now," Roan said. "I'm in boat number one, the command boat."

"Anyway, Henry Dread keep you by him," Iron Robert rumbled. "Good. You stay close, keep head down when shooting start. Henry Dread not let you get hurt, maybe."

"He wants me on his boat so he can keep an eye on me. He thinks I'll try to run away, but I won't—not until you can go, too."

Boots clanged at the far end of the corridor. Henry Dread, tall in close-fitting leather fighting garb, swaggered up. He wore an ornate pistol at each lean hip and carried a power rifle in his hands.

"I figured I'd find you here," he grated. "Didn't you hear my orders?"

"I heard," Roan said. "I was just saying good-by."

"Yeah. Very touching. Now if you can tear yourself away, we've got an action to fight. You stay close to me. Watch what I do and follow suit. I don't expect much static from the natives, but you never know—"

"Roan should have gun, too," Iron Robert rumbled.

"Never mind that, Iron Man. I'm running this operation."

"You nervous as caged dire-beast, Man. If everything so easy, what you afraid of?"

Henry narrowed his eyes at the giant.

"All right, I'm edgy; who wouldn't be? I'm hitting what used to be the capital of one of the greatest kingdoms in the Empire—and me with a seven-thousand-year-old hulk and a crew of half-breed space-scrapings. Who wouldn't be a little nervous?"

"Give Roan gun; or does lad make you nervous too?"

"Never mind, Iron Robert," Roan said. "I'm not asking him for anything."

Henry Dread's jaw muscles worked. He jerked the power rifle. "Come on, boy. Get down to the boat deck before I change my mind and give you a job swabbing the tube linings!"

"You bring Roan back safe, Henry Dread," Iron Robert called. "Or better not come back at all."

"If I don't, you'll have a long wait," the pirate growled.

In the cramped command compartment of the assault boat, Henry Dread barked into the panel mike: "Now hear this, you space scum! We're dropping in fast, slick and silent! I'm giving you a forty-second countdown after contact, then out you go. I want all four Bolos to hit the ramp at the same time, and I want to see those treads smoke getting into position! Gunnery crews, sight in on targets and hold your fire for my command! Heli crews . . ." The pirate captain gave his orders as the boats dropped toward the gray world swelling on the forward repeater screen. The deck plates rumbled as the retro-rockets fired long bursts, correcting velocity. Atmosphere shrieked around the boat now. Roan saw the curve of the world swing up to become a horizon; a drab jungle continent swept under them, then an expanse of sparkling sea, and a white-surfed shoreline. There was a moment of vertigo as the vessel canted, coming in low over green hills; it righted sluggishly, and now the towers of a fantastic city came into view, sparkling beyond the distant forest-clad hills.

"Remind me to shoot that gyro maintenance chief," Henry growled. Roan watched as treetops whipped past beneath the hurtling ship. Then it was past the wooded slopes, and the city was close, looming up, up, until the highest spires were hazy in the airy distances overhead. The ship braked, slowed, settled in heavily. A ponderous jar ran through the vessel. The torrent of sound washed away to utter silence. From below, a turbine started up, ran sputteringly, smoothed out. Henry looked at the panel chronometer.

"If one of those slobs jumps the gun . . ."

A light blinked to life on the panel.

"Ramp doors open," Henry murmured. "Thirty-eight, thirty-nine, forty!" He whirled on Roan.

"Here we go, kid! With a little luck we'll be drinking old Terry wine out of Terry crystal before the star goes behind those hills."

Roan stood with Henry Dread at the foot of the ramp, looking out across a pitted and crumbling expanse of ancient pavement. Far across the field, four massive tracked vehicles aimed black gun muzzles at the silent administrative sheds. Nothing moved.

"Empty emplacements," Henry said. "Missile racks corroded out. It's a walkover . . ."

"Iron Robert said the 'zoo played here once," Roan said. "He said the natives have guns and bows, and know how to use them."

"The carny was here, eh? Who'd it play to, the rock lizards?"

"People," Roan said. "And they wouldn't have to be very smart to be smart enough to stay out of sight when they see a shipload of scavengers coming."

"Corsairs," Henry barked. "We don't scavenge, boy! We fight for what we take. Nothing's free in this universe!" He thumbed his command mike angrily.

"Czack! Wheel that tin can of yours over here!" He turned to Roan. "We'll go take a look at the city." He waved his rifle toward the towers beyond the port. "This was one of the last Terry capitals, five thousand years ago. Men built the place, boy—our kind of Man, back when we owned half the Galaxy. Come along, and I'll show you what kind of people we came from."

There was a high golden gate before the city and at the top, worked in filigree, was the Terran Imperial symbol, a bird with a branch in its mouth, and a TER. IMP. above it.

"I've seen it a million times, in my books back on

Tambool," Roan said. "That bird and the TER. IMP. above it. Why a bird, anyhow?"

"Peace," Henry Dread said. "Czack!" he barked into his command mike. "Bring that pile of tin up here and put it in High." Then he turned back to Roan. "TER. IMP. means Terra ran the show. And any bird that didn't keep the peace got his guts ripped out. That's how Men operate, see?"

Peace, Roan thought, turning it in his mind, trying to smooth off the sandpapery edge Henry Dread gave to the word, watching the massive combat unit rumbling up beside him.

"Take it slow. Put it in Maximum now," Henry Dread said to Czack. "That fence is made of Terralloy and nothing'll tear it down but a Terry Bolo."

"But it's stood like this for five thousand years and nobody can put up another one," Roan said, wanting the TER. IMP. and the bird to stay there another five thousand years. "Why tear it down? Couldn't you just blast the lock?"

"Maybe. But this impresses the Geeks more, if they're watching. OK. Take it, Czack."

The gate screamed like a torn female, bent slowly, and finally went over with a horrible clang, and the Bolo, a crease along its top turret now, went on through and Czack traversed his guns, looking for natives.

The quick silence from the fallen gate and the dead city was eerie. Czack appeared at the upper hatch and swore at the gate and the Bolo and Aldo Cerise in general. He spotted the dent in the Bolo turret and swore worse.

"Maybe we'll find more Bolos in the city," Henry Dread said. "Never seen an Imperial city without 'em and this was a great one. Get you a nice, new Bolo and some nice, new guns. Now get back in the tin can and keep us covered while we do some ground reconnoiter. Shoot anybody you see."

Henry Dread tucked the mike under his tunic. His heavy boots rang on the mosaic of the walkway they took beside the road, and he gestured with his gun as they went along.

"Those buildings," he said. "Ever see anything that high for beings that don't have wings?"

The Terran buildings climbed into the sunlight, incredibly straight and solid. From here it all looked perfect. But at Roan's feet the tiles of the intricate mosaic were broken and missing in spots, and Henry Dread kicked at the loose ones as he walked along.

Roan paused to watch a fountain throwing rainbows into the air, spinning shifting patterns of water and light.

"They *built* things in those days," Henry Dread said. "That fountain's been running five thousand years. More, probably. Anything mechanical breaks in this city, fixes itself."

Roan was looking at the house beyond the fountain, with the TER. IMP. symbol on the door, and he gaped up at row on row of floors, windowed and balconied.

"It looks as though that door might open," Roan said. "People might walk out. My people." He paused, wondering how he would feel if this were home. "But it's all so perfect. So wonderful. If they could be like this, how could anyone beat them?"

"The Lost War," Henry Dread said, coming up to the fountain and drinking from a side jet. He wiped his mouth on his sleeve. "They call it the Lost War but we didn't lose it. Terra never lost a war. A stalemate, maybe—we didn't win it, either. Anybody can see that. But we broke the power of the Niss. The Niss don't rule the universe. There's supposed to be the Niss blockade of Terra, and they say there's still a few Niss cruisers operating at the far side of the Galaxy. But that's probably just superstition. I've never run into a Niss. And never met anybody that did—Man, Gook, or Geek."

Henry Dread got out his microphone. The men had come in through the ruined gate and were scrambling over the Bolo, perching on its armored flanks and hanging off the sides.

"Fan out in skirmish order," he barked. "Shoot anything that moves."

Roan followed Henry Dread. "Empty," Roan said. "I don't see anything that looks like natives might be living here. I wonder why not? With all this . . ."

"Superstition. They're afraid of it." Henry Dread's eyes were darting in all directions. "But that doesn't mean there might not be a few natives inside the fence. And they may be right to be afraid of the city. Look over there."

There was a deep hole, blackened at the edges.

"Booby-trapped," Henry Dread said. "Don't know how many might be around the city, or where. So watch out."

They came to a high wall, set with clay tiles, and between the tiles grew tiny, exquisite flowers.

"Park," said Henry Dread. "Full-blown memento of Terran luxury. Maybe have time for it later."

"Tank here!" one of the men called from behind a nearby building. "Bolo Mark IX, factory fresh—"

"Don't *touch* her, you slat-headed ape!" Czack's voice crackled from his Bolo. "I don't want nobody's filthy hands on her until I see her."

Henry Dread laughed. "It's not a woman, you rackskull. And it's *my* freaking tank and *I'll* see it first."

"Look, I'm going in that park," Roan said. "Call me when you want me."

Henry Dread stopped, looked back at Roan, frowning.

"I won't desert," Roan said. "Not as long as you've got Iron Robert back there in the hold."

"Maybe," Henry Dread said. "Maybe if you go in that park you'll find out the difference between Geeks and Men. Maybe you'll see what I'm after."

"Boss!" Czack called. "Take a gander at this. Full fuel tanks and magazines and . . ."

"Don't touch anything!" Henry Dread called. "These damned Gooks have scrambled eggs for brains," he added.

"OK," Roan said, starting to climb up a gnarled old tree that looked over the garden wall. "Fire three shots when you want me to come out."

"Watch out, boy," Henry Dread said, and stopped

again. He took out his Mark XXX blaster and handed it over to Roan.

"You'll come back," he said. "And you'll know more than you do now."

Roan balanced the gun in his hand, sitting on a lower limb of the old tree. He felt the solid metal of it, the waiting, repressed power, the cold steel with the flaming soul. He looked briefly at Henry Dread, who laughed, knowing what Roan felt with the gun.

Then Henry Dread was striding away across the plaza and Roan clambered up the tree, thinking as he climbed of the gracyls and how he'd climbed to follow their flights, and of the circus and the tree he'd climbed to see it, the Never-never tree, little thinking it was his last day on Tambool. And at the height of the wall he thought of Stellaraire and the tightrope and his eyes stung, but then he looked over the wall toward the park.

And there was no room for thoughts of the past. Here lay the Terran civilization that Henry Dread talked of rebuilding.

Within the park green grass spread and flowers bloomed and Roan could see small automatic weeders moving along the paths where fountains rose and splashed untouched by time.

And across the manicured precision of the lawn, a fallen statue lay—a vast statue with a tunic draped around its hips. It lay face up, one arm raised, an arm that had once pointed at the skies.

It was a Terran. Pure Terran.

And made just like Roan.

Roan leaped down from the wall onto a bank of springy grass, and ran to the statue. Feature for feature—eyes, ears, nose, the connections of muscles—this was Roan. Terran.

Did my father look like this? Roan wondered. Who was this Man? Where did he come from? He walked around to the base of the statue. TER. IMP., it said, with the dove and the branch. And then:

ECCE HOMO, July 28, 12780.

"Ecce," Roan said to the statue, touching it, wondering how the name was really supposed to be pronounced.

Then he became aware of sound scenting the air; the sound and scent seemed the same, both swirling faintly through the still air, and he followed the melody. The scent was not the heavy perfume Stellaraire used, nor were the sounds the coarse sounds of the circus noise-makers. It was all something else. Something that stirred memories—hints, odors of memories—far in the deeps of Roan's mind.

Sunlight he'd never drowsed in, winds he'd never felt, peace he'd never known.

Peace, he thought, knowing Henry Dread had said it wrong.

The razored, spring-green turf came down to the edge of the pebbled path and ran between gardens of jewel-bright flowers. A wide-petaled blue blossom, with black markings like a scream in its throat, opened and closed rhythmically.

The music stopped briefly and then changed, as though drawing out things in Roan's mind. In the small pause Roan heard the play of a fountain, the silver sound of music.

Then, more silver still, came the faint call of horns rising and loudening and loosening old locks in Roan's mind. A smokelike drift of stringed music floated into the horn motif, countering it softly, then running away and coming back a little differently, so that the horn challenged it and took up the string song itself and then a further, tinkling sound joined the horn and strings and built an infinite, convoluted structure in Roan's mind that spread through his whole being and finally broke into a thousand crystals, leaving Roan almost in tears for the old, old things that are lost and the beautiful, infinitely beautiful things that never existed.

A fat bee droned past, bumbled inefficiently into a flower, and hunted nearsightedly for a drop of honey. The flower folded a maternal petal over the bee and he emerged covered with yellow pollen and bumbled away looking triumphant and ridiculous.

Roan laughed, his nostalgia broken.

The music laughed, too. A little flute giggling and teasing and running away.

Roan went after the sound.

The park went on and on and the flower scents changed and interwove like their colors. Roan came to a still, blue lake, floated with flowers and enormous, long-necked birds that swam like boats and drifted up to him inquiringly when he came to the edge of the lake.

Roan turned from the lake into a wood where the vines made bowers—thorned vines heavy with sweet berries—slim, curled vines bright with wide-faced flowers. He walked through sunny slopes where tall grasses rolled like water in the wind, and deep groves where the moss grew close and green in the still shade of warm-barked trees. Then the grove narrowed to a dark, arching tunnel of branches that ended suddenly in sunlight.

Ahead of Roan was a wide, white flagstone walk that curved between fountains of flying water and led finally to a colonnaded terrace. From the terrace rose a fretted cliff of airy masonry. A house the wind blew through.

Roan, thirsty now, scooped up a handful of smooth, cool water. It had a taste of bubbles, a smell of sunshine.

But the water had not been put there for any purpose, even to drink. It showered into the air merely to fall back into the pool. It pleased Roan somehow to think that the mighty Terrans made the water go up just so they could watch it coming down.

He went up the wide, shallow steps, into the airy building that up close seemed as solid and lasting as time itself. The marble floor within was an intricate design of reds and blues that moved into purple and led the eye straight to a ramp slanting up to a gallery on the left.

Roan listened for a moment to the ringing stillness, then started up the sloping way.

The house was a maze of rooms within rooms, all neatly kept. The air filters whispered noiselessly, doors opened silently to his presence, lamps glowed on to greet him, off to bid him good-by. On polished tables were set objects of curious design, of wood and metal and glass. Roan picked each up and tried to imagine its use. One, of green jade, grew warm as he held it, but it did nothing else and there were no buttons to press. So he carefully replaced it and went on.

Then Roan noticed the pictures. He stood in the middle of a room and his eye was caught by a picture in sinuosities of blue, as interwoven and complex as the music he'd heard. Every time he looked at the picture the lines caught his eye a different way, led them along a different trail, and he looked at the picture so long the blue disappeared and then the picture itself until finally he was left following tortuous convolutions in his own mind, and it was a shaft of late afternoon sun, burning through a high window, that brought him to himself and made him blink hard to get the sun glimmers from his eyes.

Some of the pictures were like the Blue; others seemed to project out from the walls, or were sheer patterns of light hanging in empty air. And some—as Roan looked and noticed—some were pictures of Terran places and houses and . . . people? The figures were so tiny and distant. Hunt though he did, he couldn't find any close-ups of Terran people. It didn't really matter. But it was what he most wanted to see.

Roan went on, walking right through a misty Light Picture in the middle of one of the rooms. All this. What was it for? Just to look at? Just to enjoy?

It seemed a human way to be. A Terran way to do things. Roan felt a kinship with all this. He knew how to look at the paintings, how to enjoy the music.

Then Roan walked into a room wide with windows, so that the sunshine shimmered clearly in it. Marble benches stood beneath the low windows and green plants hung over a scoop-shaped sunken pool. As Roan went over to stand on the edge of the empty pool there was a soft click! and water began foaming into the pool.

Roan laughed with pleasure. It was a bath! An enormously magnified version of the one Stellaraire had had in her quarters with the 'zoo. He stripped off his shabby, ill-fitting tunic, realizing suddenly how dirty he was.

He stood by a jet of soapy foam and scrubbed himself thoroughly. The pool carried off his dirt and dead skin cells in eddies of black and whirled in renewed, clean water. Roan luxuriated in the bath for an hour, watching the chasing clouds and the blue sky through the windows, and wondering at the delicate veining of the Terran plants that nodded over the water.

And thought wistfully of Stellaraire and how if she were here they'd splash water at each other and be foolish and afterward walk in the garden and make love with timeless joy in the deep grasses. And live here forever in this enchanted place where there was no violence, no raspy, alien voices, no ugly, misshapen faces, no one hating or despising or envying Roan his Terran ancestry, his Terran inheritance.

But there was no Stellaraire. Only a memory that overfilled him now and then, like a bud with no room to open into a flower.

Behind a colored glass panel Roan found simply designed but beautiful clothes, of some close-woven material that sprang to fit him as he put it on. There were silver tights that fitted from his ankles to his waist and were cool to the touch. Then a short, silk-lined scarlet jacket, soft to the skin but stiff outside with gold and jewel embroidery. He found boots that fitted softly like gloves, and protected his feet without heavy soles or heels. All this he put on, though there were other things. Thin white shorts and singlets and short cloth boots that were too thin to be used for walking.

The only other thing Roan took was a magnificent, massive jewel, engraved TER. IMP. It hung around his neck from a gold chain and where it rested against his bare chest, between the edges of his scarlet jacket, it warmed him, almost seeming to throb like a beating heart.

I look the way a Terran ought to look, Roan thought, looking at himself in the enormous mirror that backed the door to the bathing room. The jewel glowed on his browned chest and his freshly washed hair clustered in dark red curls over his forehead.

Roan wondered if a Terran would think him handsome. A Terran woman. Oh Gods, how long since he'd had a woman!

Roan buckled back on his old link metal belt. He wondered why he thought it brought him luck, because it didn't really. Then he reluctantly picked up the Mark XXX blaster. Here, it didn't seem right. But he shoved it into the belt, which stretched to hold it.

Roan retraced his steps through still corridors, down to the echoing concourse, out onto the broad terrace.

Far in the sky the lowering sun flashed orange from the towers of the city—where Henry Dread was searching for loot now with his vicious crew of cutthroats. It was soiled, grubby—all of the universe—but here it didn't exist. He didn't want to call it into being again.

Roan took a new path, beyond the house, walking quickly because he didn't have much time left. Night was coming. He'd seen, perhaps, most of what there was to see, and one more quick turn—

Roan drew up short.

Because reflected in a round mirror pool, among fragile violet flowers, was a human woman.

She was flushed pink in the sunset, pouring water from a long-necked jar. The water, sparkling pink, too, in the light, rippled over her slim neck, between her lifted breasts and around her softly bent body over her flanks, and finally ran murmuring into the mirror pool making no splash or ripple.

"Oh. Please," Roan said, not meaning to speak, and went up to the woman. But it was a statue, smiling its dreamy, carved smile, thinking the secret thoughts of stone.

Roan reached out and touched the soft curve of the hard, marble cheek.

And far away came the violent stutter of guns. Then a single shot—a power rifle.

Perhaps it was the anger against life that filled him or perhaps it was a premonition of what was really happening, but Roan was running. Along the curved paths and then straight across the middle of the park where there was a wide concourse and through a small grove where night had already come, and up the fence, holding to the nearest heavy vine, and slowing to be quiet now, along the fence to the tree.

A gun rattled, paused, fired again. A voice shouted.

Roan looked from the top of the wall. The streets were violet shadows now, the towers bright-edged silhouettes against the orange and purple sky. There was a faint movement in the gloom below the tree and a face, a white blob in the darkness, looked up toward Roan, the glint of a knife in the teeth.

There was a sharp hiss. Something chipped at the tiles and then another hiss and whoever it was starting up the tree fell back and slumped to the ground.

Roan hefted the gun out of his belt. His Mark XXX that he'd all but forgotten in the park. Well, that dream of peace was over now.

Roan waited, heard a few shots, distant now, saw nothing moving. He dropped softly from the tree, squatted, turned the body on its back. The coarse, slack features of a bald Minid stared past him with dead, surprised eyes. The stump of a broken-off wooden shaft poked from the Minid's chest just below the edge of the sheepskin vest.

One of the crew. A mean, dirty creature, but somehow one of *his* . . . Roan stood, trying to see through the dark streets; the firing was becoming steadier now, coming from locations to the north and east. A cold evening wind blew up, and one brilliant orange star came out. Probably the next planet of the sun Aldo.

Roan crossed the street, started up one of the dark avenues toward the north. Lights came on suddenly to illuminate the city; mists of light that seemed to hang in the air like clouds.

There was a sharp hiss. Something struck the doorway of the house near Roan and clattered on the steps. Roan dropped, rolled, brought his gun around and fired at a figure bounding from the shadowed doorway across the street. The figure fell, under the misting streetlight.

Roan retreated to crouch in the angle between the

steps and the Terran house. Three long-legged, round-shouldered creatures emerged from the side street. He saw the thick, recurving bows in their hands, the lank hair that dangled beside their oddly flat faces, the heavy quivers slung at their backs. They paused, fanning out. One saw the dead bowman, made a hoarse noise. At once, the three whirled, angled off quickly in different directions. One was leaping toward Roan. He brought his gun up, fired, swung and fired on a second savage as the first slammed to the curb of the mosaic sidewalk, almost at his feet. The second bowman reeled, stumbled, went down. Roan swung to the third and it dived for the black shadow of the building at the corner as his shot sent blue sparks from the door of the Terran house.

Roan was up instantly, dashing for the corner, rounding it as a heavy arrow touched his shoulder, skipped high, flashed off into darkness. Roan skidded to a stop, stepped back to the corner, dropped flat, thrust himself out. The native was charging from cover. Roan's shot caught him full in the chest and he fell with a tremendous heavy slam, an impact of utter finality. Roan let his breath out in a long sigh, slumped against the pavement, listening. There were no sounds, no moving feet, no stealthy breathing, only the intermittent rasp and crackle of guns, nearer now but still, he guessed, a street or two away.

He got to his feet, moved off quickly, following a side street that would bring him to the scene of the action by a roundabout route.

From a low balcony which he had reached by clambering up the shadowed carved front of a peach-colored tower, Roan watched as a party of a dozen or so bowmen assembled almost directly below him in a narrow way. The sounds of firing came closer from along the wide avenue. Roan could see the blue flashes of power guns now, the yellow stabs of pellet throwers. Below, the leader of the ambushing party spoke, and his bowmen set arrows, crouching silent and ready. Down the avenue, Roan made out Henry Dread's tall figure among a huddle of humanoids. There were not more than fifty in the party, he estimated—out of over eighty who had landed; a straggling band of cursing, frightened raiders, caught off guard, retreating under a rain of arrows that flew from the darkness without flash or sound. A bald Minid screeched, spun, fell kicking. The others passed him by, firing at random into the shadows, coming closer to the ambush.

Below Roan, the bowmen gathered themselves; there was a single, grunted syllable from the leader. He stepped forward—

Roan shot him, swept the gun across the others as they sprang back gaping; three more fell, and the rest dashed for the deep shadows, disappeared between close walls. No one in the retiring ship's party seemed to have noticed the byplay. They were formed up into a defensive ring, watching each side street as they passed. Henry Dread held up a hand, halted the group fifty feet from Roan's vantage point. Lying on the balcony, he had a clear view of the pirates, and the empty streets all around.

"Belay firing!" Roan heard Henry Dread's voice. "They've pulled back for now."

There were snarls and mutters from the crewmen. They shifted uneasily, watching the dark mouths of side streets. A gun winked blue, a harsh buzz against silence.

"I said belay that!" Henry Dread grated. "We'll hold up here for ten minutes to give stragglers a chance to join us."

"To the Pit with stragglers," the crewman who had fired his gun cut in. "We should stay here and let these local slobs surround us? We're moving on—fast."

"Shut up, Snorgu," Henry Dread snapped. "Maybe you've forgotten I busted you out of a Yill jail after you were dumb enough to get caught flat-footed strangling an old female for her nose ruby. And now *you're* going to do the thinking for my crew—"

"*Your* crew my hind leg, you lousy Terry. We've taken enough orders from your kind. What about it, boys?" Snorgu glanced around at the watching pirates. Henry stepped up to the heavy-shouldered crewman. "Hand over your gun, Snorgu!"

Snorgu faced Henry, the gun in his fist aimed at the pirate leader. He laughed.

"I'm keeping my gun. And I'm firing when I feel like it . . ."

A crewman beside Henry moved suddenly, caught the pirate captain's arms from behind; another struck out, knocked Henry's gun from his hand. A third stooped, came up with it.

"Here's where we get a new captain," Snorgu growled. "Lead us into a ambush, hah? Some captain you are. I guess us Gooks have got just about a gutful of fancy Terry ways."

"I seem to remember giving some orders about looting parties posting sentries," Henry drawled. "And about skeleton crews on the Bolos—"

Snorgu snarled and jammed the gun hard against Henry's chest. "Never mind all that. Hand over the keys to the chart room and the strong box in your cabin."

Henry laughed, a hard sound like ice breaking. "You're out of luck. You think I carry a bunch of keys around for stupid deck-apes like you to lift the first time you see a chance? They're combination locks. Kill me and you'll never get 'em open."

"You'll open 'em," someone barked. "A couple needleburns through the gut, and a couple of days for the rot to set in, and you'll be screaming for somebody to listen to you sing, and all you'll ask is a fast knife in the neck before your belly explodes."

"Meanwhile, how do you plan to get back to the ship?" Henry Dread cut in. "There might be a few natives between here and there that don't want to see you run off after such a short stay."

"Gun him down," someone suggested. "We've got enough on our hands without we got to watch this Terry."

"Sure. We can beam them locks open."

"Suits me." Snorgu grinned, showing large, widely spaced teeth in a loose-lipped mouth wide enough to put a hand in sideways. He stepped back a pace, angled the gun down at Henry's belt buckle—

Roan took careful aim, shot Snorgu through the head. The pirate's gun flew into the air as his hand jerked up; he stumbled back and fell, and Henry stepped forward, caught the falling gun out of the air, held it aimed from the hip. The crewmen gaped.

"Anybody else care to nominate himself captain?" Henry's sharp voice cut across the silence. The men were craning their necks, looking for the source of the shot. Roan saw one ease a gun around, aim it at Henry Dread; he shot him through the chest. As he fell, another brought a gun up, and Henry, whirling, beamed him down.

"Next?" he said pleasantly. No one moved. The crewmen stood stiffly now, cowed, worried. Henry laughed shortly, lowered his gun.

"All right, spread out in a skirmish line and let's get moving." He motioned them past with his pistol. Roan lowered himself over the balustrade and climbed quickly down. Henry Dread watched him come. His narrowed eyes were on the gun at Roan's hip.

"Found out how to use it, eh?"

"Comes in handy," Roan said casually, imitating Henry Dread's manner. He stood with his thumbs hooked in his belt, looking at the older man. Henry's eyes went from Roan's scarlet vest down the length of the silvery trousers, back up. His eyes locked with Roan's.

"You had a good chance to shoot me then," he said. "But when it got right down to it, you sided with me." His face broke slowly into a smile. "I knew you'd figure out which side you were on, boy. You picked a good time. Something you learned in that park?"

"I found a garden," Roan said. "It was perfect; the most perfect place I ever saw. I wanted to stay there. There was everything you could ever need. And then I saw a statue, and I touched it, and all of a sudden I saw that it was all dead, frozen, just a fossil of something that was alive once. Something that could live again, maybe. I decided then. I want to make it live, Henry. I want to do whatever I have to do to make it come to life again. I want that stone girl to turn to living flesh and walk in that garden with me."

Henry's hand thrust out. Roan took it. "We'll do it, Roan," the pirate said. "Together, we'll do it."

Smiling, Roan said, "Want the gun back?"

Henry Dread's smile was grim. "Keep it," he said. "From now on, you walk behind me. Keep the gun on your hip, and your right hand loose."

He turned and followed the huddle of pirates, and Roan trailed him, walking with his head up, liking the feel of the heavy gun in his belt.

12

"These past two years have been good, Roan," Henry Dread said, refilling his heavy wine mug. "Seven raids, all successful. Enough new men recruited to more than cover our losses; and our fuel and ammo reserves are at the best level in years—"

Roan looked at his half-full glass sullenly. "And we're still no closer to starting a new Terra than we ever were. We haven't found even one more Man to add to the roster. There's still just you and me; two Terries, two Freaks, talking about what we'll do some day—"

"Look here, Roan, we've followed every rumor of a Terry we've run across. Is it my fault if they didn't pan out? We'll find a colony of Terries yet; and when we do—"

"Meanwhile Iron Robert's still chained. I want you to release him, Henry."

The pirate's hand came down to slam the table. "Damn it, are we going to start into that again? Haven't I explained to you that that man-eater's a symbol aboard this vessel? My cutthroats saw him stand up to a blaster; they heard him threaten to pitch me through the side of my own ship! And I let him live! As long as he's chained to the wall his talk is just talk; maybe a blaster can't touch him—but Henry Dread has him under lock and key! But turn him loose—let him stamp around this ship a free Geek—well, you get the picture!"

"I get the picture," Roan said. "For over two years now I've been living off the fat of the land while my friend sits in the dark with half a ton of steel welded to his leg—"

"Hell, let's be realistic, boy! He doesn't mind it—not like you or I would! He says so himself; he sits and goes off into some kind of trance; doesn't even eat for days at a time. He's not human, Roan! By the Gods, with Man's Galaxy at stake, you worry about one damned Geek!"

"Set him free; he won't cause any trouble; I'll be responsible for him—"

"That's not the point," Henry said in a hard voice. "You'd better settle for having him alive. He's the first Geek I ever let live aboard my ship!"

"That's what your grand dream really boils down to, isn't it, Henry? Killing Geeks . . ."

Henry swiveled to stare into the view screen that curved above the command console. "Somewhere out there, there's a Niss warship," he said quietly. "We're closing the gap, Roan; the stories we've picked up these last couple of months all tell the same tale: The Niss ship is real, and it's not far off. We'll pick it up on our long-range screens any day now—"

"More Geeks to kill. That's all it is. It isn't a war; the Niss were beaten—at least as much as the Empire. They're no threat to us—or to anybody. They haven't attacked anyone—"

Henry swung back. "Haven't they? What about the Mandevoy patrol boat they vaporized last year—at a range of twelve thousand miles—"

"The Mandevoy went out looking for trouble. They admitted that. The Niss haven't attacked a planet, or any ship that stayed clear of them. Let's forget the Niss. It's Terra we're interested in. Let's look for Terra—"

"Terra!" Henry snorted. "Don't you know that's just

a name, Roan? A mythical wonderland for the yokels to tell stories about! The Terran Empire isn't some two-bit world somewhere at the far side of the Galaxy; it's humanity—organized, armed, and in charge!"

"There *is* a Terra," Roan said. "And some day I'll find it. If you've given up on it, I'll find it alone—"

"Given up!" Henry Dread roared, coming to his feet. "Henry Dread never gave up on anything he set out to do! I'm not chasing rainbows! I'm fighting a live enemy! I'm facing reality! Maybe it's time you grew up and did the same!"

Roan nodded. "You're right. Just set me down on the next inhabited world with my share of the spoils. I'll leave your grand scheme to you; I've got a better one of my own."

Henry's eyes were fierce fires blazing in a face purple with fury.

"By the Nine Gods, I've got a good mind to take you at your word! I picked you out of a damned 'zoo, a Freak in a cage, and made you my second-in-command— and tried to make you my friend! And now—"

"I've never asked you for anything, Henry," Roan cut in, his blue eyes holding the pirate's. They stood face to face, two big, powerfully built Men, one with gray hair and a face of lined leather, the other with a mane of dark red curls hacked short, the clean features of youth, a flawless complexion marred only by a welted scar along his right cheek where Ithc's talons had raked him, long ago.

"But you've taken plenty!"

"I was content with the 'zoo. I had friends there, a girl, too—"

Henry Dread snarled. "You'll befriend any lousy Gook or Geek that gives you the time of day; but me, a commander in the Imperial Terran Navy—I'm not good enough for your friendship!"

Roan's expression changed. He frowned.

"You said—the Imperial Terran Navy . . ."

Henry Dread's eyes held steady. "That's what I said," he grated.

"I thought," Roan said carefully, watching Henry Dread's eyes, "that the ITN was wiped out, thousands of years ago . . ."

"You did, eh?" Henry was smiling a tight, hard smile. He looked at Roan bright-eyed, enjoying the moment. "What if I told you it wasn't wiped out? What if I said there were intact units scattered all over the Eastern Arm when the shooting stopped? What if I said Rim Headquarters had taken over command control, reorganized the survivors, and held the Navy together—waiting for the day a counter-attack could be launched?"

"*Are* you saying that?" Roan tried to hold his voice level and calm, but it broke on the last word.

"Hell, boy, that's what I called you up here to talk about, before you started in on your pet Geek!" Henry clapped Roan's shoulder. "I've watched you close, these last years. You've done all right, Roan—better than all right. It's time I let you in on what you're doing here—what we're doing. You thought I was just a pirate, raiding and looting just for the hell of it, getting fat off the leavings of Geeks and Gooks—and you thought my talk about getting the Galaxy back for Man was just talk. I know . . ." He laughed, with his hands on his hips and his head thrown back.

"I can't say I blame you. Sure, I've got a hold full of heavy metal and gem crystals and old Terry cloth and spices and even a few cases of Old Imperial Credit tokens. But that's not all I've got tucked away. Come here."

He turned, walked across the broad command deck of the ancient battlewagon, tapped keys on the panel. An armored door swung open, and Henry stepped inside, ducking his head, came out with a wide, flat box. He lifted the lid with a flourish, held up a garment of close-woven blue polyon, shook it out. Roan gaped.

"My uniform," Henry Dread said. "As a commander in the Imperial Terran Navy. I'm assigned to recruiting and fund-raising duty. I've done all right as far as funds are concerned. But this is my first recruitment . . ."

Roan's hungry eyes held on the rich cloth, the glitter

of ancient insignia. He swallowed, opened his mouth to speak—

Henry Dread stepped back into the vault, came out holding a second box in his hands. He tucked it under one arm.

"Raise your right hand, Lieutenant Cornay," he said . . .

Roan stared into the mirror. The narrow-cut, silver-corded black trousers fit without a wrinkle into the brightly polished ship boots. Over the white silk shirt, the short tunic was a swirl of braid, a gleam of silver buttons against royal blue. A bright-plated ebony-gripped ceremonial side arm winked at each hip against the broad, woven-silver belt with the big, square buckle adorned by the carved TER. IMP. and bird symbol.

He turned to Henry Dread. "I've got about a milliard questions, Henry. You know what they are . . ."

Henry Dread laughed again. "Sure, I know." He keyed a mike, snapped out an order for a bottle and glasses. "Sit down, Lieutenant. I think you can forget about Geeks for a few minutes now while I tell you a few things . . ."

Iron Robert stirred as Roan called to him. His heavy feet scraped the rusted deck plates; chains clashed in the gloom and his green eyes winked open.

"What you want, Roan," the heavy voice growled. "You wake Iron Robert from dream of youth and females and hot sun of homeworld . . ."

"I . . . just came to see how you are," Roan said. "I've been busy lately; I guess I haven't gotten down to see you as often as I'd like. Is there anything you need?"

"Just need to know you well and happy, Roan. I think now you and Henry Dread friends, you have good time, not be so sad like before."

Roan gripped the two-inch chromalloy bars of Iron Robert's cell. "It's not just a good time, Iron Robert. I'm doing something: I'm helping to put the Terran

Empire back together. I know, it's not much—just one ship, cruising space, looking for Terrans, or rumors of Terrans, and collecting funds for the Navy, gathering intelligence to use when we're ready to launch our counterattack—"

"Counterattack against who, Roan? You already attack all Gooks and Geeks you find, take all guns and fuel and money—"

"You have to understand, Iron Robert! We're not just looting. We need those things! We're cruising according to official Navy orders, hitting every world in our assigned sector. Captain Dread's already been out twelve years. Two more years, and we finish the sweep, and report back to Rim Headquarters—"

"Just so you happy, Roan; have good time, live to full, eat good, drink good, have plenty fight, plenty women."

"Damn it, is that all living means to you? Don't you understand what it is to try to build something bigger than you are, something worth giving everything that's in you for?"

"Sure, Roan. Iron Robert understand big dreams of youth. All beings young once—"

"This isn't just a dream! The Terran Empire ruled this Galaxy once and could rule it again! Haven't you seen enough suffering and torture and death and indifference and ruins and greed and hate and hopelessness to understand how it is to want to change all that? The Empire will bring back peace and order. If we left it to the damned Geeks it would go on like this forever, only worse!"

"Maybe true, Roan." Iron Robert's voice was a soft rumble. "Fine thing, build towers up into sunlight, squirt water, make pretty sounds—"

"Don't make fun of my garden! I shouldn't have told you about it! I might have known a Geek couldn't understand!"

"Hard thing for Geek to understand, Roan. What place Geeks have in Terry Empire? Geeks get to walk in pretty garden, too?"

"The Geeks will have their own worlds," Roan said sullenly. "They'll have their own gardens."

"Iron Robert have garden once too, Roan. Fine black stones, and pools of soft mud to lie in, and hot, stinky water come up out of ground. But I think Roan not like my garden. I think hard thing for Roan and Iron Robert to walk in garden together, talk over old times. Maybe better have no garden, just be together, friends."

Roan leaned his head against the cold bars. "Iron Robert, I didn't mean—I mean . . . We'll always be friends, no matter what! I know you're locked in here because of me. Listen, Iron Robert, I'm going to tell Henry Dread—"

"Roan not tell Henry Dread anything! Iron Robert made deal with pirate; Geek keep word as good as Man—"

"I didn't mean it when I called you a Geek, Iron Robert—"

"Just word, Roan. Iron Robert and Roan friends, few angry words nothing. Iron Robert not 'shamed to be Geek. Fine thing to be royal ferrous strain and have friend like Roan. Human flame burn short but burn hot, warm old stone heart of being like Iron Robert."

"I'm going to get you out of there—"

"No, Roan. Where else I go? Not like Terry cabin, too small, too weak chair. And only cause trouble. Henry Dread right. Crew not like see Iron Robert free being. Better wait here, be near Roan, and some day maybe we make planetfall together. Meantime, you got destiny to work out with Henry Dread. You go ahead, chase dream of ancient glories. Iron Robert be here by and by."

"We'll be at Rim HQ soon—in a year or two. I'll make them give me a ship of my own then—and you'll be my second-in-command!"

"Sure, Roan. Good plan. Till then, Iron Robert wait patient—and Roan not worry."

Roan stood up, stretched, rubbed his eyes, drained the mug of bitter brown coffee, clattered the empty cup down on the chart table.

"I'm tired, Henry. Over thirty-six hours we've been hanging over the screens, and we've seen nothing. Let's admit it's another wild-goose chase and turn in."

"They're close, Roan," Henry snapped. His face was grayish and hollow in the lights of the panel. "I've chased the Niss for forty years; another forty minutes and maybe I'll see them in my sights."

"Or another forty days—or forty years, or a thousand, for all we know. Those clodhoppers back on Ebar probably just gave us the story to get rid of us before the boys got bored and started shooting the town up again."

"They're out there. We'll close with them this time."

"And if they are—what about it? We're on a recruiting and fund-raising mission, aren't we? What's that got to do with launching one-man attacks against Niss warships—if there is any ship, and it really is Niss."

"They're there, I said! And we're a fleet boat of the Navy! It's always our job to seek out and destroy the enemy!"

"Henry, give it up. We don't know their capabilities. I know we've got special long-range undetectable radar gear, but they may still blast us out of space like they did that Mandevoy scout a few years ago, before we even get close—"

Henry Dread whirled, stared up at Roan from his seat. "Scared, Lieutenant?"

Roan's tired face smiled humorlessly. "Sure, I'm scared, if that's what you want to hear. Or maybe I've just got common sense enough not to want to see all you've worked for—all *we've* worked for—destroyed just because you've got the itch to fire those big batteries you've been keeping primed all these years."

Henry Dread came to his feet. "That's enough out of you, Mister! I'm still in charge aboard this tub! Now get on that screen until I give the order to leave your post!"

"Slow down, Henry—"

"Commander Dread to you, Mister!" Henry's face was close to Roan's, his square jaw, marred by a slight sagging of the jowls, thrust out. Roan straightened, settled his gun belt on his hips. He was an inch taller than Dread now, and almost as heavy through the shoulders. He looked the older man steadily in the eye.

"We're just nine months out of Rim Headquarters, Henry. Let's see if we can't get there in one piece—both of us . . ."

Henry Dread's hand went to his gun. He half drew it, looking into Roan's eyes, his teeth set in a snarl.

"I gave you an order!"

"You're a big enough man to take an order back, when you see it's a mistake," Roan said flatly. "We both need rest. I know a couple of crewmen who'd like to see the pair of us out on our feet." He turned away. Henry Dread's gun cleared the holster.

"Stop right there, Mister—"

A clanging alarm shattered the stillness into jagged fragments. Roan spun; his eyes leaped to the long-range screen. A bright point of blue light glowed near the lower left corner. He jumped to the panel, twisted knobs; the image centered. He read figures from a ground-glass plate.

"Mass, five point seven million standard tons: velocity, point oh-nine light, absolute; nine-eighty MPH relative."

"By the Nine Devils, that's it!" Henry Dread's voice choked. He stared across at Roan, then grabbed up the command mike, bawled into it:

"All hands, battle stations! Secure for action! All batteries full-arm and countdown! Power section, stand by for maximum drain!"

A startled voice acknowledged as he tossed the mike aside, looked across at Roan. His eyes were wide, bright.

"This is it, Roan! That's a Niss ship of the line, as sure as I'm Henry Dread!" His eyes went on the screen. "Look at him! Look at the size of that devil! But we'll take him out! We'll take him out!" He holstered his gun, drew a breath, turned to Roan.

"For the first time in five thousand years, a ship of the Imperial Navy is engaging the enemy! This is the hour I've lived for, Roan! We'll smash them like a ripe fruit . . . !" He raised his clenched fist. ". . . And then nothing will stop us! Are you with me, boy?"

Roan's eyes held the long shape growing on the screen. "Let's break it off, Henry. We've established that we can get in range, and we have them located. When we reach Rim Headquarters, we can . . ."

"DAMN Rim Headquarters!" Henry Dread roared. "This is MY action! I tracked that filthy blot on the human sky halfway across the Eastern Arm, and now I'm going to burn it clean—"

"You're out of your mind, Henry," Roan snapped. "The damned thing outweighs us a hundred to one—"

"Crazy, am I? I'll show you how a crazy Man deals with the scum that challenged Terran power at its peak—"

Roan gripped Henry's shoulders, eyes on the screen. "It's not just you and me, Henry! We've got eighty crewmen below! They trust in you—"

"To hell with those Gooks! This is what I was born for—" He broke off. A tremor rattled the coffee mug on the table. There was a sudden sense of pressure, of impending violence—

The deck rose up and struck Roan a mighty blow. Instrument faces burst from the panel, screens exploded in smoke and white light. He had a glimpse of Henry Dread, spinning past him. A thunderous blast rolled endlessly, and then it drained away and Roan was whirling in echoing silence.

He was on the floor, looking up at a soot-smeared figure in rags, bleeding from a hundred cuts, hunched in the command chair, square fists clamped on the fire-control levers. Roan coughed, raised himself on one elbow, got to his hands and knees. The walls spun dizzily.

"How bad are we hit?" he choked.

"Filthy, sneaking Niss," Henry Dread chanted. "Let 'em have another broadside! Burn the devils out of the sky . . . !"

Roan's eyes swept over the shattered panel, the smashed instruments, fixed on the controls in Henry Dread's hands. They hung slack and useless from broken mountings.

154 Keith Laumer and Rosel George Brown

"Henry—let's get out of here—the lifeboats . . ."

"Maximum beam," Henry Dread shouted. "Forward batteries, fire! Fire, damn you!"

"We've got to get out." Roan staggered to his feet, grasped Henry's shoulder, pulling him away from the devastated control console. "Give the order—"

Wild eyes in a white face stared up at him. "Are you a fighting man of the Empire or a dirty Geek-loving spy?" Henry tore himself free, lunged for the command mike, dangling from its socket.

"All hands! We're closing with the enemy! Prepare to board—"

Roan tore the mike from Henry's hands.

"Abandon ship!" he shouted—and threw the dead mike from him as Henry yelled, swung a wild blow. He leaned aside, caught the other's wrists.

"Listen to me, Henry! We've got to get to the boats! We can survive to fight again!"

Henry stared into Roan's eyes, breathing hard. Swelling blisters puffed the left side of his face. His hair was singed to curled stubble. There was blood at the corner of his mouth. Quite suddenly, the wildness went out of his eyes. His arms relaxed; he staggered, caught himself.

"Two boats," he mumbled. "I've fitted 'em out as raiders; armor, an infinite repeater each, two torpedoes . . ." He pulled free of Roan's grip, pushed past him toward the lift doors, stumbling over the debris littering the deck.

"We're not beaten yet," he was shouting again. "Slip through their screens—hit 'em in close . . ." Smoke swirled from the lift as the doors clashed open. Henry Dread lurched inside, and Roan followed.

On the boat deck, a dense-packed mob of shouting, struggling crewmen fought for position at the two escape locks.

"It's Captain Dread!" someone yelled.

"Here's the Terry swine now!"

"Open up!"

"Get the boats clear!"

Henry slammed his way through the press, gun in hand. He smashed it down over the skull of a horned bruiser in blackened sheepskin, whirled to face the mob. Behind them, the glare of raging fires danced against the bulkhead visible at the end of the long corridor.

"Listen to me, you swabs," Henry roared. "There's room in the two boats for every gutter-spawned rascal here—but by the nine tails of the fire devil, you'll form up and board in a shipshape fashion or fry where you are! You there! Gungle! Let him be! Get back there! Askor! Take number one port!" The pirate chief bellowed his orders, and the frantic crewmen broke off their struggles, moved back, taking places in two ragged lines.

Roan pushed through them, coughing, blinking through the smoke.

"Here, where do you think you're going!" Henry Dread bellowed after him. But Roan was clear of the press, into the transverse corridor now; the smoke was less here. He ran, bounded down a companionway, leaped the crumpled form of a Minid with a short knife standing in his back; someone's grudge settled, Roan thought as he dashed along the cargo level way.

He skidded to a halt at Iron Robert's cell. Through the layered smoke, he made out the massive figure, seated stolidly on the steel-slab bench.

"Iron Robert! I'll get you out! The keys are in Henry's cabin—"

"Just minute, Roan," the rumbling voice said calmly. "What happen? Iron Robert wake, hear engines dead, plenty smoke in room—"

"We tried to attack a Niss warship! It hit us before we even got close, smashed our screens, burned out our circuitry; we're a hulk, on fire. We're abandoning ship!"

"You want Iron Robert go free out of cell? Don't need key, Roan. Easy . . ." The giant stood, brought his massive arms forward, and snapped the chains as easily as loops of wet paper. He stooped, tore the ankle chains from the wall, then peeled the massive welded collars from his ankles.

"Stand back, Roan . . ." He stepped to the grating, gripped the wrist-thick bars, ripped them aside with a screech of metal, forced his nine-foot bulk through the opening like a man brushing aside a beaded hanging, and stood in the corridor, looking down at Roan.

"You could have broken them—any time," Roan stuttered. "You stayed there—in chains—for five years—on my account . . ."

"Good place as any to sit, think. Now fire grow hot; time to go, Roan."

Roan whirled, led the way along the smoke-fogged corridor, up the companionway, along to the boat deck. Half the crew had entered the lifeboats now. Two dead men lay on the deck, blasted at short range by Henry Dread's guns. The grizzled Terran caught sight of Roan.

"You're taking number two boat! Where in the Nine Hells have you been—" Iron Robert lumbered from the smoke behind Roan.

"So! I should have figured!" The gun swiveled to cover the giant. "Get aboard, Roan! We're running out of time!"

"I'll load when my crew's loaded." Roan walked past Henry, ignoring the gun, to the gangway where burly humanoids pushed, crowding through the port.

"I said get aboard!" Henry bellowed.

There were half a dozen more crewmen. They pushed, shouting; answering shouts came from inside the sixty-foot boat, cradled in its massive davits in the echoing, smoke-filled hold. A broad-faced Minid thrust his head from the lock of number one boat.

"We got a full load!" he roared. "You load any more in here, they'll be standin' on each other's shoulders!"

Henry's gun swung. "I don't care if you have to stack 'em like cordwood! Get 'em in, Askor!" He spun back to face Roan. "What the hell are you waiting for, boy? Get aboard that boat—now! Can't you feel that heat? This tub will blow any second—"

"Iron Robert," Roan called past him. "Go aboard—"

"There's no room for that hulk!" Henry shouted. "That was an order, Mister!"

Three frantic crewmen struggled at the port of number two boat.

"No more room!" a hoarse voice bellowed from inside the lock. A broad foot swung out, kicked at one of the men. He fell from the gangway, and the two behind leaped forward. A fight developed in the lock. Henry Dread took a step, aimed, fired once, twice, a third time. Two dead crewmen fell, rolled onto the hot deck plates. A third was lifted, tossed from inside.

"Fight your way in there, Roan," Henry yelled. "Shoot as many as you have to!"

"Iron Robert—"

"I said he's not going aboard!"

Roan and Henry Dread faced each other, ten feet apart across the blood-spattered deck. The pirate captain's gun was aimed unwaveringly at Roan's chest.

"He goes or I stay," Roan yelled above the clamor.

"For the last time—follow your orders!" Henry bellowed.

"Iron Robert, go aboard—" Roan started.

"Roan—" Iron Robert took a step, and Henry Dread wheeled, and blue fire lanced, splashed harmlessly from Iron Robert's chest.

"You board boat, like Henry Dread say, Roan," the giant rumbled.

Henry took a step backward, his gun covering Roan again.

"Listen to Iron Man," Henry grated. "He's telling you—"

"Let him board, Henry!" Roan said.

"Over my dead body," Henry grated. "Not even you can—"

"Roan, no—!" Iron Robert cried.

In a motion too quick to follow, Roan's hand had flashed to his gun, brought it up, fired, and the pirate leader was staggering back, his knees folding, the gun dropping from his hand. He seemed to fall slowly, like an ancient tree, and he struck, rolled over, lay on his back with his eyes and mouth open, smoke rising from a charred wound centered on his chest.

"Roan! You big fool! No room on boat for Iron Robert! Now you kill Henry Dread, true Man who love you like son!"

Roan tossed the gun aside, went to the fallen pirate, knelt beside him. "Henry . . ." His voice caught in his throat. "I thought—"

"You wrong, Roan," Iron Robert's voice rumbled. "Henry Dread not shoot you in million years. Try save your life, foolish Roan. You go now, quick, before ship explode—"

Henry Dread's open eyes flickered. They moved to Roan's face.

"You . . . in command . . . now," he gasped. "Maybe . . . right . . . Iron Man . . . OK . . ." He drew a ragged breath and coughed, tried to speak, coughed again. "Roan," he managed. "Terra . . ." The fight died from his eyes like a mirror steaming over.

"Henry!" Roan shouted. Two mighty hands clamped on his arms, lifted him, thrust him toward the port.

"You go now, Roan, live long life, do, see many things. Think sometimes of Iron Robert, and not be sad, be happy, remember many good times together—"

"No, Iron Robert! You're coming—"

"No room; Iron Robert too big, not squeeze through port." Roan felt himself propelled through the narrow opening into the noise and animal stink of the crowded lifeboat. He fought to regain his feet, turned to see the wide figure of Iron Robert silhouetted against the blazing corridor. He lunged for the port, and a dozen pairs of horny hands caught at him, held him as he kicked and fought.

"You got to navigate this tub, Terry," someone yelled.

"Dog down that port," another shouted. Roan had a last glimpse of Iron Robert as hands hauled him back. The heavy port swung shut. Then he was thrust forward, passed from one to another, and then he was stumbling into the command compartment. Rough hands shoved him into the navigator's chair. The cold muzzle of a gun rammed against his cheek.

"Blast us out of here, fast," a heavy voice growled. Roan shook himself, forced his eyes to focus on the panel. As in a dream, his hands went out, threw levers, punched keys. The screens glowed into life. Against the black of space, the long shape of the immense Niss war vessel glowed no more than a thousand miles distant, its unlighted bulk blotting out the stars.

Roan gathered himself, sat upright. His teeth were set in a grim caricature of a smile. He twirled dials, centered the image in the screen, read numerals from an instrument, punched a code into the master navigator panel, then with a decisive gesture thrust home the main drive control.

13

Roan slumped in the padded seat, let his hands fall from the controls.

"We're clear," he said dully. "I don't think the other boat got away. I don't see it on our screens—"

A clay-faced creature with the overlong arms and the tufted bristles of a Zorgian pushed through the crew packed like salted fish in the bare, functional shell of the lifeboat.

"Listen to me, you muckworms," he hooted in the queer, resonant voice that rose from his barrel chest. "If we wanta make planetfall, we got to organize this scow—"

"Who asked you?" a gap-toothed, olive-skinned crewman demanded. "I been thinking, and—"

"I'm senior Gook here," a bald, wrinkled Minid barked. "Now we're clear, we got to find the nearest world—"

Other voices cut him off. There were the sounds of blows, curses. Scuffling started, was choked off by the sheer cramping of the confining space.

"I don't, we don't wanna all die," a hoarse voice yelled. "We got to pick a new cap'n!"

"I won't have no lousy Minid telling me—"

"Button yer gill slits, you throwback to a mudfish—"

Roan stood, turned on the men. "All right," he roared—an astonishing shout that cut through the hubbub like a whiplash through cotton cloth.

"You can belay all this gab about who's in charge! I am! If you boneheads can stop squabbling long enough to let a few facts into your skulls, you'll realize we're in trouble—bad trouble! There are forty of us, crowded into a boat designed for an emergency cargo of thirty! We've got enough food for a few months, maybe, but our air and water recyclers are going to be overloaded; that means tight rationing. And you can forget about the nearest planet; it's nine months away at fleet-cruise acceleration—and we've got less than ten percent of that capacity—"

The Zorgian bellied up to Roan. "Listen, you Terry milksop—"

Roan hit the humanoid with a gut punch, straightened him out with an upward slam of a hard fist, pushed him back among the crewmen.

"We've got no discharge lock," he grated, "so if anybody gets himself killed, the rest of us will have to live with the remains; think that over before you start any trouble." Roan planted his fists on his hips. He was as tall as the tallest of the cutthroat crew, a head taller than the average. His black-red hair was vivid in the harsh light of the glare strip that lit the crowded compartment. Coarse faces, slack with fright, stared at him.

"How many of you have guns?" he demanded. There was muttering and shuffling. Roan counted hands.

"Sixteen. How many knives?" There was another show of hands, gripping blades that ranged from a broad, edge-nicked machete to a cruel, razor-edged hook less than six inches long.

"Where are we going?" someone called.

"We'll die aboard this can," a shrill cry came.

"We can't make planetfall." Roan's voice blanketed the others. "We're a long way from home, without fuel reserves or supplies . . ." The crew were silent now, waiting. "But we've got our firepower intact. There are two thousand-megaton torps slung below decks and we mount a ten millimeter infinite repeater forward. And there's food, water, fuel, and air just a few miles away . . ." He stepped aside, pointed to the forward screen, where the Niss ship swelled now to giant size.

"We're inside her defenses now," he said. "They won't be expecting any visitors in a hundred ton dinghy—"

"What do you mean?" a one-eyed crewman growled. "You're asking—"

"I'm asking nothing," Roan said harshly. "I'm telling you we're going in to attack the Niss ship."

At five miles, the Niss dreadnought filled the screens like a dark moon.

"They don't know we're here," Roan said. "Their screens aren't designed to notice anything this small. We'll close with her, locate an entry lock, and burn our way in. With luck, we'll be in control of the COC before they know they've been boarded."

"And what if we don't have luck?"

"Then we won't be any worse off than we would be eating each other and dying of foul air aboard this tub."

"Four miles, rate of closure twenty meters per second," called a crewman assigned to the navigation panel.

"Slack her off there," Roan ordered. "I want you to touch down on her as soft and easy as if you were lifting a purse back on Croanie."

The crewman showed a quick, nervous smile. "Sure. I don't want to wake nobody up."

"What's these Niss like, Terry—"

Roan turned and slashed his forearm across the mouth of the speaker.

"That's 'Captain' to you, sailor! I don't know what the Niss are like, and I don't give a damn. They've got what we need and we're taking it."

"The size of that scow—there must be a million of 'em aboard . . ."

"Don't worry—just kill them one at a time."

They watched the screens in silence.

"Two miles," the navigator hissed. "No alarm yet . . ."

The lifeboat drifted closer to the swelling curve of the

miles-long warship. The scrawl of great alien characters was blazoned across the dull black of the hull. Complex housings set at random caught the faint glint of starlight. Roan selected a small disk scribed on the metal plain below.

"Match us up to that, Noag," he ordered. "The rest of you suit up."

He hauled a stiff vacuum suit from the wall locker, settled the helmet in place, flipped switches. Stale air wafted across his face from the suit blower.

The lifeboat's engines nudged her, positioning the lock directly over the hatch of the Niss ship. Roan stood by, watching the maneuvering on a small repeater screen.

"Quiet now, all of you," he said. "Any noise we make will be transmitted through the hull."

The two vessels touched with a barely perceptible rasp of metal on metal.

"Nice work, Noag. You're learning," Roan said. "Hold her right there and magnetic-lock." He listened. Through his deck boots he could feel the vibration of the engine; nothing more.

"Cycle her open," he ordered.

"Hey, what kinda air these Niss use?" someone called. "My tanks are low."

"What's the matter, you gonna stay here if it ain't to your liking?" another came back.

Air hissed as the lock cycled. Roan's suit plucked at him as the pressure dropped. Through the opening the iodine-black curve of the alien hull blocked their way.

"Cut into her, Askor," Roan commanded. The crewman pushed into the opening, set a blaster on narrow beam, pressed the firing stud. The dark metal reddened, turned a glaring white, went bluish, then puddled, blowing away, driven by the pressure of released gases. The soft spot bulged, blew out under the pressure of the Niss ship's internal atmosphere. Askor worked on, widened the opening, cut out a ragged hole a foot in diameter.

"Shut down." Roan stepped past him, reached through, found a release, tripped it. The Niss lock rotated up and away, exposing the lightless interior of the enemy ship; icy air gusted into the lifeboat, bringing a faint, foul taint. Frost formed on the metal where it touched.

"Let's go." Blaster in hand, Roan stepped through the opening; the beam of his hand light lanced ahead, picked out curving walls, complex shapes fitted to what should be the floor. Festoons of odd-sized tubing looped across the room. There was a scattering of heavy dust over everything.

Silently, the boarders followed through the broached hull, gathered in a huddle around Roan. Their breath made frosty puffs before their faces.

"Where do we go from here?" Noag muttered.

Roan threw his light on a narrow vertical slit in the wall. "That might be a door," he said. "We'll try it."

The corridors of the Niss ship were high, narrow, lit by dim strips that had glowed to reluctant life in the minutes after the invaders had boarded. The walls seemed to press in on Roan. It was hard to breathe, and there was sweat on his forehead, in spite of the chill that cut at his exposed hands and face like skinning knives.

"She's pulling a half-G," Askor said. "There's power on somewheres . . ."

"I don't like this," Noag muttered behind Roan. "If they jump us now, we're stuck like mud-pigs in a deadfall . . ."

"Shut up," Roan said. His heart was pounding high up under his ribs, and what Noag was saying made it worse. He strode on, careless of sound now, emerged from the constricting passage into a wide chamber walled with honeycombed storage racks. The crewmen gathered, staring around. One went to the nearest niche, drew out a heavy bundle wrapped in stiff, waxy cloth. He plucked at the bindings, tore the covering away, blinked at a grotesquely shaped metal casting, peppered over with tiny fittings. The others craned, took the object as the finder passed it around.

"What th' Nine Hells is that . . . ?"

"Hey, how about the next rack—"

"Can't you slobs even wait until after the fight to start looting?" Roan snapped. "Put that back where you got it—and cut out the chatter." The men fell silent, listening for the enemy they had, incredibly, forgotten for the moment.

"Come on." Roan led the way out of the storeroom along another narrow way that stretched into darkness.

"These passages," a crewman whispered hoarsely. "There's miles of 'em. What if we get lost in here . . . ?"

"That's easy," another offered. "We just pound on the walls until the Niss come to see what's the matter."

"Where they hiding, anyways?" Noag shifted his power gun from his right fist to his left. "We been prowling this tub for an hour . . ."

The corridor ended at a blank wall ahead. Roan raised a hand.

"Hold it up," he said. He indicated the passage along which they had just come. "I've been counting paces. We've come about half a mile along here. That puts us on the opposite side of the ship from the hatch we came in by. All we've seen is cargo, supply, and utilities space. We're going back to the big corridor we crossed and move forward. I'm guessing we'll find the personnel areas in that direction. We're going to string out now, and keep our eyes open. The first man that talks without something important to say will get a mouthful of pistol butt. Let's go."

Roan led the way back a hundred yards, turned left into a wider passage like the others, gray, featureless, faintly lit by a feeble glare strip set in the ceiling, stretching on and on into remote distance.

"I'm freezin'," a crewman whined. "I ain't gonna be able to fire my gun, my fingers is so stiff."

"Holster your guns and get your hands warm," Roan said quietly. He went to a narrow door set in the wall, pushed at its edges. It yielded at the center, swung inward in two panels. He looked into a square room with papers scattered across the floor, a slanted table attached to one wall. There was a saddlelike seat mounted on a four-foot stand before the table. Roan picked up one of the paper scraps; it crumbled in his fingers. There were strange characters printed on the fragment he held.

He stepped back out of the room, continued along the wide passage.

In an immense, dim-lit hall, Roan looked at ranked hundreds of saddlelike perches arranged in endless rows on either side of foot-wide counters that ran the length of the vast room. A hint of a vile odor hung in the still air. Dust stirred underfoot as nervous-eyed men stared around, fingering guns.

"This is an eating room, I think," Roan said. "We're getting closer."

"Closer to what?" a voice grumbled.

"We'll take the next ramp up. The crew quarters will be somewhere near the mess—"

"Hey—what's that . . . ?" A short-necked round-backed crewman pointed a blunt finger. Roan walked over to look. What looked like handfuls of fish bones were scattered in a mound seven feet long, inches wide, half-buried in dust. The crewman dug a toe in, uncovered a dull metal object like a strap buckle. He kicked again, and a curious double-bladed knife with a knobby grip at the center skidded across the floor. The finder exclaimed, jumped after it, picked it up.

"Neat!" he stated. He gripped the weapon, one stubby blade protruding on either side of his rocklike fist. "Ya get 'em goin' and comin'—"

"Cripes," another grunted, eyeing the heaped dust and the fish bones, "that's one of 'em; what's left of a Niss . . ."

Roan looked around the broad room, saw other mounds here and there.

"Let's get moving," he said. "I want to see what's up above."

They were in a long, narrow, high-ceilinged room lined with saddles before racks and dusty screens interspersed with panels of tiny glasslike buttons. One screen glowed faintly, showing a greenish image of stars against space, and a tiny oblong that drifted, turning on its short axis. Above the screen, scattered beads of light glowed. On the floor below the panel lay two of the long dust heaps that had been Niss. The crewmen were busy picking ornate metal objects from among the fish bones.

"This guy must of been a big shot," Noag rasped. "Look at this knickknack!" He held up a starburst done in untarnished yellow metal with a giant jewel at its center.

"Chief, this must be the command deck, right?" Askor muttered. He was a hulking hybrid of mixed Minid and Zorgian blood, with the stiff, tufted hair of the latter scattered incongruously across the typical broad Minid skull.

"I think so," Roan said. "And that's *Warlock* on the screen there."

"I don't get it . . ." Askor looked around the long room. "Where are they? What are they waiting for?"

Roan stood, staring at the screen. As he watched, the blip that had been Henry Dread's ship expanded suddenly into a vivid sphere that swelled, spreading out in ragged streamers . . .

"She blew," Askor stated. "It's kind of a funny feeling. I lived aboard her for thirty years . . ."

"In reply to your question," Roan said in a harsh voice, tearing his eyes from the screen, "they're all around us. We've seen forty or fifty of them in the past three hours."

"Yeah, but them was just bones. I'm talkin' about—"

"You're talking about the Niss—the crew of this vessel," Roan cut in. He pointed to the scattered remains on the floor. "There they are. Meet the captain and the mate."

Askor furrowed his heavy brow. "Somebody fired that broadside that knocked out *Warlock*," he growled.

Roan jerked a thumb at the glowing lights. "The automatics took care of that," he said. "They were set to blast anything that came in range. I'd guess the power piles are nearly drained. That's why her bombardment didn't annihilate us completely."

"You mean—they're all dead?" Askor looked down at the dust and fine bones. His face spread into a broad grin. He chuckled, then put his wide hands to his chest and laughed, a booming guffaw.

"That's rich, hey, Chief? Us pussyfooting around like that—"

"Chee," a bystander commented. "Think a' that! How long's this tub been floating around like this?"

Roan kicked the bones aside, hoisted himself into the saddle before the command panel, began punching keys at random.

"I don't know," he said. "But I think it's a fair guess she's been cruising for the best part of five thousand years, with a full complement of corpses aboard."

In a cramped, metal-walled chamber lost far aft of the immense engines, Askor looked sideways at Roan.

"Look like the Niss had a few captives aboard, eh, Cap'n?"

Roan looked down at the scattered bones of men, and the smaller bones of women, and in the far corner, two small skeletons of children—human bones; Terry bones, moldering among chains.

"Gather up the identity disks," he said emotionlessly. There was a clump of feet in the corridor. The horned head of Gungle appeared in the doorway, his eyes wide with excitement.

"Cap'n, we found something! A slick thousand tonner, a Navy job, banged up a little but spaceworthy! She's slung in the boat deck . . . !"

Roan followed the man along dark ways littered with discards from the looting parties ransacking the ancient vessel, now and again passing the scattered remains of a long-dead crewman.

"Wonder what killed 'em all, Cap'n?" Askor kicked a mound, sent foul dust flying.

"Disease, starvation, suicide. What does it matter? Dead's dead."

Askor cast a quick glance at his grim-faced captain, said nothing.

On the boat deck, Roan studied the businesslike lines

of the sleek vessel poised in a makeshift cradle between malformed Niss scout boats, the numerals printed across her bows, the ITN crest.

"Looks like she took a hit aft." Noag pointed out areas of fused metal beside flaring discharge nozzles. "But they made repairs. Musta been getting her ready for some kind of sneak job . . ."

Roan mounted the access ladder, shouldered through the narrow port. There was an odor of mildew and dust. He flicked on lights, went forward, climbed a companionway to the surprisingly spacious command deck, stood looking around at the familiar Terran screens, instruments, fittings. He threw open a wall locker, choked at the dust that flew, hauled out a ship suit. He thumbed the tarnished TER. IMP. affixed above the pocket, read the name stenciled below.

ENDOR.

"Hey," Askor said from behind him. "That's the same as it says on one o' them IDs we took off them bones . . ." He sorted through the bright metal disks, handed one over.

"I didn't know you could read Terran." Roan eyed the half-breed.

"I can't exactly read, Cap'n—but I'm good at remembrin'. They look like the same marks to me."

"So the captain died in chains." Roan tossed the disk back. "I think his suit will fit me."

"How about it, Cap'n?" Noag called from the entry. "How's she look?"

"Check her out," Roan said. "If everything works, load her up and figure out how to get those hull doors open."

Askor rubbed calloused palms together with a sound like a rasp on rough wood.

"She's a sweet tub, Cap'n. Not as big as *Warlock*, but we never needed all that tonnage anyways. I'll bet she's fast. We can hit and get out before the dirt-huggers know what hit 'em—"

"We're through raiding for a while," Roan said. "There's more loot aboard this hulk than we can haul— enough to make every man aboard rich."

"Not gonna raid . . . ?" Askor scratched at his bristled scalp. "Where we goin' then, Cap'n?"

"Set your course for a world called Tambool. It'll be listed in the manual." Roan indicated the glowing face of the index set in the navigator's panel.

"Tambool? What's there?"

"My past—maybe," Roan said, and turned away to pore over the ancient star maps on the chart table.

14

Askor sat beside Roan, staring into the wide, curved panoramic screen that filled the wardroom wall. He sipped his Terran coffee—a drink that it had taken many months to develop a habit for—then cleared his throat self-consciously.

"It's been a long cruise, Cap'n," he said.

Roan didn't answer.

"A few more hours," Askor went on. "We'll be touching down at Tambool. Not much of a place, but there'll be a few kicks—"

"I'll distribute a few kicks myself if you don't shut up," Roan said.

Across the table, a crewman named Poion laid down his ever present stylus, closed his pad; he flickered his translucent eyelids down over his bulging eyes, fingering a wineglass delicately.

"Gee, Chief," Askor tried again. "It's been nine months now since the fight with the Niss ship and all. You been snappish as a gracyl in molting season ever since you took over as captain. You didn't used to be this way, back when you was Cap'n Dread's Number Two—"

"I'm not anybody's Number Two now," Roan said.

"I'm Number One, and don't ever forget it." He drained his glass, refilled it.

"What do you seek on the minor world Tambool, Captain?" Poion asked in his soft, breathy voice. "Henry Dread's mission was not there. . . ."

Roan looked at the Beloian curiously. Poion seldom started conversations, and never personal ones.

"I thought you could read minds."

"I read emotions. I compose with emotions. It is the art of my people. I am now scoring a composition for ten minds and a dozen experimental animals—"

"Let's hear you read my emotions." Roan cut him off abruptly.

Poion shook his head as though to dislodge a trouble-some thought. "I cannot. That's why I asked you the question. I haven't the talent for Terran emotions. They're not like the others. They're in a different . . . mode. More powerful, more brutal, more . . . primitive."

Roan snorted. "So you can't tell anything from my mind?"

"Oh, a little," Poion said. "You engaged in a *noston*, a return home. But your nostalgia is not the nostalgia of any other creature in the universe." He sipped his wine, watching Roan. "Because you have no home."

On the screen Tambool rose on the left and the ship turned on its gyros and an arrow swung. Roan gripped his glass, watching the world swell on the screen.

"Perhaps," he said, at last.

The vibrations of landing stopped and Roan rose and walked back through the crew compartments. He found Askor by the exit port, rattling a gun nervously against his belt.

"I told you this wasn't like other ports," Roan said sharply. "You'll keep the men under control. They're to pay for what they take. And no shooting."

Askor muttered but Roan ignored him. The port cycled open; Askor ducked his head and peered out at the puddled field, the drab row of sheds, the dismal town straggling up the hillside.

"Cripes, Chief, what's this crummy dump got that's so hot?"

"Not much; but such as it is, I don't want anybody bleeding all over it." The other men had crowded around now, decked out in their shore-going clothes, guns and knives in belts, anticipatory grins in place.

"My business won't take but a few hours," Roan said. "While we're here, forget looting. There's not much you'd want anyway."

The men muttered and shuffled their feet, but no one said anything loud enough to take exception to.

"No reception party," Sidis commented as the men followed Roan down the ramp. "At least not in sight . . ." He licked his lips and watched the windows of the sheds and peered at every shelter that might house an ambush.

"Anybody that wants to land here can land," Roan said. "Nobody cares and you shift for yourself. It's not rich enough to loot and it's useless as a base. It's a place for outcasts to come and lose themselves."

Poion glanced sideways at Roan. Roan saw the glance. He was talking too much—more than the men expected of their taciturn captain. It was a sign of nervousness, and it made the men nervous too.

He walked on in silence, heading for the jumble of shacks behind the port. Had it been this derelict—this dirty and depressing when he'd left it as a boy?

It didn't matter. He was returning as a Man, and he'd come for a purpose, and let anyone who got in his way look out . . .

Roan marched the men past the tented Soetti Quarter, under the walls and towers of the Veed section, into the gracyl slums. He almost marched past his old house without recognizing it. Everything seemed smaller, dirtier than he remembered. A group of unwashed gracyl infants dug morosely in their instinctive way in the dust of the yard, and Roan thought fleetingly how strangely each gracyl reenacted his race's evolution from a primitive burrowing rodent. The flower garden was gone and no one had whitewashed the house for years.

A suspicious gracyl mare peered from the window where Bella had once flapped a towel to call Roan to meals.

He swallowed a nostalgia that he hadn't expected to have and marched the men on past the garbage dump, now bigger than ever. No one knew, or asked, why he took that route. He walked confidently, his head up, his guns strapped to his hips, his boots kicking up decisive splatters of mud as though he knew where he were going.

He had no friends to look for, no hint as to how to find Bella. But Uncle Thoy hoy had had a favorite haunt—a tumbledown bar where he had been wont to huddle with other hard-bitten slaves, sipping at vile Yill drinks and muttering unknowable Yill secrets. It would be a starting place.

Roan turned a corner, and the men behind him murmured, and he could picture the grins spreading. This looked more like it, the pirate's part of his mind noted automatically. Ahead a carefully trimmed wine vine made an enclosure, and beyond could be seen the spangled tops of rich houses. A small party of Veed petty nobles was coming through the gate; some had iridion clasps on their pleated skirts and one had a diamond class badge attached to his neck. The only weapons they carried were daggers and whetted talons, and their slithering gait had the native insolence of those who think daggers are enough. Roan felt the men slow behind him, watching the Veed; he turned and gave them the look of ferocity that came so easily now.

"All right, you hull-scrapings, I've warned you! The first man that gets out of line gets a bullet in the guts."

"Those Geeks friends of yours?" Noag inquired loudly, watching the Veed move past. Noag was a Gook and he had no use for Geeks.

"I have no friends," Roan said. "If you think I'm kidding, try me."

The Veed had paused and now two of them swaggered over.

"Get you gone from the places of the noble Veed," one said in a flat, badly accented Standard.

"And take these mud-swine of half-caste Terries with

you," the other added. They stood with their hands resting on their knives and they looked as though they hoped someone would give them some slight cause to draw them.

"OK if I kill these two?" Sidis asked hopefully. He was grinning and his polished teeth shone like silver.

"No killing," Roan said. The other men moved up and began to ring in the two Veed; they moved together, suddenly nervous, realizing that these were not local outcasts.

"Be gone," Roan said in the faultless Yill Bella had taught him. "My slaves scent easy blood."

The two Veed took their hands from their knives and made inscrutable Veed faces. "Take your vile scent with you," one said, but he moved back.

"Before you go," Roan said, "give me news of T'hoy hoy, the Yill bard and teller of tales." He put his hands on his guns to show that it was no idle inquiry.

"It is said the one you name can be found over his cups in any pot-house so undiscerning as to accept his custom," the Veed snapped the answer.

Roan grunted and turned on toward the gate. He remembered that once the Veed Quarters had been sacred and taboo, and that he hadn't been good enough to be allowed there except when he ran messages or delivered merchants' goods. But now he was Roan the Man and he went where he liked. He strode through the gate, and Veed faces turned, ready to hiss their anger; but a silence fell over them as the small party tramped past. There were a few half-hearted catcalls, but no one moved to intercept them. The Veed had seen the byplay at the gate with the two dagger men, and understood that it was a time for discretion.

On the far side of the Veed Quarter, in the swarming artisans' section of the city, Roan halted the men at a tavern under the battered red, green, and purple symbol of an all-blood establishment.

"You wait out here," Roan said. "I'll send out a round. And keep your hands off your guns and other people's belongings."

There was a Yill inside; he wasn't Uncle T'hoy hoy but he was the Twix caste, one of those inconspicuous ones who were always to be found in public places sitting unobtrusively in a corner to pick up information, compose their strange Yill poems, and be available in case there were messages to be sent.

Roan slid into the cracked seat across from the Yill, ordered Bacchus wine for himself and Fauve for the old Yill, then took out an oblong coin and put it on the table.

The Yill winked his eyes at Roan and let the coin lie there. There were many things a Yill would do for money and other things nothing could make them do, and the Yill was waiting to find out which kind of thing Roan had in mind.

"First," Roan said, coming directly to business in the Yill fashion, "I want to find my mother, Bella Cornay. Then I want to find T'hoy hoy, my foster uncle."

The Yill took the coin with pointed fingers from which the fighting talons had fallen long ago, deposited it under his tongue, and watched while the clumsy, frizzle-haired waiter brought the wine. He smelled the Fauve, looked keenly at Roan, and said, "I am L'pu, the Chanter of Verses. I know you: the flame-colored Terran boy who filled the empty life of the faded beauty Bella. You were a small, wild flame of a youngling, and you have lived to become a fire of a man. Your mother's heart would have leaped for your beauty, which is that of all great beasts of prey."

"Mother is . . . dead?" Roan felt a slow sadness. He had never loved his mother enough, and it had not been fair. All he'd ever thought about was Raff.

"She is no longer alive," the Yill said. He was being precise about something. Roan waited to see if he would say more, but he didn't and it was no use to ask.

"Uncle T'hoy hoy?"

"At this moment, T'hoy hoy listens at the house of the autocrat of the noisome Soetti. Would you have me fetch him?" Roan nodded and the Yill drank off his wine and slipped away. Roan sat and waited in the small, dank tavern; the room smelled of a hundred liquors,

poison to each other, and of alien sweats. Outside the
flaps of the cellophase windows the men were bored,
talking too loudly and throwing knives carelessly at
each other's feet. Rain started up and drummed on the
tin roof. It reminded Roan suddenly, overwhelmingly,
of Bella. But he thrust the emotions back under a gulp
of strong wine. Home was gone, had never been.
Tambool was a place like any other and in a few hours
he'd be on his way. He had another drink and waited.
Bella was no longer alive, L'pu had said. What did that
mean?

Finally he heard the men jibing at someone outside,
and the tavern lighted with an opening door and feet
shuffled. It was Uncle T'hoy hoy. He had gotten old, so
old, and his gray face was like shriveled clay, but it rose
into smiles for Roan.

"My boy," he said. "Oh, my boy." And Roan saw that
if a Yill could cry, Uncle T'hoy hoy would have cried.

Roan embraced the old slave and ordered two more
Fauves.

"I guess I've changed," he said. "Would you have
known me?"

"You have changed but I would have known you,
Roan. But tell me the story of your years. Have you
killed and have you loved and have you hated?"

"All that and more," Roan said. "I'll give you my
story for your collection. But my mother. What happened to Bella?"

Uncle T'hoy hoy reached under his belt, inside his
tunic, brought out a thick gold coin and offered it to
Roan. "Your inheritance," he said. "All that remains of
a once-fair flower of the Yill . . ." Uncle T'hoy hoy was
a storyteller and he couldn't help being poetic, Roan
told himself, suppressing his impatience.

"Where did Bella get gold?" Roan fingered the coin.
It was an ancient Imperial stater, and represented a lot
of money in the ghettos of Tambool.

"She had nothing for which to live, with Raff dead
and you stolen. She sold herself to the Experimental
College for vivisection. This was her pay, and she left it
for you in case you should ever return."

"And . . . she left no message?"

"The deed speaks all that need be said, Roan."

"Yes . . ." Roan shook his head. "But I don't want to think about that now. I have to hurry, Uncle T'hoy hoy. My men are itchy for action and loot and if anybody even looks at them sideways they're going to cut loose. I came here to find out who I am. I know Dad and Ma bought me at a Thieves' Market here on Tambool, but I don't know which one. Did they ever give you a clue?"

"No clue was needed, Roan. I was there."

"You?"

"I came here, all the way from a far world, to kidnap you," T'hoy hoy said, remembering an old irony and smiling his strange Yill smile at it.

"You!" Roan was grinning too at the unlikely image of the old Yill as a hired adventurer.

"Ah!" T'hoy hoy said. He shook his head. "Better it were perhaps if all this were left untroubled under the mantle of time—"

"I want to know who I am, Uncle. I *have* to know. I'm supposed to be of Terran blood—Pure Strain. But who were my parents? How did the dealer get me?"

Uncle T'hoy hoy nodded, his old eyes remembering the events of long ago.

"I can tell you my story, Roan. Your story you must find out for yourself."

"I've shot my way in and out of a lot of places," Roan said. "But you can't shoot your way into the past. You're my only lead."

"We came here," T'hoy hoy said, "following orders. We were minutes late at the bazaar—but the dealer talked a little. We trailed the purchasers, and they went to earth in a closed place where tourists never venture. When we saw them, we laughed at how easy it would be; a frail Yill woman and an old hybrid Terran in an ill-fitting suit . . ."

"Raff was never old."

"So we discovered. It was incredible. He fought like a fiend from the Ninth Pit, and even after his body bones were broken, he fought on, and killed all the others, and he would have killed me, but the lady Bella saw that I was Yill, like her, and that I would yield; and she needed me, so my life was spared. Then by my oath I was forever bound to her, and to Raff. And to you."

Outside the men had begun a game of rolling the tankards their drinks had been served in, and shooting at them. Inside there were only Roan and T'hoy hoy, and the bartender frowning worriedly over his pewters, and casting glances toward the door.

"Send out a refill," Roan called. He poured his and T'hoy hoy's glasses full.

"Dad used to say I was Pure Strain; but whenever I asked him what made me any more valuable than any other more or less pure Terran, all he said was that I was something special. What did he mean, T'hoy hoy?"

"Special you were, Roan, for many men died for the owning of you. But how, I cannot say."

"This market where I was bought, tell me where it is; maybe the dealer who sold me knows something."

"As to the bazaar, tell you I will, but as for the dealer . . . alas, he died of a throat ailment."

"A throat ailment?"

"There was a knife in it," T'hoy hoy said a little guiltily. "Ah, I admit, Roan, I was not so even-tempered then as now." T'hoy hoy told Roan the location of the Thieves' Market on the far side of Tambool. "But let me advise you to stay clear of the place, Roan. It was an evil haunt of the scum of the Galaxy twenty-five years ago, and the neighborhood has since deteriorated . . ."

Roan was watching through the window as a large company of Veed gentry went by outside; his crewmen stood silent, watching, but everything in their stance suggested disrespect. Sidis was tossing his knife in the air and catching it without looking, and grinning his steel-toothed grin.

"They're like children," Roan started, and broke off. A lone Veed had hurried past, trailing the group, and the diamond at his throat had glinted like a small sun, and from the corner of his eye Roan caught a sudden movement and now he heard an almost silent thud.

He was out in the street in a moment, in time to see

Noag's short cloak flutter at an alley mouth. Roan sprang after him and whirled the lumbering Minid around, but it was too late. The young Veed noble's head dangled at a fatal angle. An angry buzzing was growing among the gathering bystanders. They didn't like Veed nobles, but strangers killing them in the public street was too much.

"Come on, you brainless slobs!" Roan yelled. "Form up and let's get moving." He looked at Noag, and the Minid fingered his knife and looked back.

"You can stay here with your Veed and his diamond," Roan grated, and passed him by.

"Huh?" Noag looked puzzled. "You can't do that! It'd be murder," he roared, starting after Roan. "I got no Tamboolian money! I don't know the language! I won't last a hour!"

"Tough," Roan said. "Cover him, Askor, and shoot him if he tries to follow us."

T'hoy hoy was trotting beside Roan, looking back worriedly. "Cleverly done," he puffed. "The sacrifice will satisfy them for the moment, but you'd best not tarry. Farewell, Roan. Send word to me, for I would know how your saga ends."

"I will, Uncle," Roan said. He pressed a heavy Imperial Thousand credit token into the old Yill's hand and hurried after his men. At the gate he looked back; Noag was squatting at the alley mouth. Tears were streaming down his face but he was cutting the diamond off the dead Veed.

15

It was a steaming, screaming color blaze of a bazaar, and the dust was like yellow poison, and as Roan marched his men through the narrow, twisting ways between stalls, no one gave them a second look. No one gave anything a second look in the Thieves' Market unless it was something he wanted to steal.

They came out into an open plaza and wended their way across it among sagging stalls with sun-faded awnings. Merchants too poor to rent booths squatted by heaps of tawdry merchandise and gold and green death-flies buzzed everywhere, and the air reeked of opulent perfumes and long-rotted vegetables and sweat and age and forbidden drugs. They passed a scarlet and blue display of Tirulean silks that were worth fabulous amounts and a spread of painted esoterica that was worth nothing at all and came up to the crumbling wall of the chalky ocher rock face that towered over the square. A hand-painted sign beside a dark stair said YARG & YARG, LIVESTOCK. Under the first sign, another hung by one rusted pin. It said FOR SALE—VIABLE HUMAN EMBRYO. Something had been painted beneath the words, but the letters had been scratched out.

Roan turned to the men. "Go shopping," he said, and they stood and looked amazed.

"Go shopping. Spread out so you don't look like an army; and don't start anything."

"Where you going, Boss?" Askor inquired.

"I'm going to see how easy it is to become a father."

Roan climbed the narrow, hollowed steps, pushed past the remnant of a beaded hanging into a dark and smelly room lit by a crack in the ceiling. From behind a desk, a mangily feathered Geek in tarnished bangles looked at him with utter insolence.

Roan kicked a broken chair aside and leaned on the desk.

"What do you want?" the creature rasped in a scratchy, irritable voice. "Who referred you here? We deal wholesale only, to selected customers—"

"I don't go through channels," Roan interrupted. "I came to inquire about buying an embryo: a human one, like you advertise outside."

"We have thousands of satisfied customers," the dealer said automatically, but in a tone that indicated that it had no need of another. It was looking Roan over distastefully. "How much are you prepared to pay—if I should happen to have something in stock?"

"Money doesn't matter—just so it's the real thing."

"Your approach appeals to me." The dealer fluffed out its molted face ruff and sat up a little straighter. "But you have to have at least one wife. Sodomate law. The Feds would get me."

"Let me worry about that. What have you got?"

"Well, I could offer you a good buy in a variety of FA bloodlines—"

"What does FA mean?"

"Functionally adapted. Webbed digits, heavy-gravity types, lightly furred—that sort of thing. Very nice. Guaranteed choice, selected—"

"I want genuine Terry type."

"What about our number 973? Features the cyclopic maternal gene, rudimentary telepathic abilities that could be coaxed along—"

"I said Terry type, the original variety."

"Nonsense. You know better than that. It doesn't exist—"

"Doesn't exist, eh?" He bent close to the dealer. "Take a look. A *good* look."

The dealer clacked its tarnished beak and looked at Roan worriedly. Its large round Rheops eyes were watery.

"My goodness," it said. Then: "The feet. You'd be surprised how often it's the feet."

Roan stepped back and pulled a boot off and planted his bare foot on the massive old desk.

The dealer gasped. "*Five* digits! One might almost think—" It looked up into Roan's face with a sudden alarm. It slid off its stool and hopped back.

"You're not—oh, no—"

"Sure I am," Roan said. "I came from right here. Twenty-five years ago. And now I want to know all about the circumstances surrounding my presence on your shelves."

"Go away! I can't help you! I wasn't here then! I know nothing!"

"For your sake," Roan said, "you'd better know something." He took a gun out of his belt and hefted it on his palm.

"My . . . my uncle. Uncle Targ. He might—but he left word he wasn't to be disturbed . . . !"

"Disturb him," Roan said ominously.

The dealer's eye went to a corner of the room, flicked back.

"Tomorrow. Come back tomorrow. I'll check the files, and—"

Roan came around the desk and headed for the corner the Rheops had glanced at. There was the tiny glint of an oculus from a shadowy niche. The feathery alien skittered across to intercept Roan.

"Uncle Targ isn't active in the business any more! He's not a well being! If you'd just—"

"But I see he still retains an active interest." Roan swept the dealer aside and raised the gun and fired a low-power blast at the wall. Plaster shattered all around the Eye, exposing wires which led down toward a circular hairline crack in the fused-sand floor. Roan brought the gun up and fired at the crack. The dealer jumped at him and hauled at his arm, squawking. Abruptly, the trapdoor flew up and a tiny, old voice screeched in five languages: "Stop, cease, desist, have done, give over!" A naked ancient head popped up from the opening, its three remaining feathers in disarray. "Break off, check, stay, hold, cut short! Chuck it, I say!" it shrilled. "Terminate—"

"I've already stopped," Roan said. "Uncle Targ, I presume?" He tossed the dealer aside, stepped to the opening. Spidery stairs led down. He holstered the gun and descended into the heavy reek of sulphur dioxide. Uncle Targ danced on skinny, scaled legs, screaming curses in at least four tongues it hadn't used before.

"You swear with great authority," Roan said when the oldster paused for breath. "Why all the flummery?"

The creature skittered to the wall and plugged a wire dangling from its wrist into a socket.

"I should have let you rot! I should have decanted you at the first sight of that accursed box with its crests and jewels and its stink of trouble! Because of you, my very own pouch-brother was hacked to spareribs in the flower of his dealership! But instead, I maintained you at the required ninety-eight degrees Fahrenheit for days, and this is the thanks I get!" It stopped and breathed heavily for a moment. Then:

"Go away," it piped in a calmer tone. "I'm an old being."

"You're an old windbag, but that's your problem," Roan said carelessly. "All I want to know is who am I?"

"All that shooting! You could have shorted my metabolic booster unit!"

Roan looked around at the dim-lit room. There were no windows, but the walls were paneled in pure gold and somebody kept it polished. There was a chandelier hung with diamonds and a burl desk that must have cost a couple of thousand Imperial to import from Jazeel. The creature's flimsy old body was swathed in yards of silver damask, and in one side of its beak it wore a ruby that looked like the heart of a rare red wine.

"You've got a right nice sickroom," Roan said. "And

it's a matter of no moment to me whether you're evading the Feds or the tax collectors or if you just like to be alone. But I'm still waiting for an answer." He tossed the gun impatiently and motioned with his free hand at Uncle Targ's wires. "I can either plug you," he said, "or unplug you."

Uncle Targ squeaked around in the back of its throat as though it were pulling out rusty file drawers in its head.

"I'll have to get your records." It hesitated. "Don't look now." It sounded as though it had them in its lace bra.

Roan went on looking, but Uncle Targ played a tune with its fingers on a solid piece of wall and a drawer slid out. A card flipped up.

Roan reached over Uncle Targ's shoulder and grabbed the card. Somehow, he'd expected to see names on it: his father's name or his mother's. Or a country.

Instead, it said, *Pure Terran, Beta. ITN Experimental Station Alpha Centauri. (special source d.g.)*

"What does 'Beta' mean?" Roan asked.

"Beta is you. Alpha was somebody else. And then there was Gamma, and the others."

"Others. Pure Terran . . ."

"They weren't viable."

"Were they my brothers?"

Uncle Targ shrugged. "Alien biologies have never been a hobby of mine."

"But what else do you know?"

"What's the difference? Why do you care? You're you and it seems to me you're pretty lucky. Suppose you were me, getting older and older and all the money I've got won't buy even a minute of the pleasures you can get free." The screech was a whine now.

"Why I care is my business. Telling me is your business."

Tremulously the old creature unplugged itself, teetered across to its stool, perched, and lit up a dope stick. It was obvious from the way it caressed it that it wasn't allowed to have them very often.

"So long ago," it murmured, looking at the ceiling.

"Did you know I was stolen?" Roan asked.

"You *are* crude," Uncle Targ said distastefully. It pushed a button and the trapdoor slammed shut in its nephew's face peering from above.

"I'm waiting," Roan reminded it.

"I, ah," Uncle Targ said. "That is, so many of one's usual sources had withered away—you understand—"

"What made me so valuable?"

"You? Valuable? You retailed for a miserable two thousand, if I recall correctly."

"Still, there *was* your brother. And someone went to considerable trouble to come after me."

Uncle Targ blew smoke from orifices in the sides of its head. "Who knows? You do seem to be a more or less classic specimen of Man, if anyone has an interest in such matters." It sighed. "I envy anyone who cares that much about anything at all. With me it was money, but even that palls now."

"The card said I came from Alpha Centauri; can't you tell me any more than that?"

Uncle Targ rolled one beady eye at Roan. "On the flask," it said, "there was a name: Admiral Starbird, and the notation 'Command Interest.' I have no idea what that might mean."

"Are there Terrans on Alpha?"

"I know nothing whatever of this Alpha place," Uncle Targ piped. "And I do not care to know. But there are no Terrans living there—or anywhere else, for that matter. The Pure Terran is a myth. Oh, ten, fifteen thousand years ago, certainly. They kept to themselves, lords of the universe, practiced all sorts of racial purity measures—except for the specially mutated slaves they bred. But then they had the poor judgment to lose a war. Since then the natural tendency toward environmental adaptation has had free rein. And with the social barriers down, the various induced mutations inbred freely with the Pure Strain. Today you're lucky if you can pick up what we in the trade call an Eighty X; a reasonable superficial resemblance to the ancient type."

"What about me?"

"Umm. If I were to cut into you, I daresay I'd encounter all sorts of anomalies. How many hearts do you have?"

"I don't know. I thought you said alien biology wasn't a hobby of yours."

"One can't helping picking up a few—"

There was a loud thud from above and plaster fell down on the burl desk. Uncle Targ screeched and jumped for the trapdoor button. The lid sprang open and a solid slug wanged off the gold wall by Roan's ear and the ancient being's profanity cut off in midcurse. Roan yanked out his gun and flattened himself against the wall; through the trapdoor he could see Askor holding Uncle Targ's nephew by the neck and slamming the feathered head against the desk. A small ragged slave was scrabbling frantically for the beaded hanging, but Sidis' unsheathed claws held him pinned by a trailing cloak. Roan fired a shot into the ventilator grill. It made an echo like eternity bursting.

"All right, boys, break it up," he called, and clambered up into the shop. Sidis looked at him, grinning his metallic grin, and the slave broke free and bolted from the room. Askor waved the dealer in a wide gesture as though he had forgotten he was holding him.

"Poion seen you come in here and we thought we heard some shots and then we couldn't find you."

"So all you rowdies could think of was to shoot the place up. I told you to go shopping."

"*Pay* for stuff?" Askor tossed the dealer aside; it struck with a clatter of beak and claws and bangles and crept to a neutral corner. "We figured you was kidding."

Roan glanced down into Uncle Targ's private retreat. The ancient Rheops lay on its back, glazed eyes wide, with its mouth full of blood.

"Come on," Roan said. "Let's get out of here."

Back in the plaza the bazaar had died as though a sudden storm had slammed it shut. Roan could feel the eyes staring at him from behind blind shutters and past barely parted hangings at narrow windows and through cracks in sagging façades. Askor glanced around, strutting.

"I guess they know we been to town, hey, Chief?"

"Shut up and march," Roan said.

This is what I always leave behind me, he thought. Fear . . .

"I don't get it, Chief," Askor grumbled, sitting beside Roan in the eerie light of the central panel. "For better'n a year and a half now—ever since we lost *Warlock*—we been bypassing dandy targets, blasting balls to bulk-heads from one two-bit world to another. And when we get there—no shooting, you say. Go shopping, you say. The boys are getting kinda fed up—"

"We stopped and took on supplies once or twice," Roan said. "But I suppose that wasn't enough to satisfy your sporting instincts."

"Huh? Aw, that was peanuts; just grocery shopping, like."

"With a few good-natured killings thrown in, just to keep your hand in. Well, you can tell the crew there'll be plenty of action from now on."

"Yeah? Say, that's great, Cap'n! What you got in mind? A run through the Spider Cluster, maybe, and knock off a few of them market towns that ain't been hit for a hundred years—"

"Nothing so pedestrian. Set your course for Galactic East . . ."

Askor scratched at his hairless skull. "East? Why do we want to head out that way, Chief? That's rough territory. Damn few worlds to hit, and them poor ones."

"There'll be plenty of worlds; and after the first couple years' travel, we'll be in a part of space no one's visited for a few thousand years—"

"A couple years' run out the Arm? Cripes, Cap'n, that'll put us in No-man's-space. The ghostships—"

"I don't believe in ghostships. We may run into Niss, though. That's where the last big engagements were fought—"

"Look, Chief," Askor said quickly. "What about if we talk this over, huh? I mean, what the hell, there's plenty good worlds right here in this sector to keep us eating good for the next two hundred years. What I say is, why look for trouble?"

"You're afraid, Askor? That surprises me."

"Now wait a minute, Cap'n! I didn't say I was scared. I just . . ." His voice trailed off. "What I'm getting at is, what the hell's out there? Why leave good hunting grounds for nothing?"

"Alpha Centauri's out there," Roan said.

"Alpha . . . That's the place you said the ITN was. Cripes, Chief, I thought you said we was through with that chasing around—"

Roan came to his feet. "What do you think this is, a ladies' discussion circle? I gave you an order, and by the Nine Hells, you'll carry it out!"

Askor looked at him. "You sound more like old Cap'n Dread all the time," he said. "I'll follow your orders, Cap'n. I always have. I know I need somebody with brains to tell me what to do. I just made the mistake of thinking we could talk about it—"

"We've talked enough," Roan cut him off. "You plot your course to raid every second-rate planet between here and Alpha, if that's what it takes to make you happy. Just don't forget where we're headed."

Askor was grinning again. "That's more like it, Chief," he said. "This is what the boys been waiting for. Boy, what a cruise! It'll be a ten-year run, cutting into new territory all the way!"

"And no more talk about ghostships—or live Niss either."

"OK, Cap'n. But with some good targets in sight, it'll take more than a shipload of spooks to scare the boys off."

After Askor left the bridge, Roan sat for a long time staring into the main view screen, with its spreading pattern of glittering stars.

So much for the next ten years, he thought. After that . . .

But there'd be time enough to plan that when the sun called Alpha Centauri filled the screens.

16

Roan sprawled in his favorite deep-leather chair in the
genuine wood-paneled officers' lounge of the heavy
cruiser *Archaeopteryx*, which had served the free-booters
as home for seven years now, since a stray missile had
uncovered the underground depot in which the retreating ITN had concealed it, fifty-seven hundred years
before. Sidis sat across from him, his grin ragged now
with the absence of five front teeth, carried away by a
shell fragment in an engagement off Rastoum the previ-
ous year. Poion perched in his special seat, fitted up to
ease the stump of his left leg, toying with a massive
silver wine goblet. Askor was tilted back with a boot on
the mahogany tabletop, paring chunks from a wedge of
black cheese and forcing them into his capacious mouth.

"I called you here," Roan said, "to tell you the cruise
is nearly over. The story that last batch of prisoners told
fits in. The sun ahead is Alpha."

"Not many of the old bunch still around, hey, Cap'n?"
Sidis observed. "Bolu, Honest Max, Yack—all gone."

"Whaddaya expect?" Askor inquired, with his mouth
full. He lifted his alabaster chalice and washed the
cheese down with green Bacchus wine, then belched
heartily. "We been on, lessee, twenty-one raids in the

last eleven years, and fought three deep-space engagements with wise-guy local patrols—"

"You can reminisce later," Roan said. "I expect the ITN to pick us up on their screens any day now. I don't like that, but it can't be helped. If they let us alone, however, I'm making planetfall on the fourth world of the system. According to the records, ITN Headquarters is on the second."

"From the stories we been hearing, I got my doubts the ITN has a cheery welcome for nosy strangers," Askor said. "What you want with them Terries anyways, Chief?"

"I'm a Terry myself," Roan said. "I've got business with the ITN."

"In his origins a being finds hints of his destiny," Poion murmured. "Alas, our captain knows his not . . ."

"You'll wait for me on Planet Four," Roan went on, "and stay under cover. If I'm not back in ten days—you're on your own."

"Hey, you mean . . . ?" Sidis' grin was sagging, hooked up on the bad side by twisted scar tissue. He looked from Roan to Askor to Poion. "You're talking about letting the captain walk in there alone? And where does that leave the rest of us—?"

"You'll be all right," Roan said. "You'll be happy; you can raid back down through the Eastern Arm and shoot up everything in sight, without me to nag you."

"Just like that, huh? Thirteen years together, and then, *srrikk!*" He made a cutting motion across his throat.

"I didn't take you to raise," Roan growled. "I remember you, the day we met: you were pounding some Ythcan's brains out against the bulkhead. You were doing all right."

"Back out through the Ghost Fleet, alone?" Sidis' grin was a grimace now. "To the Ninth Hell with that! I'm going with you, Cap'n!"

"I'm going alone," Roan said flatly.

"Then you'll have to shoot me, Cap'n," Sidis said distinctly.

Roan nodded quietly. "That could be arranged."

"And me too," Askor said. "Count me in."

"And I," Poion said. "I shall go or die, as my captain wills."

Roan looked from one to another. He lifted his glass and took a long draft, put it back on the table.

"You're *that* scared of the ghosts of departed Terries?"

Nobody spoke.

"You Gooks amaze me," Roan said. "All right, we four: but no more."

Sidis' grin was back in place. Askor grunted and carved off another slab of cheese. Poion nodded.

"It is well," he said. "We four."

"Gungle," Roan asked, "you think you can navigate *Archaeopteryx* now?"

"Yeah, Chief," Gungle said, grinning his snaggle-toothed grin. "Yeah, I think. You show me what to feed in, I feed it in."

"Suppose you were captain now. What course would you set?"

"No offense, Chief, but I'd plug in a straight line back outa East Sector. Me and the boys, we heard back on Leeto about the Terry Ghost Fleets, and there ain't no civilization for parsecs. Just these dead worlds like Centaurus Four here, without even no air."

"What are your coordinates for the nearest all-blood joy city?"

Gungle grinned wider, flicked a chart of the Eastern Sector on the navigation screen, and punched out a course to Leeto.

"OK," said Roan. "You're captain in full charge until I get back."

"Huh?"

"I'm taking Poion, Askor, and Sidis with me to Centaurus Two."

Gungle gaped. Roan took the heavy gem he'd worn on his chest since Aldo Cerise and tossed it to the newly appointed captain, who hung it around his neck and threw his shoulders back and stood proud, the grin turning into a stern look of dignity.

"Now pipe the crew up," Roan told him.

"Men," he said, when they had all assembled, "I'm going to leave you for a while—" and raised a hand to still the muttering that started up. "Meanwhile Gungle's captain and he'll do any gut-splitting that's necessary. And anybody that's got any ideas about anybody else being captain had better think twice. That's my Terran magic jewel Gungle's wearing. As long as he wears it nothing can touch him."

The men rolled their eyes at Gungle and made magical signs in twenty-four different religions, but no one raised any objection.

"That thing really magic?" Sidis asked, as the scout boat nosed on toward the brilliant star that was Centaurus Two, with *Archaeopteryx* four days astern, outward bound for Leeto.

"It created magic in the heart of Gungle," Poion answered. "He is now a man and a leader. It created magic in the hearts of the crew as well. They fear him. All this I could feel very plainly."

"Yeah, but that's not what I mean—" Sidis started.

"Look!" Roan was pointing at the forward view screen.

"A ship," Askor said. "Heavy stuff, too . . ."

"It didn't take 'em long to spot us," Sidis said. "Somebody's awake in these parts."

"We'll hold our course steady as she goes," Roan said. "Leave the first move up to them."

"What if the first move is a fifty megatonner amidships?" Sidis inquired.

"That'll be a sure sign we ain't wanted," Askor grunted.

Roan turned the all-wave receiver, picked up star static, a faint murmur of distant planetary communications. Then the drone of a powerful carrier came through.

"Inbound boat, heave to and identify yourself," a voice barked in a peculiarly intonated Standard.

"Survivors from the merchant vessel *Archaeopteryx*," Roan transmitted. "On course for the second planet. Who are you?"

"This is the Imperial Terran Navy talking. Ye're in

Navy space. Stand by to receive a boarding party and no tricks or we'll blow ye to kingdom come."

"Are we glad to see *you*," Roan transmitted. "Any hot coffee aboard?"

But there was no answer and the four ex-pirates watched the Terran vessel growing in their tiny view screen.

"Ah, Captain," Poion observed sadly, "again the Terran Navy is a disappointment. You look for home and there is no home."

"Your emotion receiver's working overtime," Roan said. "But I admit our welcome lacked a certain something."

"Me, I feel like a fly that's about to get swatted," Sidis said. "Why don't you ever read my emotions, Poion?"

"You're too stupid to have emotions," Askor said. "We shoulda brought *Trixie* in; she could handle that Terry tub."

The ITN vessel came in, paced the tiny scout boat at a distance of fifty miles and then came alongside, looming like a dull-metal planetoid. There was a heavy shock as its magnetic grapples embraced the boat.

"Open up there," the harsh but strangely cultivated-sounding voice said from the communicator.

Roan nodded to Askor. He operated the control and the four pairs of eyes watched the lock cycle open. Hot, dense air whooshed into the boat from the higher-pressure interior of the naval vessel, bringing odors of food and tobacco and a pervading animal stink.

Askor snorted. "Terries! I can smell 'em!"

Boots clanged against metal decking. A tall, lean Man wearing an open blue tunic over a bare chest ducked through the lock. He had a lined, triangular face and there was sweat glittering across his forehead and chest and his pale eyes were restless. He gripped a power rifle with both hands and looked at the three massive humanoids and then past them at Roan.

"Who are ye?" he demanded of Roan, ignoring the others.

"Roan Cornay, master of *Archaeopteryx*."

"Who're these beauties?" He jerked his chin at the three Gooks, not looking at them.

"My crew. We were all that got out, and—"

"You go aboard," the Man said to Roan, keeping the power rifle pointed at him. "These others stay here."

Roan hesitated a moment. Poion caught his feeling and nodded imperceptibly at Askor. Then Roan stepped accommodatingly toward the port behind the Man, and as he passed he half turned quickly, slammed the gun from the Terran's hands with a lightning blow. Askor caught it, flipped it up, and let it point at its former owner.

"I prefer to keep my crew with me," Roan said calmly.

The Man had flattened his back against a bulkhead and his mouth was open. "Ye're stark, raving mad," he said. "I'm Navy. One yell . . ."

". . . and I'll have your guts plastered on the ceiling," Askor said, grinning. "Whattaya say, Cap'n. Let him have it?"

"Oh, I don't know," Roan said, watching a rivulet of sweat that was crawling along the Man's neck. "Maybe he's going to be nice after all. Maybe he'll decide to extend the hospitality of his ship to all of us. How about it, Terry?"

And Roan smiled an ironic grin at himself. This was the first time he'd called anybody else Terry. And it came out like a dirty word.

Askor nodded. "He'll need to point his popgun at us." Askor pushed a thumb against the firing stud of the Man's power rifle and bent it out of line. He tossed it back to the Man. "Don't worry," he said. "We won't tell nobody it don't shoot."

Roan walked close behind the Man as they went through the port into the Navy ship. "No need to be nervous," Roan told the Terran. "Just say all the right things when you see your buddies."

A small, roundly built Man with a high, pale fore-head stood waiting for them in the hold. He wore the tarnished silver leaf of an ITN commander on the shoulder of his uniform and he was flanked by four armed Men. He had small, dim eyes and they squinted at Roan and his companions, as though the brilliant lighting of the hold blinded him.

"Some reason why ye didn't dump 'em back out into space, Draco?"

Draco cleared his throat. "Distressed spacemen, Commander Hullwright."

Commander Hullwright frowned, still looking hard at Roan. "Aren't they all. But I see. This one seems . . ."

"Yes, sir," Draco said quickly. "He's Terran, but I don't think he even knows it. That's why I brought him in to you."

Hullwright grunted, but to Draco's obvious relief he was looking at Roan and ignoring the others.

"Ye speak a little Standard?" the commander asked Roan.

"Yes, I recognized your voice."

"Then why didn't ye answer me hail?"

"I did."

"Hmmmph. Blasted receiver's prob'ly out again. Draco, see to it." Draco drifted back, eyeing Askor and Sidis nervously, and Commander Hullwright forgot about him again.

"Don't know you're Terran, eh, lad?" Hullwright asked Roan. "Ye must be pretty overwhelmed with all this," indicating with a wave the Navy ship and himself and his officers.

"I've seen ships before," Roan said.

"Um. Got an ugly tongue in your mouth. No doubt ye're a dirty spy from Rim HQ. Blan send ye?"

"No."

"Fat chance ye'd tell me if ye *were* a spy. What's your story? What are ye supposed to be doing in ITN space?"

"My merchantman *Archaeopteryx* blew up a couple of parsecs back. I was outbound for Leeto for shore leave. We had a brush with pirates off Yount and I guess they mined us. We four escaped in the boat; I was afraid we'd drift forever."

"Left ye'r ship and crew to fend for themselves, eh?" Hullwright's lip curled. "All right. I'll give ye a berth and ye can start in the Navy, swabbing decks. Maybe ye can work up to something. Maybe ye can't. Take care of him, Draco . . ." He shot a look at Askor and Sidis. "And put the animals back on their boat."

"Wait a minute," Roan said. "These are my men and they're hungry and thirsty. And I don't swab decks. I'm a master."

"Right now you're the most insignificant swab in the Imperial Terran Navy, you puppy," Hullwright barked. "And as for your 'men,' they'll have to find their own animal feed in space. Put 'em back and cast 'em loose, Draco."

Draco shuffled his feet unhappily. "Uh, Commander. They claim to be distressed spacemen . . ."

"What's this—pretty sentiments about distressed Gooks? What's going on, anyhow? Are ye in on this mutiny I keep hearing rumors about? What . . ."

The four armed men with Hullwright had tightened up their ranks and one drew the gun from his holster. "Drop that power rifle, Draco," he said.

Draco dropped it. Sweat dripped from the end of his nose. "Listen, Commander," he said hoarsely, "they made me—" Roan took a quick step while attention was centered on Draco; his right hand made an expert chop across the throat of the Man with the unholstered gun. Askor leaped like a cork from a bottle, seized two of the Men in his vast hands, slammed their heads together in his favorite tactic. Sidis caught the last of the four as he was bringing up his gun, yanked the weapon from the Terran with such force that the Man skidded across the hold and slammed against the bulkhead screeching, clutching a bloody hand.

"Hey, look," Sidis said cheerfully, holding the gun up, "his finger's still stuck in the guard!" Sidis dislodged the amputated member and tossed the gun up. "What do we do with these nancies, Chief?"

"Poke them in the ship's lazaret. Commander Hullwright's coming with us for a little pleasant conversation, aren't you, sir? We'll go to the bridge where we can talk in privacy and comfort."

Askor gathered up the guns, gave the best one to Roan, handed the others to Poion and Sidis.

Commander Hullwright's ineffectual little eyes were frightened. "What," he began, "what are you . . ."

"Now, now, be calm, Commander," Roan said. "If you play it cleverly, you may even live through this."

Roan sat in the captain's padded chair, gnawing a roasted leg of fowl and studying the charts of the Space Traffic Control Area surrounding Nyurth, the second planet out from Centaurus, and other charts showing the layout of the vast headquarters complex.

"You know, Commander," Roan said, "I'm impressed with the Imperial Terran Navy after all. I'll just want a few details from you so I can be even more impressed. Care for another piece of bird?"

Hullwright snarled. Sidis cracked him across the shins with the power rifle.

"Answer nice when the cap'n speaks to you," he admonished.

"No, I don't want a piece o' bird, you pirate!" he roared.

"Tell me about the defenses, Commander," Roan said.

"I'll tell ye nothing, ye murdering mutinous cross-breed Geeks!"

"Our captain objects to adjectives," Poion said mildly, giving Hullwright a gentle but telling twist of the ear. "And I find your emotional radiation both primitive and appalling. Answer the captain correctly and succinctly."

"I'd eat me own tongue first!"

Roan tossed the chicken leg aside and began peeling a banana. "Umm. Now, about these charts. How many of the emplacements are operative and which ones?" He held the chart for Hullwright to see.

Hullwright was silent. Sidis jabbed him roughly with the end of the gun.

"Ye think I'd betray me uniform, ye scum?" Hullwright snarled.

"That's right," Roan said. "Unless you'd rather die—one piece at a time."

"Ye wouldn't dare lay a hand on me, ye filth! I'm an officer of the Imperial Terran Navy!"

"I killed a captain once," Roan said. "It's just as easy as killing a Gook."

Hullwright tried to keep his defiant look in place, but the spirit had wilted from him.

"Damn ye'r eyes," he said, "ye won't get through anyway. Untie me right hand and I'll point them out to ye on the chart."

Hullwright sagged in the chair. His little eyes were closed and he rubbed his sparse eyebrows with his right hand. Empty glasses and plates littered the plotting board and chart table, the remains of meals brought up from the galley at the commander's reluctant request, and passed in through the service slot.

"I've told ye all I know," Hullwright said hoarsely. "Ye've sucked me brain dry as a mummy's tongue."

"You've done very well, Commander," Roan said. "Askor, what's the plot for Planet Three?"

"Twenty-seven million miles abaft our port beam, Cap'n."

"Fine. Now, Commander, I've got just one more little favor to ask, and you've been so nice. Pass the word to your second officer to assemble the crew on the boat deck in fatigues for calisthenics in exactly ten minutes."

"Hah? Whazzat?"

Askor applied the butt of the rifle. "Jump, Terry!"

After two more prods of increasing severity, Hullwright complied. With the cold muzzle of Askor's rifle against his left temple, his ragged voice sounded through the vessel.

"And now, good-by, Commander," Roan said. "Askor, you and Sidis take the commander to join his men; they'll be in their skivvies and unarmed, so you shouldn't have to kill many of them. Dump all but two kilotons of reaction mass from our lifeboat; then load the commander and his men aboard and cast them off."

"That's cold-blooded murder, ye swine . . ." A crack across bloody shins cut Hullwright off.

"You'll have enough fuel aboard to reach Centaurus Three. According to your charts, it has a breathable atmosphere. There are forty-three of you and the supplies and water should last you a couple of months, if you're not careless. And if I find you've been honest with me about the information you gave me, I'll see that you're picked up in good time."

"Wait a minute," Hullwright said blurrily. "I just remembered. About that picket line, the outer one . . ." The commander corrected a few errors he had made. Then Askor took him away, followed by Sidis with his toothy grin.

Alone Roan sat in the bridge and knew he was a fool. He could have gone on looting the universe, or set himself up for life on some pleasant planet, with never another care in the world. Instead, here he was alone with three Gooks, going in to face the Imperial Terran Navy. And why?

I'm still looking for Terra, Roan thought. Poion says I'm looking for home and I have no home to find. Man has no home. Perhaps there is no Terra. But that's something Poion wouldn't know—and the Imperial Terran Navy might. They might know the truth of the story of the ancient Niss blockade of Terra. Roan thought of the dead Niss ship firing its last volley, and that made him think of Henry Dread, and even now he couldn't remember Henry Dread without pain. He had had blood on his hands before, but Henry's was the only blood that stained.

Poion came in with his silent tread. "Let that memory die, my captain," he said, "and gird yourself for the future."

Roan felt the boat lurch slightly. That would be the lifeboat kicking free. Askor and Sidis came back into the control deck in high good humor. Their laughter was like a cannonball rolling over an iron grill.

"That was cute, Chief," Sidis said. "The tub's all yours. What are you going to do with it?"

"First we're going to scuttle her," Roan said, smiling grimly at three astonished expressions. "Then we're going to ride what's left into ITN HQ on Nyurth."

"And after that?" Askor asked.

"After that we start taking chances."

17

It took nine hours to burn a carefully aligned series of holes through the bulkheads of the ITN destroyer, so arranged as to destroy food and water supplies and smash unimportant portions of the control system, while leaving intact the vital minimum of instruments and fuel reserves. The final punctures through the outer hull plates were bored by Sidis, cramped in a too-small ITN regulation vacuum suit, at points marked by tiny pilot holes cut from within. When the job was complete, crude patches were rigged and the foursome gathered in the now sealed-off control deck, surrounded by heaps of supplies placed there before the work was begun.

"Get the story straight," Roan said. "We're from an ITN detachment on Carolis. That's far enough away they won't know any better. We found this tub derelict, beyond the fourth from Centaurus, driving out-system at a half-G. We boarded her and sealed off the leaks, restored atmosphere to the conn deck, and headed her for her home station for salvage."

"What were we doing nosing around this sector?" Askor asked, levering the cap from a can of compressed quagle eggs.

"We were lost," Roan said. "And next time you get a yen for quagle eggs go in the john. They smell like a corpse's armpit." There were a few things the Minids ate that Roan could never get used to. "We left our scout ship in orbit around fourth from Centaurus. We were out of supplies and almost out of fuel. When we first saw the Navy ship we thought we were being rescued. Then we found out it was a ghostship. We're distressed spacers—nothing more."

"We'll be more distressed yet, when the ITN gets hold of us," Askor said.

"I get distressed every time you open your ugly mouth," Sidis said. "Why don't you shut up and let the cap'n do the worrying?"

"It's a good forty-hour run into the Planetary Control Area," Roan said. "We'll stand watch two on and four off. Every half hour we transmit our Mayday signal. We'll keep our receivers open; I doubt that we'll pick up anything, but if we do, ignore it."

"What if we hear an order to heave to?"

"Our receivers are out. We keep going."

Roan keyed the transmitter to the ITN distress channel.

"ITN vessel *Rage of Heaven*, under salvage crew, calling ITN HQ at Nyurth," he called. "We're headed in-system on course for Nyurth; our position is . . ."

At the center of a box of four heavy destroyers which paced the damaged vessel at a distance of one hundred miles, Roan steered the scuttled and patched *Rage of Heaven* in past the tiny outer moon of Nyurth, crossed the orbit of the massive inner moon, descended, braking now, into the turbulent upper reaches of the deep atmosphere. The escort moved in to fifty miles, then ten. On the screens, the telltales winked with the incoming pulses of long-range sensors aimed from the planetary surface nine hundred miles below.

"They're tracking us like we was a missile volley from a hostile super-D," Sidis growled through his carefully polished teeth. He was sharpening a new toothpick with a steel file, and sweat beaded his low forehead.

"At least they've laid off hailing us," Askor pointed out. "I thought maybe the bastards meant it when they gave us that final warning."

"Their emotions when we emerge from the ship should be fascinating," Poion said, delicately whetting an ever finer edge on his already razor-sharp stiletto.

Sidis eyed the business end of his power gun and blew any possible dust out of it. Then he took out his whetstone and started honing his double-bladed Niss knife.

"You know, Cap'n," Askor said, "I dunno if it was a good idea, tricking us out in these Terry suits. A Gook ain't a Terry, no matter how you slick him pot."

"You're honorary Terries," Roan said. "Now shut up and follow my lead."

The ship grounded clumsily at the extreme edge of the vast port complex. Roan watched on the screens as two of his escorts settled in nearby, gun ports open and energy projectors aimed. The others hovered a mile or two above.

"They must think we got a army in here," Askor said.

The three crewmen looked at Roan. "Do we walk out there—just like that?"

"You know a better way?" Roan adjusted the set of the collar of his ITN uniform, hitched his gun belt to center the buckle.

"No weapons out," he said. "We can't buck the whole Imperial Terran Navy. Right now all we've got is my brains. So keep your traps shut."

"Well," Askor said, eyeing the bright sky, "it's as good a day as any to take a swig from the Hellhorn."

"I begin to sense their emotions," Poion said. "Not death lust, but a mixture of curiosity and excitement and violence restrained. Something's afoot, Captain. Walk carefully among these Terries."

Roan led the way down the landing ramp, squinting at bright sunshine, sniffing the alien scent of fresh air. Across the field, an official, uniformed contingent of the Imperial Terran Navy was drawn up in a rank to greet him. Their shoulder insignia glittered in the sun, and their metal belts shone. Striding at the head of his hulking companions, Roan snapped over his shoulder:

"If one of you thugs disgraces me, I'll have his guts an inch at a time." The ranked Terrans stood rigidly waiting, and Roan admired their precise formation, their disciplined silence and stillness. And briefly he hated himself because he wished he were one of them, a Man among Men, and not a Terry Freak surrounded by blood-thirsty Gooks.

Then he was closer, and he saw they were not all the same height, as they had appeared to be, but were artfully arranged in graduated rows with the tallest on the right and the near-midgets at the far end. His step almost faltered, but he went on, seeing the alien faces now, the wrong-colored eyes under the regulation helmets, the queer-colored skin of wrists showing above six-fingered and four-fingered gloves, the slashes in polished boots to ease wide, webbed feet, the misshapen bodies that bulged under the uniforms of glory.

At twenty feet, he barked the order to halt. A heavy body bumped him from behind. He whirled, bellowed at the trio who were spreading out, gaping at the strangers.

"Back in line there, you bone-skulled sons of one-legged joy-girls!"

He turned again, saluted stiffly as a short, pink-faced Terran came up, casually returning Roan's greeting with a wave of a soft hand. He was wearing the insignia of a lieutenant commander, and he tucked a short swagger stick under his arm, glanced past Roan at his crew, wiped his nose with a forefinger.

"Commodore Quex would like to welcome you and your men and requests the honor of your presence at Imperial Naval Headquarters at your earliest convenience," he said in a high, melodious voice. A civilized voice.

Roan nodded, staring at the strange Terran's face. Except for Henry Dread, this was the first Terran face he'd ever seen. There were two heavy-lidded eyes— pale blue, Roan noted, with a small lift of excitement—a blob of a nose, a puckered mouth, folds of fat under the small chin. For some reason it reminded Roan of a baby Fustian, before its shell grew. It didn't look like the kind of face Roan had pictured conquering a Galaxy. But he concealed his disappointment and motioned his crew to follow him as the Terran led the way across the field.

"What do you get from them up close, Poion?" Roan asked softly as they marched behind the Terran officer, flanked by a squad of Men.

"Some sort of fear, oddly enough," Poion said.

"Fear? Of four ragged spacemen?"

"Not exactly of us. But that is the emotion I read."

The Headquarters of the ITN was a craggy many-towered palace built ages before by a long-dead prince of a vanished dynasty. It loomed like a colossus over the tumbled mud houses of the village. A vast green window like a cyclopean eye cast back brilliant viridian reflections as Roan and his crew marched in under the crumbling walls along a wide marble walkway, went up wide steps flanked by immaculate conical trees of dark green set among plants with tiny violet blossoms. It was faintly, sadly reminiscent of the garden on Aldo Cerise.

Inside, the sun glowed in long rectangles along the echoing floor of a wide, high room. Terries in fitted tunics of navy blue stood at rigid attention by elongated doors at the sides of the room. Above, a vaulted ceiling arched up into shadows where gold and blue mosaics caught occasional sun gleams among masses of hanging brass carvings, all polished, which dangled like earrings from a hundred peaked corners, clanging as the wind moved them. They went under a vast arch of enameled brass, across a wide floor of gleaming brass plates; far up among darl-rafters, echoes of more brass clashed softly.

As the men marched by, Geek slaves prostrated themselves. They were lean, ribby, deep-eyed creatures, with vestigial scales across high shoulders, long, finger-toed feet, and draggled manes of lank hair along their prominent spines. They wore only loin cloths in spite of the chill, and some of them trembled violently as Roan looked at them, from cold, or fear.

The small Terran officer trotted ahead, disappeared through high doors with a sign for Roan to wait. His men clustered close behind him, drawn together and suddenly alert, almost disciplined.

"We could jump 'em now," Askor growled. "I get jumpy just waiting."

"There is a certain pleasure in the experience of mortal suspense," Poion said. "In such moments the current of life runs deep and swift."

"You'll actually enjoy dying, you poetic bastard," Askor grunted.

Roan hissed at his men as they began to mutter. Waiting came hard to them. But there was no need to worry about them. They could smell danger at half a parsec—and it was an odor they were fond of . . .

Roan's guide reappeared and beckoned to him.

"Wait here," Roan said to his men, "and don't shoot anybody before I get back!" He followed through the bossed, agate-studded door into a shadowed, high-vaulted room in which ancient magnificence hung like rotted velvet drapes. A spider-lean, white-haired man in a rank-encrusted uniform rose from behind a desk like a beached freighter, offered a bony hand. Roan took it, and felt the stitching along the fingers where the webbing had been removed. He had a wide mouth and a strange, small chin; his ears were odd, and at close range Roan could see that they were edged with pink scar tissue.

"I am Commodore Quex," the man said in a soft, almost feminine voice. He was slight, delicately boned, but the cruelty in the slits of his too widely set eyes was that of a wolf, not of the cat.

Behind Roan, the Terran saluted and went out and the door closed behind him.

"I'm Roan Cornay," Roan said. "Lieutenant Cornay," he added.

"Ah, yes. From Carolis. What a pleasure to welcome you, ah, Lieutenant." A finger like a parchment-wrapped bone brushed at a red-edged eye. At close range, Roan could see a whitish crust at the corners of the puckered mouth. An unpleasant odor hung about the Man. He settled back into his chair, snapped his fingers. Something moved in the shadows, and Roan saw that it was a slave, face down on the thick, moldy carpet. It rose and scuttled to swing a heavy chair around for Roan to sit in.

The commodore glanced at a paper before him, then looked at Roan, his hand hovering near his eye. "Your ship, ah, Navy 39643-G4. Our records . . ."

"I captured her. After *Warlock* was lost."

"Ah, yes. So you said. Hmmm. *Warlock* was a valuable vessel. I don't believe your reports made it clear precisely *how* she was lost . . . ?"

"In action—" Roan paused, thinking of what he had been about to say about the Niss ship, and deciding quite suddenly not to say it. He let the sentence hang.

Quex was looking thoughtful. "Surprising . . . and fortunate that you were able to obtain a replacement. And you say Captain Dread was lost as well?" The old voice was a purr. Roan felt tension creep along the back of his neck. He shifted in his chair so as to keep the door in view. "That's right," he said.

"And before his, ah, death, he tendered you your appointment?" The red eye peered past the finger at Roan.

"That's right."

"Ummm. And how did you happen to enter into your, ah, association with Dread?"

"He took me from a ship he captured."

Quex sucked in his dry lips. "Another naval unit?" he asked sharply.

"No; it was a traveling show. I was one of the Freaks—I—"

"You were a captive of non-humans?" Quex was digging at his ear now, angrily.

"Not really. I was, at first, but—"

Quex leaned forward. "You lived among them willingly?" There was an edge on his voice like a meat saw.

"They treated me well enough; I had good quarters and plenty of food—"

"Beware of Geeks bearing gifts," Quex said flatly. He leaned back, his thin fingers on the edge of the table.

"And what is your ancestry, Cornay? If you don't mind my asking." His voice indicated that he didn't care whether Roan minded or not.

Roan opened his mouth to say that he was genuine Terrestrial strain, but he heard himself saying, "I'm not sure. I was adopted. My folks didn't talk about it much."

"Mmmm. To be sure," Quex murmured meaninglessly. He poked at the papers on his desk.

"I want to get back in space as soon as possible," Roan said. "Who do I see about a new ship, and provisioning?"

Quex's mouth was open, showing inflamed gums and the tip of a white tongue.

"Provisioning? For what?"

"For my next cruise; my new assignment."

"Ah, of course." Quex showed the false face again. His finger was back at his eye. "But we can discuss these details later. I've laid on a dinner in your honor tonight. You'll want to prepare. Real Terran fare again, eh?"

"I take it most of the fleet is out on space duty now?" Roan said.

"Why do you say that?" Quex shot Roan a darting look.

"I only saw half a dozen ships at the port. Some of them seemed to be half dismantled. How big a force does Alpha command?"

Quex lifted the paper from his desk and dropped it again. "Ah, an extensive force, Cornay. Quite extensive. Rather extensive . . ."

"You have other bases here on-world?"

"Oh, ah, assuredly, Lieutenant. Why," Quex waved a hand toward the draped window, "you didn't imagine these few rusting hulks were our entire fleet?" He curved his puckered lips in a smile that crinkled the cruelty lines around his eyes. "Most amusing. Most. But . . ." He rose. "I suggest we allow these matters to wait until after our celebration of your happy return—"

Roan stood. "Certainly, sir. But I'd like to ask when

the counterattack is planned. I want to know how to set up my cruise—"

"Counterattack?" Quex gaped.

"The massive offensive in force against the Niss. How many of them are there? Where have they set up their headquarters? What—"

The commodore held up two quivering hands. "Cornay, need I remind you that all this is highly classified?" He shot a look at the nearest slave, crouched against the floor.

"Oh." Roan glanced at the slave. "I didn't think . . ."

Quex rounded the desk. "Not that we have any trouble with our slaves. They know their place, don't they, old one?" He kicked the slave hard in the ribs; it grunted and glanced up with an almost human smile, then stared at the floor again.

"Still, I shall have to dispose of this fellow now. Pity in a way. He's been with me for twenty years and is well trained. But getting old. Ah, well . . ." Quex took Roan's elbow, guided him toward the door. "Until tonight, then?"

"What about my crew?"

"Your crew. Of course. Do bring them along. Yes. Capital idea. Your entire crew, mind you. How many did you say there were?"

"Just the four of us," Roan said.

"At second moonrise then, Cornay. Don't be late."

"We'll be there," Roan said.

Vast grins broke across battered faces as Roan rejoined his crew.

"Glad to see you, Boss," Askor said. "We was about to come in after you."

"Relax. I'll call the plays," Roan said.

A small, neat Terry with an elegant walk flicked ashes from a dope stick, came toward Roan and his men. The guard officer came to attention.

"That will do, Putertek," the newcomer said gently. He looked Roan over, smiling faintly, glanced at the others.

"But, sir . . ." the guard protested.

"And your watchdogs, too," the dandy said. He was carefully dressed in immaculate blue polyon with silver-corded shoulder boards bearing the winged insignia of a captain. His blond, rigidly waved hair shone with oil and he touched it with polished fingernails. His perfume reminded Roan distantly of Stellaraire.

"My name is Trishinist," he said with a small flourish of one manicured hand. "Sorry about the reception. These commissioned peasants—no finesse. Perhaps you'd like a bite to eat and then we can have a little chat?"

"My men are hungry, too," Roan said. "They never seem to get invited anywhere."

"The enlisted men's mess is . . ."

"They're officers."

"My apologies. Of course." Captain Trishinist led the way along a side corridor, chatting easily about the weather, the servant problem, the inadequacies of the mess cuisine.

The dining room was quiet with deep rugs and moss-green drapes and immense, intricate chandeliers. Waiters sprang forward to draw out chairs at a long, white-linen table.

Askor and Sidis sat down awkwardly, then relaxed and grinned at each other.

Trishinist murmured an order to a servitor, waited and turned contentedly to the table as the waiter brought a loaded tray.

"Champagne and honeydew," Trishinist said as Roan's men eyed the frosted bottle and the breakable-looking glasses. "I hope you find it adequate."

Askor reached half a melon from the tray as the waiter passed, took a vast bite.

"Hey," he said, chewing juicily, "pretty good. But the skin's kinda tough."

"Wipe your chin," Roan said.

Askor used his sleeve. "Sorry," he muttered. Sidis had plucked the bottle from the tray and rapped it on the edge of the table to knock the top off. He jumped to his feet as the wine foamed out.

"Uh-oh," he said. "This one's went to the bad."

A waiter rescued the bottle with an impassive face,

mopped up the wine. Poion took the bottle, sniffed it, then took a swig from the broken neck.

"An interesting drink," he said. "Effervescent, like the human mind. And worth a brief sonnet."

"What's the matter with you?" Roan snapped. "Offer the captain a drink."

Poion blushed and pushed the bottle along to Trishinist, who waved it away with a smile.

Roan picked up his melon and took a bite. "Good," he said around a mouthful of melon.

Trishinist's hand hovered over a spoon. Then he picked up his melon with delicate fingertips and nibbled its edge. "So glad you enjoy it," he said.

Waiters cleared away the last of the dishes and filled glasses with mysterious-smelling brandy. Sidis slapped his belly and belched.

"A great feed," he said.

Askor plied a fingernail on a back tooth. "First real Terry chow I ever had," he commented. "Unless you want to count—"

"Thank you, Captain." Roan cut him off hurriedly. "It was a good breakfast."

Trishinist offered dope sticks all around and lit up as the waiters cleared the last of the dishes.

"Now, about *Rage of Heaven*," Trishinist said. "You say you found her abandoned. May I ask how it happened that you were cruising in this area?"

"We heard there were inhabited worlds in this area," Roan said carefully. "My ship was blasted by a time mine and we were drifting when we spotted the cruiser."

"You knew this was ITN controlled space?"

"Yes." Roan was watching Trishinist's face carefully. He wished Poion could tell him what Trishinist was feeling. It would help.

"And you encountered the derelict—where?"

Roan repeated the coordinates of the imaginary rendezvous beyond fourth Centaurus.

Trishinist glanced around; the doors were closed now and the waiters gone. He leaned across the table and his languid expression was gone. So were thousands of years of culture. It was as though suddenly all the waves went out of his hair.

"You're early," he hissed. "Four months ahead of schedule."

Roan sat perfectly still, holding the interested smile in place.

"As it happens, we're ready here," Trishinist went on, licking his lips. "But I dislike Blan's imprecision. If we're going to be working together—"

"Hey, Chief," Sidis began.

"Hush," Poion murmured.

Trishinist squinted at the three crewmen and took out his pistol from its holster. "What about these?" he asked Roan.

"They do what I say," Roan said.

Poion smiled. "It is true," he said.

Trishinist frowned. "I had expected rather more . . . ah . . . representative individuals."

"They're as representative as I need them to be," Roan said.

"You have your identification?"

Roan reached inside his tunic, brought out an ITN identification disk on a chain, handed it across. Trishinist looked at it carefully.

"Endor," he murmured. "Blan's never mentioned your name to me, Captain."

"No doubt," Roan said.

"Blan is proposing no changes in the scheme at this date, I trust?" Trishinist said sharply. "I've fulfilled my part of the arrangement. I assume he's done as well."

"You see me here," Roan said.

"Where are his squadrons now?"

"They're in position," Roan improvised.

"Is he prepared to move at once?"

Roan frowned. "That depends on you," he said.

"On *me!*"

"Of course. We're early. You say you're ready, Captain. Just what do you mean by that? In detail."

Trishinist's jaw muscles were tensed up. "I told you, I've complied with our agreement in every respect."

"I can't work with you if you refuse to tell me anything. I want to know just *how* ready you are."

Trishinist relaxed his jaw muscles with a visible effort. "The organization among the rank and file is now over the eighty per cent figure. Sixty-four of the ninety-eight senior officers are aligned with us. Over ninety per cent of the junior corps. Our men control communications and three of the five major supply depots. . . ."

Roan listened, taking occasional sips from his glass. Askor and Sidis sat, mouths slightly open, listening. Poion was smiling behind his hand. But Roan didn't kick him because it took some practice before a stranger could tell Poion was smiling.

"The units on maneuvers are, of course, those including high concentrations of unreliables," Trishinist concluded. "The base garrison has been carefully selected over the past three years and can be counted on absolutely. Now, what of your group?"

"We're ready," Roan said.

"At full strength?"

"I have triple the number of volunteers I expected."

"Excellent!" Trishinist pursed his lips. "How soon can you be in jump-off position?"

"We're already *in* position."

"You mean . . . you mean that literally?" The captain moved uneasily in his chair.

"Absolutely."

"Certainly you don't mean—today . . . ?"

Roan put both hands palms down on the table. "Now," he said, because all this was having such an extraordinary effect on Trishinist.

Trishinist's face seemed to fall apart as a look of comprehension and shock came over it. Sweat popped out on his forehead and his eyes went to Sidis, who was polishing his teeth, and Askor, who was just sitting, and Poion, who all of a sudden began to look as though there was something important about him.

"Oh, I see now," Trishinist said. "I see why you brought *them*. I . . ." A sick expression passed over his eyes. "You really think it's necessary to go that far?"

"What's the alternative?" Roan asked steadily.

"You're right, of course. Still . . . he *is* Pure Strain."

Roan stood up. "We've spent enough time talking about it. I'd like to meet him now."

"Meet . . . ?" Trishinist looked almost wild for a moment. "Oh . . ." He relaxed. "Just to . . . ah . . . assess him, of course."

"Of course."

"Very well." Trishinist rose. "Things are moving a trifle rapidly for me. But you're right. There's no need to delay."

At the door he hesitated, glancing at Askor, Sidis, and Poion.

"Ah . . . which one . . . ?"

Sidis grinned his jagged grin; Trishinist shuddered and went on out into the hall.

18

Guards in bright-plated helmets snapped to attention as Captain Trishinist halted Roan and his men at a massive carved door.

"I'll introduce you as a new arrival from one of the Outer Towns," he said to Roan. "He likes to meet the new recruits. There are so few these days. The others will wait, of course."

Askor looked at Roan; Roan nodded. "Stay here," he said. "Don't wander off looking for liquor."

"Gee, Boss," Sidis said.

Trishinist opened the door; Roan followed him into an ivory-walled anteroom ornamented with a pale blue floral cornice. A harried-looking staff lieutenenat came in from the room beyond, exchanged quick words with the captain, then motioned them through the arched way.

The room was wide, silent, deep-carpeted in dusty blue, with light curtains filtering the yellow light from tall windows. There were deep chairs, cabinets and bookshelves of rich polished wood, and a vast desk behind which an ancient Man with snow-white hair sat, his gnarled hands gripping the arms of his massive chair.

"Good morning, Admiral Starbird," Trishinist said. "I've brought a caller. . . ."

* * *

Starbird waved Trishinist and the aide from the room, indicated a chair, sat studying Roan's face in silence.

"Have I not met you somewhere, once, young Man?" His voice was the rumble of subterranean waters.

"I don't think so, sir," Roan said. He was staring at the other's lined face. He had never seen an old Man before, and he was remembering Henry Dread and the expression, at once that of the hunter and the hunted, that Henry had worn and that the old Man had too.

"That fellow." Starbird jerked his head toward the door through which Trishinist had gone. "He a friend of yours?"

"I just met him today."

"Vicious little ferret," Starbird said. "He's up to something. Thinks I don't know. He has picked men all over my headquarters. But it doesn't matter. No guts. That's his trouble. Oh, yes, he'll plan; he'll talk. But there's no steel in the man." The admiral's eyes were on Roan's face, as though searching for a clue to something.

"From the Outer Towns, eh? What were your parents like?"

"I don't know, sir. I was raised by foster parents."

"And you want to fight the enemies of Imperial Terra."

"I've thought about it."

"If I were young again," Starbird said with sudden vigor. His fingers twitched on the chair arms. "I remember *my* first day. Ah, those were great times, young man! There was something in the air, a feeling of things to be done, goals to strive for. . . ." He sat, looking beyond Roan into the past.

"My father was on fleet duty then," he went on, talking to himself now, communing with the dead. "He commanded a five million tonner, gunned out of space by the Niss. Three hundred years ago that must be now. I was just a lad, then, on border duty in the north. I was to have been with him on his next sweep. He was a bold one; too bold. Who else would penetrate all the way to Sol? Nobody!" Starbird pounded his chair arm and looked at Roan. "Now look at the trash you see disgracing the uniform today! They're a cruel lot, young Man! And gutless. . . ."

Roan sat silently, waiting.

"Revenge," Starbird said. "I swore I'd have it! But no suicide run, by God! Plenty of smirks and snickers thrown my way. All talk, they said. Talk! But I wasn't jumping off half-ready. I needed the rank first. Then reorganization, weeding out the corruption, the twisted element that was choking the service like Venusian Tangle-weed! Measure a man's genes instead of his guts, that was their way! Damn his genes! It's the dream that makes a Man, not the number of his toes!"

Starbird fell silent, his face twitching with the pain of old memories.

"I had my star at last," he said suddenly. "I put my plan before the general staff. The plan I'd worked out over all those years. Five hundred ships of the line, a million picked Men. We were to move in two echelons, blast our way past the Niss picket lines beyond Pluto, strike with our full power all the way in past the Neptune and Jupiter orbits—then—when they massed to meet us—split! Our probes had given us plenty of information on the Niss defensive patterns! I analyzed their data and saw the answer: We'd split beyond Mars, break up into two hundred and fifty pairs, and carry a running fight right in past Luna—then regroup in a beautiful maneuver I'd worked out as carefully as a ballet—and hit the Niss blockade with a spearhead that could blast its way through the walls of Hell!" The old Man's eyes blazed with a fierce light; then he let out a long breath and leaned back. He raised his hands, let them fall.

"They laughed at me," he said flatly. "We weren't ready, they said. The Niss were too powerful, we didn't have the firepower to stand against them. Wait, they said. Wait!" He sighed. "That was almost two hundred years ago. We're still waiting. And four lights away, the Niss blockade of Terra still stands!"

Roan was sitting bolt upright. "Terra?" he said.

"Ah, the name still has magic for you, does it, lad?"

"Only four lights from here?"

Starbird nodded. "Sol's her sun; the third planet, the double world, Terra the Fair. Locked up behind a wall of Niss!" Starbird's fist slammed the desk. "I'll never live now to see my plan used! We waited too long; somehow, the fire that we carried died while we talked—and the dream died with it."

Roan sat forward in his chair. "Admiral, you said you weren't worried about Trishinist. What if he had outside help?"

Starbird's eyes narrowed. "What outside help?"

"A man named Blan."

"Blan? That warped imp out of Hades? Is he still alive?"

"His forces are due here in four months."

Starbird was sitting erect now, the force back in his voice. "How do you know this, lad?"

"Trishinist mistook me for Blan's emissary. He's ready to make his move now; today. He thinks one of my crew is assigned to assassinate you. I'm here now to size you up for the killer."

Starbird rose and walked across to the door. He was a tall, once-powerful Man with square, bony shoulders and lean hips. He flipped a lock, threw a wall switch that snicked locks on outer doors. He came back and sat behind the desk.

"All right, young fellow: Maybe you'd better tell me all you know about this plot."

"That's as much as I was able to get out of him," Roan said. "With half the men backing him, he's in a strong position, even without Blan's reinforcements."

Starbird stroked the side of his jaw thoughtfully. "That timetable suits me very well. Let Trishinist go ahead with his plans; when he discovers his allies are missing, he'll collapse."

"I can't stay much longer, sir." Roan got to his feet. "Trishinist will begin to suspect something. What do you want me to do?"

Admiral Starbird thumbed his chin. "When's the assassination scheduled?"

"Tonight, after the banquet."

"Make it late! I'll be ready; just follow my lead. In the meantime, arm yourself. How many men do you have with you that you can trust?"

"Three."

Starbird nodded. A smile was growing on his seamed face. His hand slammed the table. "Young fellow—what was your name again?"

"Roan. Roan Cornay."

Starbird was cackling. "Terra excites you, does it?" The old Man turned to a wall safe, punched keys with trembling fingers. The door swung open and he took out a sheaf of many-times-folded papers.

"My attack plan," he said. "The ships are ready— over four hundred of them, in concealed docks on the other side of the planet. I've kept them ready, hoping. I needed a leader, Mr. Cornay. Trishinist has supplied the men. Let him try his coup! Let him send his killer to me! Then, when he comes along a little later to see for himself, I'll be sitting here, laughing at him! And the orders will be waiting! I have a few loyal officers; they'll command the five squadrons of the flotilla. And you, lad! You'll take command as acting Admiral of the Fleet!"

"You'd trust me, Admiral? You don't even know me—"

"I've known many Men in my years, boy. I can judge a fighting Man when I see one. Will you do it?"

"That's what I came here for," Roan said softly. "That's what I've lived the last eleven years of my life for."

Roan's thugs clustered about him in the windy bronze-and-mosaic hallway outside the grand dining chamber. They were splendid in new clothes of bright-colored silky cloth spangled over with beads and ornaments of glass and polished copper, and they smelled incongruously of flowers.

"Keep your guns out of sight," Roan ordered. "Keep your hands off the females and don't kick the slaves; that's a privilege we'll leave to our hosts. No rough stuff unless *I* give the word, no matter what happens. And any man that drinks so much he can't shoot straight will deserve whatever he gets." He settled his palm-sized power gun against his stomach under the wide scarlet cummerbund that had been wound around him by his assigned slaves in the dust-covered splendor of his quarters.

"Let's go," he said and pushed through the high mother-of-pearl inlaid doors. The clang and thump of noisemakers burst out; dancing girls sprang into motion, whirled forward strewing flower petals. A thousand tiny colored lights gleamed from chandeliers and winked from tiny fountains that sparkled on long tables spread with dazzling white cloths almost hidden under gleaming plates, polished eating tools, slender glasses as fragile as first love. There were hundreds of Terrans seated at the tables, and they rose, clapping their hands. Commodore Quex came forward, his eyes, set at the extreme edges of his face, flicking over Roan and past him at his crew. He took Roan's arm and tugged him toward the nearest table. "You'll sit with me at the head table, of course . . ."

Roan held back without seeming to. "What about my men?"

"Oh, they'll be well taken care of." When Quex smiled, he kept his upper lip pulled down to cover his teeth, but Roan caught a glimpse of widely spaced points. A crowd of humanoid females with slender bodies and immense eyes and huge bare breasts were crowding around the men, taking their arms possessively, giggling up into surprised Gook faces that broke into vast, bristly, snaggle-toothed smiles.

"Belay that," Roan snapped. "You men will sit with me—or I'll sit with them," he amended, turning back to Quex. "I have to keep an eye on them," he explained.

"Ah, but, yes, as you wish, Lieutenant." Quex dithered for a moment, then signaled, and crouching slaves darted in, shuffled chairs and place settings about. Roan took the deep armchair Quex waved him to and looked around. Strange faces stared at him curiously.

"Where's the admiral?"

"He is unfortunately indisposed." Quex toed a slave aside and took the chair opposite Roan. "Chavigney '85 or Beel Vat?" he inquired brightly.

"Chavigney '85," Roan said, because he'd heard of it. "Indisposed how?"

"Admiral Starbird is getting on. He can't stand much . . . excitement." Quex showed his pointed teeth again and watched the slave pour ruby liquid into glasses. He picked his up and flicked a libation on the marble floor and nosed it. Roan drained his and thrust it out for a refill. No doubt the Chavigney '85 had a magnificent bouquet, but at the moment he didn't care.

Quex was staring at him; he remembered his smile when Roan looked at him. "I don't believe I've ever seen hair just like yours before," he said. "Quite . . . ah . . . striking."

"We all have our little peculiarities," Roan said shortly, and let his eyes rest on Quex's. They seemed to sit at the corners of his head and bulge.

"No offense," Quex said. "One sees a new face so seldom . . ."

"How many Terrans are there here at HQ?" Roan asked, glancing at the obvious Gooks along the table.

Something touched his shoulder and his hand went to his gun and then there was a choking cloud of perfume and a lithe, blue-trimmed girl was sitting on his lap. She had soft, round breasts with blue-dyed tips that poked through her beads, and she squirmed up against Roan's chest and nudged his wineglass against his lips. She looked a little like Stellaraire, and for an instant Roan felt a lost emotion clutch at him, but he took the glass and put it firmly on the table and palmed the female gently from him.

"Stand over there," he said sternly. "If I need anything, I'll call you."

The girl looked stricken, and then she looked at Quex and shrank back. The commodore slapped his hands sharply together, and the girl turned and was gone.

"I don't want her to get in any trouble," Roan started. "It was just—"

Quex hissed. The points of his teeth showed plainly now. "We do our best with our Gooks," he said. "But they are so abysmally stupid."

Slaves came with the food then. It was marvelous, and Roan forgot his problems for the moment, savoring the fabulous Terran cooking. The wine was good too, and Roan had to force himself to sip it carefully. Along the table, his men spooned in the delicacies, and then when they grew impatient with the small bites, used their hands. Their girls kept up a constant shrill giggling, slopping wine against big alien teeth, spilling it down across stubbled jaws. Beside Quex, Askor took a glass from his neighbor's girl's hand and poured the contents down his girl's throat. She choked and sputtered, and Askor caught Roan's eye and winked.

The noisemakers kept up their cacophony. Roan watched them, behind a screen of bushy potted plants, sawing and pumping and puffing at the gleaming, complicated noisemakers.

"You like music?" Quex asked, leaning across the table. There were purple, juicy stains at the corners of his mouth and his eyes bugged more than ever. He had loosened his collar, and Roan saw red scars down the sides of his neck where something had been surgically removed.

"I don't know," Roan said, because he had never heard the word before. "Is it something to eat?"

"The sounds," Quex said. He waved a hand at the orchestra, bleating and shrilling in the corner behind their screen of foliage.

"It's all right, I suppose," Roan said. "Back in the 'zoo, they were louder."

"You want it louder?"

"I remember a sound I heard once," Roan said, thinking quite suddenly of the deserted park in the Terran city on Aldo Cerise. "Real Terran sounds. Pretty sounds." He was feeling the wine, he realized. He took a deep breath and sat up straighter, and felt for his gun with his fingertips.

"Terry music?" Quex clapped his hands and a slave popped up and leaned close to get Quex's instructions, then slipped away. Roan glanced at his men. They were still chewing with their mouths open, reaching across each other's plates for juicy gobbets almost out of reach, wiping thick fingers on now-greasy silks. Henry Dread had picked his Gooks for size, not beauty, he was thinking, when he became aware of a sound penetrating the bellowed talk and laughter. It was an elfin horn, picking its way lightly above the uproar, and then it was joined by other sounds, deep and commanding, like the tramp of marching armies, and now the horns darted and flickered above like the lightnings of a coming storm while a bugle called demon troops to the attack. Roan pushed his glass aside, listening, searching for the source, and his eyes fell on the noisemakers behind the flower boxes.

"Are *they* doing that?"

"A clever group, eh, Lieutenant? Oh, they know any number of tricks; they can make a sound like a wounded dire-beast charging—"

"Shut up," Roan said, not even noticing he'd said it. "Listen . . ." Now a lonely horn picked out a forlorn melody of things beautiful and forgotten, and Roan remembered the glimpse he'd almost had, once, of how life must have been in the days of the Empire. The music faded to silence, and the players mopped at their faces with soiled handkerchiefs and reached for clay mugs. They looked tired and hot and ill tempered and frightened, all at once.

"How could a crew of ugly Geeks make sounds like that?" he wondered aloud.

"You like it?" Quex said coldly. He was fingering the braid on his sleeve rather pointedly.

"I'm sorry, Commodore," Roan said. "I was quite carried away."

Quex managed a sour smile. "It's some ancient thing about a Prince called Igor," he said. "Would you like to hear another? They do a rather clever thing called *Jivin' Granny*—"

"No." Roan shook his head to clear away the vision.

Quex chose an attenuated cheroot from a blue-and-orange inlaid box a cringing slave offered him. The slave lit it, and when the lighted match fell on the floor from the creature's trembling hand, Quex planted a solid kick in its side. It grunted and crawled over to Roan and he took a cigar and watched the slave crawl away. When it thought it was out of sight, it patted its injured side and wept silently.

"Now, Lieutenant . . ." Quex blew out smoke impatiently, as though he enjoyed knowing he was smoking a rare weed, but was annoyed with the actual process. "You've just reported in from a long cruise. You deserve to relax—"

"I don't want to relax," Roan said. "I'd like to know about the Niss. What kind of fleet can they put in space?"

"Surely all that can wait," Quex said blandly. He waved his glass and wine slopped on the floor and a slave scrambled to lick it up. There were other slaves under the table, eating scraps, and still more crowded in, offering finger bowls. Another girl had gotten into his lap somehow, and she was breathing erotica into his ear. Roan was aware that he was dizzier than he should be, and he pushed the slaves away and forced his eyes to focus.

"I've waited long enough," he said. He could feel the thickness of his tongue, and he worked on getting angry enough for his temper to boil the lethargy away.

A slave shoved a vast plate of foamy stuff in front of Roan. Quex was clapping his hands again and there was a stir, and two immense dull-faced troopers were hauling someone small and struggling into the open space at the center of the square of tables.

"Sorry if I seemed to have been dilatory in handling this matter," Quex was saying, "but I always think executions go better with dessert . . ."

Roan blinked while the two troopers held the girl down on a short bench with her head over one end. He recognized her as the one who had first gotten into his lap. Her gold-dusted hair was in disarray now, and her thin pantaloons stuck to her legs. One of the men holding her down got out a knife with a foot-long blade and casually thrust it into the side of her neck. She screamed once, and then she was slack, and the trooper was sawing away, holding the head by the hair. He got it free and held it up. There was blood on his hands to the elbow, and more was spreading out on the floor. Roan got to his feet, and his girl pulled him back, laughing.

"Clumsy oxes," Quex said. He picked up his cigar and drew on it, and then tossed it into the soup tureen.

"You'd think they were butchering swine. Try your ice cream. It's rather good, considering."

Roan's men were staring at the body of the girl. They were used to bloodshed, but they'd never seen anything like this. The executioners trooped off, one with the head and the other with the body, and a slave came with a bucket of water and a nauseous-looking rag. It was a female slave, and her row of teats dragged along the floor as she scrubbed.

"What—what—" Roan stuttered.

Quex raised his plucked eyebrows. "The creature annoyed you. That's something we Terrans don't tolerate in slaves . . ."

Roan got to his feet, and the girl on his lap squalled and slid off onto the floor.

"All right, men! Up!" he bawled. "The party's over! Let's march!"

In the sudden silence, Sidis laughed foolishly. The ITN personnel stirred at their places, glancing toward Quex. Roan went along the table to Sidis and slapped him so hard it hurt at the other end of the room. He jerked him to his feet and turned, and Quex was holding a long-barrelled nerve gun in his hand, aimed at Roan.

"Not so fast, Lieutenant—or whatever you are," the commodore said in a voice like chipped glass. "You made a poor choice of identities." The identity disk Roan had produced dangled from his finger. He tossed it to the floor. "Lieutenant Commander Endor was lost in action some six thousand years ago. You're under arrest for mutiny in Deep Space and the murder of Commander Henry Dread."

Roan looked along the table and caught Askor's yellow eye. The men were still in their places, waiting for the word. The garrison men were getting to their feet, gathering in clumps, watching. Some of them had guns out now.

Roan moved toward Quex and his gun, staggering a little more than was necessary.

"What do you want with me?" he said thickly.

"That's neither here nor there. Now, before we go any further, if you'll take off your jacket, please . . ."

Askor stirred, and Roan flickered an eyelid at him, and the half-breed settled back. Roan stripped off his braid-heavy jacket and tossed it on the floor. The Imperial Terran symbol over the pocket made a loud clink when it hit.

"To the skin, please," Quex insisted. Roan pulled off the silky white shirt, and the crowd staring at him drew in quick breaths. Quex got up and came around the end of the table, not bothering even to kick the crouching slave, and his eyes were round, taking in Roan's smooth, unscarred hide, the scattering of reddish hair across his chest.

"Your feet," he ordered. Roan pulled out a chair and sat down and pulled off his boots. The spurs clanked as he tossed them aside. Quex leaned close and stared.

"Unbelievable," he said. "You're a Terran. A *real* Terran. A textbook case." He looked into Roan's eyes with an expression almost of awe. "You might even be a Pure Strain . . ."

"Hurry up and shoot, if you're going to," Roan said. He picked up a glass and drained it. It would have been easy to toss it into Quex's face, but he wasn't ready for that yet.

"Where did you come from? Who were your parents?"

"My parents bought me as an embryo." Roan was watching Quex's face.

"Where?" Quex snapped.

"At the Thieves' Market on Tambool."

Quex raised a hand and brought it down in a meaningless gesture. "Of course. There is a certain fantastic inevitability to it! A Pure Terran, cast among Geeks; naturally, he would seek out his own—"

"What do you know about me?" Roan interrupted Quex's soliloquy.

Quex stepped back, signaled for a chair, sank down, watching Roan over the gun. He laughed shortly, a silly laugh. "I suppose I shall have to abandon the idea of shooting you. I'll make it up by planning something rather special for these animals of yours who've had the effrontery to plump themselves down at table with gentlefolk." And Quex tittered again, enjoying himself now. "In a way, I'm almost a sort of parent to you myself." He crossed his legs, swinging his foot.

"I was rather active in my younger days. The admiral honored me by dispatching me as his personal agent among the renegade pigs of the Gallian World. It was they who initiated the experiment. I took a chance—don't imagine I wasn't aware of the risks! I lifted the entire lot—the wealth of the Nine Gods, and you could hold it in your hand! The fools were careless, they practically invited me. And I made my error. Trusting Geeks! I was an idiot!"

Roan saw Quex's finger tighten on the firing stud, and he tensed, ready to jump, but the commodore drew a shuddery breath and calmed himself.

"I was fool enough to divulge the nature of the consignment to the stinking animal who called himself captain of the Gallian vessel on which I had arranged passage. It was necessary, actually; I demanded refrigeration facilities, and one explanation led to another—

"He tricked me. At the end of a tedious run, I discovered he had changed course for his own world. He landed and he turned me and my so carefully guarded prize over to his Shah. This heathen considered that it would be a tremendously impressive thing to parade a palace guard of Terrans—Pure Terrans, and all identical. Can you imagine it?" Quex held out his hand and a glass appeared in it, and was filled. He looked at Roan. "Am I boring you?"

Roan let out a breath. "Go on," he said.

"Alas," Quex continued. "At this crucial moment, a spontaneous popular uprising broke out. The Shah, his two hundred and thirty-four frightful little whelps, and anyone else who happened to be standing about were killed."

"Spontaneous?" Roan asked. He looked at the nearest slave, who crouched away, quivering.

"It was as spontaneous," Quex answered, smiling with his bright, cruel slits of eyes, "as the ITN could make it. My messages to Rim HQ had gone through before landing, of course; the forces arrived within a week to restore order. Of course, the natives were not so well domesticated then; they had a certain animal spirit which had to be curbed before they were made useful possessions. I was only one hundred and fifty-two at the time—some twenty-five years ago now, Terry reckoning—but I had a natural bent for such things." He waved a hand. "The rest is history."

"And how did I get to Tambool?" Roan cut in.

Quex frowned. "The discussion begins to tire me," he said. "You're a valuable though insolent property, and Admiral Starbird will be delighted when I report that I've recovered the breeding stock that slipped through our fingers all those years ago—"

"No, he won't," Roan said. "One of his spies has already slipped out by the side door to report on you—"

Quex jerked around to look where Roan had pointed and Roan's foot caught the gun, knocked it high in the air. With a bellow, Askor went into action in the same instant, and then Poion and Sidis were on their feet, reaching for the nearest ITN man. One aimed a gun at Askor and the giant half-breed dropped his first victim and charged for the man, knocked him spinning under the table, then whirled on a group of backpedaling dandies, cracked their heads together, tossed them aside, caught two more. Roan was holding Quex by the neck now, and drinking wine from the bottle with the other hand. The ITN men in the rear milled in loud confusion, unable to get a clear shot.

"You Gooks stand back, or we'll shoot!" A frightened-looking Navy man had climbed on a chair and was pointing a fancy power pistol wildly around the room. Sidis took aim, shot him in the head; he leaped back in a spatter of blood and fell among his fellows.

There were more shots now as the astonished hosts realized that their outnumbered victims intended to fight back. It was a mistake. Four pirate guns went into action, blasting wholesale into the screaming, panicked diners, who jammed into the corners and against the doors, making effective resistance by the few determined men among them impossible.

"Belay that!" Roan yelled over the din as a glass smashed beside him. He hauled Quex into a chair, shouted again. There were moans and howls from the wounded, bellowing from the enraged crew, the buzz and crackle of guns. Smoke poured up from smoldering hangings ignited by wild shots. There was a stink of blood and spilled wine in the air. Roan jumped on the table and shouted for order. By degrees the tumult abated.

"All right," Roan said. "They shot first and I don't blame you for getting annoyed, but I don't have any time to waste. I've got a few more questions to ask old rabbit-ears here." He stepped down from the table as the men began rifling the bodies and pulling fancy ornaments off the living. Quex stared at him with wide, shocked eyes.

"You can't—we outnumber you fifty to one—a hundred to one . . ." The commodore's voice rose. He started to his feet. "Attack them!" he screeched. Roan put a foot against his chest and slammed him back, then pulled a chair up and sat in it. There were two slaves mewling under the table; as they realized they were in view, they scuttled farther back. There was blood trickling down into Roan's right eye and around his face and onto his neck. It annoyed him, like an insect.

"Pardon this little interruption, Commodore," he said. "You had just come to the part where the ITN arrived to restore order. What did they do with the embryo—or should I say with 'me'?"

Quex babbled. Roan tossed a wine bottle to him, and it fell in his lap, bubbled down over his knees. He groped it up, drank, lowered the bottle with a sob.

"They . . . we . . . it wasn't there. It was gone . . . stolen . . ."

"It seems to have been remarkably hard property to hang on to. What made it so valuable?"

"A specimen of Pure Terran stock? Do you jest?"

"Sure—but there are some fairly pure Terries around, like Henry Dread. What made me different?"

"You *were* different. Oh, yes, different! You're Pure Strain; unbelievably pure strain—"

"All right. Who stole me?"

"One of my spies, the rotter! A creature I trusted!" Quex warmed to the memory. "He'd finished his work for me, and when I sent a couple of men with knives to advise him I had no more need of his services, he was nowhere to be found! He'd skipped out—and the special bejeweled incubator unit was gone with him! I searched—oh, how I searched! I tore the tongues from a hundred Men and five hundred Geeks, and then at last I got a hint—a word babbled by a former officer of the Shah's guard in his dying delirium: Tambool. I dispatched a crew at once—led by a sturdy Yill scoundrel. The best I could find among the rabble that follow the uniform of the Empire—but none of them ever returned. I heard tales, of how they were set upon by a horde of madmen—but the embryo was lost—"

"That horde of madmen was my dad, Raff Cornay," Roan said. "We'll drink to him." He raised his bottle and took a long swig.

"You're not drinking, Commodore," he said. "Drink!"

Quex took a halfhearted sip.

"Drink, damn you! Or do I have to pour it down your neck?"

Quex drank.

"Hey, this stuff is all junk, Cap'n!" Askor called, tramping over to where Roan sat with one foot on Quex's chair. He tossed a handful of brass jewelry on the table. "Let's load up on Terry wine and shove off. And, uh, a couple of the boys was asking, OK if we take along a few broads too?"

The wounded were making a dismal sound from the heaps where they lay. Sidis went over and started shooting the noisiest ones. The rest became quieter.

"You know better than that," Roan said. "You louts would be cutting each other's throats in a week."

"Yeah." Askor scratched an armpit with a blunt finger. "It figures."

"Round the boys up now. I'll be through in a minute." Askor turned away with a roar of commands. Quex trembled so violently his seat bounced in the chair.

"What are y-you g-going to do with m-me?"

"Have another drink," Roan commanded. He watched while his victim complied.

"I—I'll be sick," Quex slobbered.

Roan got to his feet. He pulled his shirt and jacket back on, jammed his feet into his boots. There was a dead officer lying behind his chair. Roan paused long enough to take a handsome sheath-knife with the ancient Imperial Eagle from the body, clip it to his own belt.

"Askor, Poion; lock all the doors," he ordered.

Quex came to his feet. He pulled at the edge of his tunic, swaying. His eyes were like blood-red clams.

"You can't leave me here with them! Not after this!" He looked past Roan at the bright, staring eyes in the pale faces of his men. "They'll tear me to pieces . . . for permitting myself to be tricked!"

Askor and the others were by the main door now. They looked to Roan.

"Go ahead, open her up!" Roan called. He looked back at Quex. "Thanks for the dinner, Commodore. It was a nice party, and I enjoyed it—"

"Lieutenant!" Quex's voice had found a hint of a ring suddenly. He straightened himself, holding onto a chair back. "I'm not . . . Pure Strain . . . like yourself . . . but I have Terran blood . . ." He wavered, thrust himself upright again. "As a fellow officer . . . of the Imperial Navy . . . I ask you . . . for an honorable death . . ."

Roan looked at him. He shifted his pistol to his left hand, squared off and saluted Quex with his right, and shot him through the heart.

19

Roan and his three men walked, guns in their hands, along the echoing corridor. No one challenged them.

"Why don't we pull out now, Chief?" Sidis demanded. "We can take our pick of the tubs on the ramp—"

"That isn't what I came for," Roan said. "I have unfinished business to take care of."

"Why bother knocking off any more of these Terries?" Askor queried. "Not much sport in it, if you ask me."

"I didn't!" Roan snapped. "Keep your mouth shut and your eyes open! We're not in the clear yet. Trishinist wasn't at the party—"

A thunderclap racketed along the corridor. Roan spun, went flat.

"Hold your fire!" he roared. Trishinist tittered, stepped out of the half-open door that had concealed him. There were at least a dozen more Men, emerging from the shelter of tattered drapes and chipped marble columns, peering down from a wrought-metal gallery, guns ready.

"I heard the, er, sounds of celebration," the Terran confided. "It seemed wise to have a chat with you before you, ah, continue with what you're about."

"We've already talked," Roan snapped. "Tell your Terries to put their guns away before my men get nervous and shoot them out of their hands."

"Umm. Your Gooks *do* look efficient. Still, I daresay one or two of my chaps would live long enough to dispatch the four of you. So perhaps we'd best call a truce."

Roan got to his feet. His men stood, facing outward in a tight circle.

"I have an appointment with Admiral Starbird," Roan said. "Or have you forgotten?"

"I remember," Trishinist said quickly. "You haven't, um, changed your plans?"

"Why should I?"

"I thought perhaps—after all the excitement of the banquet—"

"You knew about Quex's plans for the evening?"

"I suspected something of the sort might take place. After all, strangers. . . ."

"Thanks for letting me know."

"Well, if you couldn't handle that situation, what good are you to me, ummm?"

"We're going on now," Roan said.

"Just so," Trishinist agreed. "But leave the guns."

Roan looked at Trishinist; there were small bubbles at the corners of his mouth.

"All right," he said. "Put 'em down, men."

"What for, Boss?" Askor inquired cheerfully. "Sidis still has his knife. That's all he needs."

Trishinist shuddered. Roan tossed his gun aside. The others followed suit.

"Now what, Chief?" Sidis asked.

"Now we get on with the job." Roan turned on his heel and started toward the apartment of Admiral Starbird.

It was silent in the corridor. The guards on the admiral's door were gone. Roan stopped, faced Trishinist.

"Send your Men away," he said. "You can stay. Keep your gun, if you feel like it."

Trishinist lifted his lip to show his pearly teeth. "You're giving *me* orders?" he said in a wondering tone.

"You want them to see it?"

Trishinist started. "I see," he murmured. He turned,

gave crisp orders. All but four of the Men turned, formed up in a squad, marched away.

"They'll be waiting," Trishinist cooed. "Now—"

The door behind Roan clicked and swung in. Admiral Starbird stood in the opening, a gun in his hand—" 'Ten-*shun*," he commanded.

Trishinist's Men instinctively straightened and in the instant's pause, Askor, standing nearest them, swung and brought his hand down like an ax across the neck of one, caught his gun as it fell, swiveled on the next as he brought his gun around, and the two weapons fired as one. The guard spun, falling, his gun still firing, and a vivid scar raked the wall and door-jamb and caught Admiral Starbird full in the chest. The old man slammed back against the wall, fell slowly, sprawled full length in a growing stain of brilliant crimson.

Trishinist made a noise like repressed retching and stumbled back. Askor brought his gun around as the remaining two guards backed, white with shock but with guns leveled on Roan and his crew.

"You've killed him," Trishinist gasped. "The admiral is *dead!*"

"I can nail the pair of youse, easy," Askor grinned at the gunners. "Who's first?"

Roan knelt at Starbird's side, ignoring the confrontation of guns.

"Admiral . . ." He tried the pulse at the corded veins of the wrist, felt a faint flutter. "Get your doctors, Trishinist!"

"Yes . . . yes . . . Fetch Surgeon Splie, Linerman! Hurry!"

A Man turned and darted away.

Starbird's eyes opened. He stared at the Men holding guns aimed at Roan. "At ease," he said, and died.

"You killed the admiral," Roan said slowly, looking up at Trishinist.

"Not I," Trishinist gasped, backing. "It was an accident. I won't have that on my conscience—it was them!" He pointed at the two guards. "Blunderers!" he croaked. "You've killed a Man of the True Blood!"

"Not me, Captain. Strigator was the one!" The guards

looked shaken, still covering Roan and Poion while Askor covered them.

"Shall I kill them, Chief?" Askor inquired.

"Cover Trishinist." Askor's gun flicked to point at the small Man's chest. He licked his lips and eyed the gun on the floor.

"Don't try it," Askor rumbled.

"You have no chance," Trishinist said weakly, his eyes on the gun in Askor's hands. "Surrender and I'll deal leniently with you."

"Give us a ship," Roan said. "We'll go quietly."

"You with the gun," Trishinist addressed Askor. "Give up that weapon and you'll go free."

"What about the Cap'n and these two lunkheads?"

"*You'll* go free. Never mind about them."

Askor grinned, holding the gun steady.

"Very well, then. There's been enough bloodshed. You'll all go free."

"I'll keep the gun," Askor said. "But I won't use it unless I have to. How about that boat now?"

"Certainly." Trishinist licked his lips. "I'll give the orders. But only after you surrender the gun." Sweat was trickling down the small Man's face.

"What about it, Cap'n?"

"Do I have your word as a Man?" Roan asked. "A ship, and no pursuit—for all four of us?"

Trishinist nodded quickly. "Yes, of course, my word on it."

"All right, Askor," Roan said.

"Wait a minute, Boss—"

"Don't do it, Chief," Sidis barked. "Askor can get the both of 'em while they're shooting us! Then him and you can take fancy pants here fer a hostage—"

Roan shook his head. "Put the gun down."

Askor made a jabbing motion toward Trishinist, and the captain jumped back. Askor laughed and tossed the gun aside with a clatter. Roan faced Trishinist; the Man took out a handkerchief, mopped at his face.

"Very well," he said. He made a curt gesture to the two armed men. "Take these stupid pigs to D level."

With a bellow, Poion jumped, and the guard's gun

shrieked and spouted blue lightning, and Poion whirled and fell, smoke churning from a gaping, blackened wound in his chest. He groaned and rolled on his back, and charred ribs showed before the blood welled out to hide the sight.

"Askor! Sidis!" Roan snapped. "Stand fast! That's an order!"

Roan looked at Trishinist, smiling. "You surprise me, Captain," he said. "I didn't think even a traitor like you would disgrace his Manhood in front of a couple of crossbloods."

Trishinist tore his eyes from Roan's. "There's been enough killing. I'm ill with killing. Take them away—alive." He turned back to Roan. "I have every right to execute you—all of you—out of hand. I'm sparing your lives. Consider yourselves lucky. You'll be questioned, of course—later." He turned and stalked away.

"Poion," Roan called. "Are you . . . can you . . . ?"

"I have taken my death wound, Captain," Poion gasped. "How strange . . . that so many years of life . . . can end in such . . . a little moment . . . and the world go on . . . without me . . ."

"So long, Poion," Sidis said. "Take a pull at the Hellhorn for me."

"Nice try, old pal," Askor said hoarsely. "I think maybe you're the lucky one."

The Man who had gone for the doctor came up with a short fat Man in tow. He glanced at the admiral, shuddered, shook his head.

"What about him?" A guard pointed at Poion. The doctor pursed his lips at the wound. "No chance," he said and turned away.

"Surgeon—have you . . . no medicine to cure the pain of living . . ." Poion whispered.

"Hmmmph." The doctor opened a small case, took out a hypospray, pressed it briefly against Poion's laboring chest. A breath sighed out and then there was silence.

"Let's go," the guard said.

Askor reached up, gripped the chain that linked the

manacle on his left wrist to a ring set high in the concrete wall, pulled himself up high enough to see through the foot-square barred opening in the cell wall. He grunted and dropped back.

"Nothing, Cap'n. Some kind of tunnel, I guess. We're fifty feet underground anyways."

Sidis squatted at the end of his tether near the door, angling the blade of his polished machete through the bars to catch the faint light from along the corridor.

"They's a guard post about thirty yards along," he said. "One Terry with a side arm."

"You shoulda let us jump 'em, Cap'n," Askor said. "It woulda been better'n this crummy joint. It stinks." He wrinkled his wide nose to dramatize the odor.

"I can smell it," Roan said. "And as long as we're alive to smell things we still have a chance."

Sidis was eyeing the barred door. "Them bars don't look so tough," he said. "I bet I could bend 'em—if I could reach 'em."

"What do you figure'll happen, Chief?" Askor said.

"As soon as Trishinist recovers his stomach, he'll be along to find out who sent us and why."

Askor guffawed. "That'll be a laugh," he said. "He'll twist and slice us till he makes a mess a mudpig would puke at, but we won't tell him nothing. We can't. We don't know nothing! That'll gravel him."

"If we was to bend them bars," Sidis said, "one of us could slide out and get to the joker with the blaster. Then he could come back and burn them chains off."

"Wise up," Askor said. "You got to get the chain off the first one first."

Sidis hefted his machete. "They left me this," he said thoughtfully. "Them crazy Terries. I guess they're so used to guns they forgot a knife's a weapon too."

"So what? It won't cut chromalloy."

Sidis backed from the wall until the six foot chain attached to his wrist came taut.

"How much time you think we got, Cap'n?" he asked.

"They'll be along soon."

Sidis licked his lips. "Then I better get moving." He

brought the machete up and with one terrific stroke severed his left hand.

They stood in a dark room, amid a jumble of piping and tanks.

"Smells like a derelict's bilge," Askor snorted.

"Dead end," Sidis grunted. His stump was bound in rags torn from Askor's shirt and there was a tourniquet around his massive upper arm. His face looked pale and damp.

Roan went to the center of the room, studying the floor. "Maybe not," he said.

Askor came up. There was a three-foot metal disk set in the floor, with a ring near its edge.

Roan gripped the ring and lifted the lid, exposing a dark hole and the rungs of a corroded ladder. Water glistened at the bottom.

The voices outside were suddenly louder. Askor stepped to the door, looked out. "Oh-oh! They're right on our tail . . ."

"I hope they get here quick," Sidis said. "I don't want to miss nothing."

"Do you feel well enough to travel?"

Sidis nodded. "Never better, Chief." He took a step, staggered, then stood firm.

"Askor, you go first," Roan said quickly. "Sidis, you follow him."

"Too bad we had to burn the door; we could maybe have foxed 'em." Askor started down the ladder. "Come on, Sidis; shake it up."

"I'll stay here," he said. "They got to pass the door one at a time, and Gut-biter'll get all the action he wants."

"Down the hole," Roan snapped. "Fast!"

"Cap'n, I ain't—"

"That's an order!"

Sidis started down, awkwardly, one-handed.

"Hey, Chief, wonder where this thing leads to?" Askor's voice echoed from below.

Roan knelt at the manhole. "If you're lucky, it will take you out to a drainage ditch in the open."

Sidis turned his tattooed face up. "What's that mean, Boss? If *we're* lucky—"

"I'm covering you," Roan said. "I'll give you a ten-minute start and then follow—"

Sidis started back up. Roan put out a hand. "If you get clear, wait for me ten minutes. Maybe they'll miss the door—"

Below, Askor was shouting: "Hey, what's that? What's Cap'n saying?"

"Shut up and get moving," Roan snapped. "If you get through, come back and get me. With our cruiser you can blow this place wide open—"

"We ain't going without you, Cap'n. You know better'n—"

"They won't kill me," Roan said. "I'm Pure Strain, remember? They'd burn you two down on sight—"

"We come this far, we ain't—"

"Did you ever hear of discipline?" Roan said harshly. "This is our only chance. If I've tried to teach you anything, it's how to follow orders like Men instead of behaving like a bunch of Geeks!"

Sidis looked at Roan. "If that's what you want, Cap'n . . . But we'll come back. You stay alive, Cap'n."

"I'll stay alive. Get going!"

When they were gone, Roan slid the manhole cover back in place and turned to face the door.

Captain Trishinist lounged behind the wide desk in the office recently vacated by Admiral Starbird.

"Why?" he repeated sourly. "Seventy-two hours, holed up in a filthy sewage pumping room, without food, drink, or sleep, aiming a gun at the door. Why? You must have known you'd be taken in the end."

Roan blinked at the fog before him. His head ached and his throat was like dried husks.

"Was it just for that precious pair of animals?" The captain's eyes seemed to glitter as he stared at Roan. "What hold had they on you?"

"Did they get clear?" Roan asked. His voice was blurry with fatigue.

"You're a fool," Trishinist said. "But you'll talk to me

in time. There are methods for dealing with recalcitrants —effective methods."

"I'll bet they got through," Roan said. "Your kind couldn't stop them."

"Oh-hoh, you think to tempt me to angry disclosures!" The captain smirked. "How really quaint."

"You're so quaint you stink," Roan said. "But you can't touch me. You're afraid to. You'd gut your own grandmother and make bonfires out of children, but you can't kill a real Terry."

Trishinist glowered. "Don't press me too far, spy—"

Roan laughed aloud. "You're a poor half-breed with pretensions, Trishinist. You're pitiful. Even my poor Gooks got past you—"

Trishinist was on his feet, shaking with rage. "Your wretched creatures died in unspeakable agony an hour after you saw them last!"

"You're a liar," Roan said.

Trishinist spewed saliva and fury. "Dead!" he screeched. "I took them and stripped the hide from them alive—"

"Prove it. Show me the bodies."

"I'll show you nothing! Slave! Traitor! Spy! What need have I to prove—"

Roan laughed in his face. "Good for Askor. I knew he'd get through. I hope he stole one of your better ships."

"Take him away!" Trishinist screamed. "Put him in the Hole! Let him rot there!"

The Man holding the rope looped around Roan's neck jerked it, and Roan stumbled and almost fell.

"And when you're ready to tell me your heart's secrets, beg, and perhaps! Perhaps! I'll find time to listen!"

Trishinist was still fulminating as Roan was led along the corridor. The rope urged him roughly through a small door into a paved court, across it and out onto dry hard-packed dirt. The air was cold here, and the sparse stars of the Rim gleamed through mist. Roan stumbled on, determined not to fall and be dragged.

The tugging at the rope stopped at last, and a rough hand shook him.

"Don't go to sleep standing up, you. Grab the rope— unless you want to hang!"

He took the slack rope in his hands, looping it around his forearms, and a blow on the back sent him reeling forward—and then he was falling, and his arms felt as though they had been torn from their sockets as he brought up short. He felt himself descending, the taut rope trembling in his grip. Above, the circle of dark-glowing sky dwindled. Down, down—

He slammed the mucky bottom with a force that knocked him flat. There was a whistling, and the coils of rope fell down about him. Far above, someone called:

"Trishinist won't kill ye, maybe, bucko! But if you die on your own, that's yer privilege!"

At first, Roan was hungry all the time. He was so hungry he chewed on the rope, and so thirsty he licked at the water that dripped everlastingly along the muddy circumference of the pit. And he tried, again and again, to climb the slimy sides of the hole. He scraped hand and footholds with his fingers, even after his nails had broken off, and always the crevices he made oozed away. And once, when he'd gotten several feet up, someone flashed a light in to watch him, and laughed when he fell, and Roan lay where he'd fallen, listening as the laughter echoed down the hollow hole.

One evening the old man threw down bread and then something else, something alive and bristly that struck Roan on the arm and sprang away, and as it leaped across his hand, it bit him. It was hard to make out the shape of the thing in the dim twilight of the hole, but it had red eyes that glittered and it was bigger than Roan's foot.

Its frightened bite made a vicious, screaming kind of pain and Roan could feel the blood oozing from his hand. He found the bread and then sat in the dark, his back against the cold, wet mud of the wall that clotted in the tatters of his clothes, and ate. He no longer longed for a bath, just as he no longer felt hungry all the time. He watched the red eyes glitter in the dark, listened for the scrabble of its claws. It leaped at the walls again and again and fell back with a thud and a splash. Once in its panic it ran over Roan's lap and then leaped at the slime of the wall again.

Then, finally exhausted, it stopped, and crouched across the floor from Roan, panting horribly, loud as a man. The panting slowed, and Roan watched, his hand aching, thinking of ways to kill the thing—later, when he felt better. . . .

Roan awoke with a start. The rodent had crept to his foot, attempted to gnaw his ankle. He kicked out, cursing. The rat retreated a few feet, sat watching him, sensing his weakness.

Roan felt the gashed skin of his ankle, the slippery blood. The bite on his hand ached, a swelling, throbbing ache. He was dizzy and hot now and, wiping his forehead, Roan realized it was dry, feverish. He shut out from his mind every thought except the need to survive. He wasn't going to be eaten alive by a rat at the bottom of a dark hole. Somehow, he was going to escape, and get to Terra. And if it was impossible, he'd do it anyway.

"Ye still alive, boy?" came the voice, and Roan, startled, came out of his sleep. He saw the head silhouetted against the dark sky above.

"Yes, curse you. I'm still alive and so is the rat. Double the rations."

The old man laughed. "Got no orders to double the ration."

The bread struck one side of the hole, bounced to the other, and the rat ran out, went for the crumbs that the bouncing had dislodged.

Roan stood, shakily, pulled off his heavy metal-link belt, tied his trousers in a knot at the top. They were inches too wide for him now, and the blades of his hips jutted out like knives. His dizziness turned to nausea whenever he moved. His strength had gone out of his body and into the earth . . .

Roan held the belt by one end, walked toward the rat, then swung with all his strength. He caught the rodent as it turned to dart away, and it screamed a woman's scream, kicking in the mud, filling the already fetid air with its smell of fear. Roan felt his knees going. He fell, lay in the mud, listening to the death struggle. Roan was afraid to believe it even when he could feel the death in it, so he strangled it again with his hands.

And knowing his weakness and starvation were probably going to kill him, feeling half insane but knowing he must have nourishment, he skinned the rat with the sharp edge of his belt buckle and ate it.

It was three days and nights before the fever went away; Roan tried to rebuild his strength by pacing the circumference of the hole and swinging his arms, but he found it harder to exercise his mind, and sometimes all day would go by and it would seem like a minute, and other times a night would seem like centuries and the only time anything different happened was when it rained and the water rose knee-deep before it drained away. And time passed. . . .

Then, one evening the old man didn't come with the bread. And Roan could do nothing but wait, wait eternities. The stars came and went and then the stars again, and Roan, trapped for so long in the dark, slimy pit, wondered if indeed he had died and this was what death was—an aching and a waiting forever and all of the world a small hole and a circle of changing sky fifty feet above. Roan lay in one spot against the wall and ignored the pain in his stomach and tried to sleep, and perhaps dream of Stellaraire and of food. Stellaraire bringing him food, feeding him the delicacies of a hundred worlds washed down with ancient Terran wines, Stellaraire smiling . . . and fading. The food disappeared and Gom Bulj was yelling and Henry Dread was yelling and . . .

Someone *was* yelling up above, a head silhouetted against dark sky. Roan saw the rope dangling in front of him. Was it real? For a long time it didn't seem worth the trouble of reaching up to find out. He had waited so long . . .

But he did reach up, almost without hope that it was a real rope, real people calling him to loop the rope around his waist. But he complied, and the rope pulled, lifting him, and it hurt, and he gripped the rope, think-

ing he would never reach the top. Probably there was
no top.

Then hard hands were on him, lifting him up, and a
broad, ugly face was bending over him, and he saw the
glint of light on filed steel teeth.

"Gee, Boss," Sidis said. And Roan had the strange
thought that it must be raining, because there was
water running down the leathery face.

"You Gooks . . . took your time . . ." Roan said. And
then Askor was there, grinning a meat-eating grin, and
their faces were prettier than any faces Roan had ever
seen, and he smiled, and smiling, he let it all go and
whirled down into the bottomless soft night.

"Eat slowly," a testy voice said from somewhere;
Roan's eyes were almost shut against the bright light.
"And not too much."

Roan sipped a brothy soup, the bowl trembling in his
hands. After the soup the doctor poked him, shone
lights in his ears and mouth, and whistled. "I'm giving
you a walloping shot of Vitastim," he said. "You'll feel
human in about an hour. But don't overdo it. Unless, of
course, you want to," he added.

Askor and Sidis hustled him into a hard shower, gave
him a brush to scrub with. Then they let him sleep. By
the time Roan had on a uniform which almost fit his
bone-thin body, he'd come back to himself. The face
that looked back at him from the mirror was a stranger's. A gaunt, old-looking, deep-eyed stranger. And the
hair above his ears had silver streaks in it. But Roan
grinned at the reflection.

"We're alive," he said. And behind him, Askor and
Sidis smiled, too.

"Let's go, men," Roan said. "There's nothing more
here for us."

Aboard the stolen light cruiser *Hell's Whore* and after
an hour's run in space, Roan relaxed in the big padded
first officer's chair, studying the pattern of lights on the
screen.

"I'm glad you two showed up when you did," he said.

"But it was pretty stupid of the two of you to try it alone."

"We wasn't alone, Boss," Sidis corrected. "We had their best bucket here. Though we had to wait around out there on Four for three months to get a crack at her, but you know there wasn't much left of the old *Rage of Heaven*."

"Nice work, taking a cruiser with that hulk," Roan said. "Maybe you're learning after all."

"Nothing to it. They thought they was taking us."

"I wish I'd been there—instead of where I was."

"You didn't miss nothing." Sidis flashed his teeth and examined the tip of the steel toothpick with which he had been grooming them. "It was kind of pitiful, them bums pulling guns on us."

"And that's what they call the Imperial Terran Navy," Askor snickered. "Them nancies—"

"Those weren't real Terries," Roan said. "That was just some sort of ragtag gypsy outfit using the name. The real Terries are on Terra."

"I heard of it," Sidis said doubtfully. "But I thought— Hey, Captain, we ain't going *there*, are we?"

"Why shouldn't we go there?"

"I dunno. I figured maybe you was still working for the ITN, like Cap'n Dread—"

"I've seen enough of the ITN for now," Roan said shortly. He rose and picked up the folded garments of blue and silver polyon which he had replaced with the old familiar ship clothes, tossed them to Sidis.

"What'll I do with this stuff?" Sidis asked, holding the Terran uniform.

"Burn it," Roan said.

20

Sol was a brilliant jewel to starboard of *Hell's Whore* and now the tiny, faint points of light that were Sol's planets could be seen. Roan tried to pick out the one that might be Terra. But he couldn't be sure. It was a double planet, Starbird had said, but the faint companion, Luna, would be too dim to see at this distance.

There was the usual buzz of interstellar noise as he switched the receiver on, but nothing else. He took the microphone and began transmitting. "Imperial Terran Cruiser *Hell's Whore* calling Niss headquarters . . ."

"What makes you think they speak Standard, Boss?" Sidis asked nervously. He had been nervous ever since they sighted the great, silent Niss ship.

"They did five thousand years ago," Roan said.

"How long's it been since anyone tried to run the blockade?" Askor inquired.

"Three hundred years," Roan said. "They didn't make it."

"Swell," Sidis muttered.

"We ought to be in detector range now," Roan said calmly. He adjusted controls; a meteorite flashed around the repulsion field of the ship's hull. The image grew on the screens.

"She's a big baby," Sidis said.

"No bigger than the last one," Askor pointed out.

"Yeah—it was dead," Sidis conceded. "But what if this one ain't?"

"Then we'll get blasted into the Nine Hells. Why?"

"Just asking," Sidis said, and then they watched the screen in silence.

Up close, the Niss ship looked familiar, even to the characters scrawled across the dark curve of the hull; it was a twin to the dreadnought they had boarded after Henry Dread's death, so many years before—immense, ancient, dead. It took an hour with a cutting torch to force an opening. Dead air whistled, stilled. Inside, sealed in his atmosphere suit, Roan and his men walked along the narrow, empty, dim passageways, remembering the route, passing the little piles of dust and fish bones that had been Niss warriors.

In the control room there was an ancient, abandoned-looking uniform jacket hanging over the back of the pilot's chair—the first garment they had seen. Roan came closer to the control board.

"Terran!" an echoing voice said. "Stand where you are!"

Roan slipped his power pistol from its holster.

"Drop your weapon!" The voice was hollow, alien as not even a Geek's voice was alien, and filled with an inexpressible weariness.

Roan stopped breathing for a moment. Askor and Sidis stood behind him, silent.

"Never mind," the voice came again. "Keep your gun, Terran. I cannot keep this up; and I am dying, so there is no need to shoot me." The chair moved, swung around. In it was draped a creature that looked like a long, crushed polyon bag with something rotten in it. The part that moved, Roan decided, must be the mouth.

"My form shocks you," the voice said. "It is because my energy level is so low. But how did you come here? Where are my people?"

"I don't know," Roan made his voice sound. "You're the first Niss I've ever seen."

"I am over-great-one Thstt, Commander of Twelve Hordes; the alarm energized my far-traveler, and I came awake, here, in the stink of loneliness. I called, but none answers. Only you, Terran. . . ."

"I've waited years for this," Roan said. "I always thought it would be very satisfying to kill a Niss. But now I don't seem to care."

"Did the armies of Terra arise then and destroy us? I see our dreadnoughts, all in station, orbiting the enemy homeworld. But no one answers my signals . . . and when I tried to call my home planet, I got only . . . listen."

The Niss floated out a portion of his polyoid body, threw a switch. "Listen!"

Roan could hear nothing. But out of the receiver came a swirl of purple smoke. No. Not purple. Some inconceivable color. It writhed into the room and disappeared without dispersing.

Thstt screamed, and his scream turned finally into a smoke of the same color as that coming out of the receiver. The Niss's odd, formless body twisted and swelled, pulsating, and then shrank, slacker than before.

Roan stepped over, switched off the microphone. "I don't know what that means," he said in a shaken voice.

"It's the sound of desolation," Thstt said. "Don't you see? There is no one left but me. We had planned to seize your galaxy because our own was infected with a parasite that consumed Niss vital energies. But we have lost, and so we died—all but me, waiting here in alert stasis . . ."

"The Niss were never conquered," Roan said. "They just disappeared, as far as anyone knows. And the machinery has run down, over the eons."

"And so, I, too, die," said Thstt. "And with me the ancient and mighty dream that was the race of Niss. But do not shoot me or I will implode and you, too, will die. There is no need to watch me. It is not pleasant. We Niss are strong, and strong is our hold on that mystery we know as life. . . ."

But Roan did watch. The polyoid body first grew, expanding as high as the ceiling and half as wide as the room, exchanging an alien rush of terrifying colors within itself. Fascinated, Roan found himself hypnotized by the horror of the colors and by something else, as though the death agonies of this alien being were being breathed into his own nostrils, stuffed into his own ears, touching nerve endings . . .

Thstt began to shrink now, the colors becoming denser and slower and coagulating into painful scabs and Roan felt himself gasping painfully for breath and his mind reeled at the horror he felt—and then, suddenly, it was over. Roan let out his breath in a long sigh. He went to the crumpled polyon on the floor, and when he picked up the shrunken, pathetic thing, something clanked inside of it, like bones.

"Gee, Boss." Sidis spoke for the first time.

Askor wiped his face with a horny hand. "Let's get out of here, Chief."

Roan nodded silently and turned away, feeling a strange loneliness, as though a part of his life had died.

Even from a hundred miles up it was beautiful. At twenty miles the night side was misted with lights and the day side was a soft harmony of blue and green and russet. Roan could feel the leap of his heart, the shine in his eyes. Terra. Home. If only Henry Dread could have seen it like this.

Roan dropped deeper into atmosphere, and his men leaned close, scanning the scene on the high mag screen.

"Look, Boss," Sidis pointed. "They're coming up to meet us. Maybe we better arm a couple batteries."

Roan watched the atmosphere planes, flashing their wings in the sun, far below.

"They're coming to meet us, as you said," Roan pointed out. "Not to shoot at us."

A jet flyer barreled past, rolled like a playful fish, then shot away toward the west.

"Hey!" Askor was studying the charts and comparing them with the screens. "That there is Americanada. Only it's upside down."

Sidis keyed the communicator and called, for the

twentieth time. There was no answer. The jet was back, circling, then streaking away again.

"He wants us to follow," Roan said. He altered course, trailed the tiny ship. It led them over a dazzling blue and green coastline, across green hills, over a sprawling city, down to a wide paved field as white as beach sand. Roan lowered the ship carefully so as not to disturb the wide bands of colored plants massed beside the ramp. The ship grounded gently, and the rumble of the drive died.

Roan stood, feeling his mouth dry, his knees trembling slightly. It wasn't like fear; it was more like the feeling he'd had the first time he saw Stellaraire: wanting her, and afraid that somehow he'd do some small thing wrong, and lose her . . .

Askor was buckling on his guns.

"Leave 'em here," Roan said. "This is home. You don't need your gun at home."

"Us Gooks got no home, Cap'n," Sidis said. "But maybe we can pretend."

Roan took a deep breath. "Maybe we'll all have to pretend a little," he said.

They descended from the ship into a world flashing with sunlight. Beyond the flower beds were trees that fluttered silver when the wind blew, and the air smelled of a thousand perfumes. It was so familiar to Roan's dream that tears came to his eyes.

"Where's all the Terries?" Sidis wondered aloud.

Faint but pervasive, as though sounded by the motion of the air, came a gentle music.

"Come on." Roan led the way across the glass-white concrete, past Terran planes, blind and closed, past a row of empty, bright-colored buggies, used no doubt to convey passengers from the long-range planes to the building ahead where helicopters waited on the roof.

There was a wide, color-tiled walk between whispering, silver-leafed trees. Roan followed it and bumped into the door before he saw it. It was absolutely transparent glass, as was the wall. Only a faint line showed where the glass door joined the glass wall, and beyond it was a garden of thin-petaled flowers. Within he could see solid panels, walling off rooms, and more flowers and streams and fountains.

But no people.

Roan thought for a panicked moment of Aldo Cerise, of the beautiful, sad, dead city and the woman who was only a statue. But no. There were obviously people here. People? Could it be that the Niss had taken it over, that there were now only Niss?

He pushed at the door, but it didn't open and there wasn't a handle.

He heard running steps and through the trees came a child, a human child, and after the child a large white animal that Roan recognized as a dog, from the picture book he'd seen as a child.

"Paulikins! Paulikins!" called the dog, and then barked wildly, seeing them.

The child stopped before Roan, rocking a little after the run. He stared mercilessly, a beautiful pink and gold child with round blue eyes.

The dog ran up, panting, and cringed with his tail between his legs. "It's only a child, sirs," he said and trembled all over. "A youngling. I don't know how he got . . ."

"It isn't old Niss," the child said. "It's just a funny man. Look at his funny hands. See, Talbot?"

"Of course we're not Niss," Roan said, and patted the child on the head. "We're human, like you."

Talbot was sniffing the air, and edged closer, trying to sniff at Roan without seeming to. His eyes rolled to take in Sidis and Askor, standing silently by.

"Is it a mama or a daddy?" Paulikins asked. "It smells funny, doesn't it, Talbot?"

"There's been a mistake, sir," Talbot said. He had lost his fear and sat on his haunches, looking serious. He was a big woolly white dog, spotlessly clean, and Roan could imagine that Paulikins rode on his back and afterward curled up on the grass and rested his head on his furry stomach.

"I see," Roan said. "We landed in a spaceship and naturally everyone would think we were Niss."

"If you could wait here a moment, sir, I'll inform the

Culture Authorities. You see, they're fetching a Niss scholar; they didn't want anyone else to greet you."

"We'll wait," said Roan.

A helicopter hesitated and lighted easily as a fly on the roof. Askor and Sidis got up from where they had been sitting under a tree, smelling flowers they had picked. Roan was pacing under the trees, practicing Terran in his mind. The dog's accent had been smoother, much more precise than his own. Many of the words Roan had had to strain or guess at. Also, there was a rising inflection that Roan's language lacked.

The woolly dog was back and made a deferential noise in the back of his throat. "If you would come this way, sir, so that you can be properly received."

Roan turned to follow the dog and Askor and Sidis fell in beside him. He waved them back.

"You two wait here," he said. "I'll handle this."

"How come, Chief?" Askor frowned. "Up to now we always stuck together."

"I don't need a bodyguard here," Roan said. "And I don't want the sight of you two to scare anybody. Just stand by."

The glass door opened silently at a touch. Roan followed the dog into a paneled-off room which looked as transparent from the inside as the glass door had looked from the outside. The room was planted with a lush, green lawn that sprang softly under his feet. A breeze blew through the room, though there were no openings in the one-way glass.

A door slid open soundlessly across the spacious room, and a handsome young woman—no, a handsome young Man with bright brown hair that curled around his head like a cap stepped through and smiled. A dog followed, silent and watchful.

"I am Daryl Raim, the Niss expert," the Man said; his voice was low and controlled, as though he tuned each phrase before he spoke it. Roan felt his face looking angry.

"I'm no Niss," he said in a voice that sounded harsher than he intended. "I'm a Man."

"Of course; I see you are not Old Niss."

When Daryl smiled, a dimple broke in the smooth, white skin of his left cheek. Roan found himself for the first time feeling a mixture of embarrassing emotions and to his horror, he blushed. There was something feminine and appealing about the dimple, and the smooth white skin glowed as though it wanted to be touched.

Daryl sat down gracefully, motioned Roan to a chair entwined with trumpet vines.

"I . . ." Roan didn't know how to begin. How to explain who he was. "I am a Terran," he said finally.

Daryl nodded, smiling encouragingly. Roan felt foolish. Always before, "I am a Terran," had been an impressive thing to say.

"Of course," Daryl said. "I assume you have some important message from Old Niss?"

Roan's mouth opened and closed. His face hardened. "No," he snapped. "I'm a Terran, coming home. The Niss are dead."

"Oh?" Daryl's voice was uncertain. "Dead? I'm sure this news will interest many people. But if you're not from Old Niss . . . ?"

"I was born on Tambool, out in the Eastern Arm," Roan said. "Out there Terra is a legend. I came here to see if it was real."

Daryl smiled apologetically. "Geography was never a hobby of mine . . ."

"Tambool is another world. It's half a lifetime away. Its sun is so far away you can't even see it in the sky from here."

Daryl smiled uneasily. "You've come from Beyond? You've really . . . returned from the dead?"

"Who said anything about being dead . . . ?"

"I can't believe it." Daryl seemed to be talking to himself now. "But you *do* look—and your ship is like—and—and I've seen your face before—somewhere!" He finished up with his voice almost on a note of fright. Roan thought he shuddered—but the smile never left Daryl's face. He held out his arm. "Look. Goosebumps!"

Roan got to his feet. The chair was too comfortable, the conversation too unreal. He looked around at the perfect lawn, the perfect invisibility of the walls, the perfumed and curled Man.

"Don't you realize what this means? The Niss blockade is over. Terra's an open world again!"

Daryl took out a thin golden cylinder, drew on it, blew out pink smoke through delicate nostrils. He rearranged his body with a subtle excitement.

"I haven't felt such a thrill in years," he said. "I half believe you really did come back from Beyond." He stood, a smooth, flowing motion. "I want you to come with me, talk to me. I promise you such a night as you've never experienced on either side of the grave. My equipage is waiting. Come along to my place . . ." He put a slender hand on Roan's arm. Roan knocked it away.

"Just tell me where to find your military leaders," he said harshly. He pushed past Daryl, who shrank back, his painted eyes wide. Roan groped, looking for the door. He slammed against the invisible wall, cursed, felt his way along it, banged his knee at an invisible corner. He whirled on Daryl.

"Get me out of here!" he roared. "Where in the Nine Hells are the people who ought to be out here to hear what I have to tell them!"

Daryl huddled against his chair; Roan stared at him, feeling the anger drain away as suddenly as it had come.

"Listen—Daryl," he said, forcing his voice low. "I grew up among aliens, fought my way through aliens to come here. I've gotten what I've had out of life by force, by guile, by killing. Those are my methods—the way to survive on the worlds out there." Roan rammed spread fingers at the sky, accusing the worlds, accounting for himself. "I'm sorry if I hurt you," he finished.

Daryl smiled through glistening tears. He rose, all assurance again, touched his hair.

"You're quite wonderful," he said. "And of course you'll want to meet—oh, ever so many fascinating people."

"The place looks deserted," Roan said. "Where is everybody?"

"They're a little shy—you understand. We weren't just sure about Old Niss."

"You didn't seem to be afraid of me—at first," Roan said bluntly.

"Afraid? Oh, I see what you mean. No, of course I wasn't afraid. The restrainers are focused on you, of course."

"What's a restrainer?" Roan said in a tight voice.

Daryl giggled. "They're trained on your two—associates—too," he said. "Shall I give you a demonstration of what it does to them?"

"No!" Roan looked out across the flower beds beyond the glass. Askor and Sidis were standing together, squinting up at the strange blue sky of Terra.

"We need a place to stay," he said. He was looking around the room now, trying to pick out something that looked like a restrainer.

"Oh, you'll find many charming compositions to choose from," Daryl said. "But why don't you accept my invitation? It would be such a coup to have you all to myself this first evening."

"What about my friends?" Roan demanded.

Daryl arched his neck gracefully to look at them. "Such strange-looking, er, persons," he said. "If you don't mind my saying so."

"Why should I mind?" Roan snapped. "It's true enough, I guess. But there are a lot stranger, out there." He waved at the sky.

"They'll be quartered wherever you choose," Daryl said stiffly. "So long as you're sure they're not . . . Lowers . . ."

Roan rounded on him. "No, damn you! They're my friends!" And he hated the reluctance he felt in claiming them.

Daryl frowned. "Your manner is somewhat abrupt," he said stiffly.

"Too bad about my manners," Roan snapped.

"But I suppose you forget such things, Beyond." Daryl dimpled forgivingly, and led the way out through panels that opened before he touched them to the accompaniment of musical tones that shimmered in the air like soap bubbles. Outside, Roan beckoned Askor and Sidis over.

"This is Daryl," he said. "He's fixing us up with a place to stay—"

"Boss, did you say *he* . . . ?" Sidis grinned.

But Roan was staring at the heavy-maned, two-legged animals that pulled the open chariot. The chariot itself was a work of art—a composition of airy, fluted columns that supported a latticed roof. The columns were gold and the latticed roof seemed to be of glass or a plastic and changed color constantly, always glittering. The chariot had large wheels of gold, spoked with the same glittering lattice-work, whose convolutions suggested the forms of half-remembered dreams. And Roan would have stood puzzling over the lattice, except that his eyes kept going back to the heavy-maned draft animals . . .

"They're Men!" he cried suddenly, watching the dog adjusting their harness neatly. "Terrans, pulling your chariot!"

"Only Lowers," said Daryl. "You wouldn't have dogs do it? My charioteers are very well treated. Come, give them a sweet and see how happy they are." He smiled benignly, went over and took something from the pouch at his waist.

Roan watched, feeling something in his heart rip. Terrans! The magic that word had been, all across the universe. Askor and Sidis gaped, mouths open.

Daryl handed a square, white bit of food to one of the hairy Terrans. "Here, Lenny. Good boy."

Lenny took the candy and popped it into his mouth, then grinned happily. "Good master!" He almost jerked the chariot over as he got down to kiss Daryl's sandaled foot.

"Now, now, Lenny," Daryl reproved softly. "Such a good boy," he said, turning to Roan. "Would you like to give the other candy to Benny?"

"No, damn you!" Roan roared. "I'd . . ." and then stopped in shock when Benny—the other draft-human— burst into tears.

Daryl started to say something to Roan, sighed, and gave Benny the candy himself. "Roan is not familiar with our customs," he told Benny, patting him on the shoulder. "Good Benny. We all love Benny. Benny is pretty. Roan, *could* you tell Benny he's pretty?"

Roan bit his lip. Benny looked at him in agony, holding the sweet and too upset to eat it. Benny had wide, innocent eyes that went oddly with his square beard and intricately plaited mane.

"Benny is pretty," Roan choked out. Lenny was watching, looking confused and frightened.

"The slaves of Alpha Two at least hated being slaves," Roan said. "And they weren't even human."

"Hmmm," Daryl mused. "You feel that because Benny and Lenny have the same basic form as you that they should be in all ways the same as you? Whereas if they were a different shape . . . ?"

"I don't know," Roan cut him off. He avoided the eyes of Askor and Sidis. "Come on, load up," he snapped.

"In this play-pretty?" Sidis growled.

"Unless you want to walk!"

"Yeah," Askor said. "We'll walk."

"I guess we can walk as fast as Benny," Sidis said.

"And Lenny," Askor added.

"Then walk."

The car moved off.

"You'll need a dog, of course; I'll see to it as soon as I have you situated. You'll have time for a bath and a nap." Daryl gaily flicked the flower-decked reins over the broad tan backs. "And then—but you'll see for yourself—tonight!"

21

Roan awoke in utter darkness, and his sleep had been
so deep that it was still heavy on him, like a weight of
blankets. For a moment he strained his ears for noise,
hearing only silence that crowded his own heartbeat
into his ears. Then he remembered; he was on Terra, in
a room like a garden with flowers, high in a glassy
tower. In the darkness, a breeze was blowing from
somewhere and it smelled like a drowsy afternoon.

Then suddenly the darkness lightened and Roan looked
up to see a large, short-haired brown dog, which nodded politely.

"Good evening, Master. I am Sostelle. I am to be
your dog—if you approve, sir?"

Roan grunted, sat up. "My dog," he said. He had
never owned a living creature before.

"I'm sorry to have disturbed you, Master—but Master Daryl was emphatic about the party—"

"That's all right. I'm hungry. Can you get me something to eat?"

Sostelle moved gracefully on his overlong hind legs,
trotted to the wall, pushed a button, and a tray of hot,
glazed fruit came out. He pulled the legs down on the

tray and rolled it over to Roan, pulling up a chair for Roan to sit on. He had hands like a Man's.

"Is this all there is?" Roan asked.

"It's usual," Sostelle said. "But I'll get you something else, if you wish."

"How about meat and eggs?"

"Dog food?" Sostelle looked as though he didn't know whether to frown or laugh.

"I can't live on candy," Roan said.

"I'll do my best, Master," Sostelle said. "Cutlets in Sun Wine and pheasant eggs Metropole?"

"OK," Roan said. "Anything."

"And shall I prepare a bath, Master?"

"I had one yesterday," Roan snapped.

"Still—it's customary . . ."

"All right." Roan looked at the dog. "I'm pretty ignorant, Sostelle. Thanks for trying to help me."

Sostelle's tongue came out in a canine smile. "I am sure that you will be a great master. I sense it. If you'll forgive a dog's foolish fancy, sir."

"Keep me from looking like an idiot in front of these pretty creatures and I'll forgive you anything."

The fete was held in a vast, silver-and-glass walled space where fragile columns as slender as reeds ran up to arch out and meet in a glitter of jeweled-glass panels high overhead. The floor was a polished expanse of pale violet glass, and the music was as stirring and as lovely as a flight of swans, as martial as the roar of lions, as gay as a carnival.

To Roan's left and behind him, Sostelle stood in his stiff formal jacket, quite graceful on his hind legs, and whispered, "Hold your glass by the loop with one finger, Master, not with your whole hand."

Roan nodded, feeling awkward and almost naked, for Sostelle had depilated his face and dressed him in a silky, green and gold garment that folded and tied together and felt as though it might fall off if you moved too quickly in it. The guests carefully avoided staring at him and Sostelle pointed them out as they whirled past, their dance a dainty posturing in which neither partner touched even the fingertips of the other; Roan watched, overwhelmed by the blaze of light, of color, of movement across the vast expanse of multitiered transparent floor that made the throng of fancifully gowned men and women appear to be floating in the air. He finished the drink and another was there at once. Daryl appeared, transformed in a pink garment, silver-dyed hair, and feathery wings attached to his ankles.

"Roan—how marvelous you look . . ." He glanced at Sostelle.

"And Sostelle—an excellent son of a bitch. But didn't he offer you a choice of hair tints and scents? And what about decorative touches—"

"He offered them," Roan cut in. "I didn't want them. Look, Daryl; I can't afford to waste any more time. When will I meet your governmental leaders, your military men?"

A small crowd was gathering in Daryl's wake, watching Roan curiously. Someone tittered and discreetly stopped.

"Waste time?" Daryl's nose got a pinched look.

"I seem to have offended everybody again," Roan said in the silence. "Didn't you warn them I'd forgotten my manners?"

A nervous laugh went through the group.

"Is that what it means to you?" he almost shouted. "Manners? Don't you care that Terra's a free world again—that the Galaxy is open to you?"

Daryl put a hand on his arm. "No one here is much on mythology, Roan. They—"

"Mythology, hell! I'm talking about a thousand worlds—a million of them—and once Terra ruled them all!"

A ripple of applause broke out.

Daryl joined in. "Charming," he said. "So spontaneous." He flicked his eyes at the others. "Roan's going to be wonderful," he said.

A girl was looking at Roan. If she had been done by a bad artist in brass, she would have looked like Stellaraire. She was the statue in the garden on Aldo Cerise, but her body was warm human flesh instead of cold stone, and her mouth by its very existence begged to be kissed. She had smiled when the others laughed. Her lips barely curved but her green eyes seemed to tilt up at the corners.

"I'm Desiranne," she said. "I don't understand what you've said—but it's exciting."

"Desiranne will entertain tonight," Daryl said. "It will be the high point of the evening." His eyes moved over her like a lecherous hand.

"Look," Roan said to the girl. "It's nice about the party and you're so beautiful a man almost can't endure it, but someone's got to listen to me. This is the biggest thing that's happened to Terra in five thousand years—but before long the ITN is going to realize the blockade is over. There's a fellow named Trishinist who'd give his hair to be the one to lead an invading force in here. They think of Terra as one big treasure house, ripe for looting—the richest prize of all."

Daryl laughed with a mouthful of smoke and ended up choking. Sostelle came immediately with a glass of water and a scented, gossamer tissue. People were turning away, already looking bored.

Daryl smiled knowingly, took out a cigarette. "I wouldn't," he said. "Not so soon. I'm sure you'll become a great favorite, but if you try to push yourself forward right away, people will resent it."

Roan growled and Daryl jumped. "Really," he said almost sharply. "You'll have to learn a few of the graces. And I'd also suggest you let your fingernails grow out a bit more gracefully and a few things like that which Sostelle will advise you about." He rose in a smooth ballet-like movement.

"And now, I think Desiranne and I—"

"She'll dance with me," Roan said roughly. He finished his wine with a gulp, tossed the glass aside, walked past Daryl to the girl's side. She looked around, wide-eyed, as Roan took her in his arms. She was as light as a handful of moonbeams, Roan found himself thinking, suddenly struck dumb by her fragile loveliness.

But there was no need for talk. He was suddenly aware of the music, swelling louder now. There was a deep, booming throb that matched the cadence of the human heart, and a dazzling interplay of horns that repeated the rhythms of the human nervous system, and an intricate melody that echoed forgotten human dreams. Stellaraire had taught Roan how to dance, long ago; he had not forgotten. All around, the Terrans had drawn back, and now they stood, watching, as Roan responded with a lifetime's pent-up emotion to the call of the music and the girl and the strong wine of Terra.

And then the music ended on a fading susurration of cymbals and the high wail of brass. Roan swept Desiranne almost to the floor, and for a moment he held her there, looking into her perfect, half-frightened, half-enraptured face.

"I think I know now why I came here," he said. "I think I knew I'd find you. Now I don't think I'll ever let you go."

There were sudden tears in her eyes as Roan set her on her feet. "Roan," she whispered. "Why . . . why didn't you come sooner . . ." Then she turned and fled.

Suddenly, there was deafening applause. Shouts of bravo! and splendid! rang out. Everyone seemed to be staring at him with eyes that were bright with . . . fear? They came toward him almost cautiously, as though approaching a tame beast, led by a small, lithe brunette with long hair done into such a complex system of plaits and curls that her head looked too heavy for her small body. She had a sinuous, elongated walk, and her dress was the color of . . . of air with sunshine in it.

"Mistress Alouicia," Sostelle whispered to Roan, "a dancer, and a very clever woman."

"Marvelous," she said. "Such a spectacle of primitive savagery! For a moment I thought you were going to . . . to lose control and kill her, tear her throat out with those great strong teeth." She shuddered, showing Roan a smile that was just a little long in the tooth.

"I'd never understood ancient music before," a Man said. "Now I think I do. . . ."

"The way he sprang at her," someone else offered. "And then putting his hands on her that way. It *was* intended to represent a tiger seizing his prey, wasn't it?"

"No, it was just a dance," Roan said; and turned to Sostelle and asked in a loud voice, "It's all right, isn't it, to say what you mean instead of making people guess?"

Sostelle, knowing this wasn't to be answered, kept a discreet silence and straightened the folds in Roan's chiton.

"Does everyone dance in that way in your homeland?" Alouicia asked, smiling a bit stiffly now.

"On every world there are different dances. Once I was with a circus and my girl did erotic dances in several different cultures."

"Erotic? How interesting . . ."

Roan was glad to have found a subject of interest. He was feeling the wine, wanting to put everyone at ease, and then go find Desiranne.

"It frequently led to public copulation," he added.

"To . . . to . . . what *did* you say?" Alouicia's eyes widened.

"What does it mean?" a high voice whispered loudly. Someone tittered. "Like dogs. Imagine!"

"Really! What sort of . . . animal . . . would perform such a dance?"

"She was beautiful," Roan said, remembering Stellaraire, and feeling that something should be said out of loyalty. "I loved her."

"He's not merely a savage," a voice said loudly behind him. "I do believe he's a Lower."

Roan turned. A tall, wide-shouldered Terran stood looking at him with an expression of distaste. He was deep-chested, well-muscled.

"Master Hugh, the famous athlete," Sostelle murmured.

"Hugh!" Alouicia said, her voice carrying the faintest edge of shrillness. "What an exciting confrontation: The strongest man on Terra, with your interest in the ancient athletic arts—and this . . . elemental man from—wherever he's from!"

"Please," Daryl said, putting a hand on Roan's arm. "I think—"

"Never mind," Roan said. "I'm not very good at remembering all the things that are too ugly for you pretty people to talk about. I'm a Man; I sweat and bleed and eat and excrete—"

"Roan!" Daryl said. Alouicia drew away with a small cry. Sostelle gasped.

"Go away," Hugh said. "I don't know who brought you here. You're not fit for the society of civilized people—"

"There's nothing civilized about the ITN," Roan said. "What would you do if *they* showed up? If they came storming across those pretty gardens and in through the pretty door; what would you do?"

"I'm sure that thirty thousand years of culture have prepared us to deal with whatever a barbarian might do," Daryl said uneasily.

Roan doubled a fist and held it before him. "Do you know what this is?"

Hugh eyed the doubled knuckles. His nose wrinkled. "Of course; the dawn-men—Romans, I think they were called—had a primitive sport in which they flailed one another with their hands held in that way. This was done in a coliseum called Madison Square Garden, and the winner was awarded a fig leaf, or something of the sort—"

Roan drew back his fist and hit Hugh square on the nose, taking care not to put too much power back of the blow. Hugh went down, blood streaming down across his lip and into his mouth. He cried out, dabbed at his face, stared at the crimsoned fingers. There were little shrieks all around.

"You—you *brute!*" Hugh said.

"All right," Roan heard himself shouting. "What do you do, with your thirty thousand years of culture?"

Hugh came to his feet; all round, people stared, eyes bright, lips parted. Roan stepped to Hugh and hit him solidly on the side of the jaw. Hugh fell down again, his mouth open and a look of utter amazement on his face.

"You're supposed to be an athlete," Roan said. "Get up and fight back."

Hugh got to his feet; he folded his fingers over his palms and held them in front of him; then he stepped up to Roan and struck out with an overhand blow; Roan casually brushed Hugh's arm aside and hit him in the stomach; as Hugh doubled over, Roan planted a left and right to the face. Hugh sprawled on the floor and began to cry.

Roan reached, caught his garment by the shoulder, hauled him half erect, slapped him across the cheek.

"It may surprise you," he said. "But members of an attacking army don't stop when you cry. They just laugh at you. And they don't fight nicely, like I do; if you're on the floor"—he let Hugh drop—"they kick you—like this." And he planted a solid blow in Hugh's ribs with his toe. Hugh scrambled back, tears streaming down his face; he was sobbing loudly.

"Get up!" Roan said. "Get mad! That's the only thing that will stop me!" He followed Hugh, dragged him to his feet, hit him in the eye, then, holding him up, punched him in the mouth. Hugh's face was a bloody mask now.

"Fight!" Roan said. "Hit back!"

Hugh broke away, stumbled back against the watching crowd. They thrust him back toward Roan. He saw their faces then, for the first time. They were like hungry Charons, waiting for an old gracyl to die.

"Kill him, savage!" a man called; saliva ran out of his mouth and down into his perfumed, pale blue beard. Alouicia held out her hands, the gold-enameled nails like raking claws. "Bite his throat!" she shrilled. "Drink his blood!"

Roan dropped his hands, feeling a thrill of horror. Hugh broke through the ring and ran, sobbing.

"Master," Sostelle said. "Oh, Master . . ."

"Let's go," Roan said. "Where's my crew?" He staggered, feeling the room tilt under his feet. Terran wine was made for Terran nervous systems; it hit hard.

"Master—I don't know. I heard—but—"

"Find them!" Roan shouted. People scattered before him. He was out in the wide entry hall now. The polished black floor threw back reflections of chandeliers and of the stars above the glass-domed ceiling. Sostelle hurried ahead, bounding on all fours. Two tall, wide shapes stepped from the shadow of a slender supporting rib ahead, stood silhouetted against the sweep of glass front.

"Askor," Roan called. "Sidis!"

"Yeah, Boss." They came toward him. They were dressed in their soiled ship clothes. Sidis wore a pistol openly at his hip.

"Thought I said . . . no guns," Roan said blurrily.

"I had a hunch you might change your mind," Sidis said; his teeth gleamed in the gloom.

"You did, eh?" Roan felt an unreasoning anger rising in him. It was almost like joy. "Since when did you start doing my thinking for me?" He took a step, swung what should have been a smashing blow to the Minid's head, but he missed, almost fell. Sidis hadn't moved.

"Gee, Chief," Askor said admiringly. "You're drunk!"

"I'm not drunk, damn you!" Roan planted his feet, breathing hard. "And what are you doing here in those rags? Why haven't you washed your ugly faces? I can smell you from three yards away. . . !" He could feel his tongue slurring over the words, and this made him angrier than ever. "You trying . . . 'scrace me?" he roared. "Get out of here and don't come back . . . 'til you look like human beings!"

"That could be quite a while, Chief," Askor said. "Look, Cap'n, let's blow out of this place. It's creepy. And I can hardly keep my hands off these Terries of yours—"

"They're not mine," Roan yelled. "And I'll say when we leave—"

"He's right, Boss," Sidis cut in. "This world ain't good for us. Let's shove off, Cap'n. Just the three of us, like before—"

"I'm captain of this bloody menagerie," Roan yelled. "When I'm ready to lift ship, I'll tell you. Now get out of my sight! Get lost!"

"Master," Sostelle whispered.

"You, too, you Freak." Roan staggered, wiped a hand across his face. It was hot, feverish. Everything seemed to be spinning around him; his mind seemed to be floating free of his body, like a captive balloon. Then sky rockets came shooting up in a fiery shower and

when they shimmered away into darkness there was
nothing. . . .

Roan sat up and looked around. Noise roared in his
ears. A face swam mistily before him.

"Ah, he's awake!" someone called. Someone else thrust
a thin-stemmed glass into his hand. He drank thirstily,
let the glass fall. Daryl was there, looking at him eagerly with painted eyes.

"Roan! You looked so lovely sleeping, with your mouth
open and sweat on your face . . ."

"Where's Desiranne?" Roan said. His head ached but
he could speak clearly now.

"Eh? Why she's preparing for her performance, later
in the evening—but—"

"I want to see her." Roan stood and the table fell
over. "Where is she?"

"Now, Roan." Daryl was at his side, patting his arm.
"Just be patient. You'll see her." He laughed a high,
tight laugh. "Oh, my, yes, you'll see her. You liked her,
didn't you? You . . . you lusted after her?"

Roan took Daryl by the shoulder, lifted him from the
floor. "Keep away from me," he snarled, and threw the
Terran from him. His vision seemed cloudy, as though
the room were full of mist. There were other people
around him, but their faces weren't clear. Sostelle was
there, his face worried and homely and familiar and
dependable.

"Where is she, Sostelle?" Roan said. "Where did she
go?"

"Master, I don't know. This is not a matter for dogs."
His voice was almost a moan.

"Sure, I liked her," Roan said loudly. "I loved her!"
He kicked a chair from his path, started across the
floor. "She liked me, too, didn't she?" He rounded on
the dog. "Well, didn't she?"

Sostelle's face assumed an unreadable canine expression. "Her interest in you was unmistakable, Master."

"You think so?"

"Certainly. She is a lovely lady, Master. Worthy of

you." But there was something about his tone; something Roan didn't understand.

"I've got to find her. Can't leave this madhouse until I find her." He started on. The people before him flitted backward, just out of reach, just out of vision. The noise was like an avalanche of sound—a wild, screaming sort of music that seemed to tell of great birds of prey swooping to a feast.

"I will help you, Master," Sostelle said. "I will help you all I can."

"You're a damned good dog, Sostelle. Hell, you're the only friend I've met here—"

"Sir!" Sostelle sounded shocked. "It's not done, sir, to call a dog a friend. . . ."

Roan laughed harshly. "I guess I'll never learn the rules, Sostelle. I came too late—for all of us."

"Master—perhaps you should go now—and take me with you—"

"You, too? What is it, a conspiracy? I've told you, damn you, I'm not going until I find her!" There was a table in his path and he kicked it savagely aside.

"Roan, Roan," a quavering voice called. He stopped, steadied himself against a table, peered through the mist. Daryl darted up to him, his carefully coiffed hair awry. A smile flicked on and off like leaf shadows playing on water.

"It's Desiranne you want to see—and I promise you, you'll see her. Just wait. But now—come along with me. The party's just begun. We have wonderful things planned, and we *must* have you! It will be the greatest affair of the century—of a lifetime! And at the end of it—Desiranne!"

"Sostelle, is he lying?" Roan stared at the Terran, who was quivering with eagerness, like an Alphan slave awaiting a kick or the dregs of a wineglass, not knowing which it would be.

"Master," Sostelle whined, "Master Daryl speaks the truth. . . ."

"Then I'll come."

"You'll be glad, Roan," Daryl gushed. "So glad. And—"

"Never mind that. Where are we going?"

"First, we'll dine. After the dancing and the . . . excitement . . . we need to nourish ourselves, don't you think?" He giggled. "And then—but you'll see; there will be marvelous things—all the pleasures of Terra are waiting for you tonight!" He danced away, calling to others. Roan started after him, then turned back to Sostelle with a quick thought.

"Pleasure," he said, "is what you go after when there isn't anything else left."

22

The cold night air cleared Roan's head. He looked
down from the open flyer in which he and Daryl and
two women and their dogs sat on silken cushions, drinking from small, thin-necked bottles of spicy liquor. There
were other airboats around them, darting in and out
like a school of playful fish. Over the rush of air, thin
cries of excitement mingled with the chatter of many
voices talking at once.

The dog piloting the craft dropped it to the tip of a
tall spire of glowing yellow glass. Roan followed the
others through an entry that looked like solid glass, but
parted before him with a tinkle of gold crystals. Flushed,
bright-eyed faces swarmed around him, but none of
them was Desiranne. A tall girl with heavy golden hair
came up to Roan, her bare arms ivory-white. She looked
at him with her eyes half shut, her lips parted, her pink
tongue showing. Roan showed his teeth and reached for
her, and she shuddered and shrank back. Roan laughed
and pushed through to follow Daryl.

He was trying hard to remember where the table
was, how he had come there. He couldn't; there had
been so many tables, so much noise, so many of the

271

little bottles of spicy wine. He felt very sober, though, and his mind seemed to be working unusually clearly. Neatly dressed dogs were serving food. Roan ate with voracious appetite while his companions nibbled and watched. Roan hardly noticed them. Once he looked up to see the blond girl sitting across the table from him.

"You Terries know how to make food," he said. "This is better even than blood."

The girl—Phrygette, Roan remembered her name—looked sick and excited at the same time. She put out her hand as though to touch the hair on Roan's arm, then drew it back.

"You're strange," she whispered. "I wonder what you think about. You with your sixteen-thousand-year-old brain and your years of wandering the universe."

"I think about many things," Roan said carefully, wishing the hot feeling and the humming in his ears would go away. "I think about the Niss, and how Man destroyed himself fighting them, and how they died alone, then, and how their ghosts haunted the Galaxy for five thousand years."

"Old Niss," Phrygette said, boldly touching Roan's arm now. "I always thought he was a silly superstition."

"I did a terrible thing when I ran the Niss blockade," Roan said. "I didn't free Terra; I shattered the myth that had held the universe out for five thousand years. Now she's exposed to the sharks: Trishinist, and after him, others, until Terra is no different from Tambool."

Phrygette was looking around for her dog, Ylep, to come and fix her makeup.

"A new Navy, that's what you need," Roan said. "Trishinist can muster fifty thousand men, and he has the ships to transport them. You have ships, too—underground, waiting. You need to issue weapons and learn how to use them, prepare tactics to meet an enemy landing party."

Phrygette frowned at Roan. "Really, for someone from Beyond, you talk about the strangest things. Tell me how it feels to kill someone, Roan. Tell me how it feels to die—"

"You'll find out soon enough," Roan said roughly.

Suddenly he felt very bad. His heart was trying to climb up his throat, and his head hurt terribly. He swallowed more wine, put his head down on the table. Phrygette got to her feet, wrinkling her nose.

"I'm afraid he's becoming a bore," she said to someone. "Let's go on to the Museum, Daryl. They've probably already started—without us!"

"They wouldn't dare!" Daryl said, sounding alarmed. "Not after *I* planned it!"

"They might—"

"Roan!" Daryl was shaking him. He raised his head and saw a crowd all around him, faces staring out of a blackish haze.

"Come on, Roan!" It was Daryl, catching at his hand. "You went to sleep again, you foolish boy, but now we're all ready to go to the Museum!"

"Go where?"

"To the Museum of the Glory of Man! Come on! Oh, you'll be thrilled, Roan! It's an ancient, ancient place— just at the edge of the town. All sort of shuddery and dim—but marvelous, really! It's all there—all Terra's history. We've been saving it for a special occasion— and this is certainly the perfect night!"

"Funny place . . . for a party . . ." Roan said, but he got to his feet and followed the laughing, chattering crowd.

Out on the roof, the dogs jumped up, handing their masters and mistresses to their places in the waiting flyers, some of which hovered, waiting their turn. Roan felt as though he were moving in a dream imbued with a sense of terrible things impending. The dogs' eyes looked wide, afraid. Even Sostelle was awkward getting the flyer's door open. Roan's hand went to his belt, feeling for a gun that wasn't there.

"Askor," he said suddenly. "And Sidis. Where are they?" He half rose, sat down suddenly as the flyer jumped forward.

"They'll trouble you no more," Daryl said. "And now, Roan, just think! Objects that were held sacred by our ancestors, five thousand—ten thousand years ago—"

"What do you mean," Roan said, feeling tightness in his chest. "Where are they?"

"Roan—don't you remember? You sent them away yourself . . ."

"Sostelle . . ." Roan felt a sudden weakness as he tried again to rise. Blackness whirled in, shot with fire.

"Master, it is true. You ordered them to leave you. They laid hands on you, to drag you with them, but you fought, and then . . . then Master Daryl was impelled to . . . to call for the Enforcers."

"What are they?" Roan heard his own hoarse voice as from a great distance.

"Specially trained dogs, Master," Sostelle said in a tight voice. "Led by Kotschai the Punisher."

"Are they—did they—?"

"Your companions fought mightily, Master. They killed many dogs. At last they were overwhelmed, and restrainers were focused on them. Then they were taken away."

"Then they're alive?" The blackness broke, flushed away.

"Of course, Master!" Sostelle sounded shocked.

Roan laughed harshly. "They're all right, then. They've been in jail before. I'll bail 'em out in the morning."

They had landed on the wide roof of an ancient palace. Roan tottered, felt Sostelle's hand under his elbow.

"I'm sick," he said. "I've never been so sick, since I was burned when Henry Dread shelled the Extravaganzoo. There was a Man doctor there; he cured me. He couldn't cure Stellaraire, though. She was crushed by a chromalloy beam, and then . . . burned . . ."

"Yes, Master," Sostelle soothed.

"Gom Bulj died from the acceleration. But I killed Ithc. And I killed Henry Dread, too. You didn't know that, did you, Sostelle? But Iron Robert—he died for me. . . ."

They were inside now. The voices of the others were like birds', quarreling over a dung heap. Their faces were blurred, vague. All around, tall cases were ranged, faced with glass. Someone was talking urgently to Roan, but he ignored him, walked to the nearest display, feeling as though he were toiling up a hill.

"This is a collection of famous jewel stones, Master," Sostelle was saying. "All natural minerals, found here on Terra, and treasured by Men for their beauty and their rarity."

Roan stared down at rank on rank of glittering, faceted crystals—red, green, pale blue, violet, clear white.

"There is the Napoleon emerald," Sostelle said. "Worn by an ancient war chief. And beyond is the Buddha's Heart ruby, once the object of veneration of five billion worshipers. And there, just beyond—the Iceberg diamond, said to be the largest and finest ever found in Antarctica."

"Look, Roan," Daryl called. "These are called monies. They're made of solid natural gold, and in early times they were traded back and forth in exchange for, oh, other things," he finished vaguely. "Rather a bore, really. Come along to the next room, though. There are some fabulous things. . . ."

Roan followed, stared at looming walls decorated with objects as baroque and primitive as the crude weapons of the wild men on Aldo Cerise, others of a powerful, barbaric beauty, and still others of a glittering intricacy that his mind could not comprehend. There were more cases—miles of them, each glowing with its own soft light, each with its array of objects of metal, stone, wood, glass, fabric, synthetic.

"Look!" Daryl was poking Roan. "Those clothes were made from fibers that grew from the dirt; they scraped them clean in some way, and then worked them all together, and colored them with—with fruit juice or something. Then they sawed out pieces and looped them together with little strings. That was called sowing—"

"No, that was when they made the plants that they got the fibers from," someone interrupted. "But aren't they funny?"

Roan gazed at the display of old uniforms. Some were shapeless and faded, brown with age, curled with time, even protected as they were by the vacuum of the display cases; others, farther along, were more familiar.

"You see those long, sharp things? They used those to stick into each other," a high excited voice called. "And these odd-shaped objects made some sort of lightning and tore holes in people; there must have been a great deal of blood."

Roan stopped, staring at a tunic of brilliant blue, with narrow silvery-gray trousers, and a belt with a buckle bearing an eagle in place of a dove, and the words *Terran Space Forces*.

"It's like the ITN uniform," he said to no one. "But it was made before there was an Empire. . . ."

Daryl was beside Roan, his face puckered in thought. He looked up at Roan, his eyes snapping wide.

"You!" he said in a strained voice. "I know where it was I saw you face! Look, everybody, come with me . . . !" He turned, ran off.

"What's the matter with him?" Roan growled, but he followed.

In a small room off the main hall, a crowd clustered around a lighted case. They looked around as Roan came up, gave way, staring at him, silent now. Roan halted before the high glass panel, stared at a hazy scene, bright lit. He blinked, cleared his vision. The figure of a man stood before him, clad in a uniform like the one he had just seen, leaning against the flank of a ship of quaint, primitive design. The eyes, blue like cool fire, looked into Roan's from across the centuries. The deep red hair was hacked short, but its stubborn curl still showed. A deep, recorded voice spoke from a slot beneath the display:

"This was Vice Admiral Stuart Murdoch, as he appeared in his last solido, taken only moments before he embarked on his last, heroic mission. Admiral Murdoch is renowned as the hero of the Battle of Ceres and of the Siege of the Callistan Redoubts. He was lost in space in the year eleven thousand, four hundred and two of the Atomic Era."

"Master," Sostelle said in the silence. "It's you!"

Roan turned, looked at Daryl. "How . . . ?" he started. He put his hands on himself as though to assure himself that he was Roan Cornay, alive here and now. But Daryl and the others stared back at him as though he was himself a thing from out of the remote past, like the ancient figure in the glass case.

Roan laughed suddenly, wildly. "I wanted to know who my father was," he said. "But I never suspected he was sixteen thousand years old."

"He . . . really . . . is . . ." Daryl said, and licked at his lips. He whirled to the others. "Don't you understand? He really *did* come from Beyond, just as he said! He's returned from the dead!"

"No," a loud voice said. It was Hugh, his face raw and cut from the beating Roan had given him. "He's a dirty Lower, and he should be turned over to the dogs."

"He's returned from the dead!" Daryl screeched. "Come along! It's easy enough to prove!"

"The genetic analyzer!" someone called. "In the next hall . . ."

"Roan, this will show them all," Daryl said breathlessly. There was a strange light in his eyes. "And then—you'll tell me how it feels to be dead, and rise again!"

"You're insane, Daryl," Roan said. "You're all insane!" he shouted. "I'm the most insane of all, for being here, where I don't belong—" He broke off. "Tomorrow," he said. "Tomorrow I'll leave. With Askor and Sidis. They're my kind. I understand them. They're not pretty, but they've got the beauty of reality about them . . ."

"And you'll take me, Master?" Sostelle whispered.

"Sure, Man's best dog is his friend, eh?" Roan stumbled, almost fell. He was hardly aware of walking, Sostelle at his side, Daryl trotting ahead, under a high arch with a flame burning under it in a metal tray, on into an even bigger room that echoed with the batlike cries of the Terrans.

". . . classify persons wishing to contribute to the germinal banks," Daryl was saying. "Here in the Hall of Man, all the records were kept—"

"My genetic pattern won't be here," Roan said, almost clear-headed for the moment.

"He's afraid," Hugh said. "Will he confess his pretensions now?"

Roan looked around at gleaming equipment, towering metal panels, winking clinical lights.

"Put your hand here, Roan," Daryl urged. He indicated an opening, guided Roan's hand to it. He felt a sharp tingle for an instant, nothing more. There was a soft hum and a plastic tab extruded from a slot in the face of the genetic analyzer. Daryl snatched it, looked at it, then whirled to face the others.

"It's him! It's Stuart Murdoch, returned from beyond the crematorium!"

He didn't remember again then; not until they were in a vast room with ancient flags hanging from age-blackened rafters.

". . . minster hall," an excited voice was saying. "Over thirty thousand years old. Think of the toil, the human tears and sweat and heartache that went into building this, so long ago, to preserving it down through the ages, to bring it here—for us . . ." The voice went on, excited, rapturous.

"What's it all about?" Roan asked. "What's this old building? It looks like something on Tambool. . . ."

"It's very ancient, Master," Sostelle said. Somewhere, a bright light was flaring in the gloom.

". . . took them so many ages to create, with all its traditions and memories—and we, us! Yes, in a single night! A single hour! We can destroy it all. Thirty thousand years of human history end—now!" Roan watched as a slender man in flowing pale garments ran forward, applied the torch to the base of a hand-hewn column. Fire licked upward. In moments it had reached the faded pennants; they disappeared into smoke. Fire ran across the high peaked ceiling. Voices shouted as the crowd pushed forward. Suddenly a woman whirled madly, striking out at those around her; they fell back, yelping, and the frenzied girl tore at her garment, stripped it off, threw it at the fire. Roan saw with a dull shock that there was no hair on her body.

"Give me something sharp!" she screamed, then plunged, caught up a jagged fragment of smoking wood, scored it down the creamy white of her chest and stomach. Blood started. The woman staggered back, wailed faintly, fell, and dogs darted forward, bore her away.

"Get back!" someone was calling. The ceiling was a mass of boiling smoke and flame; each massive timber supporting the rafters blazed, crackling. Roan backed away, then turned and ran.

Behind him, the roof fell with a great thunder; a blast of scalding air struck at him, and sparks flew all around . . .

Later, he stood at the top of a broad flight of marble steps, where a group of men wheezed under the weight of a black statue of a man with a wide headdress and a straight-ahead gaze.

"See him, Roan?" Daryl called. "Isn't he wonderful? The labor, the hopes that went into that image. And now . . ."

The Pharaoh Horemheb went over with a resounding smash, tumbled down head over throne, pulverizing the steps as it struck them. The head flew off, struck a man standing below, who fell screaming, and a crowd closed around him like fish after a bait.

"Master, you're not well," Sostelle was saying. "Let me take you home . . . !"

"Wait. Have to see Desiranne." Roan shook his head, started down the stairs. Daryl skipped ahead, dragging a picture in a heavy frame. At the foot of the stairs, he raised it high, brought it down on the bronze figure of a girl with a water jar; it burst into a cloud of dry chips.

"The Mona Lisa," he caroled. "The only one in the world—and I destroyed it!" He spun on Roan. "Oh, Roan, doesn't it give you a wonderful feeling of power? Those old ones—the ones that conquered the universe—they treasured all this. And we have the power to do as we like with it. They made it—we finish it! Doesn't that make us their equals?"

Roan stared past him at a bigger-than-life white marble of a thick-bodied woman with her garment down around her hips. She was chipped and her arms were missing.

"Shame," Roan mumbled. "Shouldn't break . . . old things." He felt as though he were falling.

"I didn't do that one," Daryl said. "It was already broken—but I'll finish it!" He ran to the statue and pushed. It didn't budge. Daryl made a face and ran on to pull down a painting of a man with one ear bandaged.

"It's hot in here," Roan said aloud. The walls were sailing by, going faster and faster. He groped for support, sank down on the steps. All around, people were running like gracyls in molting time, carrying things that smashed or broke, or were torn apart. Someone started a blaze in the center of the floor, and pictures went flying into it. The floor shook as heavy marbles toppled.

"Get a cutter," a girl screamed, "to use on the bronzes!"

"What a night!" Daryl exulted. "We did the Louvre long ago, and the Grand Palais d'Arte, and the Imperial Gardens; we were saving this one for a special occasion—and your being here—it's just made it perfect—"

Roan got to his feet, fighting the blackness. "I can't wait any longer," he shouted over the din. "Where's Desiranne?"

"Roan, Roan! Forget her for now! There's her performance coming! There's lots of luscious sport to be had before then—" Phrygette was there tucking back a strand of corn-yellow hair with a white arm smudged with soot.

"I'm bored," she said. "Daryl, let's get on to the performance."

"But there are still lots of things to do," he cried, dancing around her. "The books! We haven't even begun on the books—and the tapes, and the old films, and . . . and . . ."

"I'm going," Phrygette pouted. She looked at Roan. He stared back, seeing her face dancing in fire.

"Don't look at me like that," she said sharply. "You look so peculiar . . ."

Roan took a deep breath and held one part of his mind away from the whirling dizziness that enveloped him. He produced something that could be defined as a smile.

"If you were a sixteen-thousand-year throwback, you'd look peculiar, too." He seemed to be watching everything through a view screen now; Daryl looked tiny and far away, and all around the floor curved upward. A wild singing whine rang in Roan's ears. His face felt furnace-hot. "I want to see Desiranne now," he said.

"Oh, all right," Daryl gave Phrygette an icy look. "Spoilsport!"

23

They were in a moldy velvet and chipped gilt room lit by tiny lights glaring down from above like stars as seen in Deep Space, set in a ceiling that slanted away toward a small, bright-lit platform below. There were seats ranked beside Roan's, and more rows lower down, and others swinging in wide sweeps farther up, and still more, perched like tiny balconies just above the stage, and all of them were filled with slim-necked, soot-streaked Men and Women.

"In all that you've told me of other worlds, Roan," Daryl said in a low, vibrant voice, "there has been nothing to equal what you will see Desiranne do here tonight."

"What will she do? Play some instrument? Sing?" The thought of seeing her again made his pulse throb in his head, driving back the sickness. He remembered Stellaraire and her erotic dancing. Surely Desiranne wouldn't do anything like that . . .

"Master," Sostelle whined at Roan's side. "Please— let me bring the doctor to see you now."

"The stuff you gave me is working," Roan said. "I feel better. I'm all right."

A blue mist blew across the stage. Out of it, a little blue and silver dog emerged, singing an eerie, piercing little song in a register so high it was barely within hearing. The blue color faded, and now there were pale pastels—mauve, bluish pink, sunshine-yellow, rain-gray—swirls, clouds, blown foams. The blue dog's song ended in a tiny yelp, and behind Roan, Sostelle winced. Roan could make out another figure in the mist now, dressed in diaphanous robes, swathed from head to foot. It came forward and the scarf blew from its head. It was Desiranne and her pale hair swirled down about her shoulders.

The music was low and gentle, almost a lullaby, and Desiranne ran gracefully, girlishly about in the mists, playing. Then, by degrees, the tempo changed and a drum began to beat—an insistent, commanding beat. Roan began to be aware of Daryl's breathing beside him and he also remembered the fearful beat of the drums that night he stood frozen with fear by the high wire on Chlora, when he was with the circus.

Was that it? Was that what was making the small hairs on his arms prickle, and bringing the smell of danger and the cold sweat in his stomach? Something . . . he turned to Daryl to tell him to stop the show. Whatever it was going to be, Roan could feel it beginning to stink. Something was wrong. Something . . .

But Daryl was smiling expectantly and proudly at Desiranne.

"By the way," he said. "Did I mention that she is my daughter?"

"Your daughter?" Roan repeated dumbly. "You're not old enough," he blurted.

Daryl looked astonished. "Not old enough . . ." A strange expression crossed his face. "You mean—you're . . ." He gulped. "I remember learning once that long ago, men died like dogs, after only a moment of life. Do you mean, Roan, that you—that you . . . ?"

"Never mind."

On the stage, Desiranne had begun a slow, sensuous striptease. The music became more and more insinuating, erotic, then slowed as Desiranne removed her last wisp of garment. As she pirouetted, all pink and gold in the lights, the little silver and blue dog came mincing out onto the stage with something sharp that glittered silver where the light caught it.

It was a knife, long and leaf-thin and sharp. Desiranne dipped in her dance to pluck the stiletto from its cushion, danced away, holding it high. Then the music began to change again, and now a savage tempo took over. An animal music. It went straight to some dark, forgotten part of Roan's mind and again fear began to swell in him insistently. He came to his feet—

Desiranne stopped, stood poised; she held the scalpel-keen blade in her right hand and with great grace and sure slowness, cut off the little finger of her left hand.

A terrible cry tore itself from Roan's throat. He plunged down through the crowd, not even aware of the screams and the smash of his fists on anything that impeded him. With a leap he was on the stage, snatching the knife from Desiranne's hand as she moved to stroke it across her wrist. He caught her, looked into eyes as vacant and dead as the glassless windows of a ruined city.

"Why?" Roan screamed. "Why?" Blood ran down Desiranne's arm. For a moment her eyes seemed to stir with returning life; then she wilted. Roan caught her up, whirled on the others who had crowded around the stage now, all shouting at once. The air reeked of blood; it was a taste in the mouth.

"Get a doctor! She'll die!"

Daryl's livid face was in front of him. He shook his fists over his head. His mouth looked loose and wet.

"Your daughter!" Roan said hoarsely, looking down at the small, gentle, beautiful face. "Your own daughter!"

"She felt nothing! She was drugged! Do you realize that her one chance for a perfect Death Performance is ruined forever? That this is all she has lived for and now she will never have it? I reared her for this, trained her myself! All these years I've kept her perfect, waiting for the one, the ideal occasion—and now—"

Roan snarled and kicked him brutally, and Daryl doubled over, mewing, coiled on the bloody floor.

"Sostelle—get a Man doctor!" Roan jumped down, ran toward the rear of the theater. Desiranne hung limp in his arms, her face as pale as chalk.

*   *   *

In a vast gilt room, Desiranne lay on a narrow couch of pale green silk with curved legs wrought of silver and ivory. A small crowd of eager-eyed Terrans stood by, watching. The doctor, a scrubbed-looking dog carrying a pouch, clucked and sprayed something from the pouch over Desiranne's stumped finger, looked over at Roan.

"She will survive. The tourniquet saved her from excessive bleeding. A pity; so fair she was. But, you, sir; you don't look well. Sostelle tells me—"

"Never mind me; why doesn't she wake up? Are you sure she isn't going to die?"

"She won't die. I'll see to a bud implant from self-germinal tissue, and in a year or two, with the proper stimuli, she'll be as good as new. Now I must insist, sir: Let me have a look at you."

"All right." Roan sank down in a high-backed chair; the doctor applied a smooth, cold metal object to him, muttered to himself.

"You're a sick master," he said. "Temperature over one hundred and four; blood pressure—"

"Just give me some medicine," Roan interrupted. "My head aches."

"I've heard a bit of your background, sir," the doctor said as he rummaged in his bag. "I think I see what's happened here. You've no immunity to the native diseases of Terra. And, of course, they find in you a perfect host. Now—"

"I've never been sick," Roan said, "not like this. I thought it was just the wine, but . . . ." He tottered in the chair as a wave of dizziness passed over him.

"Master!" Sostelle was at Roan's side. "They are coming—Master Hugh and many others—and with them are the Enforcers. Kotschai himself—"

"Good!" Roan snarled, showing his teeth. "I need something to fight! Terrans are no good—they just fall down and cry."

"Please, sir," the doctor said sharply. "You must stand still if I'm to administer my medicants—"

"Doctor," Sostelle whimpered. "Give him something to bring back his strength. See how he faints. . . ."

"Ummm, yes, there are stimulants—dangerous, mind you, but—"

"Quickly! They come! I smell them! I smell the odor of human hate!"

"The scent is thick here in this room," the doctor grunted. He sprayed something cold against the inner side of Roan's elbow.

"Master, you must flee now." Sostelle took his arm.

Roan shook him off. "Bring 'em on," he yelled. "I want to crush the life out of something! I want to pay them back for what they did to Desiranne!"

"But, Master, Kotschai is strong and cruel and skilled in inflicting pain—"

"So am I," Roan shouted. Ice seemed to be pumping through his veins. The ringing in his head had receded to a distant humming. Suddenly he was light, strong, his vision keen; only his heart seemed to pound too loudly.

"Oh, Master, there are many of them," Sostelle cried. "You cannot kill them all. And you are sick. Run— quickly—while I delay them—"

"Sostelle—go and find Askor and Sidis. Get them and bring them to the ship."

"If I do as you command, Master, will you make your escape? The door is there; it leads by a narrow way to the street below."

"All right." Roan let his breath out in a hiss between his teeth. "I'll run. Just get them and send them to me—and take care of this poor girl."

"I will, Master!"

"Good-by, Sostelle. You were the best man I found on Terra." He opened the door and stepped through into dusty gloom.

The street was not like the others Roan had seen on Terra. It was unlit, with broken pavement through which rank weeds grew. He ran, and behind him dogs yelped and called. There was a gate ahead, a stark thing of metal bars and cruel spikes. Roan recognized it from Daryl's description. Beyond it he saw the ominous darkness, smelled the filth and decay of the Lower Town.

Without pausing, he leaped up, pulled himself to the top, and dropped on the other side.

Roan didn't know how many hours later it was. He had run—for miles, it seemed—through dark, twisting, ancient streets, empty of people, with the police baying at his heels. Once they cornered him in a crumbling courtyard, and he killed two of them as they closed in, then leaped up, caught a low-hanging roof's edge, and fled away across the broken slates where they could not follow.

Now he was in a street crowded with faces that were like those remembered from evil dreams—Terrans, with scars, pockmarks, disease-ravaged faces, and starvation-wracked bodies. Women with eyes like the sockets in a skull held out bony hands, quavering pleas for bread and copper; children like darting brown spiders with oversized eyes and knobby knee joints trailed him, shouting in an incomprehensible language. A vast, obese man with one eye and an odor of sickness trailed him for two blocks, until Roan turned, snatched up a foot-long knife from a display before a tumbledown stall, and gestured with it.

There were no dogs here, only the warped, crooked people and the evil stench and the glare of unshielded lights and the sense of age and decay and bottomless misery. Roan could feel the strength going from his legs; he stumbled often, and once fell and rested awhile on hands and knees before he could stand again, shouting to scatter the ring of glittering-eyed people who had closed in on him.

He felt a burning, terrible thirst, and went toward a smoky, liquory, loud-smelling bar. Inside it was hot, steamy, solid with noise that sawed at him like ragged knives. He sank down at a wobbly table and a green-toothed female slid into the seat beside him and elbowed him invitingly. Roan made a growling sound and she went away.

A huge, big-bellied Man was standing before him.

"What'll it be?" he growled in very bad Terran.

"Water," Roan said in a dry whisper. "Cold water."

"Water costs too," the Man said. He went away and came back with a thick, greasy tumbler, half full of grayish liquid.

"I have no money," Roan said. "Take this. . . ." He fumbled the golden clasp from his garment, tossed it on the table.

The barman picked it up, eyed it suspiciously, bit into it.

"Hey," he grunted. "That's real gold!"

"I need . . . a place to rest," Roan said. The sickness was back in full force now, washing up around him like water rising in a sinking ship. "Get me a doctor. . . ."

"You sick, huh?" The Man was leaning toward him leering; his eyes swelled until they were as big as saucers. Roan forced his eyes shut, then opened them, fighting to hold onto consciousness.

"I know . . . where there's more. . . ." He could feel his mind cutting loose from his body again, ready to float away into a tossing sea of fever fantasies. But he couldn't—not yet. He tried to get to his feet, slammed back into the chair. The glass clashed against his teeth.

"Drink up, buddy," the thick voice was saying. "Yeah, I'll get a doc fer yuh. You know where there's more, eh?"

Roan gulped; the warmish, stagnant-smelling liquid gagged him. The Man brought more water, cold this time and in a slightly cleaner glass, as though he had wiped it on his shirt.

"Look, bo, you take it easy, huh? I'm Soup the Insider. Sure, I'll fix yuh up with a room. Swell room, bed and everything. Private. Only look around good before yuh close the door; yuh can never tell what yuh might be locking yourself in with." He guffawed.

"Got to have rest," Roan managed. "Be . . . all right in the morning. Find my friends. Hope Desiranne is all right. Then get out . . . this filthy place. . . ."

"You just take it easy, bub. I'll fix yuh up good. Then we'll talk about where to get more of these little knick-knacks. And you don't talk to nobody else, see?"

"Get me . . ." Roan gave up trying to talk and felt the big man's arm under his, leading him away. . . .

* * *

He fought his way up from a nightmare of heat and pursuit and blood and cruelty and opened his eyes to see a spotted glare panel set in a blotched ceiling, casting a sick light on a threadbare velvet wall. An ancient, withered Man stood beside the bed, blinking down at him with eyes that were polished stones set in pockets of inflamed tissue.

"Sick, ye are, true enough, lad. Ye've got every ailment I ever heard of and six or eight I haven't, you."

Roan tried to sit up; his head barely twitched, and pain shot through it like an ax blow. He lay, waiting for the throbbing to subside. His stomach ached as though it had been stamped by booted feet, and a sickness seemed to fester through his body like sewage bubbling in a cesspool.

"Sore, hey?" the oldster cackled. "Well, it might be; ye've tossed up every meal ye've et since ye learned to guide spoon to lip, you."

Through the wall Roan heard an angry scream and a slap. "For half a copper I don't even smile!" a female voice shrilled, and a door slammed.

"Got to get out," Roan said. He tried to throw back the rough blanket, and the blackness swirled again.

". . . him something to make him talk," the thick voice of the big man was saying.

"Whatever ye say, Soup—but it'll kill him, it."

"Just so he talks first."

Roan felt a cold touch on his arm, a sharp stab of pain.

"Where's the loot, bo?" Soup's thick voice demanded.

"Ye'll have to wait a little hour, Soup. First he'll sleep a bit, eh, to get back the strength to talk, he."

"All right; but if you let him die before he spills, I'll squeeze that scrawny neck of yours."

"No fear o' that, Soup. . . ."

Time passed, like a storm of yellow dust that choked and harried and would never cease. Sometimes voices stabbed at him, and he cursed them and struck out; and again he was running, falling, and far away on the floodlit stage the knife was cutting into Desiranne's white flesh, and he fought his way toward her, but always the sea of mad faces blocked his way until he screamed and clawed his way out of the dream—

". . . tell me now, before the blasted glutton comes back, he," a scratchy voice was saying. "Then I'll give ye more nice medicine, and ye'll sleep like a whelp at a bitch's teat."

"Get . . . away . . . me . . ." Roan managed. "Got . . . go . . ."

Something sharp and painful poked his throat.

"Ah, ye felt that, then, lad? Good. Now speak once more, tell old Yagg where the pretty treasures lie. Not in Upper City, eh? For the dogs would tear a man to bits if ever he ventured there. Where, eh? Is there some house that's been missed, some buried trove—"

There was a great smash, and a bull roar.

"So! Yuh'd cheat Soup, would yuh? I'll rip your head off—"

"Now, Soup—you misjudge me, you! I was just trying to find out—for you. No harm, what?"

There was a growl and a sound of two heavy blows and a squeal. Then Soup's wide face loomed over Roan, breathing foul breath and flecks of spittle.

"All right, give, bo! You ain't going to die and not tell Soup, not after he give yuh a place to die in!"

Roan croaked, and his hand moved feebly. "Tell . . . you . . . later . . ." The face faded and Soup's voice mumbled, drifted off into the insistent clamor of fever images.

Light again, and sounds.

". . . didn't you send for me sooner?" a tremulous voice was complaining. "That quack Yagg like to killed him, with his poisons! He's full of disease! Look at those sores—and see the swelling here. He'll die—mark my words, he's a goner—but we can do our best . . ."

"Yuh better. . . ."

Stellaraire was standing by the bed, looking down at him. Her hair was burnt off and her face was scarred and blistered.

"Come with me, Roan," she said urgently. "We'll

leave this 'zoo and go so far away they'll never find us. Come. . . ." Then she was running away, and Henry Dread was shooting after her, the blaster bolts echoing along the steel corridor, echoing . . .

Henry Dread holstered the gun. "Damned Gooks," he said. "But you and I, Roan: we're different. We're Terries." His face changed, became small and petulant. "I trained her," Daryl said. "What higher art form can there be than destruction? And the destruction of one's self is its highest expression. . . ." Deftly, Daryl fitted a noose about his neck, hoisted himself up. His face became black and twisted and terrible. "You see?" he said pleasantly. He went on talking, and many voices chimed in, and they cheered and the dust cleared away and Iron Robert held up his arms, melted off at the elbow.

"Iron Robert born to fight, Roan," he said. "Can't fight now. Time for Iron Robert to die." He turned and the iron door opened and he walked into the furnace. The flame leaped out of the open door, scorching Roan's face. He turned away, and rough hands pulled him back.

"Yuh can't die yet," Soup's voice said. "Yuh been laying here for two days and two nights, yelling to yourself. Now talk, damn you, or I'll choke the life out of yuh!" Hands like leather-covered stone-crushers closed on Roan's throat—

There was a terrible growling, and then a scream and suddenly the hands were gone and there were awful sounds of tearing flesh and threshing limbs and then Sostelle's face was leaning over him, and there was blood on the dog's jaws.

"Master! I came as quickly as I could!"

Roan cried out, turned away from the phantom.

"Master! It's your dog, Sostelle! And I have another with me. Look, Master. . . ."

A cool hand touched Roan's forehead. There was a faint odor of a delicate perfume, almost lost in the stench of the foul room. Roan opened his eyes. Desiranne looked down at him. Her face was pale and he could

see the faint blue tracing of the veins in her eyelids.
But she smiled at him.

"It's all right now, Roan," she said softly. "I am with
you."

"Are you . . . real?"

"As real as any of us," she said.

"Your hand . . ."

She held it up, swathed in bandages. "I'm sorry I'm
no longer perfect, Roan."

The dog doctor appeared, looking concerned. He
talked, but Roan couldn't hear him for the thunder in
his ears. He lay and watched Desiranne's face until she
faded and dissolved in mist, and then the mist itself
faded into darkness shot with lights, and the lights
twinkled like distant stars, and then went out, one by
one. . . .

Roan was sitting up in bed. His arm, resting on the
patched blanket over his knees, was so thin that his
fingers met around it, and it was scarred with half-
healed pockmarks. Desiranne sat by the bed, feeding
him thin soup. Her face was thin and paler than ever,
and her hair was cut short, held back by a simple scarf
of clean cloth. Roan lifted his hand, took the spoon.

"I can do that now," he said. The spoon trembled,
spilling soup; but he went on, emptied the bowl.

"I'm stronger now," he said. "I'm getting up."

"Roan, please rest a few days longer."

"No. We've got to get to the ship now, Desiranne.
How long has it been? Weeks? Maybe Askor and Sidis
will be there, waiting for me. We'll leave this poisoned
world and never come back." He had thrown back the
blanket and put his feet down on the floor. His legs
were so thin that a choked laugh grunted from him.

"I look like old Targ," he said. With Desiranne's
hand under his arm, he stood, feeling his senses fade in
vertigo from the effort. He took a step and fell, and
Desiranne cried out and then Sostelle was there, helping him back into the rags of the cot.

It was a week later. Roan sat in a chair by the

window, looking out at the decayed roofs and tottering walls of Lower Town. There was a sickly plant in a clay pot on the windowsill, and a fresh breeze brought odors of springtime and corruption.

Sostelle came in, carrying a patched cloak.

"This is all I could get, Master."

"I told you never to call me 'Master' again," Roan snapped. "My name is Roan."

"Yes . . . Roan. Here is a garment. But please—don't go. Not yet. The dogs are about again today—"

Roan stood, ignoring the dizziness. "We're going today. Askor and Sidis are probably waiting for me, wondering what happened. They probably think I'm dead." His fingers fumbled with the chipped buttons.

"Yes, Mas— Roan." The dog helped him with the cloak. It was a faded blue, of a rough weave that scratched Roan's pale skin. Desiranne appeared at the door.

"Roan—you're so weak. . . ."

"I'm all right." He forced himself to smile gently at her, to walk without staggering across to her. "It's not far," he said. "We can do it."

They went down patched stairs, ignoring the eyes that stared from half-concealment at the dog who had torn the throat out of the formidable Soup, and the pale Upper woman, and the sick madman. Out in the sun-bleached, time-eroded street other faces, weather-burned and life-scarred, watched as they passed; and when one of the watchers ventured too close, Sostelle bared his fangs and they drew back.

After half an hour, Roan and his escort stopped to rest at a dry fountain with broken carvings of Men with the tails of fish. Roan looked at them, and wondered on what world they lived. He and Desiranne sat on the carved stone lip of the monument, feeling the warmth of the sun, while Sostelle paced up and down, his human-like hands hooked in his leather belt. When Roan had rested, they went on.

It was late afternoon when they reached the raised avenue that ran past the port and on to the bright towers of Upper City. Roan shaded his eyes, staring past the orderly trees and the banked flowers in the distance.

"Where is it?" he said. "I don't see the ship." There was a new sick feeling in him now, not the fever of pain and infection, but the hollow sickness of terrible loss. He scrambled up the embankment, led the way along under the gentle trees. He could see parked flyers, the flash of color of moving chariots, the tiny figures of dogs at work; but *Hell's Whore* was gone.

"Perhaps the people, sir," Sostelle said. "Master Daryl and the others; they may have moved her . . ."

"They couldn't have," Roan said in a voice that almost broke. "Only Askor and Sidis knew how to open her ports—how to lift her."

"Roan—we must go back now." Desiranne's hand was on his arm. He touched the thin fingers, looking at Sostelle.

"You knew," he said.

"Roan—I could not be sure—and how could I have told you . . . ?"

"It's all right." Roan tried desperately to hold his voice firm. "At least they got away. I knew those pansies couldn't hold them."

"Perhaps one day they'll come back, Roan," Sostelle said. "Perhaps—"

"No. They're gone, back to where they belong—out there." Roan tilted his head back, looking up into the bottomless blue of the deep sky. "I sent them away myself," he said. "I betrayed them to their enemies and then turned my back on them. There's nothing for them to come back for."

24

Roan sat with Desiranne and Sostelle at a small table in the bar that Soup the Insider had once owned. It was evening and the room was filled with yellow light and the last of the day's heat. In one corner, a Man with magic fingers caressed a stringed instrument that mourned for love and courage and other forgotten things. A one-eyed Man came in silently from the street, crossed to their table.

"I seen another patrol," he said accusingly. "You and yer woman and yer dog better pull out tonight."

Roan looked at him with an expression that was the absence of all expression.

"Yer calling 'em down on us," the Man said, his lips twisting with the hates that ate at him like crabs. "When the dogs get on a man's trail, they don't never quit. And long's they're here in the Town, ain't nobody safe."

"They're not looking for me," Roan said. "Not after a year. I'm not that important."

"A year—ten years. It's all the same to dogs. They ain't like a man. They're trained to hunt—and that's what they're doing."

"He's right, Roan," Sostelle said. "Kotschai will never

forget the man who shamed him by escaping him.
Perhaps we'd best leave now, and find another place—"

"I'm not leaving," Roan said. "If they want me, let
them find me." He looked at the one-eyed Man. "If you
fought them—if we all fought them—we could wipe
them out. There are only a few hundred of them. Then
you could leave this pesthole. You could spread out into
the countryside, start new villages—"

The Man shook his head. "You was lucky," he said.
"You got clear of 'em. But that was because you was in
Upper Town, where they wasn't expecting no trouble.
When they come down here, they come in packs, with
nerve guns and organization. Nobody's going to jump
that kind of force. And neither are you." He straightened, showing his teeth. "You're going to get out, like I
said—or you ain't going to live long."

Roan laughed at him. "Is that a threat? Is being dead
worse than living in this ghetto?"

"You're going to find out pretty soon—you and your
. . . friends." He swaggered away.

"Roan," Sostelle started. "We could leave by night,
make our way to—"

"I'm going out." Roan stood. "I need fresh air."

"Roan—you're challenging the dogs—and the Men as
well . . . ?"

Desiranne caught at his hand. "They'll see us . . ."

Roan pushed her gently back. "Not us. Just me. Let
them beware."

"I'm going with you."

"Stay here with Sostelle," Roan said flatly. "I've hidden from them for a year. That's long enough."

As he walked away, he heard Sostelle say: "Let him
go, Mistress. A Man like Roan cannot live forever as a
hunted slave."

The rumor ran ahead of Roan. People stared, made
mystical signs, then darted out to follow as he strode
along, taking the center of the hut- and garbage-choked
street. Others slipped away into decay-slimed alleyways
to spread the word. The last of sunset faded and the few
automatic polyarcs that still worked came on, shedding

their tarnished brilliance on broken walks, cracked façades, and Roan, walking the night with his shadow striking ahead.

"They're close," someone called to Roan from a doorway. "Better run quick, Mister Fancy-talk!"

He was in a wide avenue with a center strip of hard-packed dirt where flowers had once grown. At the far end was the wide colonnaded front of a building the roof of which had fallen in. It gleamed a ghostly white in the glare from a tall pole-mounted light. Tall weeds poked up among marble slabs there, and rude huts grew like toadstools in the shadows of the chipped pediments.

A dog appeared on the broken steps, standing tall, curve-shouldered, cringe-legged, cruel-fanged, wearing the straps and sparkling medallions of the police. Roan walked toward him, and the trailing crowd fell back.

"Stop there, red-haired Man!" the dog yelped. He drew the curiously shaped gun strapped under his foreleg and pointed it at Roan. "You're under arrest."

"Run," Roan said in a strange, flat voice. "Run, or I'll kill you."

"What? Kill me? You're a fool, Red-hair. I have a gun—"

Roan broke into a run straight toward the dog and the animal crouched and fired and in the sudden shock of pain Roan felt his legs knot and cramp and he fell. The dog stalked up to him, waving back the gathering crowd.

It's only pain, Roan told himself. He rested on hands and knees. *Pain is nothing; dying without feeling his throat under your hands is the true agony.* . . .

He rose to his feet in a sudden movement, and the police dog whirled, reaching for the gun, but Roan's swing caught him below his cropped ear, sent him spinning. With a growl, the dog scrambled to all fours, and Roan's foot met him under the jaw with a solid impact and the shaved body rolled aside and lay still. Roan stooped, picked up the gun, as a mutter of alarm swept across the mob.

"You see?" Roan shouted. "They're dogs—nothing more!"

"Now they'll kill you for sure!" a gaunt woman yelled. "Serve you right, too, you trouble-bringer!"

"Here they come!" another voice screeched. Two more dogs had appeared from the ruin, coming on at a relentless lope. Roan took aim and shot one; it fell, yelping and kicking out, and the other veered aside and dashed for safety. The crowd shouted now.

"But these are just ordinary dogs," the one-eyed Man had come up close to Roan. "Wait until you meet Kotschai, face to face. Then you'll learn the taste of honest fear!"

"They say he's three hundred years old," a short, clay-faced Man said. "His masters have given him their magic medicine to make him live long, and with every passing year he's grown more wise and evil. My gran'fer remembered him—"

"He's just a dog," Roan shouted. "And you're Men!"

Across the square a squad of uniformed dogs burst into view, fanned out, halted, facing the crowd, which recoiled, leaving Roan to stand alone. Then an avenue opened through the police and an immense dog paced through. In silence he advanced across the plaza, skirted the injured dog, which was crawling painfully, whimpering. A dozen feet from Roan, he halted.

"Who dares defy Kotschai the Punisher?" he growled. He was taller than Roan, massive-bodied, with the thick, sinewy forelegs of a tiger and jaws like a timber wolf. His body had been shaved except for a ruff around the neck and his pinkish-gray hide was a maze of scars. He was dressed in straps and bangles of shiny metal decorated with enamel, and there was a harness studded with spikes of brass across his chest, and above his yellow eyes was a brass horn that seemed to be set in the bone of his brute-flat skull. His tail had been broken and badly set, and it swung nervously, as though it hurt all the time.

"How does a dog dare to challenge a Man?" Roan demanded.

"It is the order of my master." The wicked jaws grinned and a pink tongue licked black gums.

"Can you fight all of us?" Roan motioned toward the silent mob.

"They do not count," Kotschai said. "Only you. I see you have a gun, too. But my dogs have more."

"You and I don't need guns," Roan said. "We have hands and teeth for fighting."

Kotschai looked at Roan with his small, red-circled eyes. He lifted his muzzle and sniffed the air.

"Yes," the dog said. "I smell the odor of human bloodlust." He seemed to shiver. "It is not a scent I love, Master."

"Then you'd better learn how to crouch on all fours and heel on command, dog," Roan said loudly, so that everyone could hear.

"I have never learned such lessons, Master," Kotschai said.

"You haven't had a proper teacher, dog."

"That may be true." Kotschai motioned his dogs back. He unbuckled his gun harness, threw it aside.

"It is said that once Man was Terra's most deadly predator," he said. "I have wondered long how it was that the pretty creatures I call Master made the dogs their slaves. Perhaps in you I see the answer."

"Perhaps in me you see your death."

Kotschai nodded. "Perhaps. And now I must punish you, Master."

Roan tossed the gun to a Man, reached to his shoulder, ripped loose the clasp that held his garment, wrapped the ragged cloth around his left forearm.

"Now I'll instruct you in courtesy, dog," he said, and Kotschai snarled and charged.

Roan's padded arm struck into the open jaws as the dog's bristly body slammed against him. He stumbled back, twisting aside from the horn that raked his jaw, locked his free arm around the dog's shoulders, keeping his face above the vicious chest spikes, and together Man and dog fell. Roan locked his legs around the heavy torso, and Kotschai snarled, raking with all four limbs as Roan's locked arms and legs crushed, crushed—

With a frantic effort, the dog wrenched his jaws half free of Roan's strangling forearm, lunged for a better grip with his teeth, and Roan struck with his fist, kicked free, hurled the animal from him. Kotschai scrambled to his feet, jaws agape, the stubble along his spine erect. Roan faced him, blood on his arm, teeth bared in an ancient defiance. All around, dogs and Men stood silent, gaping at the spectacle of Man pitted against beast.

The dog charged again, and Roan slipped aside, dropped on the broad back, locked ankles under the dog's belly, wrapped his arms around the thick neck, pressing his face close to the mightily muscled shoulder. Kotschai went down, rolled, and Roan held on, throttling the breath in the dog's throat. Kotschai reared high, tottering under the weight of the Man on his back, throwing his horned head from side to side, and Roan's grip loosened—

At once, the dog twisted, the great jaws snapping a hair's breadth from Roan's unprotected shoulder. Roan doubled his fist, struck a smashing blow across the dog's face, but the jaws snapped again, and this time they met hide and muscle. Roan found a grip on the corded throat, forcing the fanged head back, and he felt the locked teeth tear his flesh . . .

The garment wrapping Roan's arm had slipped down. It flapped in the dog's face, and the animal snapped at it, and in the instant's diversion, Roan ripped free. But even as he retreated a step the dog was on him, and again the rag-snarled fist was thrust into the yawning jaws, and again Roan fell, and now Kotschai was above him, snarling and worrying the impeding rag, struggling to find a clear thrust at Roan's throat, while Roan fought to hold the fighting body close. . . .

A minute that was an eternity passed, while the two antagonists contended, chest to chest, their agonized breathing the only sound in all the wide plaza. And slowly the jaws grew closer, as Roan's grip loosened. He looked into the yellow eyes, and felt the hot, inhuman ferocity that burned an inch from his face now. And then he saw another face, above and behind that of the dog—the features set and pale, the one eye glaring—

There was a shock, and the pressure was gone. Kotschai kicked convulsively, growling; the growl became a howl, choked off. Roan thrust the two-hundred-pound body from him, got to his knees, then to his feet. Blood was running hot across his chest from the wound in his shoulder, and his breath was raw in his throat. He was aware of the Man standing before him, looking half triumphant, half afraid, and of a roar from the mob of humans, and of the dogs starting forward uncertainly, guns ready. Roan shook out his torn and bloody tunic, pulled it on.

"Thanks," Roan said, then yelled and charged the advancing dogs. He felt the wash of fire as the field of a nerve gun touched him, and then he was on the nearest dog, feeling the solid smash of his fists on hide, and then the shouting was all about him and the ragged horde leaped past him, howling out their long-pent fury. The dogs fought bravely, but as quickly as one Man fell another leaped his body to grapple his antagonist. The police had fallen back almost to the broken marble steps of the ruined building before whistles and barkings sounded from a sideway, and now more dogs arrived, long pink tongues hanging out, stub tails whipping, firing as they came; and still more Men scrambled to join the fight which had spread all across the square now.

The one-eyed Man was beside Roan. His face was bleeding from a dog bite but his single eye gleamed with life.

"I killed three of 'em!" he yelled. "Got one by the throat and choked him till he died!" He ran on.

The dogs had formed a tight phalanx, guns aimed outward to sweep the crowd, and they retreated slowly as Men rushed at them, shouting curses, leaping the bodies of the fallen, striking out with clubs, knives, fists. Now the dogs reached a narrow way, and more Men fell as the enemy retreated, leaving a trail of casualties behind them. They reached a gate and slipped through it and it clanged behind them. The Men tried to climb it, but the dogs shot them down, and they fell, all but one who hung, impaled on spearpoints.

But a wild yell was echoing along the street, across the plaza. Men and women danced, screaming their triumph. The one-eyed Man was back, seizing Roan's arm, pumping his hand.

"We beat 'em!" he was shouting at the top of his lungs.

"They'll be back!" Roan shouted. "We'll have to collect the weapons, set up a defensive position . . ."

No one was listening. Roan turned to another Man as One-eye darted away, tried to explain that the dogs had retired in good order for tactical reasons, that they would renew the assault as soon as reinforcements arrived with heavy weapons.

It was useless. The Lowers capered, all yelling at once.

Something made Roan look upward. A point of brilliant light sparkled and winked against the night sky, and Roan felt the clutch of a ghostly hand at his heart.

"A ship . . ." he said aloud, feeling his voice choke.

"Roan!"

He whirled. Sostelle was there, unruffled by the frenzy all about. "The Lady Desiranne commanded me to come . . ."

Roan clutched at him. "It's a ship!" he said hoarsely, pointing.

"Yes, Roan. We saw it from the rooftop. Oh, Roan—is it—your ship . . . ?"

A great searchlight lanced out from the port area; the finger of chalky bluish light glared on low clouds, found the ship, glinted on its side.

"No," Roan said, and the ghostly hand gripped even tighter. "It's not my ship. It's a big one—a dreadnought of the line. It's Trishinist and his plunderers of the Imperial Terran Navy."

Roan and Sostelle watched from the shelter of the causeway as the mile-long vessel suspended itself five miles over the city, like an elongated moon ablaze with lights from stem to stern. Its pressor beams were columns of pale fire bearing on smoking pits spaced at hundred yard intervals across the flower beds and glassy pavement of the landing ramps. Three smaller shapes of light had detached themselves from the mother vessel, dropping quickly toward the earth.

"They're landing about three hundred men," Roan said. "How many fighting dogs are there?"

"I don't know, Roan. Perhaps as many, perhaps more—but look there—"

From the Upper City, a flock of flyers had appeared, moving swiftly toward the port. Roan could see the crossed bones insignia of the police blazoned on the sides of the grim, gray machines. The landing craft from the ITN battleship were settling to the broad pavement now; ports cycled open; a cascade of men poured out of each, formed up in ragged columns. The police flyers closed ranks, hurtling to the attack at low altitude. Something sparkled from the prow of the first of the landing craft in line, and the lead flyer exploded into arcing fragments with a flash that lit the landscape for two miles around in dusty orange light. The other police vessels scattered, screaming away at flank speed, hugging the ground, but not before an aerial torpedo got away to burst near an ITN column, sending half a dozen men sprawling.

"The dogs are brave enough," Roan said. "But they don't know how to fight a force like Trishinist's. The ship won't fire; he'll want the city intact to loot; but the ground party will walk through them to take the city, and then they'll come on to Lower Town and from here they'll go on to the next city, and when they're finished there'll be nothing left but ashes."

"Perhaps if the Lowers joined with the dogs—"

"No use. They're just a mob, drunk on a taste of victory."

"Why, Roan?" Sostelle whined. "What do these men seek here? Surely in the wide skies there must be worlds enough for all creatures. . . ."

"They destroy for the love of it—like Daryl and his friends. Poor Terra. Her last, forlorn hope is gone now."

The landing force had advanced across the ramp to the reception buildings; a detachment broke off, and Roan saw the wink of guns as they smashed their way into the glass-walled lounge where he had met Daryl that first day, so long ago. The dogs, meanwhile, had grounded their flyers and were advancing in open order across a wide park to intercept the invaders at the causeway.

"Terra's own—her lost, wandering sons—returned to deal her her deathblow," Sostelle whispered. "In a sad world, this is the crowning sadness."

Roan was studying the advancing ITN column. Even from the distance of half a mile he could make out the hulking forms, the shambling gaits of the mongrel humans in the blue and silver uniforms. Two large men marched at the head of the column, a smaller figure between them.

Sostelle raised his nose and sniffed.

"Look there!" Roan said. "Can you see . . .?"

"My eyes are not as keen as those of a Man, Roan; but—"

Roan was on his feet. His heart beat in his throat, almost choking him. Then he was running, sprinting across a stretch of open grass, leaping up the embankment to the causeway. He heard Sostelle at his side.

"Roan—you'll be killed! Both sides will fire their guns at you—"

But Roan ran on toward the approaching ITN detachment. The leader—a huge figure in ill-fitting blues—held up a hand, halted the column, brought a short-barreled power gun around. . . .

Then he threw it aside.

"Roan! Chief!" he bellowed.

"Askor! And Sidis!"

They came together and Roan seized the half-breeds' broad shoulders in a wild embrace, shouting, while Askor grinned so widely that every one of his twenty-eight teeth showed.

"Chief, we knew we'd find you," he roared out. Sidis was looming then, his steel teeth glittering in the polyarc light.

"Askor and me came in here ready to blow this dump apart if we didn't find you OK." He clapped Roan on the back with his steel hook, and Roan seized him, danced him around, while the troops standing by at the ready gaped and grinned.

"I told that lunkhead you was OK." Askor gripped Roan's arm and pounded his back with a great, horny hand.

"Gee, Boss, you look different," Sidis said. "Your hair's got gray and you got lines in your face . . . and you ain't been eating good, neither. But to the Nine Hells with it! We're together!"

Roan laughed and listened to both men talk at once, and then other crewmen were crowding forward, and Roan caught a glimpse of a once-familiar face, now thin and dirty and streaked with tears. It was Trishinist, and there was an iron collar around his neck to which a length of heavy chain was welded.

"I knew you big plug-uglies would come back," Roan said. Sostelle was by his side, his tail wagging. "Didn't I, Sostelle?" Roan demanded, blinking back an annoying film in his eyes.

"Yes, Roan," the dog said. "You knew."

"Chief, I guess maybe we better take a few minutes to straighten out these fellows coming out from the city," Askor said. The dogs were marching across the causeway now, four abreast, advancing in defense of their masters.

"Sostelle—can't you stop them?" Roan asked.

"No," the dog said, almost proudly. "The dogs will fight."

Then Askor was away, bawling orders, and Roan stood with Sidis under a tree as delicate as a lilac as the two columns met in fire and dust.

25

It was an hour after dawn; in a half-shattered house at the edge of the city, the leader of the surviving dogs stood before Roan and Askor. His fur was singed and there was blood clotted at the side of his head, but he stood straight.

"My animals are overwhelmed, Masters," he said. "Only twenty-three survive, and all of those are injured. We can no longer fight."

"You put up a good scrap," Askor said approvingly. "You knocked off a couple dozen ITNs and even nailed one or two of my own boys."

"I request one hour's time to permit my dogs to clean themselves and polish their brasses before we are put to death," the dog said. "They wish to die like dogs, and not as masterless curs."

"Huh? Who said anything about killing you? You lost, we won, that's the breaks of the game."

"But . . . now your soldiers will loot the Upper City, which we were sworn to protect."

"Forget it. You tried. Now I got other plans for you dogs. What would you say to joining up?"

"Joining . . . ?"

"The ITN," Askor explained. "I need good fighters

. . ." He looked at Roan. "Sorry, Chief. I guess this last year I kind of got a habit of talking like it was *my* show."

"It is," Roan said. "You've earned it."

"If we hadn't found *Archaeopteryx* and our old crew cruising around near Alpha Four looking for us, we never would of made it. But what about signing up the dogs, Chief? You like the idea OK?"

"Sure; they're Terrans too, aren't they?"

The dog's eyes gleamed. He straightened his back even more. "Sirs! My dogs and I accept your offer! We will fight well for Terra, sirs!" He saluted and limped away.

Sidis came up. "Boss, uh, the boys are kind of looking around a little in the city, if that's OK. They been a long time in space, and, uh . . ."

"No unnecessary killing or destruction," Roan said. "I leave it to them to decide what's necessary."

"Them poor Terries in the dump town," Askor said. "They look worse than the Geeks back in that place, Tambool, Chief. We give 'em some food and blasted down the gates so's they could help themselves to some of the stuff that's laying around in the fancy part of town. I got a idea we could sign on a few of them, too, after the fun's over."

"Yeah, Boss," Sidis said eagerly. "With a couple hundred of Trishinist's Gooks, and the dogs, and now these Terries, we got a nice-sized little navy shaping up. We could maybe even man two ships. What you got in mind for our next cruise?"

Roan shook his head. "I'm staying on Terra," he said.

Askor and Sidis stared at him.

"This world needs every Man it can get," Roan said. "The old equilibrium's been shattered—and if I leave now, leave them to their own devices—they'll die. The Lowers outnumber the Uppers a hundred to one—but they don't know how to run a world. And if the automatic machinery isn't properly tended, they'll all starve. They'll starve soon, anyway, when the system breaks down completely. But I can help. I have to try."

Askor nodded. "Yeah . . . from what I saw, there ain't much hope for these Terries on their own."

"There's still life in the old world," Roan said. "Now that the blockade is broken, the word will spread; they'll be coming, to get in on the spoils. But with a little time and luck, I can organize her defenses—enough to give her a chance."

Askor frowned. "Defenses? What about *Trixie?* There ain't many tubs in space can take her on."

"I can't ask you to stay here," Roan said. "For me, it's different. I have a wife now. And in a few months I'll have a son. . . ."

Askor and Sidis looked at each other.

"Uh . . . you know, Boss, it's a funny thing," Sidis said. "I feel at home here myself." He waved a thick-fingered hand. "The air smells right, the sunlight, the trees—all that kind of stuff. I been thinking—"

"Uh, Chief," Askor broke in. "I'll be back. . . ."

Roan looked after him. "I guess I'm a great disappointment to him: married, settled down, no more raiding the spaceways. . . ."

"It ain't that, Boss." Sidis snapped the top off a tall wine bottle and occupied himself with swallowing. A big Gook named Gungle appeared at the door, grinned across at Roan.

"Hey, Cap'n, what you want to do with this Terry captain we got here? Askor said bring him along from Alpha for you to roast over a slow fire if you wanted to." He tugged the chain in his hand and Trishinist stumbled into the room.

"Roan—dear lad," he babbled. "If you've a heart surely you'll take a moment now to instruct these animals to release me—"

Gungle jerked the chain. "Talks funny, don't he Cap'n?"

"Maybe we should find a nice deep hole to put him in," Roan said thoughtfully, studying the former officer. "But somehow the idea bores me. You may as well just shoot him."

"Roan—no! I'm far too valuable to you!"

"He's all the time talking about something he knows,

Cap'n," Gungle explained. "Said you wouldn't never find out, if we was to blow a hole in him."

"Yes, Roan," Trishinist gasped. "Only set me free—with a stout vessel, of course—one of the flagship's lifeboats will serve nicely—and an adequate supply of provisions—and perhaps just a few small ingots of Terran gold to help me make a new start—and I'll tell you something that will astonish you!"

"Go ahead," Roan said.

"But first, of course, your promise—"

Gungle gave the chain a sharp tug. "Tell it," he growled.

Trishinist bleated. "Your word, Roan—"

"I guess I might as well go ahead and plug him, Cap'n," Gungle said apologetically, tugging at his pistol. "I shun't of bothered you." He turned on the cowering man.

"I'll speak," he bleated. "And throw myself on your mercy, Roan. I have faith in your sense of honor, dear lad—"

Roan yawned.

"You're a Terran!" Trishinist screeched. "Yes, of the Pure Strain—the ancient strain! There was a ship—oh, old, old, it was, Roan! Hulled in a Deep Space by a rock half as big as a lifeboat, and drifting through space and centuries—until I found it. There was the body of a Man—frozen in an instant as the rock opened her decks to space. They took from his body the frozen germ cells, and at my order—*my* order, Roan! our finest technicians thawed them, and induced maturation! And then—but the rest you know. . . ." He stared at Roan, his mouth hanging open, his eyes pleading.

"His name was Admiral Stuart Murdoch," Roan said. "He died sixteen thousand years ago."

"Then—you knew . . ." Trishinist's face went gray; he sagged.

"I didn't know the whole story. Tell me, Trishinist, if I let you go, will you settle down here on Terra and live a useful life?"

"Live? Life?" The former captain straightened. "Roan, I'll be a model citizen, I swear it. Oh, I'm tired, tired!

of killing, and struggle, and hate! I want to rest now. I'll till a plot of soil—Terran soil—and marry a Terran woman, raise a family. I want . . . I want to be loved . . ."

"Cripes," Gungle said.

"Get out," Roan said. "And if you betray me, I'll find you, wherever you are."

"Gee, Cap'n," Gungle said disgustedly. He dropped the chain and Trishinist caught it up, darted from the room. Roan heard a yell, then the scamper of retreating feet. Askor came in, grinning.

"I figured you'd let him go, Chief. And, uh, now I got something to show you . . ." He turned, beckoned. A girl appeared in the doorway, smiling shyly. She was small, pretty, obviously Terran. She was dressed in soft-colored garments from the Gallian World, and she held a baby in her arms. Askor went to her, put a protective hand on her shoulder, led her to Roan. A fat, three-month-old face looked up at Roan, suddenly smiled a wide, half-familiar smile.

"My kid," Askor said proudly.

Roan blinked.

"Me and Cyrillia," Askor went on, grinning. "I, uh, kind of took her along when me and Sidis left here, Chief. We was in kind of a hurry, but I seen her, and . . . you know . . ."

"You took her with you?" Roan took the baby. He was solid, heavy, with the round face of a Minid and the pert nose of his mother. "Then—this means—"

"Yeah," Askor said. "I guess that proves even a Gook's got a little Earthblood, huh? I want to stay here, Chief. With you. And the rest of the boys too. You need us here. Terra needs us to start her new Navy—and ever since Roan was born—" Askor blushed.

"We named him for you, sir," Cyrillia said in a soft voice.

"Hell's hull, Chief—all the boys are tired of this shipboard life. They all want to get a nice Terry gal and settle down. We'll keep *Trixie* shipshape—we'll cruise her enough to train the green hands and keep the crew in trim. . . ."

"There are plenty of ships," Roan said, through a smile that felt as large and silly as Askor's. "We can crew fifty of them if we want to, and stand off anybody that comes looking for easy pickings. And meanwhile, we'll be building, and learning, and growing. Give us a few hundred years—"

"Just give me now, Boss," Askor said, taking the baby and holding him in his huge hands. "That's more than any Gook ever had a right to hope for."

It was evening. Roan sat with Desiranne's hand in his on a grassy hillside above the city. Cyrillia, Askor, Sidis and Sostelle were grouped around them. Below, fires winked and glimmered in a dozen places across the dark city. Faint sounds of raucous laughter, shouts, the unmelodic harmonies of drunken looters rose like the murmur of surf.

"Roan," Sostelle said. "Shouldn't you put a stop to the destruction—"

"No!" Desiranne spoke almost fiercely. "Let them destroy it! It's false, hateful, full of hideous memories! Let it all be burned clean—and then we can start new. We still have the soil and the sun; we still have Terra!"

"But the museums—the ancient things, the treasures of Terran art. . . ."

"No," Cyrillia said. "The First Era of Man has ended. Let it be forgotten."

"But thirty thousand years of history; all Terra's past. . . ."

"Terra's past is lost forever," Roan said. "Now she has only the future."

TRAVIS SHELTON
LIKES BAEN BOOKS
BECAUSE THEY TASTE GOOD

Recently we received this letter from Travis Shelton of Dayton, Texas:

I have come to associate Baen Books with Del Monte. Now what is that supposed to mean? Well, if you're in a strange store with a lot of different labels, you pick Del Monte because the product will be consistent and will not disappoint.

Something I have noticed about Baen Books is that the stories are always fast-paced, exciting, action-filled and seem to be published because of content instead of who wrote the book. I now find myself glancing to see who published the book instead of reading the back or intro. If it's a Baen Book it's going to be good and exciting and will capture your spare reading moments.

Another discovery I have recently made is that I don't have any Baen Books in my unread stacks—and I read four to seven books a week, so that in itself is a meaningful statistic.

Why do you like Baen Books? Drop us a letter like Travis did. The person who best tells us what we're doing right—and where we could do better—will receive a Baen Books gift certificate worth $100. Entries must be received by December 31, 1987. Send to Baen Books, 260 Fifth Avenue, New York, N.Y. 10001. And ask for our free catalog!